WOLF AND RAVEN
BOOK I

WOLF

of

FURY

K. J. PEARCE

ETESIAN PRESS

Edited by Ashley Olivier of Enchanted Author Co.

Cover design by Jordan Minor

Map design by Lia Ramirez Art

Subjects: Fiction/Fantasy, Fiction/Science Fiction and Fantasy, Fiction/Romance

ISBN: 979-8-9992057-0-4

In a world full of nineteen year old mortal girls,
be the nine hundred year old queen with elemental magic.

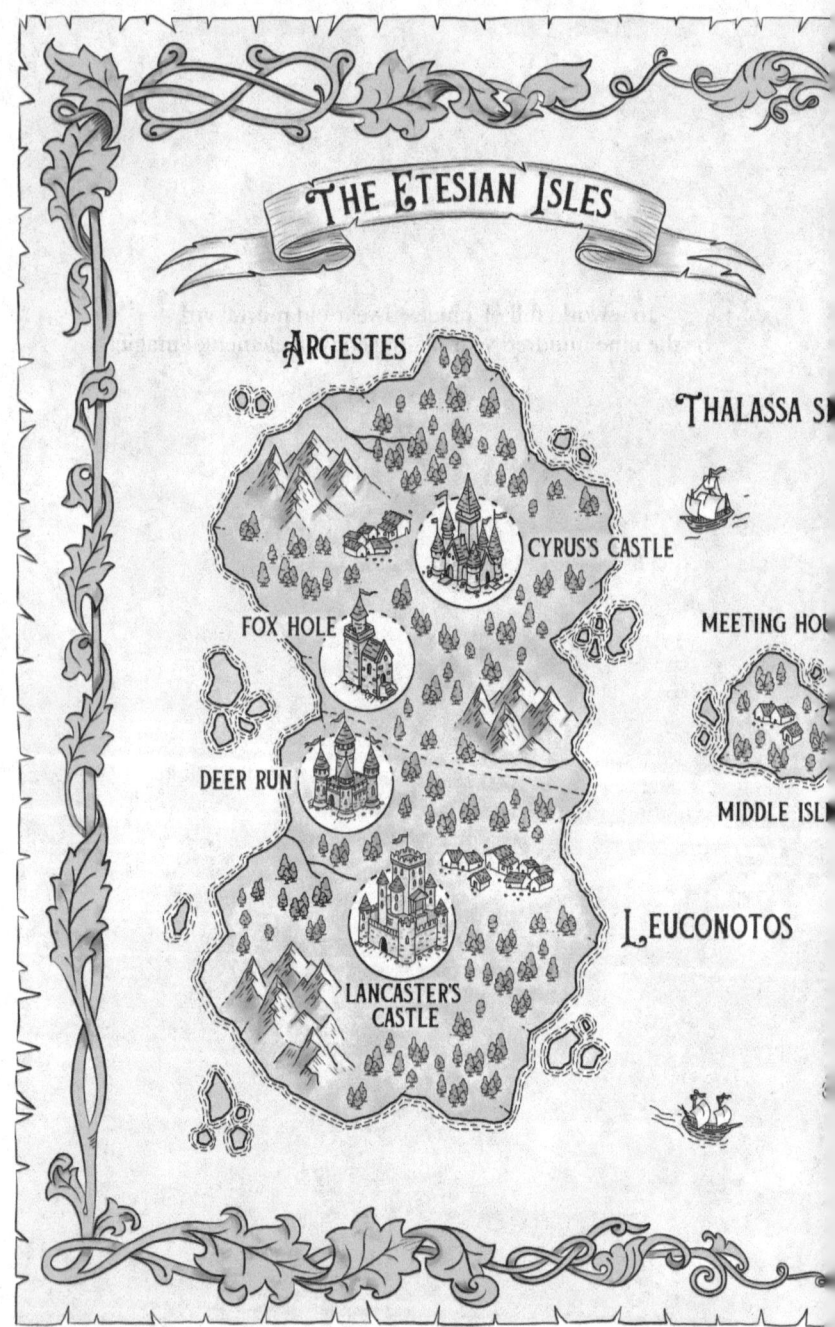

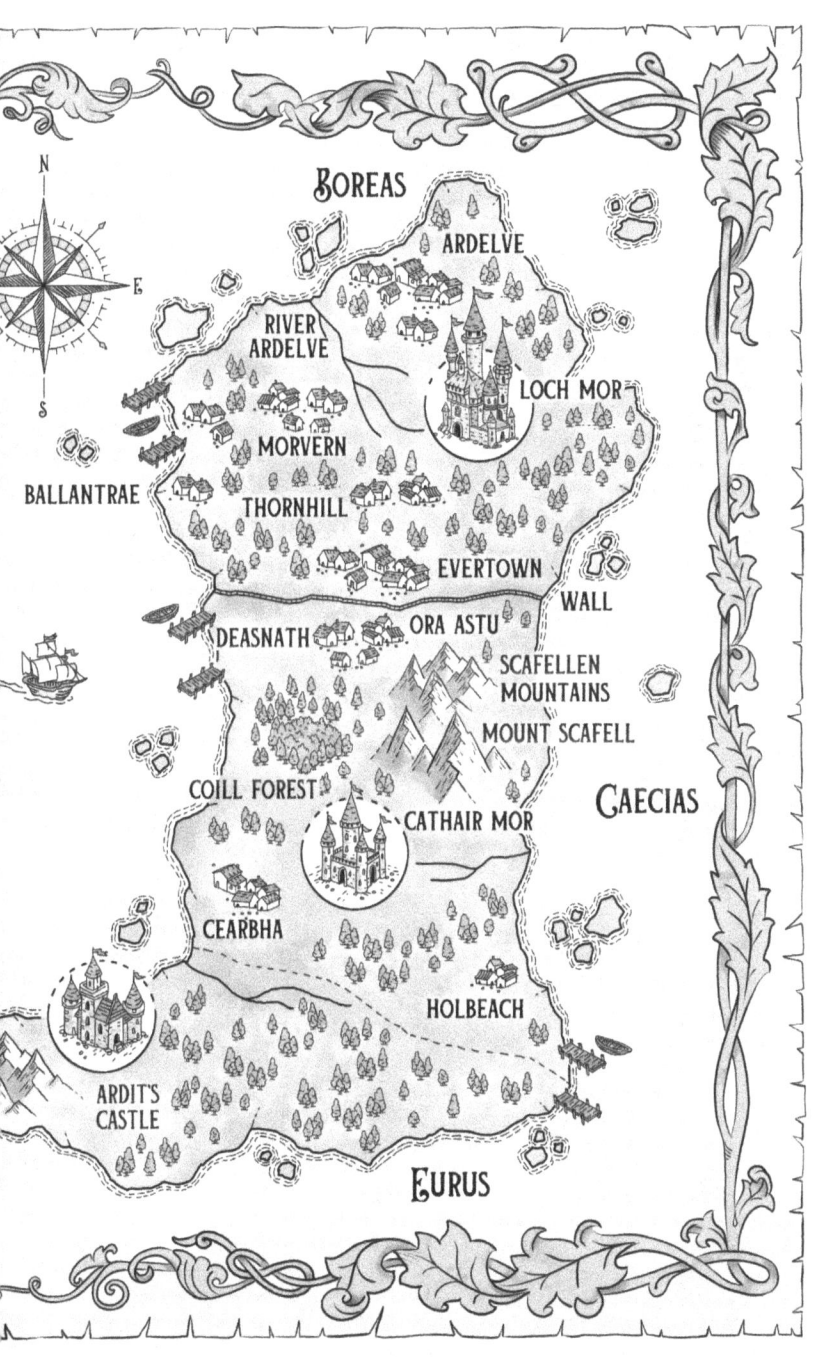

CHAPTER ONE

Faolan

"It's about time you stop hiding under your mother's skirts and learn what it means to be a leader." My father has always been an asshole.

He called me into the parlor next to the war room and stood facing the window with his back to me, his large frame a silhouette against the rising sun, his black hair shining in the morning light.

"As my new general, I want you in the meeting with the heir of Leuconotos when he arrives today," he informed me.

We buried my older brother Cathal less than a month ago. He was our kingdom's general and the largest and strongest of my three brothers, so it was quite a shock when his body was delivered back to the castle under a black shroud with a letter from the evil witch queen of the north that merely said, "This is more than he deserved."

It was the following day when my father announced that I was to take Cathal's place as the new general. He never gave me a reason for choosing me over my oldest brother, Brenhin, who is the heir to the throne and takes after my father.

They are both ruthless. He probably thought I was expendable and wanted to keep Brenhin alive to succeed him.

"I thought you'd want Brenhin in the meeting," I said through gritted teeth.

"Of course he'll be at the meeting. Are you thick?" My father whipped around, his dark brown eyes penetrating mine. He took a slow, menacing step toward me. "He's my heir, but you... well, you've been a disappointment thus far, so it's time for you to *earn* your place in this family. Become the male you were born to be."

I groaned quietly. If I was such a disappointment, then why did he choose me to take Cathal's place? Brenhin was the clear choice.

Or even Bradach, my other brother and spymaster of Caecias, our kingdom. Instead, he chose me. And as much as I may disagree with my father, I did want to earn his respect and find my rightful place in the kingdom and the family.

"Yes, Father." A deep sigh left my lips, and I slowly trailed behind him as he left the parlor and walked down the corridor.

He stopped in front of the large oak doors that led into the war room. Turning the brass handles, he swung the doors open. Reluctantly, I followed him inside to find my brother Brenhin standing by a small drink table pouring himself a glass of whiskey with a smirk on his face.

I knew that smirk well. It was the face he made when he was irritated, which happened to be quite often when I was around.

"Hello, little brother. What brings you in here today?" Brenhin was a perfect copy of my father: both stood taller than me at 6'4, they had the same dark brown eyes that lacked any warmth, black-brown hair that was cut short to show off their elegantly pointed fae ears, and tan skin covering large muscles that they had honed in battle.

"Father," I answered shortly as I nodded in his direction. I may not have wanted to be general, but I would temper my annoyance to ensure I proved myself capable of being granted this position.

"Yes, your pathetic, useless, bastard of a brother is finally going to contribute to the family," Father sneered in my direction.

Ever since my right of passage with the amarok at eight years old, my father has called me a bastard. I could never understand why he thought that, as I looked just as much like him as the rest of my brothers. The only difference between my brothers and me was that I possessed our mother's warmth.

My father turned toward Brenhin. "As you know, I appointed Faolan as the new general, so I think it is important for him to be here to hear about this *threat* the Leuconotan king seems to think we are facing." His eyes narrowed.

I took a seat in one of the deep chairs in the corner of the room, fighting to keep from scoffing at his tone. The leather was old and cracked but smelled as though it had been recently polished. I ran my fingers over the arms and gripped the corners until my knuckles turned white.

"What do you think of this so-called threat?" Brenhin asked as he turned toward our father. He picked up the letter they had received a few days prior from the desk in the corner of the room and glanced over it again.

The letter had come from the kingdom of Leuconotos on Western Etesia. There were five kingdoms in total on the Etesian Isles. The kingdoms of Leuconotos and Argestes were in Western Etesia and the kingdoms of Caecias, Eurus, and Boreas were in Eastern Etesia. Lancaster Winterbourne II was the current king of Leuconotos and had sent a letter informing my father that there had been some curious events and potential threats that had taken place in both his kingdom and the kingdom of Argestes to their north.

He also mentioned that he would be sending his son Lancaster III to meet with my father today, but he gave no specifics on the threats or reason as to why the information needed to be conveyed face to face.

Unsurprisingly, my father had little concern for the troubles plaguing Western Etesia. The only thing that concerned my father was reclaiming the Kingdom of Boreas. He had the misguided notion that the fae of Caecias were the only Sylphs that descended from a pure-blooded high fae line directly from the God of Air, Nuada, and were therefore the rightful rulers of all Sylphs.

The two of them stood over the table discussing the letter and sipping on their whiskeys. "I don't understand why the king would send his son all the way to Eastern Etesia just to warn us about threats they are facing on their own lands. Do you think he will ask for our assistance?" Brenhin asked, and my father's face soured.

"He will be sorely disappointed if he expects any assistance from us," my father replied before a loud knock on the door interrupted their conversation. "Enter," my father barked, and Crown Prince Lancaster walked into the room.

He headed straight for my father and brother, confident and unafraid, every bit the quintessential royal.

Lancaster was tall and lean, his black hair in sharp contrast to his pale skin and bright blue eyes. He was the youngest crown prince of the Etesian kingdoms at ninety-nine years of age, but he still had more than sixty years on me. Age didn't mean much to the fae. We reached the aibithe, our maturation age, around forty and our bodies stopped aging. Any physical signs of aging that we may have acquired became permanent, but no new ones would develop.

"Your Majesty, Your Highness," he said as he inclined his head slightly. "It is nice to see you again, however I wish it was under better circumstances."

Lancaster was the epitome of a fairytale prince, all charm and elegance. His tunic and jacket were immaculate in dark green and silver. His trousers were clean, save for a small smudge of dirt from where his knees gripped his saddle. His boots were polished to a shine, and there was not a single trace of mud. He looked as if he hadn't just traveled a full week to arrive in our kingdom.

"Brenhin is fine, Your Highness," my brother said dryly before forcing a thin smile. Brenhin despised titles as it denoted his position as a prince, rather than king. He coveted the crown and was not-so-patiently waiting for our father to die.

Honestly, I was surprised that he hadn't yet attempted a coup to murder our father and claim the throne for himself; it was the kind of thing our father would have done.

"Have you met my youngest brother, Faolan? He is our new... *general*." He lingered too long on that last word as he turned and waved an arm in my direction. I knew when Brenhin finally ascended the throne that my tenure as general was going to come to an end.

I didn't care, though. I never wanted to be the general anyway; I just wanted my father's respect. "Lancaster." I stood and inclined my head slightly in greeting.

"Faolan? It's nice to meet you. I was sorry to hear about your brother." He approached me and extended his hand.

His features softened, and a small empathetic smile pulled on the corners of his lips. I swallowed the lump that had suddenly appeared in my throat. If only my own family was as compassionate.

"And you can call me Cas," he continued. "I'm sure we will be working together in the future. I hope we have a long and prosperous relationship between our kingdoms going forward."

"Cas." I nodded, a small but genuine smile gracing my lips. "I look forward to that, as well."

My father cleared his throat. "So, why exactly have you come here, Prince Lancaster? Your father mentioned some troubles on the Western Isle, but I'm not sure how that concerns me. Why send you all this way when he could have simply included the details in his letter?"

Brenhin and my father took their seats in two large chairs around the low oak table that faced the fireplace. Lancaster turned and approached them again. I sank back into my chair in the corner of the room.

"The information is sensitive. My father worried what could happen should such a letter be intercepted. And since we don't know the source of the trouble yet..." he trailed off and averted his gaze from my father to the fireplace. I didn't have to be a mind reader to know that he and his father were suspicious of the monarchs in the kingdoms here in Eastern Etesia after whatever happened in their lands.

"Have you heard of the ancient portals?" Lancaster inquired as he took a seat on the sofa opposite my father and Brenhin.

"Portals?" Brenhin repeated, sounding genuinely perplexed. He leaned forward in his chair, placed his elbows on his knees, and steepled his fingers.

"Yes, the kind that act like a gate between two places. My father said that thousands of years ago there were fae who had powers strong enough to create such portals," Lancaster said, looking from Brenhin to my father.

"That's ridiculous. No fae has that kind of power anymore, not even the evil witch queen up north, Melisende," my father declared, almost choking on his drink.

It was rare that he spoke her name, preferring instead to address her as the "evil witch." The nickname wasn't unwarranted though; she was one of only a handful of fae to retain any kind of elemental powers, and she used them to defeat anyone who stood between her and the throne of Boreas. According to my father, the gods had taken away our powers for a reason and those few fae must have done something unspeakably evil to retain them.

"I assure you, it's not ridiculous. My father and I think that someone does have the power to open them and has been doing so of late." Lancaster adjusted in his chair, eyes narrowing.

"And what proof do you have of this? Have you seen one?" My father stood and stalked past the prince to refill his whiskey across the room.

"Yes, a portal opened in Leuconotos. We don't know who conjured it or where it originated, but we believe there have been others," Lancaster declared.

Father stared at him over the rim of his glass as he took a sip, then came to sit down once more. "What do you mean you *believe* there have been other portals?" He set his drink down on the side table between his chair and Brenhin's, crossed his arms, and looked down his nose at the prince. He only liked facts, not speculation.

"A few weeks back there was an attack in Argestes by a small group of warriors dressed in black and donning masks. One of the guards said it was as if the warriors had appeared from thin air. Argestes dispatched of the warriors quickly, but unfortunately, they didn't leave any alive to interrogate about where they were from or why they were attacking."

"So, they may not have come through a portal. For all we know it could have been a band of Raiders." Brenhin looked as incredulous as my father, a scoff on his lips.

"No. At first, King Cyrus believed it was an attack by Leuconotos, so he sent one of his sons to question us. I assured Prince Verano that we sent no such attack to their lands, and after hearing more about what happened, I believe the warriors arrived in Argestes through a portal. How else could they have appeared seemingly from thin air?" Lancaster took a deep breath, his expression twisting in frustration. "The king may not be convinced that the warriors came through a portal, but it would explain their mysterious appearance."

"And you have no idea where the portals are coming from?" my father sighed, his patience wearing thinner by the minute.

"No. We only know one opened in Leuconotos, but we don't know where it originated. We also know that one opened in Argestes, but the circumstances are the same. But we *do* know the warriors were fae, not the mortal Raiders.

"I firmly believe that someone has powers strong enough to conjure portals and has some nefarious plan in mind. If the portals are being created by some rogue fae and not one of the monarchs, I think it is important for all the Etesian kingdoms to be aware and possibly form an alliance to protect ourselves."

"But both attacks have been in Western Etesia. This sounds like a problem for Leuconotos and Argestes." My father glanced sideways to Brenhin before taking another long sip of his whiskey.

"But what if portals start opening up on our lands?" I spoke up. There wasn't much to go on, and I wasn't sure that I believed Lancaster either, but it couldn't hurt to be prepared. "Wouldn't it make sense—"

"Shut up, boy," my father snapped, whipping his head in my direction. He was always talking down to me; it didn't matter that we had company.

Lancaster's eyes widened in shock of my father's behavior.

Yet Father continued, "I'm still not convinced that these *portals* even exist. So, there was an attack on Argestes and a random portal opened in Leuconotos. Why should this be of any concern to me?"

I glanced over at Brenhin, seeing my brother carefully studying the young crown prince across from him.

"If you really think these portals do exist and have been opening, do you have any idea who is behind this?" my brother asked. Lancaster shifted his gaze from my father to Brenhin.

"Unfortunately, no. We don't know where the portal in my kingdom originated, so we have no idea who could have conjured it. And the King of Argestes still isn't entirely convinced their attack was from a portal, so we have no additional information from them. It would make sense if it was some rogue fae with powers in Western Etesia conjuring the portals, but we cannot be certain."

"But do you have any theories?" Brenhin pushed, clearly unimpressed that Lancaster came here with such little concrete information.

"I really wish I had more to tell you. The reason for my visit was more of a warning and an offer of help. My father and I just wanted you to be aware of what happened in our kingdom so that you could be prepared in case it also happens here on the Eastern Isle."

"Maybe we can send out some patrols, look for anything out of the ordinary in our own lands. Just as a precaution," I suggested.

"And waste our men chasing shadows while the queen slaughters more of our citizens? Hardly," my father snapped, and Brenhin chuckled; he always enjoyed watching me being put in my place.

9

Respect and honor were hard earned in my family. "Well, if you don't have any information that can actually help us, then I believe this meeting has come to an end." Father waved his hand in dismissal.

Lancaster glanced briefly in my direction before he stood up and said his farewells to my father and brother. I stood from my chair as he turned toward me, his voice quiet, "Faolan." He inclined his head slightly, then left the room.

"This was an absolute waste of time," Brenhin groaned as soon as the door closed. He leaned back in his chair and took a long swig of his drink, rolling his eyes.

"Agreed," my father grumbled. "That was a waste of time, especially since the real threat to Caecias is from that evil witch." Everyone knew that Melisende, the Queen of Boreas, had elemental powers, but whenever I asked my father what kind of specific powers she had, he became agitated, yelling incoherently and never quite answering the question.

When I was really young, I assumed that he didn't tell me because it was too scary for a youngling, but when I got older, I realized he probably didn't know what kind of powers she had, or at least he didn't fully understand them. Unexplained powers, constant attacks on our kingdom, and the fact that she killed her own father to claim the throne were reason enough to fear her.

"So, you don't plan on heeding his warning at all? We are going to continue on as if there isn't a possibility of a threat from some fae powerful enough to conjure portals?" I spoke up again.

Sometimes my father was too short-sighted, neglecting to see beyond the generations-old feud between Caecias and Boreas.

"Don't be ridiculous, Faolan." There was tension in his voice, and his eyebrows knitted together giving him a pinched expression. "I brought you into this meeting to learn how to be a general and protect our kingdom, not listen to idle gossip and lead our soldiers on a wild goose chase for shadows. Now shut the sard up and let the adults talk."

I stared at my father in disbelief. He was the one who had brought me into this meeting. I had mistakenly hoped that this could be a turning point in our relationship and that by inviting me I was slowly earning his respect. I stood from my chair and walked toward the door. Without even acknowledging my father or brother, I left.

"Faolan!" I could hear my father shouting at me from inside the war room. I ignored him and kept walking down the long corridor, past the guards standing along the wall and into an alcove.

Thunderous footsteps sounded behind me. "I didn't bring you into this meeting so you could just leave!"

I whipped around and met his eyes. "Why then? You shot down everything I had to say. Sard, you didn't even listen to the prince, and he was only trying to warn us about a possible threat," I snapped back.

"What threat? No fae has been able to open portals in over a thousand years. This is ridiculous. The true threat is from Boreas. We need to focus on retribution for your brother. Or have you forgotten what happened to Cathal?"

It was only a month ago that my father had sent Cathal on yet another raid to our northern border to retaliate against an attack from the neighboring Kingdom of Boreas. They were constantly sending troops into our lands, and Cathal was constantly defending our borders. In the process, he was slain in cold blood.

"Of course I haven't." I swallowed hard, steeling my resolve. "But do you really think the witch queen is the only threat? You're going to just ignore what Prince Lancaster came here to tell us?"

"What *did* he tell us?" My father's eyes narrowed, his question a challenge.

11

I stared at him as I replayed the conversation in my mind. What had the prince told us? He told us a portal opened on his lands, but he didn't know where it came from. He also told us about a supposed portal in Argestes, but not even the Argestan king believed that. He hadn't actually given us any concrete information.

"He talks of a portal in his lands, but what? He just happens to see a portal from nowhere that does nothing? Why wasn't his kingdom attacked? How do we know it even was a portal and not just some illusion? And this portal in Argestes, even their king doesn't believe it." Father took a step closer to me. "It is probably just cover for an attack that Leuconotos sent into their neighbor's lands. Use your head, son. Portals haven't been seen in over a thousand years. I will not get involved in a squabble between the two kingdoms of the Western Isle."

Had I really been that gullible? Prince Lancaster seemed so genuine. Why would he come all this way if there wasn't actually some kind of threat? But then again, why didn't they just put the information in the letter? What weren't they telling us? "I—"

"I am your king, and you are my general. That means you follow *my* orders. And my orders are for you to go north again. There must be retribution for your brother's death, and I won't accept anything less than the queen's head."

Shocked, I stared at him. What he was asking me to do was impossible. I blinked a few times, trying to process everything. "But Father—"

"No, I won't hear it." His cold eyes bore into mine as the corner of his lips curled, revealing his teeth. "You are my general, and you follow my commands. You will go north, to her castle if you must, and you *will* kill Queen Melisende."

My head started spinning. We constantly defended our borders from Boreas and would retaliate when they encroached on our lands, but we *never* sent our soldiers into their territory. The queen was brutal, and while it wasn't surprising that my father wanted her dead, he had never ordered an assassination attempt on her before.

But now my father was sending me into the heart of enemy lands to do the unthinkable. "But—"

"I will write to the queen and inform her that you will be headed there to form an *alliance,*"—he practically choked on the word— "with her kingdom to protect against these *portals*. I will give you one week to kill her. Without an heir, it will be easier for us to either convince her citizens to rejoin Caecias... or we will just take the kingdom back by force ourselves."

"But she has an heir. Her cousin is positioned to take the throne." I shook my head slightly, trying to make sense of what was being asked of me.

"That *girl* will never take the throne," Father snarled.

After the death of Queen Melisende's father, her only remaining family was her aunt, uncle, and cousin. Years later, her aunt and uncle were killed in a battle between our kingdoms, leaving only Melisende's cousin, Maelys, whom she later announced would succeed her on the throne.

"Regardless of how you feel, Father, *he* is the heir. Do you expect me to kill him as well?" I challenged.

"*He?*" A derisive snort came from my father. "*He* may have the support of that backwards kingdom, but *he* doesn't have the support of the other kingdoms. They will not support *him* being king, and that will pave the way for us to claim our lands back."

If it were up to my father, transgenderlings would die off like the wyverns.

"Our lands?" I almost laughed. "Boreas hasn't belonged to Caecias for over two thousand years! Why do you still insist on claiming it back?"

"Those lands are rightfully ours. Or have you forgotten how the Kingdom of Boreas came to be? Geralt was a trusted advisor of the Caecian king before he plotted a coup and stole our northernmost lands, naming himself the King of Boreas. King Patrice continued his father's war and pushed the Borean border further south into Caecias. And then Patrice had a daughter who was the worst of all of them. Melisende murdered her father to retain the crown of Boreas. And now they expect the crown to be handed over to a female who thinks she is a male.

"Everything about that kingdom is wrong. You do not question my motives. You are nothing; you are only here because Cathal died. He knew what it meant to be a Dulaine and what it meant to fight for what is right." Father took another step closer and stared down his nose at me. His voice grew deathly quiet. "If you question me or my motives again, I'll send you to meet your brother. Is that understood?"

I lowered my gaze to the floor, but I could still see my father's legs as he turned around and stormed back down the corridor. My breathing was shallow, and my body felt numb and heavy.

Could I really do what he asked of me? Could I really travel into the heart of an enemy kingdom and slay their queen?

CHAPTER TWO
Faolan

The creaking of the floorboards and the echoes of my hurried steps filled my ears as I made my way back toward my room. The castle was large and vast, and the long hallways were dark save for the torches burning every few feet.

The entire royal family took up residence in the east wing as it was the larger, newer wing and received the best sunlight year-round. I, however, chose to live in the western wing as far away from my family as I could get. Of course, I did have official rooms in the east wing with the rest of my family, but they were as empty as my aunt's rooms.

My mother and aunt had grown up in this castle as they were the daughters of the former king, Sidach Neville. With no son to inherit his throne, Sidach looked for a suitable male to mate my mother.

Not only was my father well-bred, but he was also ruthless and would continue the generations-old battle to reunite the kingdoms of Caecias and Boreas. After Sidach died due to an injury he sustained on a hunting trip, my father was crowned the new King of Caecias.

I always thought it was a stupid rule that female heirs couldn't ascend the throne. After his coronation, my father decided it was time for my aunt to find her own place to live.

Of course, he didn't *actually* kick her out of the castle, he just persuaded her that it would be better for her if she moved.

I made my way up a long stone staircase to the floor that housed my room. Thoughts of the meeting swirled through my head as I passed a large portrait of my father who looked down upon me in judgement, even in painted form.

Much of the resentment my father held for me stemmed from three things. First, he seemed to think that I was a bastard. Second, I had yet to reach aibithe and therefore couldn't officially complete warrior training. And third, I had the audacity to speak out during the very first meeting I had been invited to in the war room a few years ago.

The first was something I could never understand. Somehow, my father got this notion that I was a bastard, which was absurd as I looked as much like my father as any of my brothers. And while my mother didn't love my father, I couldn't imagine she would be unfaithful as there were serious consequences for anyone found guilty of infidelity in our kingdom. The accusation made no sense to me, but I was unwilling to broach the subject with my father in case I drew his ire.

The second wasn't something that I could control. Fae usually reached aibithe, the point where they stopped aging and reached a sort of ageless maturity, around forty years of age, and I was only thirty-two. In most kingdoms, your warrior training was completed when you faced some kind of trial within a fortnight of reaching the aibithe. In Caecias, warrior training was completed by traveling from the peak of Mount Scafell to the shore of Deasnath Beach near the border of Caecias and Boreas. You had to make the trek by yourself and could only survive on what you packed or were able to forage or fight for on your journey.

The third was the only reason that seemed like a legitimate explanation for the contention between my father and me. During the first meeting that I attended in the war room, Cathal announced that the twenty-first division of our warriors was going to be sent to Boreas to retaliate against an attack on our lands. They were to head directly toward the main fortress and stronghold on the border of Boreas. It was then that Cathal announced he would lead another division into Boreas to attack the stronghold from behind. I realized that the twenty-first division was going to be used as bait, and it was highly likely that few would survive.

"You can't sacrifice an entire division of new recruits as a diversion! They joined to defend our kingdom from attacks by Boreas. How can you betray them like this?" I was seething. I knew that war came at a cost, but to sacrifice new recruits as a diversion?

Cathal looked at me, then at our father with a scoff. "You know nothing of war."

"Not only do you disrespect your brother as general with that statement, but you also disrespect me as the king!" My father slammed his fists on the table. "Get out!"

I finally returned to my personal chambers and made my way to the washroom. Two attendants were already filling my bath with hot water and salts. There were lavender flowers and slices of bergamot floating in the water, their sweet fragrance filling the room.

As soon as they finished preparing my bath, they bowed and left. I undressed, piling my clothes on the floor, then stepped into the large tub and sunk into the water. The steam was welcoming, and I wanted to sink to the bottom and drift into oblivion.

Eventually, my bath water grew cold, and I knew I couldn't escape my future by trying to stay here in the present. Unfortunately for me, time kept moving forward.

I dipped my head back under the water and let out a breath. Bubbles escaped from my mouth and found the surface of the water. I sat back up and shook the water from my hair, then dragged my hands down my face.

With a sigh, I stood and exited my bath, then dried off with the large towel that was sitting on the bench next to the tub. I crossed the small room, tossed my towel aside, put on my trousers, and ran my fingers through my wet hair. I looked in the mirror that was hanging over the small washing basin and examined the dark circles under my eyes.

Today had not gone as expected, and I wasn't looking forward to what I was ordered to do next. I had hoped the meeting with Prince Lancaster would be the first step in earning my father's trust. I never imagined he would berate me in front of another royal, then demand I assassinate our greatest enemy.

Upon returning to my bedroom, I saw a figure sitting on a chair in the corner. I blinked quickly, willing my eyesight to adjust to the darkness of my room, and when I opened them again, I saw my closest friend, Fionn.

He was 6'4 and nearly the same height and build as my brother Cathal had been. And with his black hair and dark brown eyes he could almost pass as being Caecian, if it weren't for his brown skin and large hooked nose that closely resembled those of the Ellylldan fae of the continent rather than the Sylph fae of the Etesian Isles.

"I heard you are headed north again," Fionn said as he crossed one of his long legs over the other. He had been born into a noble family in Western Etesia but moved to Eastern Etesia a few years ago.

I met him when he was trying out for a position on the King's Guard. They were Caecias's elite warriors and protectors of the king, the royal family, and the castle. After earning a spot in the King's Guard, Fionn went out drinking in a pub, which was where I first met him. He ordered a drink and when he turned around, he stumbled into me, spilling most of his whiskey. He apologized, bought me a drink, then we spent the rest of the evening talking and laughing. We have been friends ever since.

I shook my head slightly and narrowed my eyes as I peered at my friend. I had long since stopped trying to figure out how he knew things before I could tell him. My brother Bradach was the spymaster of Caecias, but Fionn had friends everywhere and could find out even the most confidential information.

"This time, he is sending me directly into the lion's den. I am to head to the queen's castle in Boreas." I crossed my room and opened the wardrobe, fishing through my tunics.

"Shit!" he exclaimed, eyes widening in surprise. He ran his fingers through his shoulder-length black hair and shook his head. *Ah, so he doesn't know everything!*

"Yeah, your Leuconotan Prince, Lancaster, came to tell us about some new threats facing the Western Isle, but instead of heeding that warning, my father believes our biggest threat is still from Queen Melisende." I reached for my favorite black tunic and a pair of clean leather trousers. Then I walked back across my room and stopped by my bed. It was large, covered in blue blankets and a large fur, still unmade from this morning.

"She *did* murder your brother," he reminded me as I yanked my tunic over my head and shot him a glare. He threw his hands up innocently and softened his tone. "I'm not taking sides, Faolan, but your father does have a point. Unless the trouble on the Western Isle makes its way here, retribution for your brother's death will take priority for your father."

I didn't like the queen any more than my father, but I did find his obsession with reclaiming her kingdom a bit tedious. Especially with this new potential threat of portals hanging over the kingdom. *All* of the kingdoms.

I let out a breath as I finished tying the waist of my trousers and Fionn tilted his head slightly, asking, "Do you want me to come with you?"

"You really don't need to do that." I glanced at the sword rack in the corner of my room, then reached for the boots that were discarded at the foot of my bed. "I'm supposed to disguise this as a diplomatic visit, so it might be a bit suspicious if I show up with one of Cathal's top guards."

"One of *your* top guards, Faolan. Besides, I don't plan on going into her castle with you. I'll leave you to have fun with the queen all by yourself," he laughed, and I looked up from where I was tying up my boots. "I do have to head north anyway to check into some Raider activity. I could ride with you and the other guards to the gates of the castle, then do some reconnaissance work on my way back south."

The Raiders were mortals that terrorized the Etesian Isles. They lived outside of fae rule and robbed the fae to support their tribes. They were the threat we faced from the inside of our kingdom.

Queen Melisende of Boreas was the threat we faced from outside. And now we faced a possible third threat from an unknown rogue fae in an unknown location who had the power to conjure portals. I really didn't know how Cathal did it. He was always so enthusiastic about being general; I, on the other hand, was less excited about facing multiple threats at once.

"Fine, you can join me for the ride out." I finished tying up my boots and walked over to the mirror, glancing at my appearance and running my fingers through my hair again. It had mostly dried, with a few waves falling over my forehead.

"So, how should we spend your last evening of freedom?" Fionn asked.

"*I* am heading out to the Red District," I said as I put on my turquoise ring. My mother had given it to me when I turned thirty; it was her father's ring and had been worn by the kings of Caecias for generations. Why she gave it to me instead of Brenhin, I would never know.

Fionn gave me the same look he always did when he knew I was headed to the gambling district and into Etaine's bed. For the past few months, I'd been finding some comfort in the arms of a female in the village of Cearbha just outside of the capital city of Cathair Mor. "The Red District, huh? Have fun!" he shouted after me with a laugh.

"Sard off," I retorted as I left my room and shut the door behind me. I let out a small laugh and shook my head.

The castle was dark as I made my way down the stairs in the western wing and into the large entry foyer. There was a fire burning in the fireplace opposite the castle's entry doors and torches lit every few feet along the walls. The only sound I could hear was my footsteps on the hard stone floor as the castle's residents were in personal rooms on the upper floors and the servants were busy in the eastern wing cleaning and preparing tea and nightcaps.

The large entry doors groaned as I pushed them open, and a cold wind met me as I stepped out into the upper courtyard of the castle. A few guards nodded in my direction as they continued their rounds of the castle perimeter.

I followed the path past the inner gate, through the lower bailey, and out the large stone gatehouse. The capital city of Cathair Mor spread out before me, and I walked the road that led to the little village of Cearbha on the southeastern border.

Tall houses lined the roads of Cathair Mor, and I glanced at the small shops on the ground floor of the buildings. There were smiths, bakers, tailors, and healers. In the middle of the city was a lively market square where vendors could sell their wares during the day but which was currently empty except for the drunk presumably stumbling home.

As I approached the edge of the city, closer to Cearbha, where the gambling district was housed, the houses grew smaller and more tightly packed. I walked through the muddy streets and pulled my coat tighter around me against the bitter breeze.

It's not that I wasn't recognized here, but the edge of the city housed a gambling district where fae came to escape from their daily lives and responsibilities. Here, no one made eye contact and everyone became anonymous. I liked the idea of being able to slip through the streets and temporarily leave my identity and troubles behind.

Eventually, I found myself standing outside of a large house. I had been finding some comfort in the arms of a female here for the past few months. She was average height, with ample curves, bright blue eyes, and long black hair that fell in waves down her back. She was a temporary escape from the hell I endured at home.

I looked up to the last window on the right of the second floor. The light was on, and I could see Etaine's silhouette against the curtain.

I took a deep breath, trying to shake off the worries of the day, and headed inside. I hung my coat on the rack by the door and ascended the stairs to the second floor. The door opened just as I raised my hand to knock.

"Hello, handsome." Etaine stood in front of me wearing nothing but a slip of sheer fabric. My eyes widened, and I took in every curve of her body.

Her lips curled into an amused smile at my lack of response.

"Well, are you going to come in? Or do I need to drag you in?" she joked.

My eyes shot up and caught hers in a heated stare. Flushing, I pushed past her and entered her room. She closed the door behind me and turned around slowly.

"Fuck, I've missed you." I grabbed the hem of my tunic and pulled it over my head in one swift movement.

"It's only been a few days," she laughed, stepping closer to me. She slipped her fingers under the thin straps of her camisole and slid it off her shoulders. It pooled on the floor, and she stepped out of it, closing the distance between us.

"But it has been a *long* few days," I countered.

Her hands slid to the waistband of my trousers, and she started untying them. When she finished, I pushed them down my hips and stepped out of them. I grabbed her by the waist and pulled her body flush with mine.

She moaned as my lips crashed into hers. My tongue begged for entrance and when she finally granted it, I explored every inch of her mouth.

Elaine pulled back. "Where do you want me?" she asked with a sly smile.

My eyes trailed down her sinful body. I took her by the shoulders, turned her around, and bent her over the bed. Then I grabbed her hips and thrusted, filling her in one swift movement.

She moaned, and the sound was so sweet. I continued pounding into her from behind while sliding one of my hands across her hip, to her waist, and down toward her center. My fingers rubbed against her mound, and she let out a breathy gasp.

"Come for me, darling." I kept my grueling rhythm until she cried out.

Her orgasm sent ripples through her entire body, and the vibrations in her inner walls caused me to swiftly follow her over the cliff.

I climbed on the bed with her, and it wasn't much longer until our bodies met again. Being with Etaine allowed me to forget my responsibilities and the task ahead of me. She was my escape. Eventually, we were spent, and sleep took over.

When morning arrived, I opened my eyes to find Etaine's body draped over mine. I hadn't meant to spend the night, as I never had before. I glanced down at her head resting against my shoulder and her arm draped across my stomach.

Her hand was dangerously close to my cock, and it twitched at the thought of what we had done last night. *Sard.*

I slipped out of the bed and quickly dressed, trying to be as quiet as possible so I wouldn't wake her up. I knew I hadn't succeeded as I soon heard her voice from behind me when I was walking toward the door.

"Leaving so soon?" she said with a pout of her perfectly full lips.

I gave her a regretful look. "I have to go. I'm headed out of the kingdom later, and I need to pack."

"If you're leaving later, we still have time to play. You don't have to leave quite yet," she said as she sat up. The sheet slipped down to her waist, revealing her breasts.

"Yes, I do." I grabbed my boots that were sitting by the door. I didn't even bother putting them on; I just had to get out of the room as quickly as possible.

I liked Etaine. No, I liked fucking Etaine, but she wanted to be more than I was willing to let her be. She was a distraction, a way to release my stress and tension. Nothing more.

Without looking back, I raced down the hallway and only stopped when I made it to the bench at the bottom of the stairs. I laced up my boots and grabbed my coat from the rack by the door before hurrying out into the cold.

Now to face today's reality.

CHAPTER THREE
Faolan

"...It's the least that bastard can do." My father's voice echoed down the hallway as I returned to the castle and passed one of the sitting rooms on the way to my chambers.

I slowed my steps and approached the room, listening to the conversation from the crack in the door.

If my father was speaking of a bastard, he could only mean me.

"He's your son, Rian, and you are sending him to his death." It was rare that my mother stood up to my father. It was not that she was weak, quite the opposite in fact, but she was smart and knew when my father would stop listening both to her and to reason.

"Need I remind you who you are talking to?" my father snapped, and at that my mother recoiled slightly.

"It's just—"

"Just nothing. That bastard has done nothing for this kingdom. The least he can do is die trying to earn his place in this family."

My heart sank. My father often called me a bastard, but did he think so little of me to believe I had done nothing for our kingdom? Narrowing my eyes, I leaned even closer to the door.

My mother gasped loudly before quietly responding, "You don't mean that, Rian."

"I do. You know why I don't trust him, why *your* son has made me doubt him, why he'll never have my respect unless he does this and proves his loyalty to the kingdom and the family."

"Rian," my mother pleaded, but it was useless.

"Enough!" Father shouted, his loud voice making me flinch. "Leave me."

My mother's footsteps sounded as she approached the hallway. Face paling, I quickly retreated and hurried toward the stairs, hoping she wouldn't realize that I had been eavesdropping on their conversation. I stopped when I heard her voice call from behind me.

"Where are you coming from? It's a bit early to be *returning* to the castle, don't you think?" Mother said with a knowing smile.

She tried to hide her disappointment with my father behind her amusement at my returning to the castle early and in a disheveled state, but I could see the shadows behind her green eyes.

I shrugged my shoulders and turned back to the stairs when she called to me again, "Faolan…"

Pausing at the bottom step, I turned to face her. "Yes, Mother?"

"Your father told me what he has asked of you." She approached me and placed a hand on my shoulder.

My mother was my refuge, my sole source of comfort in the kingdom. When my father shunned me after my trial with the amarok and ordered that no one was to help me, she disobeyed him and snuck me a needle and thread to suture the wound on my forearm, as well as a healing salve.

"Asking suggests I had a choice in the matter," I mumbled, averting my gaze to the floor.

"Be that as it may, I wanted to talk to you before you head out today." She clasped her hands in front of her.

I had always had a much better relationship with my mother than my father or brothers. The only thing they cared about was power, maintaining it, and acquiring more. They had long ago forsaken the gods and goddesses and chose to forget that all fae were children of both the gods and mortals.

My mother was different, though. She was the eldest daughter of the former King and Queen Consort of Caecias. They had no sons, and as a female my mother wasn't allowed to ascend the throne. Her only option was to mate a suitable male who would become the new king and then she could become the queen consort and remain in her home.

She didn't care for power. Hell, she didn't even care about the castle, but she wanted to protect her family and if that meant playing political games, then she would.

"Sit with me," my mother's sweet voice called as she entered her private study. Unlike the rest of the castle, it was bright and filled with light purple curtains, beautiful floral tapestries, and vases filled with lavender. She took a seat on the bench under the window facing the forests that surrounded the castle.

I walked across the room and sat next to her, peering out at the ancient oak trees in the distance.

Mother spoke softly, "I want you to be careful, Faolan. You are my heart. I know what your father intends for you to do." She placed her hand on my cheek and pulled my head so I was facing her. She gazed into my eyes, almost pleading. "I know he wants you to kill Queen Melisende.

"For as long as I've known your father, he has wanted to be the one to reclaim her kingdom in the name of Caecias. Promise me that you will be careful. She hasn't been queen for over nine hundred years by being careless."

She gently took my right hand in hers and started rubbing the top of my hand.

"I promise." I looked up and saw worry etched across her face.

Mother added, "Everything I have done, I have done to protect you, Faolan." This confession surprised me. Of course, mothers protect their children, but her tone hinted at something else. Something she was ashamed or embarrassed of.

"Mother?" My brows furrowed.

"It's nothing. Besides, your father will be expecting you soon." She shook her head. "Just please be careful and remember, the strong may fall…"

"…but they never yield," I finished, and she offered me a half-hearted smile. I pulled her into a hug and inhaled. Her scent of lavender, sweet citrus, and warm vanilla filled me. Then I held her hands as I stood. "I'll be careful," I promised.

She turned from me to look out the window, and I retreated back into the hallway and to the stairs.

***

A loud knock on my door called my attention away from stowing my things, and I opened the door to find a servant standing on the other side.

"Your father would like you to join him in the small dining room at noon to discuss your mission." He turned and left before I could say thank you, and I watched him retreat down the corridor.

There wasn't much time before I needed to meet my father, so I quickly grabbed a few more items to add to my pack and set it by the door with my sword, a couple of daggers, and my bow and quiver.

The sun cast long shadows across the foyer that separated the west wing from the east wing of the castle. Large tapestries hung on the walls telling the heroic stories of my ancestors. One portrayed a male slaying a wyvern while another showed a male leading a battalion of warriors into battle.

Then a tapestry across the room caught my attention. It showed a male standing at the mouth of a cave holding the decapitated head of an amarok in his hands. The amarok was about four times the size of a regular wolf and also four times as deadly. I was reminded of my trial with the amarok when I was eight years old, and my left hand slid along the scar on my right forearm. A lump formed in my throat, and I swallowed it down before forcing my feet forward.

The 'smaller, more casual' dining room my father wanted to meet in was in fact neither small nor casual. Rather, I was told it was much grander than the formal dining rooms in other castles.

I stood outside the room and stared at the large double doors. My hand reached for the handle on the right door, and I closed my eyes, taking a long, slow, deep breath. When I opened them, I pushed the door open and entered the room, greeting my father.

"Finally," he barked. "Come here, boy." He was standing at the far end of the room, behind the head of the table, looking as imposing as possible. To his left stood his captain of the guard, *my* captain of the guard. I wondered how long it would be before I fully accepted my role as general.

"Faolan," Cadeyrn said as he glanced at me before returning his attention to the stack of papers on the table.

"As you know," Father continued as he took his seat and poured himself a glass of mead, "I am sending you to Boreas to seek retribution for your brother's death. The queen must pay for her crimes."

I slowly approached the long oak table and pulled out one of the chairs. The scraping of the heavy legs on the stone flooring grated on my already fragile nerves. I lowered myself onto the chair and warily looked at my father.

"Cadeyrn can spare some guards to travel with you," Father added and at the mention of his name, Cadeyrn turned and nodded his head once.

"Yes, we think it best that you travel with a small contingency. You'll be better able to avoid detection once you cross the border." Cadeyrn remained standing at my father's left.

My eyes shifted from my father to the guard, but his focus remained firmly on his reports. I got the impression that he didn't approve of me being appointed general after Cathal's death.

He continued, "I will permit four guards to travel with you on your mission."

"Four?" I blurted. Cathal never went anywhere without at least a dozen guards accompanying him, but I was supposed to venture into an enemy kingdom with only four? "That's not nearly enough. You expect me—"

"I expect you to do as you are told," my father snapped. Cadeyrn's mouth quirked slightly, his amusement obvious. My stomach curdled with dread. "Wolves are the symbol of the Dulaine line for a reason. They represent strength and loyalty, so grow a backbone and do as you are commanded."

Still, I shook my head. "But—"

"But nothing." He slammed his mead on the table. "You will take the four guards we are offering, and you will be grateful. Once you

31

arrive at the castle, you have one week. One week to kill the queen and return, or the guards will return *without* you."

Cadeyrn's amusement turned to bitterness, and he mumbled under his breath, "Should be one day. Useless sod."

My heart sank. "I understand," I said, but I didn't. My father and Cadeyrn clearly didn't approve of me, so why were they entrusting me with this grave undertaking?

If avenging Cathal, killing the queen, and reclaiming Boreas was of the utmost importance, why were they putting me in charge? I had overheard my father talking to my mother this morning, so I knew he didn't care whether I died while attempting to execute this mission. At least my father would get one thing he wanted out of this: he would be rid of his bastard son.

My father pursed his lips before taking a long sip of his drink, then he spoke again. "Cadeyrn will prepare your guards. I expect you to depart within the hour."

My breath hitched as Father rose from the table and motioned for Cadeyrn to follow him. I stood frozen as I watched them leave without saying goodbye. Finally, I released the breath I was holding and looked around the empty room that somehow doubled in size making me feel all that much smaller.

Reaching for my turquoise ring, I slowly spun it around my finger, trying to level my breathing. This was it. In an hour, I would leave my home and everything I knew to travel north to the Kingdom of Boreas. To my destiny.

CHAPTER FOUR
Melisende

After weeks of visiting the border villages, I was finally home. The last few weeks my personal guard and general, Foulke, and I had been leading separate reconnaissance missions along the southern border of my kingdom, Boreas.

Descending the hillside covered in pine and fir trees, I could see Loch Mor spread out before me. The dark blue water provided a stark contrast to the grey skies. I sighed, content to see my castle which sat on a small island near where the mouth of the River Ardelve fed into the massive lake.

I turned to look at my guard, Cyneweard. He was my third in command, behind Foulke, and had been accompanying me on my mission. "Do you think Ryder and Osborn will be able to train the villagers well enough before Caecias strikes again?" I inquired.

He turned in his saddle, his sandy blond hair—messy from weeks of traveling—covering his left eye. He smiled and replied, "They've been wanting to take on more responsibility. This is the perfect opportunity."

I scrunched my nose at his lack of answer. "But will they be able to train the villagers quickly? Caecias is always attacking our lands, and I don't want our villagers left defenseless."

Cyneweard pulled his horse to a halt. "I trust them with my life, Meli. They will be able to train the villagers well enough, but I can't guarantee they will be prepared before Caecias attacks again." He sighed and shook his head. "It would be easier if this war was being fought on a single front. Instead, we have to remain vigilant at all times, prepared to defend at a moment's notice. Ryder and Osborn will train basic defense to the villagers as quickly as possible. For now, we just need to hope for the best."

The afternoon breeze slid along the surface of the lake and chilled my cheeks, turning them a rosy shade of pink as we reached the banks of the lake and approached the stone gatehouse.

"Welcome home, Your Majesty," a guard said as he raised the portcullis.

I smiled in return and nudged my horse forward. Cyneweard and I passed the gatehouse and started along the long stone bridge that stretched between the shore and the small island.

After crossing the bridge in silence, Cyneweard spoke up, "It's been a long few weeks of travel. Let me take your horse to the stables. You can go inside, get a warm drink, and relax." He brushed his hair away from his eyes. "I'll debrief Foulke tonight, and the three of us can meet tomorrow once we are all well rested."

"Thank you, Cyneweard," I replied and dismounted my horse. A warm drink did sound nice. And a bath. And maybe some stew, as well. My stomach growled in response, and I handed the reins to Cyneweard, eager to be inside.

The castle loomed large on the island, even though it was generally considered the smallest of all the royal castles in the Etesian Isles. I didn't care, though; this had been my grandfather's home before he emancipated Boreas and remained his dwelling long after.

As I entered the castle, the heat from the various fireplaces kissed my skin and started warming me. I climbed a flight of stairs, then crossed the long corridor that separated the smaller tower from the one that housed my personal rooms.

After arriving in my chambers, I called for one of my maids to draw me a bath. When I entered the washroom, the scent of jasmine and citrus filled my nose. There were candles lit and burning along the low stone wall that sat next to the tub. A small wooden bench that sat on the opposite side of the tub held a large cloth towel, a smaller washcloth, and a bar of soap.

When the last maid was nearing the door, she paused and turned toward me. "Would you like anything to drink, Meli?"

"A glass of ratafia would be lovely," I replied. Unlike in other kingdoms, most of my staff addressed me by my name rather than calling me "Your Majesty," which was exactly how I preferred it, even if it did take centuries to get them to accede. Shortly after, she returned with a small glass of ratafia, a sweet, syrupy liquor made from grapes.

"And for your dinner? I can have the chef start preparing it now."

"Stew. He can make it with whatever he has in the kitchen. I have faith that whatever he prepares will be exceptional." I smiled, and she bowed slightly before withdrawing from the bathing chamber again.

I stepped into the bath and let the warmth seep into my skin as I slowly lowered my body into the water. The oils and salts helped to relax my muscles and wash away the past few weeks of travel. After bathing, I pulled my robe down from a hook and slipped it over my skin, reveling in the way the silky fabric felt.

"Oh, how I've missed you!" I announced to my bed as I returned to my large bedroom. There was a soft navy tunic, leather trousers, and a pair of fuzzy wool socks laid out for me.

I quickly dressed and braided my wet hair before entering my dressing room and reaching for the book sitting on my vanity, next to my crown. The crown had been discarded there before I left for the border villages and would remain on the vanity for now. There was no need to wear it in the castle when it was just me, the guards, and the servants. In all honesty, I didn't really like wearing the crown and knew I didn't need to wear it to assert my role as queen.

As I picked up the book, I glanced at my bookmark. "Nearly finished." A small frown spread over my face, and I crossed the hallway to my receiving room where there were several bookcases.

I was fond of reading and had bookcases in multiple rooms. And to my personal guard Foulke's dismay, I had also inadvertently turned one of the rooms near the armory, intended to be a guard's dormitory, into a small library.

"At least fill it with books on history or warcraft," Foulke had said, hoping I'd read something useful to my reign.

Gazing at the books, trying to decide what to read, I picked up a book about two warring kingdoms and immediately replaced it on the shelf. That was too close to home. There was a book about a princess who had met a prince in disguise, but I turned my nose up at that, as well. Fairytale romance had no place in my library; I had stopped believing in fairytales when I was much younger.

And then I saw it. A book about a warrior princess who had tamed a wyvern. My lips curled into a smile.

Wyverns had gone extinct almost 600 years ago. There was talk that drakes had also died out, but they originated on the continent, so it was harder to verify the information. Dragons still existed in the southeastern province of the continent where the Ellylldan dwelled, as well as wyrms over in the western province where the Rusalki lived.

I flipped the book over and looked at the image of a female raising a sword to the wyvern. Gripping the book tighter in my hand, I headed downstairs to the small parlor on the ground floor of the tower.

It was my favorite room in the castle, as it faced the lake and was warm from the fires that were constantly burning in the hearth. The room had the comforting scent of woodsmoke and leather, with a faint trace of sweet oranges.

My muscles relaxed as I sat in the large chair in the corner of the room between a window and the fireplace. There was a blanket draped over the arm of the chair which I pulled over my legs, then I signaled for one of my servants.

Mary, the youngest of my staff, came rushing into the room. "Yes, Your Majesty—I mean, Meli?" She flushed.

"I would like a cup of spiced orange tea, and you can tell Balfour that I'll take my dinner in the parlor here. Thank you, Mary," I replied.

She smiled and inclined her head before quickly exiting the room. Soon after, she returned with a fragrant tea smelling of cinnamon, clove, and oranges. I took a large sip and let the drink linger in my mouth before swallowing.

Finally picking up my book, I began to read. It didn't take long for me to finish my first book and start on the one about the warrior princess. I had barely begun the second chapter when I was interrupted by Foulke.

"A messenger just arrived with a letter for you, Meli." Foulke was a tall male, nearly 6'6 and built of pure muscle. He had been my personal guard for over four hundred years and his father for nearly another five hundred years before that.

While most fae entered the aibithe before their hair starts to grey, Foulke entered it with his hair and beard a salt and pepper mix of black and grey. His eyes were a warm honey-brown that complemented his dark skin. He had a scar across the right side of his forehead that started below his hairline and ended along his eyebrow. He had earned that scar in the battle that had cost him his father but gained him the title of my personal guard.

Foulke was nearly three hundred years younger than me, but as my guard he always acted like a protective father figure.

He crossed the room and stood next to me. I looked up from my book to study his face.

"Really? Do you know who it is from? Did you recognize the livery the messenger wore?" I asked, frowning slightly.

"Yes, but I don't want to say." He pressed his lips together, and the scar on his forehead deepened as he furrowed his brow.

That could only mean one thing…

"Shit. What does that cretin want now?" I slammed my book shut and set it on the table next to me, nearly knocking my empty teacup to the ground.

The only time Foulke looked like that when he delivered a message to me was when it was from King Rian of Caecias.

"Don't kill the messenger… or the guard who brings the letter from the messenger to you," he said with a slight huff that could almost be recognized as a laugh. Even though Foulke hated the asshole king, Rian Dulaine, as much as I did, I admired his ability to maintain his sense of humor.

I stood from my chair, discarding the blanket. Then I grabbed the letter from Foulke's hand and ripped it open. My eyes scanned the page as a grunt of frustration left my mouth.

"Well?" he said in an almost hesitant manner as he took a seat on the sofa across the table from where I had been sitting. "Let me guess, the king wishes to discuss reparations for his son."

"Rian has received word from Leuconotos about attacks on Western Etesia. The King of Leuconotos is suggesting an alliance amongst all the kingdoms of Etesia." I lowered the letter to my side and stared at Foulke.

"Yes, King Lancaster sent word to us, too. This is information we already had," Foulke said, and I sat back down in my chair.

"That's not it. Apparently, Rian is sending his son to broker a peaceful alliance between *our* two kingdoms," I said, spitting the word *alliance* like it was poison on my tongue.

"Really?" His voice dripped with disbelief. I nodded my head.

"That's what his letter says, but I know better than to actually believe that. It wasn't that long ago that we sent Cathal's body home, and now he speaks of peace? Doubtful. Brenhin is no better than his father. Neither of them wants peace, and neither of them would willingly form an alliance with us. What do you think the odds are that Brenhin will make an attempt on my life?"

I rolled my eyes and threw the letter into the fire. It erupted into flames, and the hearth crackled as it consumed the parchment.

"He can try," Foulke laughed, and I offered him a small smile in return.

Cathal was the largest of King Rian's brood and nearly matched Foulke's size but was still easy enough for Foulke to cut down when he came to the castle on a mission to take my life.

With the death of Cathal, it was likely Brenhin, the crown prince, would be sent here to form the "alliance," which was no doubt going to be another assassination attempt. But it didn't matter. We would cut down every son Rian sent to kill me or take my throne.

CHAPTER FIVE
Faolan

"There you are!" Fionn shouted as he ran to catch up with me.

After the meeting with my father and Cadeyrn, I had returned to my room and finished packing. It was less than thirty minutes later that I was exiting the castle and crossing the courtyard to the stables.

Fionn grinned. "Are you ready?"

"I guess," I mumbled, my mind still reeling from all that had happened.

"That's the spirit!" He clapped me on the back. "Let's just think of this as an adventure."

"An adventure where I most likely die." I gave him a sidelong look.

"See? Sounds like fun." Fionn winked before dropping his pack outside the stables. The horse master and a few stable boys were rushing around, readying our mounts for the trip.

Fionn approached the horse master, and I could see his arms pointing in various directions as he gave him orders. I set my pack down next to Fionn's before entering the stables where I saw the four guards I was allocated prepping their horses.

I smiled as I approached my steed, Dulachan. He was the largest of all the Dulaine horses, originally thought to be untrainable by our horse master, but I was able to get through to him. He was a bit obstinate, but once he started listening to me, I was able to build his trust.

I reached into my pocket and retrieved the apple I had grabbed from the kitchen earlier, and Dulachan graciously took it from my palm and started chewing.

His black coat shone in the early afternoon light, and I ran my fingers along his side. One of the stable boys walked up cautiously with a saddle, which I took from him then tacked Dulachan myself. He snickered a bit when I tightened the girth under his stomach.

"Quiet, you, or I'll feed you to the amarok," I chided.

The threat worked as Dulachan stood still as stone while I finished adjusting the saddle and tack. I attached my pack and bedroll to the saddle and looked over toward Fionn. He had left the horse master and was nearly finished readying his own horse as well.

"We're ready when you are, Your Highness," one of the guards said.

I turned to look at the male who had spoken and sighed when I realized that the four guards my father and Cadeyrn assigned to join me were all new recruits. Not that I had anything against new recruits, as they were all older and more experienced than me, it just spoke of my father's faith, or lack thereof, in my ability.

Why should he waste his top guards when he didn't expect me to succeed in the first place?

I sullenly exited the stables and mounted Dulachan, eager to start riding. Fionn sat atop his horse, followed by the other guards, and we made our way to the gatehouse.

The guard on duty nodded at me before raising the gates, and I led our little entourage away from the capital.

We rode for hours before taking a break to water the horses and stretch our legs. There was a small freshwater stream that was known for having trout, and even though it was the first day of our journey, fresh fish and meat were always preferred over the dry stuff we had packed.

I jumped down from Dulachan and loosely tied his reins to a tree near the stream where he would have equal access to water and some of the gorse bushes he favored when we traveled. The guards followed suit and dismounted their horses to relieve themselves and fill their waterskins.

"Should we try and catch some fish?" one of the guards asked. "Conleth only packed dried meat and bread for us. It might be nice catching a few trout, at least for dinner tonight."

"Agreed," Fionn said as he dismounted and tied his horse near Dulachan. He reached for the sword at his side.

"Do you really think you can catch fish with a sword?" I laughed in disbelief.

"Watch me," he snarked as he took off walking toward the stream.

As he approached, his steps were more cautious and he quieted, attempting to be as silent as possible. I tried to get closer to the stream without scaring off his prey.

Fionn placed one foot steadily on the stream's bank and the other he balanced on a rock sticking out of the middle of the water. He raised the sword and aimed toward a few trout that were swimming in the currents. I watched as he took a long, slow breath in and then as he exhaled thrust the sword down into the water.

I could hear the clash of metal on rock as his sword glanced off a stone at the bottom of the stream. "Sard it all!" he cursed.

I laughed, then slowly reached for the bow and arrow that were strapped to my back. I nocked an arrow and aimed, watching the same group of trout Fionn had vied for and taking a deep breath. I released the arrow, and it easily cut through both the air and water before landing in the side of one of the trout.

I smirked as I passed Fionn and reached down to pick up my prize. "Best two out of three?"

"Shut up, asshole!" he laughed as we continued to fish.

***

The sun was still high by the time we had caught enough fish for our dinner. We remounted our horses and rode for a few hours more until the sun began to set. The sky was dark when we finally found a clearing we could camp in.

Two of the guards started to make a small campfire while the other two males, Fionn, and I started setting up our tents and bedrolls.

After finishing, I approached the fire, the smell filling my nose and reminding me of trips to the forest with my family when I was young and before my father hated me.

Fionn handed me one of the sticks he had sharpened, and we both skewered fish and placed them over the flames. The rest of the guards joined us as we cooked our dinner.

"Do you think she's really as bad as they say?" Fionn asked, breaking the silence. Fionn had moved to Caecias from Western Etesia a few years prior and hadn't grown up hearing the stories of the evil witch queen like the children of Caecias had.

As far as I knew, he had only learned about her from what Cathal had told him and like my father, Cathal didn't talk about her much.

Other fae children grew up hearing stories of wicked wyverns, amaroks, or matagots, but the children of Caecias grew up hearing about the evil witch queen of the north.

"I don't know firsthand if she is as evil as they say, as I've never met her, but the stories are pretty appalling," I mused as I rotated a few of the fish over the crackling flames.

Fionn laughed, likely thinking the stories to be exaggerations. "Humor me?"

A couple of the guards shifted on the ground, diverting their attention to the campfire and the fish slowly cooking above it. I lowered my hand from the skewer and looked Fionn in the eyes.

"Boreas was our enemy even before the queen was born. We have been at war with them for two thousand years. But the short version of the story is that when her father was set to marry a noble female from Caecias and reunite the kingdoms, she killed him to retain the crown.

"With her father dead, she was the sole heir to the throne of Boreas, and even though females aren't supposed to ascend the throne, she took it anyway. There are also tales that she devours males whole and bathes in the blood of children as a way to maintain her powers, but that is just a story we tell children to keep them from wandering too close to the border alone."

"Sard, she murdered her own father?" Fionn's jaw slackened in shock.

"That's what they say." I lifted my hand and rotated the fish again. "I don't know if anything they say is true, but I guess it doesn't matter since I'm supposed to kill her."

Fionn erupted in laughter. I released my breath and let out a little laugh with him.

I added, "I just don't know why my father is so insistent about taking back her kingdom. It's been almost two thousand years since

Boreas was a province of Caecias; it wasn't even during his time, nor my grandfather's time. What is his obsession?"

Fionn gave me a pointed look. "Boreas does attack us quite often, not to mention she killed your brother. She's not exactly innocent in all of this."

"I know, it's just… there has to be a better way. Bloodshed begets bloodshed." I sighed heavily and pulled a fish down from the spit.

"How do you plan on killing her? She's nearly a thousand years old. I don't think she's gonna make it easy on you."

"I don't know." I ran my hand through my hair. "What am I supposed to do? I don't think killing her is necessary; I'd rather just ignore her existence completely and leave Boreas alone, but I know my father will never accept me as a member of the Dulaine line unless I finish her."

And wasn't that the point of this mission, to earn my rightful place in the kingdom and the respect and acceptance of my father?

We continued eating in silence, the guards still pretending that the food was far more interesting than the conversation Fionn and I were having. After an hour or so, we finally extinguished our fire and headed to our tents for the night.

Fionn and I had set up our tents so that the flaps faced each other, and as I crawled into my bedroll, I looked at my friend.

"How are you feeling, Faolan?" Fionn asked, an expression of sympathy on his face.

"What do you mean?"

"I know you haven't been general for that long, but how are you feeling about it? Before Cathal died, you told me that you had thought about leaving the kingdom."

"I can hardly leave now, can I?" I shook my head and let out a long breath. "I never wanted to be general, but I can't exactly tell my father no, so what option do I have?"

"There are always options, Faolan."

"It seems you don't know my father as well as I thought you did. Sometimes I hate being a part of my family." I peered up at my friend. "Would you like to switch places?"

"No, thank you," Fionn laughed. He shifted in his bedroll so he was no longer facing me, and I could hear his breathing start to slow as sleep overtook him.

I rolled over in my tent and tucked my blanket tighter around my body. I tried to imagine the warmth was from Etaine's body draped over mine, but the bitter evening wind was a harsh reminder that I was miles from her bed.

I don't know how long I lay there in silence with my eyes closed, but eventually I drifted off to sleep.

***

The morning arrived with the sound of birds chirping all around the woods, and I stretched in my bedroll. My muscles felt stiff from sleeping on the hard forest floor. I slowly turned over and noticed that Fionn was already awake, his tent empty.

The sound of shuffling reached my ears, and I realized all of the guards were awake and already packing away their bedrolls and tents.

I slipped out of my tent and reached for a chunk of bread from my pack. It was tough, not stale, but still difficult to chew. I fished around my pack for an apple; I had grabbed a few from the kitchen before leaving and knew I had one left. The apple was juicy and sweet, in stark contrast to the bread, and my tongue welcomed the taste and texture. After finishing my meager breakfast, I drained the water from my waterskin.

"I can fill that for you, Your Highness," one of the guards said. I looked up at the young male and recognized him. He had completed his warrior trial the same time I did.

"Faolan, please. And thank you..." I trailed off realizing that I couldn't remember the guard's name.

"Dafydd," he said with a smile.

"Thank you, Dafydd." I handed him my waterskin, then slowly stood up and watched as he retreated toward the stream. Another guard followed Dafydd with the rest of the waterskins while Fionn guided a few of the horses to the stream to drink.

I packed up my tent and bedroll and set them on a nearby stump with my pack. After the horses had been fed and watered and our tents and belongings packed up, we mounted our horses and continued our journey north.

The rest of the day passed with no incident. We rode through a long valley and into the vast woods of Coill Forest where I spent a lot of time as a child, a place known for its ancient oak trees and densely packed spruces. The northeast side of the forest butted up against the Scafellen mountain range, the largest mountain range in the Etesian Isles.

By the time the sun had set, we arrived at the base of the mountains and found a small clearing to camp in. We set up our bedrolls, ate dinner from our rations, and after the guards were finished sharing the stories about completing their warrior trials—as new recruits, they had all taken their trials in the past year—we all turned in for the night.

I lay on my back, staring up at the night sky. In the distance, I heard the howls of a pack of wolves and eventually fell asleep listening to their calls.

The next morning, we approached the border of Boreas and paused as we saw a stone outpost guarded by a few Borean guards.

We could only see three guards atop the watchtower but were unsure how many more were in the guard room at the base of the tower.

Rather than find out how many enemy guards we would be up against, we followed a small path west along the border until we were far enough away from the outpost to avoid detection.

Eventually, we crossed the border and as we moved further into the kingdom of Boreas, I watched the trees chang from oak and birch, whose golden leaves danced on the wind, to tall, narrow fir and pine trees as well as ancient yew trees with their gnarled branches. The forest floor was still covered in gorse, but the hawthorn bushes gave way to fragrant purple heather.

The sun started setting on our third day, and we found a clearing at the edge of the valley between two mountain ranges to set up our camp.

Like the previous days, we unpacked our tents and bedrolls, ate dinner from our rations, and chatted around our campfire. After dinner, we settled into our bedrolls for the night, but instead of staying awake listening to the sounds of the wolves howling or wind passing through the trees, it was the knowledge that we would be arriving at the gates of our enemy's castle tomorrow that kept me awake.

I don't know how long it was that I stayed up contemplating all the horrible ways in which the evil queen could kill me. Would she devour me whole like the children's stories, peel my skin and wear it as a cape, or would she simply slit my throat and have done with it?

Eventually I fell asleep and dreamt of my fate, with my dreams playing out exactly as my thoughts had.

Surprisingly, it wasn't my nightmares that woke me up but the sound of rustling in the bushes nearby. The sky was dark when I opened my eyes; it was clearly very late, but as the first rays of daylight hadn't yet started to breach the eastern hills, I couldn't be sure what time it was.

I rolled over and looked around to see if any of the guards had stirred or if there were animals nearby, but I didn't see anything that could have caused the rustling.

I tried to fall back asleep, but it was to no avail. I stared at the stars through the canopy of trees and took a deep breath. After a few minutes, I crawled out from my bedroll to relieve myself in the woods near our camp. A twig snapped under my foot as I neared a tree and started to untie my trousers.

It was then that I heard a low growl from behind me. Keeping one of my hands on my trousers to hold them up, I turned my head and looked toward the source of the sound. I scanned the bushes and couldn't see anything, but then a pair of yellow eyes caught my attention.

All the blood left my face. I took a slow step back, turning my body toward the wolf. Another low growl escaped its mouth, and I slowly raised my right hand, my left keeping a tight grip on my trousers.

The wolf took a tentative step toward me, and I took a deep breath.

"No." It came out quieter than I intended, but the wolf stopped its advance and looked me in the eyes.

Memories of my encounter with the amarok as a child flashed through my mind, and although I stopped believing I had actually talked to the large wolf back then, at this moment I desperately wished that I could talk to them.

"Please, no," I pleaded and watched as the wolf took another slow step toward me. But then it suddenly paused and peered over its right shoulder.

Something had caught its attention, something more interesting than me. It glanced back at me one last time before turning and running toward the noise in the distance.

"Thank the gods." I exhaled as I reached for my trousers again.

After I had relieved myself, I made my way back to my bedroll and stared at the sky once more. Eventually, exhaustion overtook me, and I drifted off into a dreamless sleep.

CHAPTER SIX

Faolan

The sun had yet to crest over the mountains to the east, but even from the bottom of the valley, the sky was bright with morning light.

Splashes of pinks and oranges streaked across the sky in sharp contrast to the dark silhouettes of the trees on the mountain ridge. There were shimmering waterfalls rolling down the hills and joining the sparkling river that followed our direction of travel.

Fionn had awoken before me and was filling our waterskins in the nearby stream. A few of the other guards were starting to wake as well, and I rolled over to see them stretching and sitting up.

A loud growl sounded from my stomach, and I fished through the food satchel in my pack, pulling out a few dried apricots and some nuts before turning to face the guards.

"Everard, can you make some of the porridge Conleth packed for us? The sooner we can have breakfast, the sooner we can continue on our journey."

"Of course, sir," Everard replied.

"Your Highness," Fionn corrected as he returned and handed me my waterskin.

Everard turned to glance at Fionn before addressing me again, "Sorry, Your Highness." He bowed and walked away to complete the task.

"Forgive him, he's still new." Fionn took a seat next to me and continued, "Do you think we'll make it to the castle today?"

"I talked to Warin and some of the other senior guards before we left, and they said it was less than a day's ride from this valley. I'm hoping we will make it before sunset." I stood and pulled a jacket on over my tunic. The morning air was cold, and I could see my breath before me as I walked over to where Everard was making the porridge.

After we finished our breakfast, we packed up the bedrolls and saddled the horses. I could tell that Dulachan was growing weary from not being able to rest properly in his stable.

I stroked his neck before pulling up each of his hooves to check for any rocks or roots that may cause him discomfort or slow him down. Once I deemed all four hooves ride-ready, I mounted him and turned toward the river we had been following through the valley.

We rode through the narrow gap at the north end of the valley and into a vastly more wooded area. The tall pine trees blocked most of the light, and the underbrush grew thicker the further north we traveled. We only stopped once at midday to water and graze the horses, relieve our bladders, and eat a bit of food.

After the quick break, we continued on our journey, climbing a small peak and then following along the banks of another river that fed into the lake where Queen Melisende's castle resided.

The sun was lowering in the sky when the castle finally came into view. It sat on an island, the two towers appearing to float above the lake. There was a sour taste in my mouth, and my stomach dropped.

I pulled Dulachan to a halt, and Fionn stopped his horse next to mine. I sat there and stared at the castle for a moment, reminding myself of what I was expected to do. My body shivered from chills that had nothing to do with the cold, and I rubbed my palms along my thighs to warm myself.

Even though I knew what I had to do, reality hit me like a ton of bricks with the castle looming in the near distance. I took a deep breath and looked at Fionn, faking confidence I didn't feel. "This is it."

"Are you ready?" He looked at me sympathetically.

"As ready as I'll ever be." I turned and faced the guards who had pulled up behind Fionn and me. "Stay here," I instructed. "According to the law of the Etesian Isles, it will be seen as an act of war if I approach the castle with more than just my personal servant. Fionn will accompany me to the gates and return after I enter. Camp here in the hills, and I will give you a signal in twenty-four hours to indicate that I am safe."

"What kind of stupid fucking rule is that?" Fionn sputtered, and I frowned at him.

I nudged my heels into Dulachan's sides and urged him forward. "The law was instituted after a king and his guards attacked another monarch in their own castle. I've been told it was Melisende's father who attacked in Leuconotos. King Patrice announced his visit as trade negotiations, but he and his guards attacked the first night after they arrived. If the guards are not explicitly invited, you cannot bring them into another royal estate."

"So, we are supposed to trust that the queen will not harm you?" Fionn snapped, raising a challenging eyebrow.

"The Boreans may not play by the rules, but I will." I shot Fionn a glance that said the matter was settled and adjusted in my saddle. Of course I'd prefer to have at least one guard, even a new recruit, with me in my enemy's castle, but angering the queen by not following a longstanding rule was even less preferable.

Fionn and I continued down the hill and rode along the banks of the lake. I took a deep breath to calm my racing nerves and inhaled the fragrant scent of the heather flowers.

I was surprised to see flowers blooming near winter in this desolate kingdom. When we reached the gatehouse, my eyes followed the small bridge beyond which led to the castle. The two towers seemed much larger and more ominous now that we were close. We pulled our horses to a stop, and a guard appeared.

"Who are you?" the guard shouted. He looked old and withered, and I would have wondered if he was mortal, but the points of his ears gave away his fae heritage. How old must he have been when he reached the aibithe? "Why are you here?"

"I am Prince Faolan of Caecias. My father wrote to the queen and informed her of my visit. I am here to broker a peaceful alliance between our kingdoms."

The guard rolled his eyes and turned back toward the gatehouse. His reaction wasn't surprising given that our kingdoms were enemies, but I still expected at least some semblance of respect given my royal status. After a few moments, he reappeared from within the building.

"You may enter," the guard finally said, his tone dry. "Is your *servant* accompanying you?" He eyed Fionn's uniform suspiciously as he spoke.

"No. He's not my servant, nor is he accompanying me. He is a friend and will leave as soon as I am inside the gates. I know and honor the law," I replied, and the guard just stared at me for a moment before waving his hand toward the portcullis.

I shifted in my saddle and whispered, "Thank you, Fionn. I'll send you a signal tomorrow so that you know I am alive and safe."

"Good luck, Faolan. I have a feeling you're going to need it," he said as I turned back around in my saddle. As I crossed under the now raised portcullis, I heard Fionn continue, "And remember, the strong may fall…"

"…but they never yield." I inclined my head, then continued across the bridge and toward my enemy's castle.

The small island before me was sparse. Only the castle, a stable, and a spindly yew tree occupied the land. A tall, muscular male waited at the far side of the bridge for me, eyes narrowing as I approached.

I had never met Queen Melisende's personal guard, Foulke, but his immense stature and intimidating facial scar made him easy to identify. From what I had heard, he was taller than Cathal, who was the tallest of my brothers at 6'5. I had also heard that Foulke received his infamous scar in the battle where his father was killed.

I continued my slow but steady pace until I reached the island, at which point I pulled my horse to a stop in front of Foulke, who regarded me carefully.

"Your Highness," Foulke said and slightly inclined his head. His eyes sparked a bit in surprise. "I'm sorry, but I was expecting your brother, Brenhin."

I gritted my teeth. *Not meeting expectations again. What's new?*

Dismounting my horse, I met his gaze with mine. "Sorry to disappoint. I'm Faolan, the new—"

"The new general," Foulke finished my sentence, lips thinning. "We heard of your promotion. We just didn't expect your father to send someone so… new to their role."

He turned his head and looked toward the small stone and wood stables.

A young male was standing outside, leaning against the wall, and Foulke shouted toward him, "Ethann! Come here." He turned back to me and continued, "He'll take care of your horse, as well as clean and feed him. You can follow me. I'll bring you into the castle."

I rubbed the side of Dulachan's neck, then handed the reins to the stable boy that approached. "Thank you." I smiled at him.

He was young, only about twelve years old, and appeared mortal. It was very rare to see mortals in the Etesian Isles, even less so to see them interacting with fae, let alone in a royal household. The kid was tall and gangly, and his brown skin shimmered in the last rays of sunlight. His nose was a bit crooked, and I noticed his ears were softly rounded instead of coming to the elegant points that all fae ears have.

He happily led my horse away, and I turned to look at Foulke. "Is he—"

"Mortal? Yes. A large boat carrying mortals was shipwrecked off our coast years ago. Not many survived, but we took in the ones who did. Ethann was orphaned in the incident, and the queen saw fit to take him in as her ward."

It was hard for me to reconcile the disparate images of the queen. The bloodthirsty, power-hungry female that has killed thousands of fae, including her father, and the apparently kind-hearted queen who would take in an orphaned mortal.

I watched as Ethann walked to the stables. He seemed happy and well taken care of. I wondered if all mortals were treated as well in Boreas. I also wondered how much devastation was caused by the mortal Raiders in this kingdom or if they only plagued mine.

"Follow me, Your Highness. I'll lead you into the castle," Foulke said, and I followed him along the small dirt path to the left.

We walked past a large, round guard tower covered in ivy and toward a small gate at the side of the shorter of the two towers that comprised the castle. Another guard stood at the door and nodded at Foulke as he allowed us inside.

I ducked under the door frame, and my nose was immediately filled with the combination of freshly baked bread, sweet oranges, and some kind of flower I couldn't quite place.

"I would say that I'm sorry about your brother, but honestly, he was a scoundrel." I grimaced at his description of Cathal. It's not that I didn't agree; Cathal was ruthless, but I was shocked at how casually Foulke mentioned him in my presence. "So... how are you adjusting to being the new general?" Foulke continued as we climbed the stairs.

I cleared my throat. "My father sent me on one small mission before. I think he considers this my first official mission as general even though I believe my brother Bradach is more suited to peace talks."

We finished climbing the flight of stairs, and then I followed Foulke along a narrow corridor. "Interesting," Foulke mused with a wry look.

"I am looking forward to meeting the queen, though," I said, but my voice lacked the confidence I was trying to convey. A small laugh left Foulke's mouth at my statement.

Obviously, he saw through me. I averted my eyes and glanced at the torches hanging from the walls.

He paused at the end of the hallway and turned to me. "You can wait in the reception parlor on the other side of this door. The queen will be down shortly to meet you."

Foulke looked me over one last time before turning to retreat back down the hallway.

I opened the large wooden door before me and stepped inside. The parlor was nicely furnished, if a little plain. There were paintings on the walls which I assumed were of the royal family throughout the years.

There was a portrait of a male I recognized to be Geralt Corentin, the queen's grandfather, the one who had murdered my ancestors in his bid to rule his own kingdom. Next to him was the image of his mate. On another wall was a portrait of Patrice Corentin, the late king and Queen Melisende's father. The painting next to his was of a beautiful blonde female who I assumed was his mate. She passed away shortly after childbirth.

Conspicuously absent was a portrait of the current queen, which struck me as odd since she had been on the throne for nearly one thousand years, which was more than enough time to commission a royal painting.

I had never seen her, but rumors said she was beautiful.

Beautiful and deadly.

Continuing my perusal of the room, I walked toward a side table at the far end of the space. My fingers ran across the soft, worn leather of a large sofa. There were simple blue linen curtains hanging from the windows and a large fur rug in the middle of the room. All of the couches were arranged around the fireplace.

And then I noticed her. In the corner was a single chair with a female sitting in it reading.

I didn't know who she was, but sard if she wasn't the most beautiful female I had ever seen. She had hazel eyes that shifted from green to brown as the light from the fireplace shone on them. Her brown hair was pulled back into a messy braid which fell in front of her right shoulder, and a few loose strands of hair around her face caressed her cheeks.

She was wearing a simple navy tunic and tight leather trousers that hugged her long, lean legs. My eyes slowly made their way down her legs to her boots, which were simple and worn, covered with dirt as though she had just returned from a long horse ride.

I wondered whether she was a friend of the queen and if perhaps they had been riding earlier in the day. The queen was most likely washing and making herself presentable before coming to meet me. At least there could be one good thing coming out of this mission: I wouldn't mind getting to know this beautiful female better.

She either hadn't noticed my arrival or didn't care, as she hadn't looked up from her book once. I moved toward the small side table and noticed what looked to be a bottle of wine and some glasses, so I poured myself a drink.

I glanced back over at the female reading in the corner, and her head lifted slightly as she eyed me curiously for a moment.

Her gaze traveled from my face, across my chest, then down my stomach. Everywhere her eyes followed it felt like a cool wintery breeze kissing my skin and a trail of goosebumps erupted along the path.

Her icy gaze made it all the way down to my boots before slowly traveling back up and reaching my eyes. I wasn't sure why my body was reacting to her in this way, but I was frozen in place, not wanting this surreal moment to end.

She narrowed her gaze slightly, and I raised a questioning eyebrow at her, but she just returned her attention to her book.

I couldn't help but wonder what she was reading that had her so captivated that she continued to ignore me.

Taking a sip of the drink I'd poured myself, I moved to take a seat at the couch furthest away from the curious female. I swirled the wine in my glass; it was good, really good. I took another sip and watched the flames in the fireplace dance on the pieces of wood within.

My attention shot to the door when I heard two male voices in the hallway. I watched the door open and Redwald, the queen's advisor, walked in before Foulke closed the door from the hallway.

Redwald had visited Caecias on numerous occasions. He was one of the only fae from the Kingdom of Boreas that I had met previously. Redwald indeed looked the part of a traditional advisor. He wasn't extremely tall for a fae, being only 6'1, and he was lean and pale from years spent reading indoors instead of fighting outdoors.

He had honey-toned skin that belied his Chthoni heritage. The Chthoni fae were born of Danu, the Goddess of Earth, and lived in the Kingdom of Terraviridi on the continent. His hair was dark brown and curly, the length stopping short of his shoulders, but the top had been tied back away from his face.

There was a patch of grey hair over his left eye, which made his grey eyes stand out. His nose was large and hooked which only became more pronounced when he donned his spectacles.

His gaze flicked around the room quickly before landing on me. He smiled, and his eyes crinkled around the edges.

"Faolan, it's good to see you again," Redwald announced as he took my arm in a welcoming grip, and the female in the corner looked up at me again with a curiously raised eyebrow.

"Same, Redwald," I replied, releasing his arm before taking my seat once more.

"To be honest, we were expecting Brenhin when we received your father's letter, though it is good to have you here." Redwald took a seat in another one of the large chairs surrounding the table, then looked over at the female. A smile played on his lips. "Let me introduce you to Melisende, Queen of Boreas."

CHAPTER SEVEN
Melisende

"Good boy, Phillipe," I praised my horse as I dismounted, handing his reins off to one of the stable boys and walking toward the castle.

I had been riding along the hills surrounding lake all morning and finally returned home. As I turned to make my way to the castle, I noticed two riders approaching the gatehouse.

I knew instantly that it wasn't the friend I was expecting. Jenephie had written to me stating that she would be arriving soon to visit, but she usually came with an entourage of attendants and a carriage to hold all of her trunks. She didn't know the meaning of traveling light.

It was most likely Prince Brenhin from Caecias, but I hadn't been expecting him for another day or two.

I watched as my guard, Durward, questioned the males at the gate. After a couple of seconds, one of them turned around and left, while the other passed under the portcullis.

"Do you think it's Brenhin?" Foulke asked as I passed him on my way toward the castle entrance.

"He must have left immediately after the messenger to arrive so quickly." I looked back over my shoulder at the rider as he slowly crossed the bridge, my nose scrunching in disgust. "If it is, I'll meet him in the parlor."

Foulke nodded in response, and I entered the castle.

I had met Brenhin a few times over the past couple hundred years. He was as formidable as his father and coveted power and the throne above all else. No wonder wolves were the symbol of the Dulaine family; they were dangerous and cunning.

If it was Brenhin, I expected him to talk a good game about the alliance before he made an attempt on my life. Being the one to kill me would give him the clout he needed to eventually take over the crown of Caecias.

I didn't bother to get cleaned up. If it was Brenhin, he could meet me in my dusty riding clothes.

I stopped by the kitchens on the first floor and grabbed a bread roll, taking a large bite from it as I walked across the long corridor that separated the two towers of the castle.

One of the maids was cleaning in the parlor as I arrived. I sent her away, but not before asking her to have a valet bring some wood and start a fire in the fireplace.

I took a seat in the large leather chair by the hearth and picked up the book I had been reading about a female who defeated and tamed a wyvern. I had just gotten to the beginning of a really good scene when I abandoned it for sleep the previous evening.

The valet entered the room and started the fire. Almost immediately I could feel the heat sinking deep into my bones, warming me from the outside in.

I placed my bookmark on the table next to me and read the first few lines on the page, trying to find exactly where I had stopped reading the previous evening. It took me a moment to find my place, but when I tried to read further my mind kept returning to the visitor at the gates.

Was Brenhin going to make an attempt on my life? Were the attacks on Western Etesia severe enough to knock some sense into King Rian? Did he really send his son to discuss the attacks and call a truce?

I shook my head and returned my attention to the book. A few minutes later—and having read the same sentence multiple times over—I finally abandoned hope of being able to focus.

I couldn't have been in the parlor for more than a few minutes when the door opened and a young fae male entered the room. *That's not Brenhin Dulaine*. Was this male another in Rian's brood? He had to be, as he just looked like a Dulaine.

He was tall, not nearly as tall as his brothers or father, but most likely a couple inches taller than me. His black-brown hair fell in waves over the right side of his forehead. His eyes were a dark brown like his father but held a warmth that Rian's never had.

He was wearing black head to toe, his tunic open at the neck to reveal the top of his muscular chest. The black trousers he wore were tight along his large, muscular thighs.

He was handsome, but all the Dulaine males were, devastatingly so.

He slowly walked across the room and made his way to the side table. As he reached for the bottle of wine, I noticed a large silver and turquoise ring on his right hand. I recognized it immediately as the ring his grandfather, Sidach Neville, used to wear.

I returned my eyes to my book but kept my peripheral vision on the male to see what he would do.

So, this is who King Rian decides to send? Some young, untested son?

I knew Brenhin, Rian's eldest and heir to the throne, and of course I knew Cathal. But the other sons, I hadn't met.

I knew one of Rian's other sons was his spymaster. His name was something like Bearach or Bradach. And there was another son that had been named the new general after Cathal, but I couldn't remember his name. I wasn't sure how many sons Rian had in total, but it had to be at least four.

The male looked in my direction, but I kept my eyes firmly on my book. Through my periphery, I watched as he slowly poured himself a glass of wine.

He took a long sip of the burgundy liquid, then licked his lips.

I looked up, and our eyes locked. It appeared as though he visibly shivered under my gaze. This was going to be much easier than I originally thought, and a laugh filled my head.

I wasn't sure if I should be glad Rian sent such a weak son or insulted that he thought this was all it would take.

I returned my attention back to my book and reread the same sentence for what must have been the twentieth time.

The male took his glass of wine, and sat on one of the couches opposite me. He took another long sip of his drink as he looked out the window.

No sooner did the young male sit, than the door opened, and Redwald walked in.

He noticed the young male and walked over toward him. "Faolan, it's good to see you again."

"Same, Redwald," he replied, standing to shake arms with him.

Faolan? I searched my brain until it dawned on me; Redwald had told Foulke and me that Rian had named his son Faolan as the new general. Beyond being the youngest son and being named Caecias's new general, I didn't know anything about this prince. But he was a

Dulaine, he was a Caecian, and that was enough for me to hate him.

"To be honest, we were expecting Brenhin when we received your father's letter, though it is good to have you here," Redwald continued as he took his seat.

"Sorry to disappoint." The dry tone in which he replied almost made me laugh.

Was he as much of a disappointment in his own lands as he was here? His gaze shifted slowly from my advisor to me, and I stared straight into his eyes. We stayed like that until Redwald cleared his throat, a smile pulling at the corners of his lips.

"Let me introduce you to Melisende, Queen of Boreas." Redwald waved his hand in my direction, prompting me to stand and walk over toward the young prince.

My vision raked over Faolan's body from head to toe again, sizing him up.

"It's an honor to finally meet you, Your Majesty," he said, appearing surprised. It was the first time a Dulaine had looked upon me with something other than contempt and murderous intent in their eyes. A flush of adrenaline tingled through my body before I straightened my posture and composed myself.

"Why did your father send you?" Without meaning to, my words came out sharper than intended.

"I, uh…" he sputtered, then he swallowed and started again. "I'm here to discuss an alliance between Boreas and Caecias. My father sent a letter—"

"You misunderstand me, *Little Wolf*," I interrupted him. I already knew that King Rian wasn't interested in an alliance, and I didn't want to waste my time pretending otherwise. What I really wanted to know was why Rian chose *him*. "My question isn't *why* your father sent you, my question is why your father sent *you*. Your oldest brother is heir to the throne, is he not?"

Faolan stood frozen before me, and I took the opportunity to walk around him, narrowing my eyes before coming to a stop.

"Instead, your father sends his… youngest son? Have you even reached the aibithe yet?" I challenged.

"I…" he sputtered again, seeming to be at a loss for words.

I returned to my chair and lowered myself back down slowly. Yes, this was going to be much easier than I originally thought.

"See, I think your father was afraid to send his eldest son and heir into the dangerous witch's lair, so instead he sent his spare son. Oh," I laughed as I leaned back in my chair and crossed my legs, "I guess you aren't a spare anymore… You know, since I sent your brother back under a black shroud and your father appointed you as general."

Faolan's brows furrowed at that. He seated himself on the sofa and looked me directly in the eyes. "Yes, I was named the new general, but for now my only purpose in coming here, Your Majesty, is to discuss the alliance between our kingdoms."

I couldn't help but scoff at this. "I know your father too well to believe that an alliance is why he has sent you to my door. He doesn't want peace, so you can return home. You won't find peace here."

"If you know my father so well, then you must also know that I cannot go home until I've done what he has asked of me." His voice held more confidence now.

My fingers dug into the arms of my chair. "And what exactly has he asked of you?" I stared directly into his eyes, my words a challenge.

"I already told you: he sent me to form a peaceful alliance between our kingdoms."

"We'll see about that," I replied and stood from my chair. I passed Faolan as I made my way toward the door. Looking over my shoulder to Redwald, I said, "Show the wolf pup to his room. He can stay for the night, but he leaves in the morning."

"I'm *not* leaving in the morning," Faolan fired back as he shot up from where he was sitting.

I turned around to glare at him. "Yes, you are." I exited the room without another word. Foulke was waiting in the hallway, leaning against the wall. I took a few steps toward him, and he smiled at me in amusement.

Foulke opened his mouth to speak, but Redwald's voice approached from the parlor.

"Follow me, Your Highness." He led Faolan out of the parlor and up the stairs toward the guest rooms. When they were gone, Foulke turned to me once more.

"Well, that was a surprise," he said, breaking the silence.

"You can say that again." I exhaled a loud breath through my nose.

Foulke appeared to weigh his words for a moment. "I talked to the kid a bit as I escorted him into the castle."

"And?" I pressed.

"First impressions? He's young and untested. If I had to guess, I'd say Rian sent him to prove himself. And that makes him dangerous."

I almost laughed. "Dangerous? Are you serious? This kid hasn't even reached the aibithe yet!"

"Yes, Meli," Foulke said, eyes narrowing. I stopped laughing and looked at my guard. "Rian may have made Faolan's position as general provisional. His title and position in the kingdom could be dependent on whether or not he is able to assassinate you. And *that* makes him dangerous."

"And you think he can succeed where Cathal failed?"

"Hardly, but that doesn't make him less of a threat to you." Foulke's eyes left mine as he looked toward the stairs where Redwald was making his way back down from the guest rooms.

I straightened. "Redwald, what do you know of this little princeling? You've met him in Caecias before, right?" I asked as he approached.

He nodded. "Yes, I met him on one of my visits to Caecias. He was introduced to me as King Rian's youngest son. He still has a few years before he reaches the aibithe, and I get the impression that he isn't well respected by his father or brothers." He paused for a moment. "I would be careful, Meli. If this trip is a chance for him to gain that respect and earn the position of general, he could be quite dangerous."

I looked at both of them before turning to the stairs. "I'll keep that in mind. But for now, I'm going to my rooms to get cleaned up before dinner."

There was a twitchy feeling in my hands, and I clenched them into fists. This prince was going to be a pain in my ass until I could get rid of him.

CHAPTER EIGHT
Faolan

Sard. Well, that could have gone better.

Redwald silently led me up two flights of stairs and to a floor that housed a few rooms. He opened the door at the end of the short hallway. "This is your room and that,"—he pointed toward a door across the hall—"is the washroom. Let the servants know if you are in need of anything."

I nodded my thanks and watched as he retreated back down the hallway and descended the stairs.

With a sigh, I entered the room, closed the door behind me, and immediately collapsed on the large bed. Melisende's scent was still swirling around my nose, and I sunk further into the mattress.

I laid there for several minutes wondering what I had gotten myself into and how I was going to survive an entire week in this kingdom, let alone a single evening.

The queen had made it obvious that she intended to send me back home tomorrow morning, but my father would not allow me to return home without completing my mission. He had sent me here to kill the queen, and I knew if I returned home without finishing her off, I would most likely be dead in her place.

The wind howled outside, and I slowly stood from where I had been lying on the bed to stretch my back. It had been a long few days of riding to get here, and I was looking forward to finally sleeping in a real bed again tonight.

The room was well-appointed, with a large four poster bed in the middle of the space. The dark blue linens covering the duvet were slightly rough to the touch, but the sheets underneath were comfortable enough. In the corner was a large, plush chair next to a small table under a picturesque window. In the opposite corner sat a wardrobe, and my pack was sitting on the floor next to it. I assumed the servants had brought it to my room after taking Dulachan to the stables.

I kicked my boots off and walked over to the chair in the corner under the window. Then I noticed a book sitting on the table beside it. I picked it up and examined it.

It was the old fable of the wolf and the witch. "Interesting reading material," I said aloud to myself with a chuckle as I flipped through the pages before setting the book back down. I hadn't read that book since I was a kid.

Wolves were the symbol of the Dulaine family, so it was always my favorite story growing up, and I would beg my mother to read it to me every night. She always obliged and told me that someday I would meet a princess as kind as the witch in the fable and that we would fall in love. I wanted to believe she was right, but I knew it was foolish to believe in fairytales.

Back across the room, I opened the door and stepped into the hallway. It was silent. I wondered how often guests stayed at the castle and if there were any currently occupying the other rooms, or if I was alone on this floor.

I also wondered where Foulke and Redwald slept. Melisende's castle was much smaller than any of those in Caecias. From what I could tell, the castle was comprised of two towers. The larger, taller tower made of some kind of red sandstone housed a great hall next to the reading parlor on the ground floor where I had met Melisende, a large dining room on the first floor that I saw as Redwald and I had been ascending the stairs, the guest rooms where I was currently staying on the second floor, and I assumed Melisende's personal rooms on the top floor.

I had only passed through the smaller tower on my way into the castle and assumed it housed the kitchen, armory, and servants' rooms.

The washroom was across the hallway, and I opened the door and entered. It was surprisingly comfortable. There was a large tub and jars of salts and flowers to scent the water. There was also a selection of towels hanging from racks on one of the walls, all were soft to the touch.

I walked toward the vanity and saw multiple jugs sitting beside a basin. Steam wafted from the jugs; Redwald must have informed one of the servants to bring water up for me to wash with.

I removed my tunic and placed it on a nearby stool before pouring water into the basin. My hands sunk into the steaming water, and I let the heat soak deep into my bones. I splashed some on my face and let it run down my neck and shoulders in little rivulets.

Reaching for a bar of soap that rested next to the basin, I found it smelled of sweet flowers and immediately reminded me of Melisende.

Her scent was soft and sultry, and I wondered whether her skin was equally soft. With a start, I shook my head and tried to erase all thoughts of her. *She is your enemy!* my mind screamed. I was here for a purpose, and I needed to stay focused on my task.

I lathered some soap between my hands and washed my face, attempting to scrub the long days of riding off my skin. After rinsing the soap from my skin, I reached for one of the towels and dried off, grabbing my tunic from the stool and returning to my bedroom to change for dinner.

My pack was still sitting next to the wardrobe, so I crossed the room and picked it up, fishing through it for a clean tunic. I hadn't packed much considering my stay in Boreas was supposed to only last a week, just one spare pair of trousers and a couple tunics.

I pulled out my nicest tunic, the one I wore for official, royal events in Caecias. It was black and had silver embroidery along the neck and the cuffs of the sleeves.

Pulling it over my head, I smoothed the front over my chest and stomach. I pushed the sleeves up to my elbows, revealing the tattoo of a sword on my right arm, and ran my fingers over the tattoo, feeling the ridges from the scar it covered.

I ignored the growing discomfort that sat in my throat like a lump of stone every time I thought about how I received that scar.

Instead, I took a deep, bracing breath and turned my thoughts to my mother.

She was the strongest woman I knew. *The strong may fall, but they never yield.* It was my mother's motto, and I reminded myself that I would not yield to any doubts or insecurities, nor would I yield to Queen Melisende.

My chest tightened as I thought about the task ahead of me. Was I a fool to believe that this mission, that killing the queen, would actually gain me the respect I so desperately craved from my father?

I stared at my hands in my lap and twisted my grandfather's turquoise ring around my finger as I tried to slow my rapid breathing.

No, I refused to let this mission beat me before I even started, so I decided to focus my mind on one step at a time. I needed to decide how, where, and when I was going to slay Melisende.

The when was the easiest. Melisende had told Redwald that she wanted me gone in the morning. My father had given me a week, whereas Melisende had given me the night. Unless by some miracle I could convince her to let me stay the week, I would have to kill her tonight.

But how and where would I kill her? These were much more difficult questions. There were so many guards stationed throughout the castle, and I doubted I'd be able to go anywhere without being followed or watched. Not to mention the only weapon I currently had on me was a hidden dagger I'd snuck through the gates of the castle.

The only option I saw forward was a dagger to the heart, likely in the middle of the night when the guards were off duty and less were present to monitor my comings and goings.

Well, if the queen didn't keep one posted on me at all times.

Suddenly, a loud click brought me back to the present and away from my plotting. It had sounded like a door closing, and I assumed it was from another room on my floor.

Curiosity got the better of me, and I quickly rose from where I had been sitting and crossed the room to the door. I opened it and looked down the hall but saw no one. Frowning, I returned to my room and looked out of the large picture window at the night sky.

It was then that I noticed how much darker it had grown while I had been planning how I would kill the queen.

I turned to look in the mirror, straightening my tunic. I decided to see if I could find Redwald before dinner to ask him about the castle, guards, and nightly routines.

Pausing, I rolled my eyes and knew my brother Bradach would be disappointed in my spy skills, or big fucking lack thereof. Walking out of my room, I glanced down the hallway one last time before descending the stairs.

With each step I took, I reminded myself of my mother's mantra, *The strong may fall, but they never yield.*

I could do this.

CHAPTER NINE
Faolan

Torches illuminated the spiral staircase as I made my way back down to the first floor of the castle. I remembered seeing a grand banquet hall here when Redwald had escorted me from the parlor to my room earlier in the day, so I headed in that direction.

I was surprised at how small the castle was; each floor of the red tower only contained a handful of rooms, if that. Most castles in the Isles—at least so I was told, for I had yet to visit any—were grand with multiple wings and tall towers. Melisende's castle was more of a large estate.

Part of me wondered whether Melisende possessed other larger castles further north hidden in the mountains of her kingdom.

My grandfather had a large castle built near a lake in the south. Both he, and my father after him, liked to spend winter in that castle as the weather was generally warmer than in the capital. We also had another castle in the Coill Forest that was referred to as the hunting lodge because my family didn't think it large enough to be considered a proper castle, but even that was larger than this estate.

I finished my descent down the staircase and turned to enter the banquet hall. It was dark and completely empty save for the large table and chairs that sat at the very center of the room. The table could easily accommodate twenty individuals, and I wondered how often it was fully seated. I took another step into the room and noticed that there were no dishes or cutlery present. The few candlesticks on the table were not lit, and the large fireplace was empty, with not even a grate or firewood in its hearth.

It appeared as if the room hadn't been used for quite some time, which made me wonder where we were to eat if not in the dining hall.

Curious, I exited the room and walked down the long corridor toward the smaller tower of the castle. At the end of the corridor was a short, narrow staircase leading to the entrance of a room. I peeked inside, seeing it appeared to be a smaller, less formal dining space, probably used by the servants. There was a door at the opposite end of the room, and based on the smell emanating from it and the sounds just beyond the door, I assumed it led to the kitchen.

As I took another step into the room, I noticed Redwald sitting at one end of a table reading some papers.

"Faolan, I see you've found your way." He looked up from his papers and smiled warmly at me.

It was surprising, but I deeply appreciated the kindness radiating from the male who, as the advisor to the queen, was considered as much an enemy as she was.

He continued, "I forgot to mention to you earlier that the queen and I usually dine in the servants' dining room next to the kitchens."

I took another step and looked around. The table would only seat about eight individuals and wasn't decorated like a grand dining hall in the slightest. Redwald looked at me as though he was waiting for me to say something, but I just continued my assessment of the space.

When I didn't speak, he added, "Dinner will be served shortly. Feel free to take a seat and join me."

I offered a polite smile and sat down in the chair near him, opposite the doorway.

"You said you usually eat in this room instead of the dining hall?" I looked at Redwald, not quite believing they would eat in such a modest space when they were entertaining guests at the castle, especially a royal guest.

"Yes," he chuckled. He set the papers he was reading down and turned toward me. "I'm guessing you're not used to such modest surroundings?"

"It's just that I noticed the large dining hall on my way down from my room. Why don't you dine in there? Wouldn't that be a more appropriate room to take dinner in when you are hosting guests?" I wondered.

"Appropriate? Maybe, but it seems such a large room when it's usually no more than four of us eating together. Even with guests, we rarely serve more than six individuals at a time. This room is a bit more intimate and closer to the kitchen, which is much easier for the staff."

I balked at him. The idea that any royalty would care for what is easier for the servants nearly made me laugh. Not that I wanted to make the staff's life any harder than it already was, it just wouldn't occur to my father or brothers to do something for their benefit.

Then I smiled, realizing it sounded like something my mother would suggest.

"I guess so," I mused as I reached for the pitcher of water sitting in the middle of the table and poured myself a drink. "I'm just surprised, that's all."

"Not good enough for you, Little Wolf?"

I froze when I heard the queen's voice come from just outside the dining room. My heart started racing as I looked up to see Queen Melisende enter.

She was wearing a long navy dress with a plunging neckline, and my eyes traced the narrow strips of fabric that covered her pert breasts from her shoulders all the way down to her stomach. The fabric was diaphanous and almost appeared sheer.

Every step she took revealed the slit up the front of the gown and showcased her long, lean legs. I swallowed as my gaze traveled from her legs back up her beautiful form.

Unlike when we met, her hair was now loose and fell over her shoulders in cascading waves. Also, she wore a crown, one unlike any other crown I had seen a monarch wear; it was modest and made of shards of dark grayish blue crystals.

She looked even more queen-like and intimidating than earlier today, and I felt as though she was trying to put me in my place. My heartbeat increased, and my palms were suddenly sweaty as I attempted to maintain my composure.

She came to take a seat at the table across from me, and as she lowered, my eyes wandered to her breasts. They were small, but attractive and well-shaped. It was then that I noticed a small scar on her chest. It was no more than an inch wide and sat just above her heart.

Feeling as though my gaze had lingered too long, I cleared my throat and looked up to find her eyes fixed on mine.

She shifted her gaze toward Redwald as she reached for her necklace and adjusted it so that the stone covered the small scar. I couldn't help but wonder what could have caused that injury over her heart and why she felt the need to hide it.

Someone cleared their throat, and it was then that I noticed the other female that had followed the queen into the dining room and was now seated to her left.

She was shorter and curvier than Melisende, with flaming red hair falling in waves over her shoulders and a crimson dress that clung to everyone one of her ample curves. If I had to guess, I would say she was from the Kingdom of Argestes based on her coloring. Her golden eyes sparkled as she looked at me, and I offered a reserved smile in return.

My gaze returned to Melisende, and I cleared my throat. "I was just surprised to find that you took meals in this small room, as I saw the grand dining hall on my way down from my quarters."

"Hmmm," the queen huffed. She looked toward the staff standing in the corner by the kitchen door and nodded. The servants immediately started bringing platters of food and decanters of wine to the table.

I shifted my gaze back to the woman seated to her left, wondering who this mysterious female was. Melisende noticed my gaze.

"This is Jenephie." She offered no explanation as to who this female was in relation to her or why she was at the dinner with us. My gaze returned to the redhead, and I smiled at her again.

"It's my pleasure," I replied. "I'm Faolan."

"The pleasure is all mine, Faolan," she said with a smirk, then she turned her gaze to Melisende. "Ignore my dear Meli's manners. I'm her oldest friend, and you can call me Jene."

"Jene." I inclined my head. I was surprised by how friendly she was toward me given that I came from a rival kingdom.

"Not that I am anywhere near as old as our dear Meli is, I've just known her the longest." Jenephie laughed, and the sound filled the room. Her laugh was beautiful and melodic, and I liked her immediately.

The servants continued to bring dish after dish of food to the table. They brought platters with roast pheasant and chicken, plates full of every vegetable you could imagine, baskets of freshly baked bread rolls, large wedges of hard cheese, and bowls of mixed nuts and dried fruits. It was indeed an impressive selection. My stomach growled, and my mouth started to water.

Melisende, Jenephie, Redwald, and I all piled food on our plates as the servants poured wine into our goblets. After the last goblet of wine was poured, Redwald raised his drink. "To possible new alliances."

Melisende pressed her lips tightly together behind her glass while the rest of us raised our drinks in toast. I took a sip and nearly moaned; the wine was delicious. It was big and bold with notes of black currant and cherry. I let the wine sit on my tongue before swallowing it. Melisende, however, drained her entire glass before setting it back down on the table. One of the servants quickly rushed over to refill her glass.

I watched as the others at the table started eating. Then I stared at my own plate, thinking about how to broach the subject of the fake alliance. I knew I wasn't going to get anywhere with the queen, but I still had to try. "Speaking of alliances—"

"No," Melisende said abruptly, cutting me off. "There will be no alliance between our kingdoms, Little Wolf. Let us not ruin dinner pretending otherwise." She glared daggers at me before returning to her food and attempting to stab a piece of carrot with her fork, only to have it skip off her plate.

"Tell me Faolan," Jenephie broke the silence lingering in the room, "is it true what they say about the Dulaine males?" Her lips curved in a wry smile.

I almost choked on my pheasant. I wasn't entirely sure what she was referring to, but by the smirk on her face, I assumed it was something related to what was in our trousers. I looked up at her, and she laughed.

Our dinner continued with no more talk of alliances. Every time I looked at Melisende or attempted to start a conversation, Jenephie interrupted and asked me questions about myself and my kingdom. I was starting to think her role was to distract and disorient me, which she was succeeding at.

Occasionally, Redwald added something civilized to the conversation, which I was eternally grateful for. Melisende, however, just ate her dinner in silence, watching and judging us.

After the main course was finished and the plates were cleared, one of the servants poured a caramel-colored liquid into some small wine glasses on the table.

Considering the awkwardness of dinner, I wanted nothing more than to drown the memories with whiskey. I took a long draw from the glass and started coughing as soon as the alcohol hit my throat. It wasn't whiskey.

"Are you alright, Your Highness?" Redwald asked, voice tinged with concern.

"Yes, I am... that's just not what I expected." I continued to cough, trying to clear my throat of the offending alcohol.

"And what exactly did you expect?" Melisende asked, and the right side of her mouth pulled up slightly higher than the left. There was a prickling sensation on the back of my neck. If I didn't hate her so much, I might find that smile entrancing.

"It looks like whiskey," I said, lifting my glass and examining it.

"It's called ratafia," Jenephie replied. "It's a ratified liquor made from grapes."

I took another sip of the ratafia as the servants brought out a cheese course. It wasn't as strong as whiskey, but it was surprisingly smooth and aromatic.

I reached for a slice and took a bite, swallowing slowly and preparing myself for the battle ahead. I needed to talk about the alliance. I needed to try and convince the queen of my benevolent intentions if I had any chance of her allowing me to stay longer than just tonight.

"You shut me down earlier during dinner when I attempted to talk business, but as you are intent on sending me away tomorrow, you give me no choice but to try and discuss it now."

"And what so-called business could you possibly have to discuss with me beyond what you mentioned this afternoon when you arrived?" Melisende locked eyes with me as she slowly took a sip from her glass.

"Nothing. That *is* my business. I'm here to broker a peaceful alliance between our two kingdoms ahead of the alliance among all the Etesian kingdoms. You may not believe that my father means peace with you, but I assure you, I do."

"Oh, Little Wolf, if it was only so easy to believe that." Her condescending tone made my skin crawl.

"Believe it or not, it's the truth. Did King Lancaster or his son inform you of the portals that have been opening on the Western Isle?" I retorted, raising an eyebrow.

"Yes, King Lancaster sent a letter informing me of what he *believes* happened in his kingdom, but that's not possible. There haven't been portals in over a thousand years. They must be mistaken." She looked away and placed a piece of cheese into her mouth.

My eyes landed on her soft lips and stayed there too long for my comfort.

I turned to Redwald, hoping he would see sense. "Not only is it possible, but it has happened twice already," I informed him.

"Twice?" The queen's eyes darted back to me, and she furrowed her eyebrows. "I thought Argestes blamed Leuconotos for the attack on their lands. Not some portal."

I started to wonder how thorough the letter the king had sent was. It obviously didn't contain as much information as we had been able to extract from Prince Lancaster when he visited, which wasn't much, but was more than what was contained in their original letter.

"The prince assured us that they didn't attack Argestes and that he strongly believes the attack was from a portal. He and his father want to form an alliance between the islands because we don't know where these attacks are coming from."

"I already have good relations with the Kingdom of Leuconotos. Actually, I have good relations with all the kingdoms." The queen glared at me. "Except for your father's."

That couldn't be. My father had always told me that Boreas was an outsider. That given the choice, the rest of the kingdoms in the Etesian Isles would see it restored to Caecias.

"Then that is all the more reason for me to be here. Our kingdoms need a relationship outside of the never-ending attacks." My voice started rising. "We could finally have peace between our lands while we are allied against these unknown threats!"

Melisende slammed her glass down on the table. "My biggest threat is from your father!" she sneered.

"He says the same of you!" My heart was pounding in my chest, and my breaths had become more ragged. "If only the two of you would pull your heads out of your asses, maybe we could put this feud behind us and actually address the threats that face us all!"

Melisende stood quickly, her chair skittering back on the wooden floor. "We're done. I want you to leave," she hissed between clenched teeth.

I stood, placing my hands on the table in front of me and leaning forward. "I'm not leaving your kingdom until we come to some kind of agreement. My father gave me a week, so if you want me gone sooner, you better start talking about how we can find some peace between our kingdoms."

"You're going to be sorely disappointed if you think that I'll ever agree to an alliance with your kingdom." She placed her hands on the table and leaned forward so that our faces were mere inches apart. It was then that I noticed the way the green and brown of her irises mixed, creating a tapestry of color in her eyes.

"You say your biggest threat is from my father, yet he is willing to put things aside for this alliance," I said, challenging her once more.

She scoffed. "You want me to be the villain? Let me make this clear, Little Wolf, that is a role I don't mind playing." She leaned back and brushed the skirts of her gown. "We are finished discussing this. I expect you to be gone in the morning."

With that, she pushed her chair further away, turned on her heel, and left the dining area.

I remained standing and took a deep breath before remembering that Melisende and I were not alone. What a performance we had just put on in front of Jenephie and Redwald. I slowly lowered myself back into my chair.

"Sorry, about that. I just…" I wasn't even sure how to finish my thought.

"Queen Melisende has a… *complicated* relationship with your kingdom," Redwald said, and Jenephie looked away from me, the jovial spirit from dinner long gone.

"'Complicated' is one word for it. Now, if you'll excuse me." She stood and bowed slightly toward me and Redwald, her face remaining stoic. I watched as she slowly exited the dining room and headed in the direction that Melisende had retreated before I returned my attention to Redwald.

"There has been much contention between Boreas and Caecias for generations. Melisende is reluctant to believe anything that comes out of the mouth of a Caecian, let alone a Dulaine." Redwald took a sip of his ratafia. "I'm afraid you'll be facing an uphill battle if you intend to actually form an alliance here."

At that, he stood and left the dining room.

I sat at the table alone, staring at the entryway. My pulse thrummed in my throat, and my breathing was shallow. I was used to being shut down by my father, but for some reason being shut down by this foreign queen felt different. I didn't like it, and I didn't want to look into why I didn't like it.

Frowning, I pushed down the feelings I didn't want to admit to and shook off the defeat. I needed some time alone to steel my resolve and ready myself for what I was sent here to do, what my destiny demanded I do.

CHAPTER TEN
Melisende

That insufferable male! I stormed out of the dining room, nearly knocking my chair to the ground as I left the table. He thought he could tell me what to do? He thought he knew what was best for my kingdom? He knew nothing. He *is* nothing!

I climbed the few stairs between the dining room and the long corridor that connected the two towers of the castle. When I turned a corner, I saw Foulke leaning against the wall with his arms crossed.

Sighing, I stopped in front of him. He looked like he was just dying to say something, so I raised an accusing eyebrow at him.

"Looks like you've met your match, Your Majesty," Foulke said with a little smirk I wanted so desperately to slap off his handsome face.

"Do you find this amusing, Foulke? That *child* is our enemy!" I fired back.

"I know he is our enemy. It's just that I've never seen anyone be as stubborn as you, especially straight to your face." He pushed off the wall and took a step closer to me. He looked down at me, that smirk gracing his lips again. "It didn't sound like either of you were willing to back down. And I've never seen anyone get to you the way he did, not even his father."

"Did you just call me stubborn, Foulke?" I took a step closer to him, closing the distance between us.

My eyes met his in challenge. I had always allowed Foulke to speak his mind, which was both a relief and an annoyance. As a queen, many would guard their words in front of me, so I appreciated Foulke's honesty. *Most* of the time.

"Yes?" His booming laugh came deep from his chest and helped relieve some of the tension building inside me. He placed a hand on my shoulder, and his face lit up with a broad smile.

"I hate you," I said as I brushed his hand away.

"No, you don't," he chuckled and turned to walk into the dining room. Then he looked over his shoulder and added, "You know, I don't think he's going to leave voluntarily tomorrow. You'll have to order me to escort him past the gatehouse or you are going to be stuck with the little prince for a bit longer."

I sighed, realizing Foulke may be right. And then my stomach turned sour as I realized I probably wouldn't have him escort Faolan off the castle grounds.

As much as I distrusted Caecians, especially the Dulaines, there was something about the prince that intrigued me. All the Caecian kings had been stubborn and ruthless in their desire to claim my kingdom, but Faolan seemed adamant about ending the ongoing feud. I wasn't naïve enough to take him at his word, but part of me wanted to. Part of me wanted—

"Meli!" Jenephie's voice interrupted my thoughts as she followed me along the corridor and started up the spiral staircase toward my chambers. "Well, that was dramatic."

She had a smile on her face that said she was genuinely amused by everything that had happened at dinner, and that irritated me.

I had known Jenephie since she first moved to my kingdom, and she knew me better than almost anyone, barring Foulke and Redwald. So when she offered insight into the situation I had found myself in, I generally welcomed her input. But when it came to this prince, I wasn't so sure I would welcome anyone's input.

I huffed, "I don't know why King Rian sent this *child*. I know the king has no desire for peace between our kingdoms. So why is he sending his youngest son here to talk about alliances?" I started heading up the final flight of stairs to the third floor where my private rooms were housed, with Jenephie still following closely behind. "The little prince hasn't even reached the aibithe yet."

"At least he is easy on the eyes. Fuck him and send him on his way," Jenephie said with a laugh, her amber eyes sparkling.

"Jene!" I turned on the spot and gaped at my best friend in disbelief. "He's the enemy. What is wrong with you?" I sputtered.

Her smile faltered, and she sighed loudly. "Nothing is wrong with me, and I know he's the enemy. Look, we both know his father probably sent him here to kill you in retribution for the death of Cathal."

"Probably?" I interjected with a scoff.

"Okay, *definitely*." A hint of the playful smile returned to her lips. "You could let him stay the week and see if he even attempts to talk about a peaceful alliance, or you could just send him packing in the morning. It is just a matter of how long you are willing to entertain this obvious pretense."

"I know. I think a small part of me wants to believe that an alliance is possible. I'm tired of this never-ending war, and if there truly are portals threatening us…" I trailed off as I stepped onto the landing outside of my personal rooms.

"We all want to believe an alliance is possible, but I don't think that gorgeous male is going to be the one to deliver it." Jenephie stepped beside me and offered a half-hearted shrug.

I rolled my eyes at her description of the prince. "Gorgeous. Really, Jene?"

"He is. There is no denying that," she said, her perfectly arched eyebrow raising. "Yes, he is our enemy, but that doesn't mean he isn't breathtakingly gorgeous, as well. If only he looked at me the way he looked at you."

Her eyebrows started wagging exaggeratedly while she picked up a strand of my hair and twirled it between her fingers.

"He was probably imagining twenty ways to kill me in my sleep," I groaned.

"Probably," she laughed. She dropped the strand of my hair and moved past me with the swing of her hips. She headed back toward the stairs, but before she started her descent back to her room, she looked over her shoulder and said with a wink, "Since you are not going to, do you mind if I take him for a tumble?"

My gaze snapped to hers, a slight twinge in my stomach. "Gods, you are incorrigible."

"And that's why you love me," she giggled, starting down the stairs.

Jenephie was absurd and ridiculous, and I absolutely loved her for it, even when she made completely inappropriate remarks about our enemies.

Jenephie had moved from the Kingdom of Argestes when her father betrothed her to a noble with a large trading empire on the east coast of Boreas. I met her when she and her betrothed came to the castle asking for my favor in their union. I preferred my citizens to mate for love, but I granted them my favor on the condition that Jenephie was allowed to visit me at the castle whenever she pleased.

I watched as my friend continued down the spiral staircase until she disappeared from view. The torches that lined the walls flickered, and my mind drifted as I stared at the dancing orange flames.

Returning to my rooms, I took my crown off and placed it on the small dressing table next to my wardrobe. It wasn't often that I wore my crown inside my own castle. Unlike some of the other leaders in the Etesian Isles, I didn't feel the need to assert my dominance through the use of jewelry.

I unfastened the back of my dress and let it fall off my shoulders onto the floor. Stepping out of the pile of clothes, I crossed the room to my bathing chamber. My maid had already filled the washing basin with hot water during dinner, and it was cooler than I would normally like, but I splashed the water on my face anyway.

After washing my face and returning to my bedroom, I slipped a chemise over my head and crawled under the covers of my bed.

I reached for my book on the bedside table only to realize I had left it in the parlor after meeting Faolan. Groaning, I crossed the room to my bookcase and pulled out another book to read.

I read the first sentence of the story over and over again, my brain always drifting back to Faolan and the way his jaw would feather just before he spoke.

After the millionth attempt at reading the sentence, I shut the book and let out a deep sigh, placing the book on the bedside table and closing my eyes. Against my will, visions of Faolan swirled in my mind. The way his eyes scanned my body when I entered the dining room, the way he challenged me about the alliance, the way his smell of lavender and leather mixed with something sweeter filled my nose as he leaned across the table, our faces just a hair's breadth apart.

Frustrated, I ripped the sheets off my bed, stood up, and walked to the window. Foulke was right; Faolan wasn't going to leave voluntarily, and I was going to have to accept that he was here to stay for a week or order my guards to escort him off the castle grounds.

I stared into the night beyond the window and tried to distinguish the darkness of the lake from that of the trees and sky. The small waves on the lake shimmered silver, reflecting the light from the moon as they crashed on the shore of the island.

Pulling myself away from the peaceful view, I walked across my bedroom to my small study. There was a large desk under a picture window that overlooked the hills to the north of the lake. I reached for a pen and sheet of parchment, then scribbled, *Meet me at dawn for a morning ride.*

Riding was my release and after the stress of the day, I wished for nothing more than to escape the castle and feel the breeze dance through my hair as I rode Philippe through the hills.

Folding the piece of parchment, I exited my rooms to find a servant to deliver the note to Jenephie. I reached for the torch hanging on the wall of the landing outside of my rooms and made my way down the stairs. The light from my torch bounced along the stone walls until I placed it in an empty sconce at the bottom of the staircase.

The main corridor between the two towers was quiet and dark, with only a single torch lit in the center to provide light. I walked briskly along the corridor and ducked into the small dining room.

"Your... Meli," Mary stammered, her eyes wide in surprise at finding me out of bed at such a late hour.

"Can you please deliver this note to Jenephie's room?" I asked politely.

"Of course," she replied, taking the note.

I smiled at my young servant. "Thank you, Mary."

I turned and retraced my steps back down the corridor and up the spiral stairs to the top floor of the castle. I returned to my bedroom and slipped under the covers. Tomorrow morning, Jenephie and I would get away from the castle and go for a ride.

I closed my eyes, took a deep breath, and waited for sleep to overcome me.

CHAPTER ELEVEN
Faolan

I wasn't sure how long I sat alone in the dining room after the others had left, but the castle was winding down and growing more quiet with each passing minute.

The noises from the kitchen next door slowly came to a stop, and the last of the cooks and servants passed through the small dining room on their way to their evening chores or to adjourn for the evening. Eventually, I stood and blew out all of the candles on the table but one. I reached for the chamberstick holding the last remaining candle and exited the room.

The long corridor between the two castle towers was illuminated by a single torch, and I was grateful I had taken the candle with me. I crossed the corridor and started up the spiral staircase toward my room.

It was then that it occurred to me that Jenephie was probably staying in the other room on my floor and caused the noise I had heard earlier that evening. When I rounded the last of the stairs to the floor that housed my room, I could see a small stream of light coming from under another door, which confirmed my thoughts.

Entering my room, I found it dark save for the small amount of light my candle provided. I set the chamberstick on the side table next to the bed and pulled back the covers. Then I discarded my boots and pulled the dagger from its sheath on my calf before crawling into bed.

If I were to attempt to kill the queen tonight, it would be best if I remained in my clothes and kept my boots and dagger nearby.

My body relaxed as I leaned against the pillows that were propped up against the headboard, but my mind raced. There wasn't a guard stationed directly outside of my room but there was one in the hallway leading to the stairs. On my way back to my room, I had passed another guard, as well as a few servants.

How long would I need to wait before everyone was asleep?

And just because there wasn't a guard outside my room didn't mean there wouldn't be one outside of Melisende's chambers. What would I do if she had a guard posted tonight?

My mind continued to race, and I noticed that I was absentmindedly spinning the turquoise ring on my finger, a nervous trait of mine. I straightened the ring and adjusted in the bed. Then I lowered the pillows and laid on my side, away from the light of the candle.

I didn't know how long it was going to take for the castle to fall into a silent, motionless state, but I was determined to stay awake all night if necessary.

***

The first rays of sunlight crept in through the crack in the curtains and landed on my face, waking me from a fitful sleep. Dust motes floated in the sun beam, and I blinked a few times to take in my surroundings. *Shit!* I had fallen asleep.

I tossed the blankets away, kicked my legs off the side of the bed, and stood up. I needed a new plan. If I couldn't convince the queen to allow me to stay a week, I was going to be ordered to leave and most likely escorted away by her guards.

Walking over to the vanity table next to the wardrobe, I noticed a jug full of water next to the washing basin. I splashed some water on my face, then attempted to brush the wrinkles from my clothes before crossing the room to the window overlooking the lake on which the castle sat.

The landscape was beautiful, the hillsides that surrounded the picturesque lake covered in tall green pine and fir trees, unlike in Caecias where the oak and birch trees turned brown and lost their leaves in autumn.

"The least he could do is die trying to earn his place in this family." My father's voice echoed through my head, disrupting my peace, and I clenched my jaw.

I had failed at my mission, and I wondered if he'd expected me to fail. No, if he *wanted* me to fail. There was a tightness in my chest, and I leaned forward, placing my hands on the windowsill. If he truly wanted Melisende dead, why wouldn't he have sent Brenhin? And if he truly wanted me to be his general, wouldn't he be more concerned with me training alongside my guards?

My heart pounded as anger overtook my body. My hands clenched into fists, and I slammed them down on the windowsill. *Why does my father not care if I die? Why is he so convinced of my failure?*

I took a deep breath, willing my heartbeat to slow and my mind to calm. I still had time; I could still try to kill the queen. It was barely dawn, so maybe she was still asleep.

I returned the dagger to the sheath on my calf and laced up my boots. Silently, I crossed the room and opened the door. There was no one in the hallway as I crept toward the staircase. I was about to take my first step as a voice came out of the darkness.

"I told you to leave. What are you still doing here, Little Wolf?"

Melisende was wearing a sheer black dress with a leather corset cinched at her waist. As she took another step down the stairs and joined me on the landing, I noticed that the dress had a slit all the way from the floor up to the corset, and her legs were covered in skintight black leather leggings.

My eyes traveled the length of her legs and back up to her chest and that small scar that lingered over her heart. Her lips were stained the color of blood, and her hair was tied in a low knot, with a few curls resting on her shoulder. The scent of citrus and night-blooming jasmine filled my nose.

"As I stated last night, I have no plans on leaving before the week is up." I straightened my back and stared back just as hard.

The queen huffed, "You do realize that I could just order Foulke and the guards to escort you past the castle gates, right?"

"But do you realize that your gate only guards the bridge? I could just walk along the banks of the lake before swimming back onto the island," I retorted hotly.

"And I could have you executed for trespassing."

"You could…" I rolled my shoulders back and tightened my jaw before continuing, "or you could let me stay the week before sending me on my way. I have no desire to stay here after I accomplish what I was sent here to do."

"And what is that, Little Wolf?" One of her eyebrows raised in question.

"You know that already. I don't know how many times I have to tell you that I'm here to form an alliance between our kingdoms."

My voice cracked, and I wasn't sure if it was from frustration, nerves, or something else.

"I very much doubt that is what your father sent you here to do." Her gaze drifted to the nearest torch hanging on the walls of the stairwell.

"Do you doubt his intentions or mine?" I pulled my focus back to her eyes.

"Aren't they the same?" Her tone was biting. "You are his pup, are you not?"

"I'm tired of this. Believe what you want, but I was sent here to create an alliance and as I have said multiple times before, I am not leaving until we achieve one."

"If that is what you believe, your father has put you in the impossible position of pursuing peace between two kingdoms that would see each other fall." She pushed past me and started down the stairs. "I'm going for a ride this morning. Leave before I return, or I will have the guards drag you out of the castle. Dead or alive, that's your choice."

I stood frozen on the stairwell and watched the queen continue her descent until she was no longer in view. My head dropped, and my chest felt heavy. I stared at my feet, willing them to move—back to my room, after the queen, out of the castle, I didn't know.

The only thing I knew for certain was that I had failed.

There was no way out of this situation alive.

Resigned, I slowly trudged down the stairs, the sounds of my boots hitting the stone floor filling my ears. I needed to leave the castle, but to do that I needed my horse and my weapons. I made my way to the first floor of the castle and crossed the corridor.

As I passed the small dining room, the smell of cooking food filled my nose, and my stomach grumbled in protest.

Sighing, I made my way past the dining table and poked my head into the kitchen. There was a cook standing next to a few large pots, rolling dough into balls, while a servant was retrieving some dishes from a cabinet. A large table meant for preparing food stood in the center of the room, and there was a smaller counter with stools along the wall.

I watched as steam wafted from the pots behind the cook.

"Hello," I said, greeting him.

"Good morning, Your Highness," the cook said while looking up from the dough he was rolling. "Would you like some breakfast? We can have it brought up to your room if you would like."

"That's not necessary, and please call me Faolan." I smiled at the chef. "Do you have a bread roll or something that I can take with me? I'm planning on returning home today."

"Of course," he replied as he turned to a large pot that appeared to contain boiling oil. He pulled a small round pastry from the oil and dropped it in a bowl of sugar. I watched as he rolled it around, ensuring all sides were covered with the shimmery little crystals. "Here, tell me what you think of this."

I reached for the sugary pastry and took a bite. It was the most delicious thing I had ever eaten. The fried dough was light and fluffy, and the sugar gave it a nice sweetness.

I swallowed that first bite and looked at the chef with wide eyes. "It's delicious."

He laughed a little and nodded. "It's called a doughnut. I learned about the recipe back when I lived on the continent," he explained proudly.

"What is your name?" I asked before taking a seat on a wooden stool in the corner of the kitchen and taking another bite of the doughnut.

"My name is Balfour." He was tall and had a large stomach, but also strong arms covered in tattoos. His skin was a shade darker than mine, but his eyes were a light golden brown.

"It's nice to meet you, Balfour. How long did you live on the continent? And what brought you to Boreas, if you don't mind me asking?" I inquired before shoving the rest of the doughnut into my mouth.

"I was born in Eurus and fought as part of their army during the war with Terraviridi. The Terraviridians had the most delicious cuisine I had ever tasted. After the war was over, I stayed and learned to cook. Then I traveled to other parts of the continent to learn other cuisines. I met Queen Melisende when she was on a diplomatic mission in Lacusia. She told me that I made the most delicious food she had ever eaten and that she wanted to know if I would ever consider moving to Boreas to be her chef. And here I am."

My brows narrowed. "She asked you to be her chef and you agreed? Just like that?"

He chuckled loudly. "*Not* just like that. She asked me every day she was in Lacusia. She also offered me a significantly higher salary than I was making at the time, and requested her advisor stay behind to arrange my move to Boreas. It was nice working for the Queen of Lacusia but I'm happier working for Meli than I was working for anyone else."

Surely, that couldn't be true. I believed him when he said that the queen asked him relentlessly, and I even believed that she offered to pay him more, but he's happier here than anywhere else? That was hard to believe.

I thanked him for my first doughnut then reached for a second one before leaving the castle to head for the stables.

It was a brisk morning, the cold, near-winter wind brushing my cheeks and causing them to turn shades of red and pink. I rubbed my hands together as I looked up at the sky. Clouds were coming in from the west and casting long shadows on the ground.

I walked in the direction of the stables, hoping to find a stable hand to start preparing Dulachan to leave.

As I approached the small stone and wood building, I saw Ethann, the mortal stable boy, taking one of the horses for a walk. I walked over to join them and as Ethann noticed me, he pulled the horse to a halt.

"Hello." My voice was low and soft, not wanting to scare the boy or the horse.

"Hello," he replied without an ounce of trepidation.

I ran my hand along the horse's back. "I was hoping you could help me with something."

"Sure, what did you need?" he answered quickly, and I was impressed with his fearlessness and willingness to help without context.

My eyes returned to find his staring back at me, his eyes bright and full of curiosity. "I am going to be leaving in a bit, and I would like my horse Dulachan to be ready to ride in the next few hours. Do you think you can do that for me?" I requested.

"Of course I can," he said as he pulled on the reins.

The horse resisted at first, but Ethann just clicked his tongue and pulled the reins again. The horse started forward, and the two of them entered the stables.

He added, "I was just about to put Bayard back in his pen. I have to feed and brush him, but I can ready your horse after that."

Bayard let out a breath as I followed them into the stables. I watched as Ethann opened the door to an enclosure and steered the horse inside. "Do you like living here?" I asked.

"Yes. I like working with the horses." He closed the door and removed the halter and lead from Bayard. "And sometimes Foulke gives me things to do. I like to be helpful. And Queen Meli is really nice."

I watched as he brushed the horse; he seemed genuinely to love his life here. "Good, I'm glad." It seemed odd that as the son of a king, I envied the childhood of this orphaned boy. What did it say about Boreas that a mortal servant child had more freedom and was treated with more respect and dignity than me, a Prince of Caecias?

After leaving the stables and Ethann, I made my way back to the castle to find a guard and inquire about getting my bow, quiver, and sword back before leaving. As I approached the door, I noticed a guard standing nearby.

"When I arrived at the castle yesterday, my sword and bow and arrows were still on my horse when he was taken to the stables. I am planning on leaving the castle soon and wanted to know how I go about retrieving them," I informed him.

The guard's head whipped in my direction, his eyes searching me and his mouth slightly open. "You're the prince from Caecias, correct?"

"Yes, my name—"

"I don't know anything about your weapons," he interrupted me, and I flinched slightly at his brashness. "You will have to talk to Foulke."

I stared at the guard for a moment before replying, "Alright, thank you." I stepped forward slowly, and the guard kept his sharp gaze on me as I passed him.

Once I reentered the castle, I opted to take a slightly circuitous route back to my room. Yes, I needed to pack my belongings, talk to Foulke, retrieve Dulachan, and leave the castle before the queen returned, but I was sure I had enough time, and I was curious about the castle and the staff.

I had entered the castle through a door in the basement of the smaller of the two towers. There was a guardroom near the entry door, and the guard positioned in it looked at me and curled his lip in disgust before shaking his head and mumbling under his breath. To his right was the armory where another guard was polishing swords.

Upon noticing me, he straightened his back and furrowed his brow, careful to keep his hands firmly on his sword. If that was where my weapons were, there would be no retrieving them without Foulke's permission.

Walking the short hallway outside of the armory, I discovered a small room nearby and when I peered in, it appeared to be a library. It was the last place I would have expected to find a library, almost as if Melisende had too many books and not enough space, so she shoved some down here.

Redwald was sitting in a chair reading some letters, and I walked in to join him.

"Hello, Redwald," I greeted as I approached him.

"Hello, Faolan. How are you this morning?" he asked as he set the letters aside.

"I am fine. I've just been to the stables and asked Ethann to ready my horse." I took a seat in a chair near Redwald, enjoying the warmth from the small fireplace I hadn't noticed before.

"Leaving already?" He pushed his glasses up his nose, then tilted his head slightly.

"The queen doesn't seem interested in my father's proposal." I leaned back in my chair and watched to see how Redwald would react to my statement.

"Hmmm…" He only nodded his head, then picked up his letters and resumed reading. It appeared Redwald had no interest in helping me achieve said alliance.

"Nice library," I added, changing the subject. It seemed that most of the books in this room were non-fiction, history, warfare, and philosophy books. "Does the queen read a lot?" *What a stupid question.* I could only imagine Bradach rolling his eyes at me. That was why he was spymaster and I was the disappointment.

Redwald wrinkled his brow, then leaned slightly forward in his chair and smiled. "She does. Rather voraciously, in fact."

"Well, I'd better head upstairs and pack. Do you know where I might find Foulke? I need to talk to him."

Redwald lifted his head from his letters again and adjusted his glasses. "He usually trains with the guards up the hill in Ardelve most mornings."

"Thank you, Redwald," I replied before rising to my feet.

The advisor just smiled gently before turning his attention back to his letters once again.

After departing the basement, I slowly made my way back toward my room, passing servants' and guards' rooms, storage, a ballroom on the ground floor, the kitchen, small and large dining rooms, wine storage, and a larder.

And while I appreciated that no guards were tasked with babysitting me and I could walk the castle relatively freely, a guard appeared in or near almost every room I visited.

Finally, I returned to my room to pack. The late morning sun cast shadows on the far wall of my room, and I sighed. What would my father think when I returned home unable to complete the task he'd given me? He had threatened me, saying that if I didn't kill the queen, I would be dead in her place, but did he really mean it?

Or would he just strip me of the title of general and continue to be disappointed in me? I sat with my thoughts until my stomach growled. It couldn't have been that long that I had been lost in thought, but when I crossed the room to the window, the sun's position suggested it was near midday.

I needed to speak to Foulke about retrieving my weapons. I needed to attach my pack and weapons to Dulachan's saddle. And I needed to leave before the queen returned. There was much I needed to do, and I was running out of time to do it.

I climbed down the stairs and crossed the corridor to look for Foulke when I heard his voice coming from the dining room. I peered inside and to see both Foulke and Redwald sitting at the table with glasses of mead and plates of food.

I took a seat across from Foulke and greeted both of the males.

"Hello, Faolan," Redwald said with a warm smile. "I just told Foulke that you needed to talk to him." At this, Foulke merely nodded in my direction.

The servants set a plate of food on the table in front of me, and I was about to object when my stomach growled again. "Was I a fool for coming here?" I looked up from my plate at the two males sitting across from me.

Foulke laughed, but Redwald shot him a glare.

"Peace is never a foolish endeavor, Faolan. However, I don't believe your father or Melisende are capable of peace right now. Even with the threat of someone possibly conjuring portals in the Isles, it is not enough for them to put aside generations of hate."

"Generations of *slaughter*," Foulke corrected, his tone biting.

I could tell that both of them had experienced their fair share of the hostility between our kingdoms. Redwald slowly shook his head. "I fear the wounds are too deep to be healed."

"What are you still doing here?" Melisende's voice sounded from behind me, and I flinched.

Slowly turning, I lifted my eyes to meet the queen's. "I have packed and requested Dulachan be saddled. I just needed to talk to Foulke before leaving."

The queen's eyes flashed, and she took a menacing step toward me.

"Melisende!" a voice called out from the hallway. The queen stopped her approach and turned to find the source of the voice. A distressed guard carrying a small piece of parchment in his hand stopped next to her, his shoulders slouched and his breathing uneven. "We've received a raven!"

CHAPTER TWELVE
Faolan

Melisende snatched the piece of parchment from the guard's hand, and Foulke stood so quickly that his chair slid back from the force and slammed against the wall behind him.

"What news?" Redwald pressed, and I turned to see him lean forward in his chair, his eyebrows knitting together.

The guard's eyes skipped around the room, not settling on anyone in particular. "There's been an attack in Morvern," he said warily.

"Were there any casualties?" Melisende's demeanor changed, and there was a desperate look in her eyes. She flipped the parchment over again and again as if she could find the answers she was looking for hidden on the page.

"We don't know yet. The message didn't say," the guard responded.

Foulke rounded the table and stood next to Melisende, placing a hand on her shoulder. "It's only civilians who live in the village, so

I'd expect quite a few. But before you ask, if he was one of the casualties, we would have heard."

I was at a loss. Through their conversation, I inferred that Boreas used ravens to deliver messages instead of hawks like all the other kingdoms, but where was Morvern? What was so important about this village that had the queen looking desperate? And who were they speaking of?

Before I could ask any questions, Melisende rushed down the stairs to the basement level of the lower tower. Foulke followed closely behind her, and getting caught up in the frenzy, I followed as well.

"Shit, get Marshall and the stable hands to ready the horses. I want to ride out as soon as possible," Melisende proclaimed as she raced to the armory located near the castle entrance. She returned carrying a sword and tucking a small dagger into the sheath on her thigh.

She always had an air of power about her, but seeing her now ready to ride into the unknown, she looked even more formidable and deadly than I had ever seen her.

"I'm coming with you," I declared, coming to a stop in front of her.

"No, you're not, Little Wolf. Go home. We don't need you here." She brushed past me, headed for the door out of the castle when I grabbed her wrist and stopped her in her tracks.

Her eyes landed on my hand, locked around her wrist, before slowly making their way up to meet mine. I hated when she looked at me like that, but more than that I hated how that look made me feel. How my stomach twisted and my pulse raced.

"There's been an attack on your lands, I'm offering my help, so let me help. Let me prove that I can be a valuable asset in an alliance." I looked earnestly into her eyes, and I could see the conflict brewing there. She wanted nothing more than to turn me away and send me back to the hellhole I'd come from, but there was something else. Respect maybe? I tried not to read too much into it. She looked from me to Foulke, and he nodded slightly.

"Fine." She ripped her wrist from my grip. Her chin raised, and she drew in a deep breath that expanded her chest and put her small but firm breasts on display over the top of her corset. My eyes fell upon her curves, and for a moment I was lost. "You want to prove yourself? Saddle up and ride out with us. You can see firsthand what kind of horrors your father inflicts on my citizens."

"My father?" I blinked, hardly able to comprehend what she'd just said. "What makes you think he had anything to do with this?"

I reached for her arm again, and this time the look in her eyes told me she might actually unsheathe the dagger from her thigh and stab it in my neck.

"The only attacks on my lands are made by your father." She ripped her arm from my grasp again and shoved through the large door.

I followed her out of the castle and toward the stable on the edge of the castle's island. A few guards were racing around gathering weapons and supplies while Ethann and the other stable hands were hurrying to ready the horses.

"No." I shook my head, my steps fast, trying to keep up with her pace. "He only sends warriors to the border to retaliate. He never sends them inside your kingdom. Besides, he wouldn't need to send warriors if you hadn't sent them first."

All the reports I had heard from him and Cathal were of planned attacks on the border villages. My father was ruthless, but I had to believe he wasn't a complete monster.

She stopped and turned toward me. "Is that what you've been told? Poor, poor, little prince. It's time to open your eyes. I've never sent my guards into your lands, but your father constantly sends his warriors into mine." She was toying with me; she had to be.

"That's not…" I trailed off. A cruel smile graced her lips. My body shivered slightly.

"True? Of course he would spin it that way. He tells tales of woe, of how the evil witch queen attacks your home, how you must defend it by sending your own guards to my lands to retaliate. You're his general now, so you must know how you got your position."

My eyes widened at her implication. The right corner of her lips pulled up further into smirk.

She continued, "Your father sent your brother into my kingdom to attack me here at the castle. Not the border. Here, in my home. Foulke, the guards, and I were able to dispatch some of the soldiers before Cathal tried to kill me. And yes, your brother perished, but it wasn't some honorable death defending your kingdom; it was due to your father's greed for power."

She turned on her heel and strode toward the stables.

"But…" My stomach dropped. I didn't want to believe her. Cathal had died in battle defending our border from an attack by Boreas. He hadn't been sent on an assassination mission.

I couldn't believe her side of the story. No, I wouldn't. The only reason my father had sent me on this assassination mission was to avenge my brother… that, and ridding himself of his most disappointing son if I failed.

"Don't be so naïve, Faolan," the queen called over her shoulder as she arrived at the stables and requested her horse.

My father… I knew he was ruthless, I knew he was an asshole, but I couldn't believe this. Did he really send my brother on an assassination mission merely for his own glory? Was he capable of such deceit?

This feud was older than my father, spanning nearly two thousand years. *Her* grandfather started the slaughter. He was the one that spilled blood first; he's the reason my family has had to defend our lands and retaliate. I was stunned into silence.

Servants rushed to prep the horses as Ethann approached me. He smiled, and I shook my head briefly to dislodge the negative thoughts before returning the gesture. "Were you able to get Dulachan ready for me?" I asked.

"He was ready, but you took a long time, so I took his saddle off. I can fetch it for you," he said, then turned to head toward the tack room.

"That's alright. I can fetch the saddle, but can you bring Dulachan to me?"

"On it!" he shouted before running off.

I walked into the small room on the side of the stable that housed all the saddles, bridles, and other tack. All of the saddles were astride, and I smiled realizing that meant that Melisende rode like the males. Of course she did.

It didn't really surprise me in the least. Melisende was unlike any female I had known, so why would she ride sidesaddle as females were expected?

My eyes darted around the room until they landed on my saddle at the far end. I pulled it down from the rack on the wall, and Melisende pulled down the one just below mine. Her saddle was quality-made but was unadorned and appeared very old and worn.

Melisende pushed past me, her arm brushing up against mine, and an electrical shock surged through my body. I paused my steps, willing myself to keep it together.

What was this strange feeling she gave me?

Shaking myself from my thoughts, I followed her and Foulke as they reached for their bridles and headed out to tack their horses.

One of the stable hands brought out two beautiful horses, a dark bay thoroughbred and a lighter brown thoroughbred.

I watched as Melisende approached the darker horse and ran her fingers over the hair covering its neck.

The horse turned and nuzzled up against her. She handed him a slice of apple as I heard her say, "Are you ready to ride hard today, Philippe?"

"Faolan! Faolan, I have Dulachan for you!" Ethann shouted as he approached with my horse, followed by additional servants leading more horses out of the stables for the other guards. I thanked him and took the reins from his hands.

Peering over my shoulder, I noticed Melisende watching me with a careful eye. She didn't want me to ride out with them, but I'd be damned if I let her stop me now. Besides, the joy I would get from proving her wrong would be delicious.

Despite how much I might despise my father, I knew he wasn't sending attacks into Boreas, especially while I, the general, was here meeting with the queen. *Right?*

After I saddled Dulachan, I walked around to his right side to double check the girth and make sure everything was sorted with his bridle. I ran my hands up his neck before ducking under it to find Melisende standing near Dulachan's front left leg.

She slowly ran her hand down the length of his leg and lifted his hoof. Her nimble fingers felt around the hoof for a moment before dropping it.

"Does he meet your approval?" I challenged, narrowing my eyes.

"He's a fine horse. What is his name?" she answered, and I flinched slightly, tipping my head to the side. She had nothing but contention for me but was so kind and gentle with my horse.

"Dulachan," my voice came out quieter than I intended.

"Good boy, Dulachan." Melisende ran her hand up his neck, ruffled his mane, and then pulled out another slice of apple.

He took it from her hand happily, then nuzzled her before she walked back to her horse. For a stubborn horse that liked few fae, he warmed up to her rather quickly.

"Traitor," I whispered in his ear before leading him forward and mounting the saddle.

CHAPTER THIRTEEN
Melisende

The closer we got to Morvern, the faster my heart started pounding and the more adrenaline raced through my body. My grip on the reins tightened. We had pushed the horses hard; their mouths were frothing as they continued our brutal pace.

The sounds of their hoofbeats echoed my heartbeat. THUD-THUD. THUD-THUD. THUD-THUD.

The smell of wet earth and sweat stung my nose as perspiration ran down my forehead. But I didn't care; I just wanted to get to Morvern as quickly as possible. I just wanted to get to *him* as quickly as possible.

After a three-and-a-half-hour ride, we arrived at the edge of the village, and my heart dropped to my stomach. We could smell the smoke and burnt wood before we could see the town. As we rode past, it was apparent that most of the buildings were still burning and a few were completely razed to the ground.

Piles of stone and wood now lay where houses once stood. There were dead bodies scattered around the village, their mouths twisted in grotesque displays of horror.

I looked around as adults and children alike were lying in the mud with necks sliced open and stab wounds to their chests, sending rivulets of blood to the ground. I swallowed the lump in my throat.

Even after over nine hundred years, it didn't get any easier seeing the aftermath of battles.

But this wasn't a battle, this was a slaughter.

I looked on and noticed two villagers searching through the rubble for any remaining survivors and I wondered how many were still missing and unaccounted for. Another villager was looking for any supplies that could be salvaged and creating a stockpile while another was on the edge of town collecting herbs and plants for both medicinal use as well as food.

As we continued through the remnants of the village, I noticed that only one small house on the far end remained unscathed.

Outside of the house, a couple villagers were gathering food and setting up a fire to prepare dinner for everyone. A few others were collecting blankets and setting up cots and beds for the residents. The lone house would most likely be a hotel, market, kitchen, and hospital for the foreseeable future until they could rebuild.

Just beyond the house was what remained of the market square. It had been transformed into a makeshift hospital with shoddy cots, blankets on the ground, and a few small basins filled with water. One of the villagers was ripping clean sheets into strips of fabric to be utilized on wounds. Another was making a balm from some herbs for the burns.

In the aftermath of the attack, the few surviving villagers that were relatively unscathed gathered and tended to the injured in the makeshift hospital.

As we approached the market square, I dismounted my horse and turned to Faolan. "See?" I waved my hand toward the scorched remains. "See what destruction your father sows?" I seethed.

"He didn't... he wouldn't..." Faolan stuttered.

Although I didn't like the idea of him seeing my citizens vulnerable, I was glad I could open his eyes to the horror his father constantly inflicted on my lands. I turned toward Foulke, who was already dismounting his horse.

"Foulke, send a few of the guards to put out the fires. The rest need to tend to the injured. I don't want anyone else to die." I dismounted my horse and handed the reins off to one of the village boys who ran up to us as we arrived.

"Yes, Your Majesty," Foulke confirmed with a nod. "Aric, Bevan, I need you to put out these fires as quickly as possible. After that, start setting up our encampment; we'll be staying the night here. The rest of you attend to the injured. I'll make sure that everyone is accounted for before helping with the camp," he instructed.

Faolan watched as Foulke gave the orders to the guards and waited as though he thought Foulke would tell him what to do. Then he somberly looked around the village, and I hoped he felt guilty for what pain and suffering his father had caused.

He avoided my gaze and started walking toward the market square before deciding to join the villagers who were searching for survivors.

I may have been irritated by his presence here, but I was grateful that he was another body to help.

Turning away from the market, I surveyed the charred remains of the village. It was then I spotted my cousin through the crowd.

"Maelys! Thank the gods!" I ran over to him as quickly as I could and threw my arms around his shoulders, pulling him into a tight embrace. "Are you okay? Are you injured?"

"A few scrapes and bruises, but that's it." He looked worse for wear; his brown hair was matted with what must have been a combination of blood and dirt. His eyes, which were usually a beautiful shade of blue that mirrored both of our mothers', were dim and surrounded by dark circles. His clothing was ripped and dirty, and absent was his signature smirk that pulled up the left side of his mouth.

"It was a brutal attack, and we didn't have time to prepare." He took a long, slow breath and looked back toward the casualties. "So many are dead."

"Come with me." I looped my arm through his and guided him to the edge of the encampment that the guards were setting up.

We walked over to a fallen log and sat side by side. Glancing around, I spotted Faolan busy looking for survivors in the wreckage on the edge of the village and not paying us any mind.

I leaned in, placed my hand on Maelys's knee, and looked in his eyes. "Tell me everything."

He shifted slightly on the log, trying to get comfortable, and rubbed the back of his neck. I could tell that this was weighing heavily on him.

As my only living family member, I was extremely protective of Maelys. He was also the heir to my throne, a position he was not entirely comfortable with. As hard as my journey to the throne had been, his journey as my heir had been much harder.

Maelys had been born as Maella to my mother's sister and a male fae who had descended from a human, which meant he didn't have full high fae blood. Because of these two things alone he would be considered an unsuitable heir in almost every kingdom but my own. No other kingdom would even consider letting a non-high fae ascend to the throne, let alone a trans-genderling.

"I was out for a morning ride along the river between Morvern and the next village over when I heard screams coming from this direction." He shook his head, his eyes glued on his hands in his lap. One of them had been recently wrapped, and blood was slowly blossoming on the cloth covering the wound. "I rode here as quickly as I could, and what I saw was nothing less than slaughter. The villagers were trying to defend themselves as best they could, but the attackers were vicious."

"Were you able to identify them? Did Rian send them?" I pressed.

"I don't think so, Meli, they didn't look like any warriors I've ever seen before. They definitely were not from Caecias, or if they were, they were trying to hide that fact."

"What do you mean?" I flinched slightly, my shoulders tight and my eyes wide.

"All the warriors were wearing black from head to toe and masks obscuring their faces."

"Masks..." Suddenly, King Lancaster's letter and Faolan's account of what the Prince of Leuconotos had told him rung in my head.

"Yes, they wore solid black masks which were fashioned like some kind of bird."

"I've heard about these warriors. The King of Leuconotos sent a letter about an attack in the Kingdom of Argestes that was led by warriors in masks wearing black. They didn't mention that the masks looked like birds, but it could be the same ones behind this attack."

"They didn't fight like any warriors I've ever come across before. They were brutal, uncaring of the fact that they were attacking unarmed villagers and children; they were cutting down everyone regardless, with no mercy." He raised his head slightly and stared forward as if seeing the battle play out before him again.

I put my hand on his shoulder, and his eyes shifted to mine. Maelys had faced many battles, but I could sense this massacre would haunt him for a long time.

"You didn't mention any captives, and I didn't see any masked bodies among the dead. Did you see where the warriors fled to? Were you able to send anyone to follow after them?"

"That's the weird part, Meli. I didn't see them arrive, but as they were fleeing, it looked as though they just... disappeared into a shimmery net. I tried to follow them, but by the time I caught up with them, it was gone."

"A portal... I don't believe it." I had initially laughed when I received the letter from King Lancaster. No one had been able to conjure portals in over a thousand years. It just wasn't possible. But now one had appeared in my kingdom. I may not have believed the King of Leuconotos, but I did believe my cousin.

"A portal?" Maelys asked, a single eyebrow raising inquisitively.

"Foulke!" I called my guard over to share the news. He turned to his men and gave them a few instructions before walking over to join me and Maelys.

To my annoyance, Faolan looked in our direction, and I hoped that he hadn't heard what Maelys said. I knew he would find out sooner or later, but I wasn't ready to let go of the idea that he thought this destruction was caused by his father quite yet.

"Maelys saw a portal. That's how the warriors escaped. That's why there are no enemy bodies," I informed Foulke as he took a seat across from Maelys and me.

"It can't be..." Foulke trailed off as he turned to survey the damage again with this new information. "I didn't believe it when the King of Leuconotos sent his letter."

118

"Me neither," I said, reassuring him.

"Where do you think the portal came from?" Faolan's voice sounded from behind me. I whipped around and clenched my teeth seeing the young prince chime in.

"Who told you that you could join this conversation?" I stood and glared at him.

"Excuse me? Why the sard do you think I was sent here in the first place?" He walked right up to me with a scoff. "My father and I were told about these portals, and he sent me here to help, to form an alliance against the threat they pose."

"Just because that's what you tell yourself doesn't make it true." I was seething. I hated that the portals were real because if they continued, we would probably need all the alliances we could get to figure out where they were coming from and how to get rid of them.

"When are you going to get it through your head that I'm here to help? I'm not leaving your kingdom until you agree to actually talk about an alliance with me," Faolan spat back.

At this point, Foulke stood up and put a hand on my shoulder, turning my attention back to him. "Where do we think these portals are coming from? Who is capable of conjuring one?" he asked.

I looked at him and took a deep breath before returning to sit on the log again.

"While I may think that Faolan's father is evil enough to wage warfare this way,"—I tossed a murderous glare in Faolan's direction —"I know he's not capable of summoning a portal. And since a similar attack happened in Argestes, I doubt that the portals originated from the royals in either of those kingdoms."

"Prince Lancaster mentioned the appearance of a portal in his kingdom, but Leuconotos wasn't attacked. My brother actually suggested that Lancaster may have mentioned the portal in his lands as a way to throw suspicion off of them. King Cyrus *did* believe the attack on his lands was at the hands of Leuconotos." Faolan added, looking pensive.

"I know both King Lancaster and Prince Lancaster; they are intelligent and thoughtful leaders. I don't see them using that level of deception," Foulke said carefully. He turned to look at me, adding, "Is there a way to determine where the portals are from?"

"Not that I know of. Nyneve is the only ruler who was alive the last time any fae were strong enough to open portals," I sighed.

Nyneve was the Queen of the Rusalki fae in the Kingdom of Lacusia on the continent. She was over two thousand years of age and was the oldest ruler of all the fae kingdoms. She was also the strongest fae I knew and had more control over her powers than anyone.

I needed some time with my thoughts, so I stood from where Foulke, Faolan, and Maelys sat and wandered off toward the last remaining house in the village to try and comfort the villagers.

My head was spinning as the information I had just learned swirled in my mind. As I approached the house, I could hear the cries of the villagers who had lost their loved ones. Their wails and screams felt like daggers to my heart. There was nothing I could say, no apology I could make, that would bring their loved ones back.

I knelt next to a mother cradling her young son who was covered in burns, his lifeless body limp in her arms. Tears stung my eyes at the sight.

"What was his name?" I asked thickly, placing a hand on her arm.

"Aodh." Her voice was barely more than a whisper.

"Aodh is with Nuada now, living in the islands in the clouds." I placed a hand on his small chest, which felt cold and contained no heartbeat, and she burst into tears. Tonight, many of our folk would be joining Nuada in the afterlife.

CHAPTER FOURTEEN
Faolan

The portals are real. I wanted to feel vindication that the destruction that lay before us wasn't caused by my father, but it was hard to feel anything other than devastation for the families in this small village.

Melisende was talking with some of the villagers, and Foulke and Maelys excused themselves to discuss what I assumed were plans for rebuilding the village.

I stared at my hands in my lap, feeling helpless. I needed to *do* something. I needed to help.

Sighing, I walked over to the makeshift hospital in the market square and washed my hands in one of the many troughs that had been filled with water. What once was clear was now a deep shade of crimson from all the blood.

As I glanced around at the wounded, I noticed a young male sitting on a blanket clutching at his leg with a bandaged arm. I squatted down on the ground next to him and tried to get a closer look. He noticed me looking and pulled his leg closer to his chest.

"I'm okay," he said weakly. "There are others that need more help than me."

His gaze shifted to the female across from him who was covered in rather serious burns. One of the villagers was applying a balm to her wounds and wrapping them with the help of one of Melisende's guards. The look on the young male's face made it clear that he was in love with her.

"She's getting the help she needs. Let me help you," I said, hoping to ease his mind and get him to trust me enough to let me look at the wound on his leg.

His trousers were ripped, and I could see blood seeping through. I just wasn't sure how deep the wound was and whether it would require stitches.

I reached my hands toward the ankle of the injured leg, glancing up at him. "May I?"

He glanced at me, then at the female across from him, before returning his gaze to me, then he nodded slightly. I pulled his trousers up his leg and folded them at his knee so I could get a better look, but his entire shin was covered in blood.

I winced. "I'm going to fetch a cloth and some water so I can clean this off and get a better look. I'll be right back."

He nodded slightly again, and I walked to the small cart in the center of the square. I pulled some clean fabric strips and reached for a bowl, pouring some clean water from one of the jugs. Then I returned to the young male and soaked one piece of the cloth in the water.

"It's just water, but it will probably still sting while I'm cleaning the wound. I need to get a better view so I know what we are dealing with." At my words, the young male nodded once more. "My name is Faolan. What is yours?"

"Peadar," he said. I lowered the wet cloth onto his leg, and he let out a hiss.

I slowly wiped from his knee down to his ankle before rinsing the cloth and repeating the motion until I removed as much of the blood, dirt, and ash as possible. The wound was much deeper than I expected, and I knew right away that I would need to close it with stitches.

"It's just a scratch," he insisted, trying once more to brush off his injury.

Tough kid, I thought, trying to suppress a laugh. "Peadar, this is not just a scratch. I'm going to need to stitch it up," I informed him.

"I'm okay, really." His eyes shifted from me to the young female again.

I looked over my shoulder and watched her for a moment. Her attention was on the villager that was bandaging her. Just before I turned around, her gaze shifted to Peadar.

I turned back to him. "You know, females like males who have scars."

"Really?" His voice was a bit incredulous as if he thought I was only telling him what I thought he wanted to hear.

I pushed my right tunic sleeve up to my elbow and lifted my arm to show the large, jagged scar covered by my sword tattoo. "Really," I replied with a wink.

His eyes widened a bit when he took a closer look at the skin that had been torn apart and stitched back together that spanned the length of my right forearm. Then he looked back up at me and nodded. "Okay," he conceded.

I rinsed the cloth again before returning to the cart that held the rudimentary medical supplies. I found a large needle and some thread that would make do, but it would most likely hurt like hell while I stitched him up. I reached for one of the healing balms and put a small scoop on a piece of fabric. It might not numb the pain, but it would at least help the wound heal a bit faster and hopefully prevent infection.

When I squatted down by Peadar again, I looked over at the young female. "What's her name?" I asked.

He flushed at my question. "Roisin."

I grimaced, knowing the pain I was about to inflict on him. "This is going to hurt, but I know you can be strong. Roisin is watching. You can be strong for her, can't you?"

He nodded once more, and I prepped the needle and thread. I would need to stitch up almost four inches of the wound where it was deepest.

Taking a deep breath, I looked at him. "Ready?"

Peadar bit his lip, and I pushed the needle through his flesh. Slowly, I stitched his skin back together. The coppery tang of blood flooded my nose and brought back memories of stitching my own wounds after I was attacked by the amarok as a child.

Peadar yelped, and I blinked before I finished up, tying off the end of the stitches and looking him in the eyes. "You did well, I'm proud of you."

He smiled, then winced as he moved his leg a bit. "Thank you."

I picked up the fabric that contained the salve and rubbed it over the wound, then bound it with the cloth bandage.

After I finished tending to Peadar, I cleaned wounds and bandaged burns on some of the other villagers. I listened to their stories of the attack and tried to reassure them the best I could. Some of them blamed my father and kingdom for the attack, while others made guesses about who the strangers in black were.

But hearing the majority of them talk about how much they have suffered at the hands of my father and brother made me uncomfortable. Gods, I only hoped that neither Melisende, Foulke, nor the guards told the villagers who I truly was or where I was from. All hells would surely break loose.

"Thank you. You've been a great help today." I turned to see Foulke standing behind me. Before I could reply, he inclined his head and turned to walk away.

Foulke hadn't been as welcoming as Redwald when I arrived yesterday, but he hadn't been as cold as Melisende either. I didn't know where I stood with him, but hearing him thank me warmed me from the inside.

I watched as Foulke walked over to the small campsite that had been set up, then I followed to join him, Melisende, and the guards for dinner. A few logs, tree stumps, and chairs salvaged from the debris served as our seats and our thighs served as our tables while we ate.

I was seated next to a guard named Bevan. I looked around at our small party, seeing a few faces were tired and weary, yet others were calm and even pleased despite the destruction we had witnessed.

My gaze shifted to our bedrolls, and I realized there were no tents. I had never known my father to camp without a tent; even when going into battle, he required a grand marquee and multiple bedrolls to ensure he acquired proper sleep.

"What's wrong, Little Wolf?" Melisende asked. She had paused eating and was examining me.

I shifted in my seat. "Nothing. I'm just surprised you're not sleeping in a tent," I replied, my eyes turning back to the bedrolls.

"Why is that?" she inquired, biting into a piece of bread.

I paused, weighing my words, then said, "I've just never known any queen to sleep rough."

"You must not know very many queens, or females for that matter," she declared as she took a large pull from a wineskin. I shifted in my seat and opened my mouth to speak, but she beat me to it. "Don't worry, if *you're* not used to sleeping rough you can always return home to the lap of luxury."

"Nice try, Your Majesty," I said, my jaw tightening. "I said I was *surprised*, not that you wouldn't or couldn't sleep without a tent. I think you like to purposely misinterpret the things I say."

"And why would I do that?" she challenged, her eyes locked on mine.

"Because it's easier to hate me." I returned her stare, daring her to back down.

"I don't need you to do or say anything to hate you. You are from Caecias, a Dulaine, and that is more than enough." With that, Melisende stood and walked over to a small table where she traded out her wineskin for another.

"I was washing in the river,"—Bevan's voice pulled my attention from the queen—"when I met a spirited boy carrying a large net. I asked him what kind of animal he intended to catch, to which he replied, 'I'm going to the brothel to catch your mother.' I laughed and told him 'Make sure you search the place carefully as you are likely to find yours there, as well!'"

The raucous sounds of the guards' laughter filled the air, and I smiled. I listened as Bevan continued telling jokes and stories as the evening drew on.

I appreciated his ability to bring a lightness to this dark occasion. When I spoke to him earlier, I discovered that he was often Foulke's right-hand male when they rode out with the queen as she required Foulke's second-in-command, Cyneweard, to remain at the castle to protect it while they were away.

Eventually, the guards excused themselves and moved to their bedrolls to sleep, and I followed suit. I slipped under my blanket and looked back toward the campfire to find Foulke and Melisende alone, talking.

"You know…" he said and cleared his throat. "He really helped today. He didn't have to, but he did."

A small smile bloomed over my lips. Foulke was defending me to the queen. It was the first time in my life that someone had defended me outside of my mother, and it felt bittersweet.

"And?" she snapped at him.

"I know you don't trust Dulaines…" he trailed off.

"And you know why better than most, Foulke. You know what happened the last time I trusted one and let my guard down. I won't make that mistake again." Her hand drifted to her chest, and from a distance I could just about make out that she moved her necklace to cover the small scar on her chest.

What happened to her to cause that scar? I wondered.

"I know, and I'm not saying you have to trust him. It's just… I don't think his father or brothers would have helped today. In fact, I know they wouldn't have, but he did," Foulke rebutted.

"One good deed doesn't erase generations of pain." Melisende stood, leaving Foulke alone by the campfire. My eyes followed her as she walked around the edge of the camp and crawled into her bedroll.

I rolled onto my back and pulled my blanket up tighter. Insects chittered and the campfire crackled as I stared up at the swaying trees surrounding the small encampment.

The fact of the matter was that I didn't belong here, this wasn't my kingdom, and earning Foulke's respect wasn't the same as earning my father's, but it felt surprisingly good just the same.

Things had been awkward when I first arrived at the castle. But being out in one of Boreas's small villages and working alongside Melisende, Foulke, and her guards, I felt more like I belonged and could contribute than I ever had at home. And that thought scared me. I didn't want to belong *here*; I didn't want *their* respect. I deserved the respect of my *own* family in my *own* kingdom.

Then it dawned on me that while I was helping with the village, I had completely forgotten my mission: killing Melisende. I hadn't once thought about what I was supposed to do; instead, I focused on what I wanted to do.

I'd had plenty of chances, but I didn't kill the queen or attempt to bring down her kingdom. Rather, I rode out with her to help her citizens. I dug through rubble to find survivors, and I applied balms to burns and stitched up cuts on the wounded.

I swallowed hard. What did this mean for me and my future?

Could I still do what I was sent here to do?

CHAPTER FIFTEEN
Melisende

The dappled morning light streamed across my face, waking me up from a fitful sleep. It wasn't just because we were sleeping rough on bedrolls at the edge of the burnt village of Morvern; I hadn't had a good night's sleep in hundreds of years. I was plagued with nightmares and would often wake up multiple times a night drenched in sweat, trying to catch my breath.

But last night, my normal nightmares made way for images of burning flesh and blood seeping from deep sword wounds. I heard the screams and wails of survivors as they clung to the bodies of their loved ones.

I blinked my eyes to clear the visions from my mind and took in my surroundings. Foulke was already up and preparing some food outside of the last remaining house, and the other guards were starting to wake as well.

I looked toward where Faolan had been sleeping but found his bedroll empty. I slowly sat up and pushed the blanket off my body and stood. Walking to the edge of the encampment, I noticed a few large basins filled with water from a nearby creek. I stood in front of one of the basins, cupped my hands in the water, and splashed it on my face. The cold water felt refreshing and banished my lingering exhaustion.

I opened my eyes and only then did I notice Faolan at the far basin. He had removed his tunic, and it was draped over the side of the wash basin. The muscles in his back rippled and flexed as he leaned over the basin and soaked a small cloth.

He raised the cloth to his chest, and I watched as droplets of water cascaded down his chest, past his stomach, and followed the grooves along the sharp V-shape where his trousers were slung across his hips.

He was possibly the most attractive male I had ever seen, much to my dismay.

I swallowed as I watched him continue washing his chest, arms, and face. He turned slightly toward me and inclined his head, as if noticing for the first time I was here.

I looked away quickly, heat creeping on my cheeks. The last thing I wanted was for him to catch me staring at his half-naked body.

His eyes flicked past me then, and he looked haunted. Then that stupid muscle feathered in his jaw again as he clenched his teeth and sighed. He turned back to the basin and continued to wash himself.

It was then that I noticed the tattoo of a sword on his right arm. He had a few tattoos on his arms and chest, but that one in particular caught my attention.

A vision flashed before my eyes, and I remembered being a young girl and my father reading me the story of the witch and the wolf. I had always fancied myself as the witch in the story and hoped that someday I would meet my wolf prince. The wolf in the story had a scar along its front right leg that was described as looking like a sword.

I laughed at the absurdity of my thoughts. I could never entertain the idea that this young prince, the son of my greatest enemy, could be the fairytale prince of my childhood dreams.

As I cleared the embankment on my way back to camp, I looked back toward the last remaining house in the village where Foulke was helping the villagers make breakfast.

"Good morning, Foulke," I greeted him.

He looked up from the bowl of porridge he was holding and handed it to me before reaching for another. Then he placed two scoops of porridge in the bowl and passed it to a villager.

"I'm going to keep a few of the guards here to help the villagers, but Bevan and I will be returning to the castle with you this morning," he informed me.

I knew Foulke didn't like leaving his guards behind if he could help them, but his first priority was always my safety. And as much as he might want to stay with his guards, there wasn't anything he could do that they couldn't.

At this point, the last of the fires had been put out and the last of the missing villagers had been found. The guards would help the villagers bury their dead today, then start to rebuild. I had already sent a message by raven to a nearby village to ask for wood, tools and other supplies. I also asked them to send any food from their stores that could be spared.

"Thank you, Foulke. I'm eager to get back to the castle so we can send word to the other monarchs of what transpired here. I'm sure the Winterbourne prince also ventured to Eurus to tell King Ardit of his suspicions about the portals, but I think it's important that I personally inform Ardit of the attack on my lands."

I took a large spoonful of porridge he had handed me. It didn't have much flavor, but it was thick and would sit in the stomach well into our day of travel back to the castle.

"Agreed, Your Majesty." Foulke only called me 'Majesty' in bleak situations, and my heart ached at his use of the formality. "Is there anything you need me to do before we head out?" he inquired as he passed out another bowl of porridge.

"Just make sure the horses are fed and ready to ride. We'll return to the castle today to gather proper supplies and more guards before heading down toward Eurus tomorrow morning. I'm going to check on Maelys one more time before we leave, and I'll meet you by the horses in an hour." I took a deep breath then finished my porridge before discarding the empty bowl.

Foulke nodded, then handed his ladle to another villager before he left and headed toward the horses.

I looked around at the village as it started waking up. The few survivors either spent the night in the makeshift hospital in the market square or outside of the single remaining house that wasn't burnt or damaged beyond repair.

There were bedrolls and blankets spread out in rows in front of the house. They looked a bit too much like graves for my comfort and I averted my gaze, trying to keep my breathing steady.

After thanking the villagers for their hospitality, I found Maelys sitting on the edge of the encampment, re-bandaging his injured hand.

"Baby Bird," I said by way of greeting as I took a seat next to him.

"Good morning, cousin. Are you headed back to the castle this morning?" Maelys asked as he tied off the bandage. He must have been exhausted as he didn't even flinch at my use of his childhood nickname.

I looked down at his poorly wrapped hand, then shook my head. He placed his hand in mine, and I started unwrapping his sloppy work before re-bandaging his hand properly.

"Foulke is going to have some guards stay behind to help the village, but yes, I need to make my way back this morning. I want to send word to King Lancaster about the attack here since he informed me of the portal on his lands. I also want to notify King Ardit that I will be heading to his kingdom to talk to him face to face about these matters."

I paused and took a breath. I knew that Maelys wasn't interested in the crown, but as my only living relative, he was my first and only choice of heir.

I spoke slowly, "Have you thought anymore about what we talked about?"

"I have. I just…" he trailed off, and I could tell that the attack had taken its toll. He was tired and weary, and I didn't want to burden him any more than he already was.

"I know." I put a comforting hand on his shoulder. "Stay. Help the villagers. When you are done here, come to the castle. I should be back from Eurus by the time you arrive, and we can talk more. The Winter Solstice celebration is coming, and many of the nobles and villagers will be expecting you to be part of the festivities in Ardelve."

He offered me his signature smirk I had grown so fond of. "I wouldn't miss it for the world," he replied warmly.

I walked back to the camp and kneeled beside my pack, rummaging until I located a pen and piece of parchment. I scrawled a quick message to Redwald to let him know that we had secured the village, that I had requested some supplies from a local village, and that I would be returning that day. I also mentioned that we would be traveling to Eurus tomorrow and to have him start preparing supplies and additional guards for the trip.

Then I stood and looked up at the nearby trees. It only took a moment for me to find a flash of blue-black feathers. I called for the raven and watched as it flew down from a yew tree and landed on the fence surrounding our small camp.

It wasn't unusual for hawks to be used to send messages, but even as a child I had been more fond of ravens. Eventually, I had been able to train a few enough to learn how to communicate with them. To this day, Boreas is the only kingdom that uses ravens instead of hawks to send messages.

I reached up and smoothed its feathers with the back of my fingers before handing it the small piece of parchment. "To the castle," I instructed the creature.

The raven took the parchment in its beak and immediately took off, flying in the direction of Ardelve.

***

A cold wind whipped through the pine and fir trees, which were still luscious and green, but the bracken and other shrubbery had turned brown with the colder weather.

I looked up to the sky, seeing there were some scattered clouds, but otherwise it was blue which was unusual this late in the year.

The closer to the Winter Solstice it got, the darker and greyer the skies usually turned. The sun would disappear, and we would live in darkness for a few months, but even though the Winter Solstice was the beginning of the coldest, darkest season, it was also the turning point where the days would start getting increasingly longer. It signaled the return of the sun, but also the return of hope.

As the kingdom furthest north in the Etesian Isles, Boreas celebrated the Solstice as that halfway point, knowing that the sun and warmth would eventually return and grace our land.

Foulke, Faolan, Bevan, and I headed back south toward the castle. We had ridden hard the day before, keeping the horses at a constant gallop, not taking breaks even to relieve ourselves, so today we took a slower pace, switching the horses between a trot and a walk.

We rode in silence for quite a while until Foulke suddenly spoke up. "Who do you think is capable of conjuring these portals, Meli? I thought those powers had died over a thousand years ago," he remarked, slowing his horse to be closer to me.

Foulke always rode ahead of or next to me depending on the number of guards riding with us. As it was just him, Faolan, Bevan, and myself, he took up the lead with Bevan taking up the rear. I rode with Faolan at my side, as I didn't trust having him behind me and out of my line of sight.

"I don't know," I sighed. And that bothered me.

"You really don't have any ideas?" Faolan asked from beside me.

"Well, now that you say that," I said, sarcasm dripping from my every word, "no, I don't have any fucking idea."

I glared at him, and he raised an eyebrow at me. The audacity of this kid. There was something about him that made me snap every time he talked, the desire to put him in his place overwhelming.

"Fine," he muttered, passing his hand over his face. "I just thought... well, you're one of the oldest fae in the Etesian Isles. Maybe you had heard of someone who had that kind of power or knew someone that possessed it at one point in the past."

"I wonder if maybe it is a fae from Leuconotos," Foulke thought aloud, and I suppressed a cringe. "They said they had a portal on their lands but that it didn't result in an attack. That's a bit convenient, don't you think?"

"That's a change of opinion," I reminded him. "Just yesterday you said that the Winterbournes didn't seem the type."

Foulke glanced over his shoulder at me. "I still don't think it is Lancaster or his sons, but it could be another fae from Leuconotos, not someone from the royal family."

"Do you realize how powerful they would have to be to conjure not only a portal, but a portal that spans from one of the islands to the other?" I chastised. Mounting frustration caused my skin to tingle, and my voice raised as I continued, "Conjuring portals from one kingdom to another already requires more power than you could even imagine. You're talking about a fae that would be as strong as a god-born." That thought terrified me.

I grew up hearing stories about the first fae and their powers, mainly from Nyneve. She was over twice my age and knew of fae who had more powers than any today could ever hope to possess. It's said that the gods and goddesses didn't realize that they had gifted their powers when they originally gave birth to the first fae, the god-born, and then took away the powers after the fae started abusing them.

The idea that there was still a fae out there that somehow managed to either retain their power or get it back suggested that the gods and goddesses weren't watching as closely as they once were or were getting involved in the lives of the fae again.

Either way, that couldn't be a good thing.

"Why do you think they are using portals to attack?" Faolan asked, and I realized that thought hadn't crossed my mind yet.

I had been so concerned with figuring out *who* could be powerful enough to conjure them that I hadn't stopped to think *why*.

"They obviously want the element of surprise," Bevan piped up from the rear. "You can't prepare for an attack that you can't see coming."

"Element of surprise, yeah, but why do they need it?" Faolan asked.

I looked at him and realized our problems just got a lot larger.

CHAPTER SIXTEEN
Faolan

It was a longer, slower ride back to the castle today. Foulke and I discussed the portals, and it didn't take us long to realize we had too many questions regarding them.

Foulke had the notion that it was someone from Leuconotos that was conjuring them. He thought it was a bit too convenient that they had a portal on their lands that hadn't led to an attack. And Prince Lancaster had mentioned that King Cyrus from Argestes thought the attack on their lands had come from Leuconotos, as well.

Could the first portal have been a test? And only once they were able to conjure one successfully did they attempt to send warriors through to another kingdom?

Maybe Prince Lancaster was putting on a performance to try and cover up the fact that one of their citizens was the one conjuring the portals in the first place. But if that were true, who in their kingdom possessed that kind of power?

While I was growing up, my father dismissed the idea that there remained many fae alive with powers. As far as I had known, Queen Melisende was the only one in the Etesian Isles to have any elemental magic. I later learned that not to be the truth, but still believed it couldn't be that many.

But if there were still fae who had powers and could potentially conjure portals, why would they be attacking now? What had happened that made them start? And if they were from Leuconotos, was it someone in the royal family?

Was it a noble? Or was it some stray fae? And were the Winterbournes even aware of who was responsible?

Maybe the reason that Prince Lancaster was so convincing about being unsure of the source of the portals was because he was unaware of who actually conjured them. It would explain why it seemed as though he believed someone else was conjuring them, not someone from inside his kingdom.

It was late afternoon when we finally arrived back at the castle. Ethann and another stable hand came out to greet us as we crossed the bridge onto the small island. He took the reins from both me and Melisende while Foulke and Bevan dismounted their horses. They walked with Ethann and the other stable hand to help feed and water the horses. I turned to Melisende to see her walking toward Redwald, who waited outside the castle to greet us.

"Welcome back, Meli." Redwald came over to hug Melisende. And it wasn't the first time I had seen him act so casual with her.

It couldn't just be in Caecias that individuals respected their monarchs. No, it wasn't a lack of respect, it was familiarity. A familiarity that would never be allowed in Caecias.

A familiarity I wasn't even allowed with my own father.

He added, "I received your raven, but with no news of Maelys, I'm assuming he is alive and well?"

"He is, but few others are," the queen informed her advisor as she pulled away from his embrace, her eyes downcast.

"Small mercies," Redwald murmured before pushing his glasses above the hook of his nose. "Come inside and tell me everything that happened." With a wave, he guided us back into the castle.

We made our way to the small reception parlor and took seats around the fireplace. Melisende sat in the large red chair that she had been sitting in when I first arrived in her castle. I took a seat on the settee across from her, and Redwald sat in the large chair to the left of the queen.

"The Winterbournes were correct," Melisende sighed, breaking the silence. "Someone is conjuring portals. I don't know who or how, but they are being opened. Maelys said that a small contingency of warriors passed through and killed everyone they came across. They burned the buildings, destroying what they could, then retreated.

"The portal closed before any of them could be captured for questioning. They wore masks fashioned like birds and dressed in all black. There was nothing else identifiable about them."

"I... I just never thought we'd see the day," Redwald said, expression troubled. He hadn't been alive the last time the portals had been opened.

"I'm going to send word to King Lancaster and let him know that we have had a portal attack here. He informed us of what happened in his lands and Argestes, so it's only fair we reciprocate and let him know that the threat has made it to the Eastern Isle."

"Do you want me to send word to any of the other kingdoms as well?"

"You can write to Argestes. I don't know if King Cyrus will believe that there are portals any more now than he did before, but we should still inform him. I'll write to King Ardit and let him know that I will visit his kingdom shortly."

"And Caecias?" Redwald asked as he glanced sideways at me.

"Little Wolf here can tell his father when he goes home," the queen said as she looked in my direction as well, face turning sour.

"I'd rather go with you to Eurus," I insisted.

I hadn't managed to kill the queen, and even though my resolve was wavering, I wasn't prepared to return to my own kingdom until I had finished what I was sent here to do.

I did believe that the portals were a bigger threat to the Isles, and specifically Boreas, but my father was the biggest threat to me. The longer I stayed with the queen, the more opportunities I would have to kill her.

And if I had any hopes of returning home and being accepted by my father, or at the very least not being executed for failure, I would have to do it.

"I don't care what you'd rather do. You've overstayed your welcome," the queen seethed.

It occurred to me that this wasn't the first time the queen had threatened me to leave, yet she hadn't actually done anything to make it happen. I wondered how long my luck would last.

She added, "Go home and tell your father about what happened here, or not, I don't care. And you can tell him whatever you wish about the alliance. Right now, the threat from these portals is more dangerous than anything your father could dare to throw my way."

"No." My voice came out more assertive than it had ever been with her. The look she gave me was downright murderous. The colors swirled in her hazel irises like a hurricane. A hurricane of fury.

"No?" She stood up and came to stand directly in front of me, and I inhaled her scent of sweet oranges, night-blooming jasmine,

141

and fir trees. "I don't care that you're a prince of Caecias; this is *my* kingdom. You can leave on your own, or I can send you back under a shroud like your brother."

"Meli, enough," Redwald interrupted, tone sharp.

I looked at him, and he shook his head at me, indicating I hadn't actually won this argument. He stood and placed a placating hand on her shoulder while he spoke in calm tones.

"Just let him accompany you to Eurus, and then he can return home on your way back to Boreas."

"Whose fucking side are you on, Redwald?" The queen spun on her heel and stormed out of the room. Redwald sighed loudly, then looked at me.

"I'll talk to her. She doesn't trust easily. Especially not anyone from Caecias. But I think it might be good for you to be there, as well. I think a representative from all three of the eastern kingdoms should be present if you are to talk of allying against this threat potentially coming from Western Etesia.

"And for some reason, I think you agree, despite where you come from and who your father is." With that, Redwald stood and left the room.

That comment sounded suspiciously like a compliment, and I smiled while reclining on the settee.

I looked at the flames dancing in the fireplace and took a deep breath. As much as I was enjoying getting under the queen's skin, I needed to refocus my energy on killing her. That was the entire reason I was here.

But the flames just brought my mind back to the destruction we witnessed in Morvern. I couldn't help but wonder if there had been any portals in Caecias. And would my father have even tried to notify me if one had opened? Surely if that had happened, it would have convinced him that the portals were the bigger threat and he would send for me to come home. *Right?*

I left the parlor and headed back out to the stables to retrieve my pack from the stable hands if they hadn't already taken it to my room. Ethann was walking a horse, and I immediately recognized it as the same horse he was walking when we first talked.

I smiled and nodded in his direction. "He looks good."

Ethann turned toward me, and a broad smile lit up his face. "Thanks. I'm hoping one day he will be mine. Foulke says I can start riding him when I turn thirteen."

I walked with Ethann as he returned the horse to his enclosure in the stable, then retrieved my pack from the pen Dulachan was housed in. I was walking out of the stable when I heard Ethann's voice from behind me.

"So, are you going home soon?" he asked politely.

"I don't know. It's difficult." I stopped and waited for Ethann to catch up with me.

"Come with me to the lake," he implored, then bounded toward the large yew tree at the edge of the island. I followed him and sat down on some unearthed roots, watching as Ethann collected some smooth rocks from the lakeside.

"My father sent me here to do something, and if I return home without accomplishing it…" I looked down at my hands and twisted the turquoise ring around my finger. "He's never really respected me, and I've never really felt I belong in my family, but this could be my chance. If I can do this, maybe he'll finally respect me."

Ethann extended his arm and sent one of the smooth stones skipping a few times along the surface of the lake before it dipped below and sank. "He doesn't sound nice. Why would you want his respect?" He frowned.

Why *did* I want my father's respect so much? I hadn't really thought about it before.

I hesitated before answering, "I guess I've always just assumed you should have respect from your family, even if from no one else. I've never understood why I don't have my father and brothers' respect. Maybe that's why I've tried so hard to earn it. But now it just feels like my destiny is trapping me in an impossible situation."

"Is it really your destiny? Or is it just something that you have been forced to believe? What is it that *you* really want, Faolan?" Ethann dropped the remaining stones, giving me a knowing look before leaving for the stables.

This young, mortal child was wise beyond his years. I replayed his question over in my mind. What did I want? I wasn't entirely sure.

When my thoughts drifted back to my father, my mouth felt dry, and my stomach roiled. One thing I knew for sure was that I didn't want to murder the queen. She may have been my enemy, but killing her was what my father wanted, not me. It was only after hearing the sounds of the frogs singing their evening choir that I realized the sun had set and I was alone on the bank of the castle's small island.

My arms and shoulders felt heavy as I made my way back into the castle and up the stairs to my room. I changed into fresh clothes, splashed water on my face, and ran a hand through my hair, a few loose curls falling over my forehead.

What was I going to do? If I had any hope of returning home, I would have to try and kill Melisende tonight. But after talking to Ethann, I wasn't sure I wanted to. I wasn't sure that the home I was returning to was even worth it.

A long exhale left my mouth as I glanced in the mirror before adjusting the dagger in the sheath on my leg. I wasn't sure what I was going to do, but at least I would be prepared.

I walked down the stairs and across the long corridor to the small dining room where I found Redwald, Foulke, and Jene already at the table with Melisende. The females were sitting on one side of the table in their usual seats while Redwald and Foulke dined across from them. I took a seat at the end of the table between Redwald and Melisende.

My hand brushed along the outside of my righthand boot where my dagger was still concealed, and I chewed the inside of my cheek to keep from showing a reaction.

Melisende quickly glanced at me before turning her attention back to Jenephie and continuing their conversation. Foulke ignored me, but Redwald greeted me while raising his glass in a toasting fashion. I smiled back and reached for the platter of roasted meat in front of me.

I watched silently as everyone at the table was eating and conversing. I would either have to try and kill Melisende tonight, or I would have to convince her to let me ride with her to Eurus.

It would take nearly a week to ride through Caecias and into Eurus, which would give me plenty of time to try and kill the queen. I sighed and realized how much time I had already been in her presence and had yet not been able to do it.

What was preventing me from accomplishing what I was sent here to do?

Ethann's words echoed in my head, "*What is it that you want?*"

I must have been staring at Melisende for a moment too long, for as my gaze shifted to Jenephie, I noticed her smiling at me. It was one of those knowing smiles, and she winked at me before she returned her focus to Melisende.

She couldn't have known what I was thinking about, otherwise she wouldn't have winked at me. *Strange.*

I turned to Redwald and tried to join him and Foulke in discussion.

Dinner continued as the five of us ate, drank, and conversed until everyone finished their meals and returned to their rooms for the evening. I lay in my bed staring at the ceiling, wondering if I had the resolve required to slay my rival kingdom's queen.

I knew my brother, Brenhin, would have stabbed her in the chest or slit her throat the moment he entered the castle. He and my father would probably be laughing if they knew that I had been here for a few days and still hadn't even attempted to make a move.

The image of them laughing at me danced through my head and made me feel weak and worthless. But then my mother's face replaced theirs, and a familiar warmth filled me.

Growing up, my mother was always a place of refuge and comfort. She made me feel as though I belonged in my family even when my father constantly showcased his disapproval.

My mind was spinning, and I wondered what my mother would want me to do. Did she want the queen dead and if so, would she want one of her sons to be the one to do it? I closed my eyes tightly.

No, I knew what my mother would want. She was everything that was *good* in this world, and she would want me safe above all else, but beyond that she would seek peace between the kingdoms. If only she was the ruling queen and my father was the consort, what a different life I would have had.

CHAPTER SEVENTEEN
Melisende

After dinner, I returned to my room to pack. We hadn't grabbed the proper supplies yesterday morning when we left for Morvern, as I wanted to leave immediately and there was no time.

The trip to Eurus to visit King Ardit would be much longer, and I wanted to be prepared, especially since we were going to be passing through an enemy kingdom.

I pulled out a leather satchel and stuffed it with a couple clean tunics, an extra pair of trousers, and a simple gown. After filling the satchel with everything I would need, I set it on the end of the bed and headed out to say goodbye to Jenephie.

We had left in such a hurry yesterday that I didn't get to say goodbye after our ride, and I didn't want to disappear on her again without so much as a farewell.

I moved quickly down the spiral staircase and into the hallway of the second floor. I could see small streams of light from both Jenephie's and Faolan's rooms. My lip curled at the sight of Faolan's door, and I blew out a breath before walking to the end of the corridor and standing in front of Jenephie's.

"Jene." I knocked against the door and slowly opened it without waiting for her to answer.

She was in bed with a gorgeous blonde female I didn't recognize. The blonde looked over her shoulder at me, her eyes wide and her cheeks blushed. She moved off of Jenephie and covered herself with the blankets as quickly as possible. It amused me that she was embarrassed, but this was probably the least compromising position I'd ever found Jenephie in.

As long as I had known her, Jenephie was always attracted to pretty things, whether they were sparkly jewels or attractive individuals.

"Sorry, Jen, I didn't..." My words trailed off as I turned back toward the door.

"Wait, Meli!" she exclaimed as she slipped out from the covers and pulled on the satin robe that had been discarded on the floor. She motioned toward the sitting area in the corner of the room. "Did something else happen? Is everything okay?"

I sat in one of the chairs and picked a piece of invisible lint from my trousers. The blonde was still in the bed, attempting to reach for her clothes that had been strewn across the floor. She attempted to keep her balance on the bed while simultaneously grasping the blanket to cover her chest and pick up her gown.

I glanced in her direction, and her deep brown eyes quickly darted away, a blush covering her cheeks.

I turned back toward my friend and cleared my throat. "I just came to say a proper farewell. As you know, I'm headed to Eurus tomorrow morning, so I'll be gone for a couple of weeks. Sorry I won't be here for the rest of your visit."

"You're the queen. You don't need to play chaperone to me. You know I prefer it when you don't." She winked at me. "But thank you for coming to say goodbye."

I glanced back at the blonde again. She was now almost completely dressed and lacing up her boots. I smiled at Jenephie. "You know you can stay at the castle as long as you want."

Jenephie glanced at her lover who was slipping out of the room, then frowned. "Thanks, Meli." She attempted a half smile.

"I can always leave so you can invite her back in…" My gaze traveled back to the door.

"Don't be ridiculous," she scoffed with a laugh. "Besides, I've been dying to ask you about Faolan."

I groaned. "What could you possibly want to know about that asshole?"

"Yesterday morning, you told him to leave of his own volition or you would have Foulke escort him from the grounds." She leaned forward in her chair as if she was awaiting the juiciest gossip.

My elbow was propped up on my thigh, and I rested my head in my hand. I looked up at Jenephie through my lashes. "And?" I pressed.

"Why is he still here? Isn't he the drop-dead gorgeous *enemy*?" She leaned back in her chair and adjusted the front of her robe with a conniving smirk that only served to infuriate me.

"Yes. He is the son of my enemy. *He* is my enemy, and he will never be anything more than my enemy. But he followed us to Morvern and he…" I grunted slightly, "helped."

"That's… *surprising*." Her voice pitched up at the word, turning her statement into more of a question.

I blew out a frustrated breath. "I don't know. I'm only letting him ride with us to Eurus so I can discard his ass on his father's doorstep on the way home." I waved my free hand as if dismissing him.

"His tantalizing ass," she said as she waggled her eyebrows.

"Goodbye, Jenephie. I can't be around you when you are like this." I pushed up from my chair and moved toward the door.

"Oh, come on, Meli!" she pleaded, her tone turning into more of a whine.

"What you forget, my dear Jenephie, is that regardless of how tantalizing an ass he may have, he is still my enemy," I reminded her. "I've lived nearly a millennium without a male by my side and am in no need of one to be happy."

She waved a finger at me. "Watch your words, Meli. Someday, a tantalizing ass is going to sweep you off your feet."

I shook my head at her impudence and opened the door, stating over my shoulder, "Oh, how wrong you are."

The door slammed shut behind me, and I could hear her laughter from the hall.

***

The following morning, I gathered with Foulke and the guards at the stables, ready to make our way south to Eurus. I started saddling my horse when I noticed Faolan rushing to join us. "I would say it's been a pleasure, Little Wolf, but I'd be lying," I said snidely.

"I'm going with you." Gods, his voice was growing bolder with each day that passed.

"Like hells you are!" I spun around on my heel. "I told you last night this has nothing to do with you, Little Wolf. Go home and play soldier there. You're not needed here."

"And you think you can just travel through my kingdom without harassment?" he challenged, stepping closer to me. "No, you'll need me to ensure you pass through Caecias safely on your way to Eurus."

I scowled, "I've got guards, and *you* are my enemy. What makes you think that I'd be safer with you than with them? How do I know you won't lead me into a trap of your own making?" My voice was becoming stilted, and my chest grew tight.

"I know where the training camps and strongholds are, and I can lead you around them. No one from Caecias would dare try anything with me in your retinue. Besides, there are mortal Raiders hiding in the woods throughout Caecias."

He took another step closer, and I could feel the heat of his body in such close proximity.

A deprecating laugh left my mouth. I knew he was right. It *would* be safer to travel through Caecias with him, but I couldn't find it in myself to agree with him.

"Anyone else would have already given up by now, but I don't think you want me to. I think you want me to ride out with you again..." he said as he leaned in closer to me.

Our lips were so close I could almost taste him.

I narrowed my eyes and took a deep breath, contemplating stabbing him in the neck. Foulke tried to stifle a laugh, and I immediately turned to glower at him.

"Just let him ride with us, Meli. He needs to go that direction to get home anyway," Foulke advised, giving a shrug.

I grunted as I pushed past the prince and led my horse out of the stables.

"Thanks," Faolan told Foulke from behind me, making me roll my eyes.

"You helped us at Morvern, but don't think for one second that I won't kill you where you stand if you try anything against Melisende," Foulke replied, and for the first time today, I smiled.

***

A twig snapped, and I looked at the woods to try to find its source. Foulke nodded at me and sent a guard to check the surrounding brush for any threats, but after a few minutes he returned and shook his head.

We were still in Boreas, but with the portal that had opened in Morvern, my nerves were frayed. Foulke remained in the front of our pack as we continued our ride south through the kingdom. Faolan and I were riding in the middle while Bevan and an additional guard took up the rear.

Foulke had decided that traveling with six was the perfect balance of keeping our numbers low enough that we wouldn't be seen as a threat or draw unnecessary attention, but there would be enough cover to protect me while traveling through Caecias. He also insisted it was to keep an eye on Faolan.

He didn't trust the prince, but he also didn't want to be responsible for any possible injury Faolan could obtain while we were traveling through Caecias. If anything happened to him while we were here, word would travel quickly to King Rian, and all hell could break loose.

King Ardit's castle sat on the west coast of Eurus, which meant we would have to travel south through Caecias before continuing southwest to his castle. It would take the better part of a week to reach our destination, that is if we didn't encounter any trouble from King Rian's guards or the Raiders that seemed to plague their kingdom.

After a long morning of riding, we approached a small village in the southern part of the kingdom. The village was still half a day's ride from the border of Caecias, but it hadn't escaped the brutality of King Rian's attacks on my lands.

Half of the buildings had been burnt or destroyed, and a few of the villagers had turned to sleeping in the square while they attempted to rebuild their homes.

As we rode along the road leading through the center of the village, Foulke and the guards handed some of the villagers parcels of food from our own store. This village wasn't a fortress, but it did house quite a few soldiers who would help patrol the southern border of the kingdom.

I watched as Faolan took in the sights of the village and waved toward the destruction. "Your father's and brother's work," I reminded him.

"What?" His eyes snapped to mine, but unlike in Morvern, they weren't defensive.

"Thornhill was attacked by your brother Cathal less than a year ago. Yet another one of your father's raids into my lands," I explained, and his eyes shifted back to the villagers and their destroyed houses. "And this isn't the only village. There are a handful of others in the south of my kingdom that your father has attacked."

He shook his head. "No, Cathal told me they never attacked villages in your kingdom, only the fortresses and strongholds on the borderlands," Faolan rebutted, but his voice faltered.

"None of the villages that your brother has attacked in the south of the kingdom are fortresses or strongholds. They've attacked these villages more than they've attacked the actual fortresses along the border," I snapped in return.

"But... that doesn't make sense. I was told we never attacked your lands." He leaned back in his saddle, his voice disbelieving as he turned his attention toward the village. "Why would they attack unprotected villages?"

"That's the question, isn't it? If you find out, let me know." I nudged my horse forward to put some distance between me and Faolan, tired of this conversation.

One of the villagers walked up to me, and I pulled Philippe to a stop. She was tall and muscular, her caramel-colored hair pulled behind her pointed ears, her hands rough from manual labor. Treasa was one of the village elders and had been responsible for getting food and resources from other local villages to help with the rebuilding.

"Hello, Treasa," I greeted, my voice warm despite my mood. "You've done a lot of work since I was here a few months ago. How many houses have you been able to rebuild since then?"

"Another five," she replied as she motioned for me to join her.

I dismounted and walked with Treasa while listening to her tell me about the progress they had managed to make in the village.

Foulke joined us and Faolan followed silently behind, his attention darting between the village and Treasa. His eyes widened as he took in what used to be a house, then he rubbed his forehead and shook his head.

Treasa first took us to the food stores, and we assessed the amount of food they had. "We've managed to get quite a good amount of food from the other local villages, but I don't think it will be enough for the village to make it through the winter."

"I will send a raven to Redwald and have some of our guards ride out with extra grains from the capital's supply to supplement your stores for the winter," I declared.

After visiting the food stores, Treasa took us by the weapons depot. "In the last attack, the village lost the majority of our weapons. The Caecians stole and looted as many as they could before they left. Not to mention they killed almost every warrior that lived here in the village."

"Why would they steal your weapons?" Faolan's voice was quiet, but what surprised me was his use of the word *they* instead of *we*.

He may not have been directly responsible for the atrocities in Thornhill, but it was still *his* kingdom, *his* father, and *his* brother that were to blame. He might not remember that at this moment, but I sure as sard wouldn't forget it.

"It's how they keep us defenseless. If they kill our warriors and steal our weapons, we can't defend ourselves when they return." Treasa gave Faolan an assessing once-over. I had neglected to introduce him when we arrived. "I have managed to acquire a few weapons from the neighboring villages. But the swords that Foulke had commissioned the royal blacksmiths to make for us arrived last month, and now we are fully restocked."

We finished our tour with the new healer's house.

"During the attack, the village lost both our healer and her house which held all of the balms, pastes, poultices, and supplies. I ensured that the healer's house was the first building to be rebuilt in the village. And I found a new healer before the house had been finished, so she had to work out of a temporary space until we could finish."

I was also impressed with how quickly they were able to restock their supply of herbs and make new pastes and balms. All in all, Treasa had done an incredible job putting her village back together.

Faolan continued to follow silently behind us, and I wondered how he felt seeing firsthand what his family was responsible for. He looked remorseful, but I knew better than to believe this one village would change his views.

After we finished our tour of the village, Treasa and Foulke continued to talk as Faolan walked up beside me.

"I'm sorry," he said in a low voice, rubbing the back of his neck before placing his hands in his pockets.

"Sorry?" I shot him an incredulous glare. What could he possibly be apologizing for?

"I didn't know," he admitted, glancing back toward the village.

It was the second time in a matter of days that I had blamed his father for the destruction of my villages, although this was the only time his father was actually responsible. I found it hard to believe that he didn't know what his father and brother did, but the look on his face... no.

I had to remind myself that he's a Dulaine and is just as responsible for the wrongs against my kingdom as his family.

My eyes narrowed. "You really didn't know? You didn't know that your family has laid waste to my kingdom for generations? You didn't know every attack by your brother killed civilians and robbed them of their fathers, mothers, brothers, sisters, and children? You didn't know that villages were left without food to feed themselves, weapons to defend themselves, and healers to treat their wounds?"

I turned on my heel and left him to stew in what I had said.

It had been a few hours since we had left the village of Thornhill, and Faolan and I had remained quiet, with neither one of us daring to speak to the other.

Eventually, he broke the silence between us.

"Can I ask you a question?" he asked. I turned and looked at him without answering. "You always ride out with Foulke and your guards when something happens."

I turned my focus back to the road ahead of us. "That's not a question."

"It's just... well, you're the queen. You could let Foulke and your guards take care of this. You could stay safe at the castle and wait to hear their reports. You don't need to put yourself in danger by riding out at the first sign of danger."

At that, I turned and glared at him, my grip on the reins turning my knuckles white. "Because I'm a female?" I challenged.

"That's not..." He turned forward again, shaking his head. "That's *not* what I meant."

"Then what did you mean?" I loosened my grip on the reins and adjusted my seat in the saddle, sparing him a sidelong look.

He hesitated. "You're the queen. You are the leader of this kingdom, yet you put yourself in danger on the frontlines. Most kings lead from behind their palace walls."

I couldn't help but scoff, "What kind of leader would I be if I let others die in my place? Just because most kings lead from behind doesn't mean it is the right thing to do." I took a deep, sobering breath. "Neither my grandfather nor my father ever sent their guards to do something that they could do themselves. It's the way my family has always been. We'll sacrifice ourselves for the good of the kingdom."

I glanced toward Faolan, seeing his focus was still on the road ahead of us. He sighed deeply, "I admire you." Then he nudged his horse forward, leaving me to think about his confession.

My stomach twisted and my heart picked up pace in my ribcage. I wanted to hate him, I really did.

He was from Caecias, and if my past was any indication, I couldn't trust anyone from his kingdom. But then he would do or say something to surprise me, and my heart would try to betray my head.

CHAPTER EIGHTEEN
Faolan

I didn't want to believe Melisende, but seeing the villages in her kingdom that had been attacked… that wasn't something she could make up. Someone had attacked those villages, and if it wasn't my father, then who?

I grew up believing that my father and brother only retaliated against Boreas. That they only fought on our lands and protected our kingdom from the threats that Boreas imposed. But the places we passed weren't fortresses or strongholds, they were small villages. Home to peasants, not warriors.

It wouldn't make sense for my father to send attacks to places like this. And the villages weren't even along the border. Boreas had never once attacked us beyond the borderlands. The truth of what had been happening hit me like a ton of bricks.

If my father lied about this, what else was he lying about?

I had followed Melisende and Treasa around the entire village of Thornhill and had listened to the villagers talk about rebuilding their lives. I saw the new healer's house and heard about how they had to find a new one as theirs had been slain in the attack.

How was it possible that we considered Boreas the threat when we were entering *their* lands, destroying *their* property, and killing *their* residents? How else was my father deceiving his citizens?

And did my mother know about this?

I couldn't believe that she would support this. Not that she would have much influence over my father in a patriarchal kingdom like Caecias.

My resolve had been slipping for a few days, but after seeing Thornhill, what did this mean for me and my mission? Could I still resolve myself to kill the queen who wasn't as evil as I had been led to believe? Did I still want to?

***

We crossed into Caecias on the second day of our ride. On the route we were taking, I doubted we would pass any Caecian Royal Guard patrols but knew that the Raiders had been active in the north of the kingdom.

As the sun started setting, I kept my guard up. Foulke had mentioned he wanted to find a spot to camp in the Coill Forest.

We entered the forest and circumvented a few of the smaller mountains. As we approached a clearing near the base of Mount Scafell, I started to get more and more anxious as if I could sense Raiders nearby. There were trees marked with red ribbons, the sign that this was their territory.

Foulke halted his horse in the clearing and announced, "We should stop here and set up camp for the night."

Melisende and the other guards pulled to a stop near Foulke. "Agreed," added the queen. "This looks like a good spot."

"Bevan, take a lap of the periphery and make sure everything looks quiet. The rest of us will start setting up camp, making a fire, and preparing dinner."

I glanced at the skeletal oak trees, devoid of all their leaves, and the bracken that had desiccated and turned brown in the cold weather.

Before anyone could dismount, I looked at Foulke. "I don't like it. Something feels off," I said, furrowing my brows. Usually, the robins were singing at this time of night, and you could hear crickets starting their symphony, but it was deathly quiet.

Suddenly, a wolf howled within earshot of the clearing, breaking the silence, and as I turned my attention in its direction, it ran off into the depths of the woods.

"What is it, Faolan?" Foulke asked as he looked at me, a suspicious eyebrow raised.

"It's too quiet." And as if I had summoned them with my thoughts, an arrow shot through the clearing and sunk into the trunk of a nearby tree.

It was black with red feathers, the colors of the mortal Raiders. Adrenaline surged through my body, and my mind started racing. This could be my opportunity to let the Raiders take care of the queen and her personal guard in one fell swoop. My hands would remain clean, but the deed would be done.

"Caecian guards?" asked Bevan as the guards began circling protectively around Melisende, looking in the direction from which the arrow shot.

"No, Raiders," I said, pulling Dulachan's reins sharply and glancing at Foulke, then Melisende. This was the perfect opportunity to end her, but I just froze. I continued to stare at the queen while I debated my course of action.

She narrowed her eyes at me, and I just knew. I knew that I couldn't do it.

My gaze shifted back to Foulke, and I blew out a slow breath. "Follow me, I know a cave nearby that we can defend from."

"A cave? Are you kidding? That's suicide," Foulke argued with a scoff.

"The Raiders won't go near it. No Caecian would go near it. It's the safest place for us to go." Another arrow cut through the air and almost hit one of the guards as I spoke.

"I'm not hiding in a sarding cave. We have enough guards to take them," Melisende insisted.

"It's not hiding, it's defending. And if you want all your guards to make it to Eurus, then I suggest we go to the cave." I rode up next to Melisende's side and reached for her reins, pulling her horse alongside mine and in the direction of the cave.

"Let go of my reins if you want to keep that hand," she threatened as she tried to wrestle them from my grip, but I held them firmly in my hand as I led our horses forward.

Another arrow flew by us, and Foulke deflected it with his shield. "Just go, Meli, we'll keep watch from behind," he assured her.

I kicked Dulachan in the sides and urged him into a gallop, with Melisende's horse struggling to stay by our side. Foulke and the guards followed close behind and kept watch. After a ten-minute ride, we reached the mouth of the cave in the base of Mount Scafell, and I heard the Raiders curse from behind us. They would shoot arrows in our direction, but they would go no further.

I pulled Dulachan to a halt, and Melisende's horse followed suit. I dismounted and walked to Melisende's side to help her down. "I'm not helpless," she argued as she pushed my arms away and dismounted her horse.

"You're not helpless, but you're sarding troublesome," I said under my breath, guiding our horses just inside the mouth of the cave and dropping the reins. Foulke and the guards pulled up to the mouth of the cave as a few more arrows shot in our direction. "Watch out!" I shouted, but it was too late; an arrow landed in Foulke's shoulder.

"Shit!" Foulke grimaced in pain, and Melisende took a step toward him. I grabbed her by the arm and stopped her from going any further. Foulke gritted out, "Stay in the cave, Meli. I'm okay. It's just an arrow. I've suffered worse."

The guards ran into the cave and took up defensive stances in front of Melisende. A single arrow landed with a thud on the cave floor and then nothing.

"They won't dare approach the cave," I said.

"What is so special about this cave?" Bevan asked as he turned toward me.

"It's cursed." My stomach dropped as memories of my night with the amarok flashed through my mind.

"Cursed? How lucky for us," Melisende deadpanned.

I dropped my grip from her arm, and she immediately walked over to Foulke's side. I watched as she placed her left hand on Foulke's cheek, looking into his eyes as she snatched the arrow from his shoulder with her right hand.

Foulke winced, then opened his eyes and smiled at Melisende. Foulke may be Melisende's personal guard, and it may be his job to protect her life, but it was clear that he trusted her with his life, too.

"We'll be safe here as long as we don't go too far into the cave." I motioned toward a small alcove. The last time I had been in this cave was the night I received the scar on my right forearm, and I had hoped that I wouldn't ever return.

Melisende walked arm in arm with Foulke, and they took up spots on the cave floor. One of the guards brought a small pack over and dropped it next to Melisende.

She fished through the pack and found some clean cloth. Then she poured water from her waterskin onto the cloth, next helping Foulke get his tunic off. My stomach twisted watching her undress him. I didn't want to admit to myself why that bothered me so much.

"It's going to sting," Melisende said as she placed the wet cloth onto the arrow wound on Foulke's shoulder. He hissed loudly, and the queen chuckled, "Don't be a baby." She removed the cloth and rinsed it before applying it to the wound again. "Did anyone pack a healing paste?"

The youngest guard nodded and rummaged through his pack before pulling out a small jar. He walked over and handed it to Melisende.

"Thank you, Gilles," she said as she removed the top and swiped her fingers into the paste.

She started massaging the paste into the wound on Foulke's shoulder and...

I swallowed, averting my gaze, my mind reeling with emotions I couldn't quite place. Emotions I didn't want to place.

"I'm going to get some water. There is a freshwater stream a little bit further into the cave. Bevan, do you want to come with me?" I forced out, trying to keep my expression neutral.

Melisende looked up at me briefly before she returned to tending to Foulke.

Bevan stood and reached for a few waterskins before following me deeper into the cave. "So, these Raiders..."

"They are a nuisance." I looked deeper into the cave, assessing our surroundings and ensuring the amarok was nowhere to be seen or heard, before turning my attention to Bevan. "We've had a lot of problems with them attacking and looting our villages."

"Sounds familiar." A sneer flashed across his face before he burst out laughing. "Sorry, couldn't help it."

This was the second time Bevan had ridden out with the queen since my arrival. I didn't know him well, but he seemed to be well liked by all the guards.

"How long have you been a guard?" I asked, ignoring the jab he made about my kingdom.

He scrunched his brows together and looked off in the distance. "About fifty years, I think. Like Foulke's family, I'm originally from Ardeaterra, but I've lived here since I was only a few years old."

Ardeaterra. That explained his sable-colored skin and muscular build. "And what made you want to be a guard?" I wondered.

"Why wouldn't I want to be a guard?" He leaned over the stream and started filling the first waterskin. "Wouldn't you want to protect all this? Well not *this*, but Boreas. I mean, I guess *you* would want to protect this; it is your kingdom after all."

A forced smile crossed my lips. I've never felt the way about Caecias the way Bevan felt about Boreas, and he was from Ardeaterra on the continent. We finished filling the remaining waterskins and brought them back to our camp near the cave entrance.

"So, what exactly about this cave is so cursed?" Foulke asked me as he pulled his tunic back over his head and shoulders.

"It's the home of an amarok," I said as I took a seat and set the waterskins down.

"What is an amarok?" asked Gilles, brows furrowing.

"Some call it the King of the Wolves," answered Foulke, rolling his shoulder and wincing. "It is said to be four times the size of a normal wolf."

"And it lives in *this* cave? Why the sard are we in here again?" Bevan sputtered, his eyes blinking rapidly.

"I'd rather take my odds with the Raiders," said Gilles, voice flat.

"It pretty much remains in the back of the cave unless it needs to hunt. If we stay here in this alcove, we should be fine." I hoped my assessment was accurate and that the beast would remain in the depths of the darkness behind us.

"Sardsake," Melisende muttered under her breath, and I looked at her as she adjusted her position. This was the first time I had seen her look truly uncomfortable.

"Don't worry, it won't be a problem." I glanced down at my forearm and ran a finger down the length of my scar. I turned my attention from my arm to the queen. "If I could survive a night in this cave alone as a child, we can survive a night in it now."

Meli's eyes widened ever so slightly as the realization of what I had just revealed dawned on her.

***

Birds started singing as the first rays of morning light filtered through the mouth of the cave. We packed our belongings, but before leaving Foulke, Bevan, and I checked the surrounding area for the Raiders.

"Do you think they left?" Bevan asked, frowning at the forest around us.

"No," I replied, pulling an arrow from my quiver and nocking it. "They don't give up that easily. Most likely, the tribe has moved on, but they would have left two or three scouts to monitor the cave."

We slowly slipped out and hid behind a large fallen boulder. After a couple of minutes, we could hear two Raiders speaking. Foulke snuck to the right side of the boulder while I stepped to the left. From where I was positioned, I could see one of the two Raiders.

I pulled the bowstring back and took a deep breath, letting the arrow fly. I knew I hit my target when I could hear the second Raider start yelling for a third.

Foulke left the protection of the boulder and charged toward the second Raider while Bevan and I began searching for the third. I could hear the clanging of swords behind me as I wove forward through the trees. Bevan caught my attention and signaled toward some bushes to our right. He drew his sword, and I readied another arrow as we slowly approached the Raider.

"Come out and we'll make it quick and easy," Bevan shouted. "Or don't and we'll make it slow and painful. Either way, it doesn't end well for you."

An arrow flew past Bevan, narrowly missing him as he swung his head to the right. With the Raider's attention fully on Bevan, I snuck around to the side of the bushes and spotted him.

I released my arrow and watched as it sank into the Raider's side, making him cry out in pain. He looked down at the arrow before rounding on me, rage in his eyes. He lunged forward, but not before I was able to release another arrow. This time it hit him square in the chest, and I watched the light fade from his eyes as his body slumped to the ground.

Bevan walked up to the Raider and sliced his throat, ensuring he was dead before we made our way back to Foulke. We passed the first Raider I shot, who was bleeding out on the ground but still breathing, and Bevan stabbed him through the heart with his sword, smattering the earth with his blood.

After Bevan placed his foot on the dead Raider's chest and withdrew his sword from the lifeless body, we turned and found Foulke standing over the corpse of the second Raider.

"You two return to the cave; I'm going to do one last pass before we head out," Foulke instructed.

Bevan and I nodded and retreated to join the others. When Foulke returned and declared the path safe, we continued our journey south toward Eurus.

CHAPTER NINETEEN

Faolan

Hours had passed since we had left the cave near the base of Mount Scafell, and I watched as the sky grew darker and darker, the threat of a storm growing by the minute. We were nearly out of the Coill Forest and approaching the little village of Holbeach.

I desperately wanted to stay at the inn in Holbeach to avoid the weather, but I knew I wouldn't be able to convince Melisende and Foulke, even if there was going to be a deluge.

"It's going to take us at least one more day to reach the border to Eurus. Where are you intending to make camp for the night, Foulke?" I asked, breaking the tense silence that had fallen since the Raider attack last night.

"There is a clearing south of the river not far from here. We will make camp there," he asserted, not even bothering to turn and look at me.

"I know it." My eyes shifted from Foulke to the queen, then back again. "There is a village just past the river, Holbeach. They have an inn we can stay at. Might be nice to take shelter inside tonight if these clouds turn out to be as threatening as they appear to be. I'm sure they would have a couple rooms for us."

"I'd rather pluck out my own eyes with a rusty knife and eat them like grapes than stay at an inn in your kingdom," Melisende said as she halted her horse, fixing me with a glare.

"Graphic, Your Majesty," Foulke remarked.

I smirked, and I could hear one of the guards from behind us start to snicker.

Foulke pulled his horse to a halt and turned to face Melisende and me. "You may not be an enemy in these lands, but we are. We are far safer braving the storm than staying in an inn of some Caecian who would see the queen dead."

I stiffened in my saddle, my voice coming out stilted. "But—"

"There are no buts. We will not stay at any inns while we are in your kingdom. The danger is too great." Foulke's eyes hardened before he turned his horse around and continued down our path.

Two hours later we crossed the river, skirted the village of Holbeach, and found ourselves in the clearing where we would camp. The rain had started when we were crossing the river, a sprinkle at first, but now a solid downpour. The guards moaned and grunted in protest as they set up their tents.

Foulke tried to start a small campfire, but it was useless. Everything from the branches, to leaves, to twigs was soaked through. Finally, he threw down the materials with a frustrated curse.

"How long do you think the storm will last?" asked Gilles while we were sitting under a tree eating dinner. The large oak had retained nearly all of its leaves and was providing a canopy that protected us from the worst of the storm.

"Too long," answered Bevan with a scowl. "I'm so wet, fucking a mermaid would feel like fucking a desert right now."

A few of the guards laughed, then Foulke piped up, "I think it is going to get worse before it gets better, but it shouldn't last more than a day or two."

At this, Bevan groaned and Melisende tightened her cloak.

After we finished a meager dinner, we turned into our tents. I tried to keep the inside of my tent dry, but the combination of pouring rain and gale force winds made it nearly impossible. I took my cloak, jacket, and trousers off before changing into dry trousers. Then I slipped into my bedroll and pulled my blanket tightly around me.

The rain was only getting worse as the night drew on, and I found it hard to sleep. *I should have let them brave the rain and stayed at the inn myself,* I thought bitterly.

Thunder sounded overhead, and I turned over in my bedroll. The grumbles of the guards broke through the sound of the storm, and I knew I wasn't the only one having a hard time sleeping.

Sighing, I pushed back the flaps of my tent and looked across to where Melisende's tent was.

There was no movement, but I doubted she was asleep. Foulke's tent was to the right of Melisende's, and he was currently sitting in his tent, the flaps secured up so that he could watch our camp.

CRACK.

There was a blinding flash as lightning struck Melisende's tent, setting it ablaze. Foulke quickly stood and yanked the tarp off and threw it to the ground, extinguishing the flames. I scurried out of my bedroll, scrambling for the queen.

"Melisende!" I shouted as I dove into what remained of her tent. Her eyes were wide with panic, and she gripped my arms tightly as I pulled her from her bedroll.

"Are you okay?" Foulke exclaimed as he knelt beside her, assessing for injuries.

"I'm alright, I'm alright," she replied. Her body was stiff from shock; her eyes darting around the camp before settling on where her hands were still gripping my arms.

She released her hold and pushed away from me.

"That's it, we're going to the inn in Holbeach," I asserted.

Meli's eyes grew dark. "No, we're not. I'm fine," she gritted out.

"Your tent caught fire! Who knows what else will happen if we stay out in this storm." My jaw clenched. "It is for *your* safety that we need to go."

"He's right, Meli," Foulke hesitantly agreed, and my eyes flicked from the queen to him.

"Whose side are you taking, Foulke?" Melisende challenged, fury lighting up those hazel eyes.

"I'm not taking anyone's side, Meli, but I'm also not prepared to let you get injured, or worse, killed in this storm. Your tent caught on fire. We need better protection."

The queen's eyes squinted as she considered her options. "Fine, but we leave first thing in the morning. I don't want to spend any more time in your wretched kingdom than necessary."

The guards quickly packed up the tents, bedrolls, and the rest of our supplies as Foulke pulled me to the side.

"What are we up against in this village?" he asked gravely. "How big is it? Are there any guards or outposts nearby?"

I blew out a breath before replying, "It's small. Only a handful of families live there. They are all farmers and laborers. There are no guards that live in the village, and the nearest outpost is miles away. We'll be safe."

"Safe? In Caecias?" Foulke scoffed.

"I doubt any of the villagers would recognize the queen. Hell, I doubt they would even recognize their own king. It's a forgotten village," I sighed.

"How is it that you know of this *forgotten* village?" Foulke asked, and my chest tightened. If I told him that my cousin lived in the village, there was no way in hell Foulke would let us stay there.

"Let's go, Foulke." Melisende's voice interrupted our conversation. "If you are forcing me to leave, I'd rather get it over with. I feel like a drowned rat."

Foulke turned to retrieve his horse, and I walked over to Dulachan, attaching my pack to his saddle and mounting him before following the rest of the guards.

"Ride up here with me, Faolan. You can lead us to the village," Foulke commanded, and I nudged Dulachan forward. I dipped my chin slightly toward Melisende as I passed her and joined Foulke in the lead of the retinue.

***

We rode back north for half an hour before finally arriving at Holbeach. The village was comprised of two streets that intersected each other. There were about twelve houses, a potter's shop, a small market square, and the inn. The residents would have to travel miles for a healer and even further for an outpost or assistance from the Royal Guards.

The rain and darkness of night transformed the buildings from happy honey-colored limestone to dreary grey. The inn was situated at the end of one of the streets and stood two floors high. As we approached, you could just make out the leafless vines climbing the walls and covering a majority of the front of the building.

If my memory was correct, there were ten bedrooms in the inn, with the innkeeper and her family residing in three of them. There was also a modest kitchen and dining room alongside a large sitting room.

Whenever I would visit the village and stay at the inn, the innkeeper allowed me to stay in the fourth room of the ground floor, away from the rest of guest rooms that were upstairs. Since the village was small, not on a main road, nor near anything of interest in the kingdom, the inn always had vacancies.

I led our group to the fence at the side of the inn and dismounted. Melisende, Foulke, and the guards quickly followed suit.

"The inn doesn't have stables or a barn," I explained to the others, "but there is an overhang behind the building with plenty of room for all six of our horses. There is a small hutch behind the inn that houses hay and feed, and the village well isn't far from here. The horses will be away from the worst of the storm and should be able to stay dry and comfortable enough for the evening."

"Bevan, go check the supplies in the hutch. Make sure there is enough to feed our horses. I'll take a bucket to retrieve water while I take a walk around the village and assess," Foulke ordered as he handed his reins to Melisende.

Bevan and the young guard disappeared behind the inn while Foulke and the remaining guard grabbed buckets that had been discarded by the side of the inn and started walking down the street.

Melisende and I lingered by the horses in silence, waiting for the others to return. We were under a tree that provided little protection from the rain, and I watched as a raindrop fell on Melisende's forehead and trailed the contours of her face. She noticed me staring, and her nose scrunched up slightly as she turned her head away.

After a couple of minutes, Bevan returned. "We found the hutch and put some hay in a trough under the overhang. It should be enough for our horses."

Melisende and I joined him and Gilles in bringing our horses to the back of the inn and loosely tying up their reins. By the time we finished getting the horses settled, Foulke and the other guard rounded the back of the inn carrying buckets of water.

"What's your assessment?" Melisende quietly asked Foulke, worrying her lips.

"It's a really small village. We didn't see anyone, but that's most likely due to the storm. I don't think we'll have any trouble, but keep your hood up just to be safe." Foulke leaned closer to the queen slightly and reached for the hood of her cloak, raising it to cover the top of her head and partially conceal her face.

We returned to the front of the inn and walked toward the door, but before we reached the stoop, the door opened and a beautiful female with black hair and brown eyes that mirrored my own emerged.

There was a wide smile on her face, and she opened her arms in a welcoming manner.

"Hello, Orlagh!" I nervously greeted as I approached her and wrapped her in a tight hug.

"Cousin, it's so good to see you!"

CHAPTER TWENTY
Melisende

Cousin? Did she just say cousin? I shot a look at Foulke to see if he knew this interesting fact, but the shock on his face reflected my own. How did I let them talk me into this?

Lightning flashed across the sky, and the resulting thunder was deafening.

"Come in, come in! You poor souls must be freezing," Faolan's cousin said as she glanced at us and waved us indoors. She either didn't recognize me or my cloak was doing a better job of hiding my face than I imagined.

Faolan kissed his cousin on the cheek before entering the house. Foulke stepped up to her next. "Thank you," he said politely. She nodded, her smile never faltering.

Foulke glanced warily over his shoulder at me, then entered the inn. The other guards and I followed suit, joining him and Faolan in a large sitting room. There were two couches in front of the massive hearth, which currently held a roaring fire. I walked next to the fire, letting the heat attempt to dry my clothes and warm me. It didn't succeed.

"You must be freezing. Let me show you to your rooms so you can change out of those wet clothes. And my mate slaughtered one of our pigs today, so I can make a stew from the leftover meat that won't take long." I couldn't deny the female was beautiful; her dark hair and eyes matched Faolan's, a clear resemblance. "I hope you don't mind sharing rooms. I only have four vacant."

Faolan's cousin started ascending the stairs to the second floor, and I heard Faolan say, "Thank you, Orlagh. I know it is late, and I didn't inform you that I would be coming with others."

"You never have to announce yourself. You know you're welcome any time, Faolan," Orlagh reminded him.

We followed her in silence up the stairs and into a hallway which was the length of the entire house. There were seven doors and small oil lanterns hung between them illuminating the way. Orlagh passed the first two doors, then stopped at the third.

She explained, "This is the washroom for guests. The next four rooms are vacant, so you can decide amongst yourselves who will share."

Bevan and Gilles took the first room, and Foulke and the other guard took the one across from it. I walked to the end of the hallway and opened the door to the room next to Foulke's.

"Thank you." I inclined my head to Orlagh before entering the room and closing the door behind me. I pulled the hood of my cloak off my head and slumped against the door, exhausted from the day and the storm.

"So, who are your friends, Faolan?" I heard Orlagh say from the hall.

I turned around and placed my ear against the door.

"Just some folk I am escorting. They are traveling to the southern border and were concerned about the Raiders. I'm riding with them to ensure they arrive there safely."

Orlagh hmmm-ed as if she was pondering the truth to what Faolan said. "How noble of you," she finally replied. Faolan offered a weak laugh in response, then Orlagh spoke again, "Get changed into some dry clothes, and I'll see you downstairs for some stew."

***

The rain pounded against the window on the opposite wall of my room as I stared into the darkness beyond. I walked toward the bed and set down my pack. Luckily, my pack was water resistant and the contents inside were dry.

I fished around for the only dress that I had packed for this trip. It was rather simple, an azure dress with a high neckline and long sleeves as well as a low, plunging back. I pulled the gown out of my pack and placed it on the bed.

Quickly, I removed my wet clothes and draped them over a chair. I doubted they would dry by the time we left tomorrow, but I had a spare tunic and trousers. Still, I would need to ensure my cloak and boots were dry. I reached for a towel near the washing basin in the corner of the room and wrapped it around my dripping body.

Then I heard a knock on the door, and Orlagh poked her head in, startling me. "I thought you would like me to start a fire for you. It will help dry out your clothes and keep you warm through the storm tonight."

She crossed the room and knelt on the ground in front of the fireplace.

Why was a member of the royal family lighting fires and making stew for strangers in a small inn in an even smaller village?

After a couple minutes she got the fire going, then she stood and smiled at me. "There, that should keep you nice and warm," she said, voice kind.

Orlagh walked back to the door, but before she left, I blurted, "Thank you."

She looked over her shoulder and smiled again before leaving.

I returned to the bed and discarded the towel in favor of my gown. This occasion didn't warrant a dress, but the dry fabric was a welcome change from the sopping wet clothes I had been wearing for hours.

I ran my fingers through my soaked hair, detangling the waves that had formed. Then I pulled a small comb from my pack and used it to secure the hair away from the left side of my face, looking at my reflection in the mirror.

Voices sounded from outside my door again, and I opened it to find my guards lingering in the hallway between their rooms. Shortly after, Faolan exited his room as well, and the six of us made our way downstairs.

He led us to the dining room, and the guards took seats around the table. Faolan stood behind a chair, then glanced at me. I was still in the doorway of the dining room, frozen, just watching the others. Faolan offered me a weak smile, then pulled out the chair next to him, motioning for me to take a seat.

As I sat in the chair, his hand brushed against my back and shoulder, and I could feel a tightness low in my stomach. I took a long, slow breath to steady my suddenly racing heart.

Orlagh entered the room with a large bowl and set it in the middle of the table. "Sorry there isn't more, but it is late, and I figured stew would warm you up before bed." She grinned at Faolan and me before crossing the room toward the hallway. "I am heading back to bed, but let Faolan know if you need anything; he knows where to find me."

Just as I was about to reach for the ladle in the bowl of stew, my hand brushed against Faolan's. My eyes snapped to his as a weak, "Sorry," left my lips.

I could feel a blush blossoming over my cheeks. What the sard was this male doing to me? He was supposed to be my enemy!

Clearing his throat, he picked up the ladle and scooped heaps of the stew into my bowl before handing it back to me. "For you," he said with a nod. I pulled my gaze from my bowl in his hand to his deep brown eyes.

The intensity I saw there made me swallow, and I looked away. *Pull yourself together, Melisende, you're a godsdamn queen not a simpering female.*

Faolan continued to serve up food for everyone, and we ate in companionable silence. Slowly, the stew heated us from the inside out, and we relaxed in our chairs. I poured water from the pitcher into my glass and drank it down before refilling my glass again.

I glanced over at Bevan, who was in quiet conversation with Foulke. Knowing my guards, they were coming up with a contingency plan in case things at the inn went sideways.

After dinner, Foulke and the guards returned to the sitting room and took seats in front of the large fireplace, but after the storm, the fire, traveling to the inn, then being surprised by the fact that the innkeeper was Faolan's cousin, I just wanted to go to sleep.

Faolan stood up, but then he paused. "Will you join us, Melisende?" he asked gently.

I waved him off. "No. It's been a long day, so I'm going to retire to my room." I stood from my chair and left the room without another word. I climbed the stairs, leaving Faolan alone in the dining room.

When I reached the top of the steps, I could hear Faolan's voice from behind me, "Melisende."

I paused and turned back to look at him. I didn't say anything, merely watched as he finished ascending the stairs to join me on the landing.

He explained, "I didn't tell her who you were. This isn't some kind of trick. I just wanted to keep all of us safe from the storm." His eyes softened, and he leaned infinitesimally closer.

I couldn't help but scoff, "Safe? There is nowhere safe for me in your kingdom." I sucked in my cheeks and leaned away from him, trying to put some distance between us.

His face fell. "I know what it is like to be in an enemy kingdom, but for what it's worth..." he trailed off for a moment as he licked his lips and took a step closer to me. My heart started racing as adrenaline coursed through my body. "I'm not my father, nor is my cousin; there are some in my family that aren't as wretched as you may think we are."

With that, he turned and retreated down the stairs.

I stood frozen in place and watched until Faolan was out of view. There was a prickling sensation down the back of my neck, and I worried my bottom lip.

"Goodnight, Little Wolf," I whispered to the empty hallway.

After what seemed like an eternity, I walked the length of the hall and opened the door to my room. As I closed the door, I sank my weight against it. I could still smell Faolan, his heady scent of leather, lavender, and bergamot swirling in my nose.

I ran my hands over my face and down my neck. My fingertips interlocked behind my neck, and I lowered my gaze to the floor. This could be problematic.

Faolan was my enemy. He was a Dulaine. He was from Caecias. I couldn't trust Caecians. I can't...

***

The following morning, I awoke not to the sound of birds singing but the pitter-patter of rain hitting the window.

The worst of the storm had passed overnight, and gone were the thunder, lightning, and gale force winds. Today would still be dreary and wet, but at least we were no longer in danger. Well, not from the weather.

I pushed myself up and out of bed and crossed the room to the window. Even through the clouds and rain, I could tell that the sun was just starting to rise. I dressed in a clean white tunic and trousers and headed downstairs for breakfast.

When I entered the dining room, I saw Orlagh setting the table with her children. It hadn't occurred to me before this moment that Orlagh had a life beyond being a member of the royal family. She had a mate and children, an inn that she ran; she wasn't just another member of the Caecian upper class wishing to see me and my kingdom destroyed. At least, not only that.

"Good morning," she greeted when she noticed me. "You're up early."

"I didn't sleep well." At my words, the look on her face dropped. I hurried to assure her, "The room was perfect, and the bed was comfortable. My mind was just too unsettled, and the storm was loud."

Her expression softened. "It was one of the worst storms we've had." She glanced up from the plates she was setting, a half-hearted smile spreading on her lips. "And I've had nights like that."

I wondered what would keep her up at night and if it had anything to do with the fact that she was living in this nondescript village far from the capital. From the palace. She motioned for me to take a seat, and I sank into a chair facing the hallway.

"Would you like some tea?" she asked.

"I would love some," I replied, forcing a polite smile.

Orlagh left to retrieve a pot, and my smile faded. She was perfectly nice, but I was unsettled being in her house. She was a member of the Caecian royal family, and that made her an enemy.

Nervously, I looked toward the hallway and waited for someone, anyone, to join me. The sooner we had breakfast, the sooner we could leave and head toward Eurus and out of this miserable kingdom.

The rest of the house eventually trickled in to join us for breakfast. Foulke sat across from me, his eyebrows raising slightly in the same way they always did when he wanted to ask me how I was doing without speaking a single word.

I inclined my head slightly, and he relaxed in his chair. Faolan joined us next and sat in the chair next to me. I couldn't help adjusting in my seat and leaning slightly away from him. He noticed, and a questioning look appeared on his face. I looked away from him and absentmindedly reached for my necklace, adjusting it above my scar before grabbing my tea and taking another sip.

Eventually, the guards made it down, and we ate breakfast in relative silence. None of us wanted to give away who we were—if Orlagh and her mate hadn't already figured it out.

Swallowing, I finished my last piece of sausage and thanked Orlagh for the food and hospitality.

She beamed. "It's nothing. Any friend of Faolan's is a friend of mine. Feel free to stay again any time." Orlagh's smile was so sweet and genuine I wondered if she really didn't know who I was. How was it possible that the granddaughter of the former king was unaware of what her kingdom's enemy looked like?

After breakfast, we packed up our belongings and readied the horses for another day of hard riding in the rain. I hoped we would be able to make our way to the Eurus border today and leave Caecias behind us.

Orlagh came out and bid Faolan farewell as I approached Foulke.

"I know what you're thinking. I'm thinking the same thing," Foulke said quietly.

"And what is it that I am thinking, Foulke?" I asked, my eyes narrowing in suspicion.

"That Orlagh hates Rian more than she fears you."

I took a deep breath. What he said didn't make sense, but somehow…

What if Rian had forced Orlagh and her mother out of the castle when he became king? What if he had demanded they leave the castle and stripped them of their possessions? What if he was just as unkind to his family as he was to me and my citizens?

"Fuck the patriarchy," I finally said. "Faolan's mother should be queen, and her family should be able to live in the castle with her. Maybe if Faolan's mother had become queen this vicious cycle of war would have ended. Why is it that females always see more sense than males?" I looked at Foulke, anger bubbling under the surface.

"As a male, I don't know if I agree with *always*, but I've also only lived under you as a queen and can agree that at times you have more sense than the kings in the Isles."

"At times?" My nostrils flared, and he laughed.

"I always think you have more sense than Rian; he's an idiot. But I do like King Ardit. He has more reason than the other kings."

"True," I agreed. Ardit was a wise king, but more than that he was a kind king and took good care of everyone in his service. He also loved to laugh. I hardly remembered a time when there wasn't a broad smile on Ardit's face.

Foulke patted me on the shoulder, then turned to check on the rest of the guards.

I ran my hand down my horse's neck and whispered in his ear, "Let's get out of this gods-forsaken kingdom."

Foulke, the guards, and I were all mounted and waiting on our horses when Faolan finally finished saying goodbye to his cousin and approached us.

"Ready, Little Wolf?" I asked as he mounted Dulachan.

"Always." He pulled on the reins and led us away from his cousin's inn and back into the wilderness of the Caecian forest.

CHAPTER TWENTY-ONE

Faolan

"Someday you are going to tell me how you ended up on my doorstep with the Queen of Boreas." It was the last thing my cousin, Orlagh, said to me before we departed her inn in the village of Holbeach and headed back south toward Eurus.

It was naïve of me to think that my cousin wouldn't recognize Melisende, of course. I hadn't lied when I told Foulke that I doubted the villagers would recognize a foreign queen, let alone their own king.

But my cousin wasn't a villager. At least, she hadn't always been.

The bulk of the storm had passed, but there was still a constant drizzle that soaked through you and chilled you to the bone. I pulled my cloak tighter and looked up at the grey sky, which was imperceptibly lighter to the west and though we were traveling south, it gave me hope that it would dry out before we made camp for the night.

Foulke had taken up the rear of the group today and let Bevan take the lead. As usual, Melisende and I were in the middle of our retinue.

It was clear that Foulke wanted to keep an eye on me, and keeping me in the middle of the group was the easiest way to do that. Movement caught the corner of my eye, and I glanced over to see Melisende adjusting her grip on the reins. My gaze traveled from her hands, up her arms, past her shoulders, to her face.

She was looking straight ahead, and if I wasn't mistaken, avoiding me. I wasn't sure why, but the fact that I had essentially tricked her into staying at my cousin's inn probably had a lot to do with it.

I would say that I was surprised how kindly she acted toward my cousin, but after having spent nearly a week with the queen, I'd started to realize that everything my father had said about her was wrong. And even though she spoke tough around me and often joked about punishing her guards, she was kind and even caring to everyone in her employ.

Unlike any other nobles I had met, she was willing to not only take mortals into her lands but also to look after them. She was kind to her villagers, especially the poorest and neediest. She always rode out into trouble and was the first to gather forces. And she was far kinder to my cousin than my father had ever been or would ever be to any Borean citizens.

After seeing the destruction my father and brother had wrought her lands, after he swore they only retaliated against Boreas along the border, and after he sent me on an assassination mission to kill the queen, I started to believe that I was on the wrong side.

I'd always known my father lied and treated not only his citizens, but his own family, like shit, but I also believed he was doing what he needed to protect our kingdom.

But now, why should I believe anything he said? It hurt to think of everything that had been done in Boreas, and the other Etesian kingdoms, at his word.

He claimed to be the victim while playing the villain.

And what did this dawning realization mean for my mission? I was sent to kill Melisende because she was a threat to my kingdom. But that's what I was starting to realize: she wasn't the threat, my father was.

Ethann's words echoed in my head, *"What is it that you really want?"*

What did I want? Part of me was afraid to answer honestly because of what it would mean.

We continued riding for hours, and all my thoughts were consumed with the question of what I really wanted for myself. All this time I believed that I needed my father's approval and respect to be happy. That my happiness was something I could earn. That I *needed* to earn.

I had always struggled with my relationship with my father; he was a ruthless man, but I always wanted him to respect me. But now I was questioning if I even wanted his respect anymore.

Was he even worth mine? I had given him my respect without question because he was my father.

And I thought as a part of the royal family that I deserved his respect in return. But then he sent me on this impossible mission and while talking to my mother alluded to the fact he wouldn't be upset if I died.

So now... well, now I wanted more from my life.

I started to realize that my happiness didn't depend on my father. That maybe, just maybe, I could belong somewhere that respect was given without having to jump through hoops to earn it. That I could find a way to acquiesce to Melisende but not yield my own strength.

That maybe being in Boreas with Melisende had actually made me stronger.

And maybe, just maybe my place could be here, by Melisende's side.

***

The sun had vanished below the horizon long before we set up camp for the evening. I sat by the fire and watched as it crackled and small plumes of smoke curled in the night air. The stars shone in the sky through the canopy of trees, unburdened by storm clouds any longer.

Foulke and the guards had already turned into their tents for the night, leaving Melisende and me alone sitting around the dying campfire. Silence stretched between us, taut and unwavering. I looked down at my hands, playing with the turquoise ring my mother had given me.

Sighing, I reached down for the small flask by my feet and took a long draw of whiskey.

"I know the stories you've heard about me…" the queen said, interrupting the silence. "They are not true."

"What?" My gaze traveled from the fire to her face. I wasn't quite sure what she was referring to or where this train of thought had suddenly come from.

She chuckled darkly. "It's no big secret that your kingdom hates me. My family stole lands from you, sure. But the stories about me aren't true. I'm not some all-powerful witch queen who kills for fun and devours children whole."

"I think it's *devours men*," I replied. She looked at me, and the corners of my mouth raised slightly.

"Well, that's true." A brief smile graced her lips before disappearing. "I barely even have powers. And I wouldn't even know what to do with the limited magic that I do have."

"My father never spoke of your magic," I said quietly. "I think he is too afraid of you to even mention it."

"Your father doesn't fear me. He fears what he doesn't understand." She twisted a strand of hair around one of her fingers. "Do you know if anyone in your kingdom has residual powers?"

"No, I mean, not that I know of. But I'm starting to doubt that my father would tell me even if he did know. That, or he'd just have them jailed or banished, if not killed."

Melisende took a deep breath before lowering herself from the stump she was sitting on to the ground. She rested her hand on a small pile of dirt. I watched as her fingers trailed over the dirt, leaving little patterns in their wake.

After a few seconds, she dug her fingers into the ground, picking up some of the dirt. She turned her hand over so that her palm was facing upwards. Her fingers slowly unclenched, and I could see the small mound resting on her palm.

My eyes traveled from her hand back up to her face. "What…?"

She closed her eyes before I could finish forming my thoughts. I looked back down her face, briefly stopping on her lips before continuing down her neck, shoulders, and arm before landing back on her upward turned hand. I could hear her breathing, deep breaths in and out.

My skin began to prickle as if there was static electricity in the air. It was then that I noticed the small mound of dirt in Melisende's hand started to move.

I watched as the dirt formed a whirlwind above her palm. The dirt danced and swirled in a circle a few times before Melisende opened her eyes again and it fell to the ground. She brushed her hands together a few times, loosing the remaining bits of dirt.

I looked from her hands up to her face, seeing she was looking directly into my eyes. She bit her lip, then looked down at the ground, her shoulders slumping slightly.

"It's not much. Fae used to be much more powerful and have far more control over the elements," she mused as she looked back toward the fire. "The Sylphs of the Etesian Isles used to control the wind and the weather."

"I never knew."

"My powers are nothing compared to my parents. I was told my mother could control the wind, like me, but that she was much stronger than I am. She could create hurricanes from still air. My father... he could control the weather. The strongest Sylphs could control lightning itself."

"It wasn't nothing. It was beautiful." I looked up at her. "You're beautiful."

"Little Wolf..." Her eyes met mine, and she held my gaze.

But the tone in her voice told me everything I needed to know. She only saw me as an enemy, someone she couldn't trust. I would never be what she wanted nor what she deserved.

CHAPTER TWENTY-TWO
Melisende

The last morning of our travels had finally arrived. The sun rose behind clouds and cast defused shadows on the ground. We slept on the moor in the clearings between the bracken and gorse bushes. The moor was vast, and up here there wasn't much cover.

After eating a meager breakfast, we packed up our tents and bedrolls and watered the horses from small streams. This time tomorrow, we would be waking in real beds and eating breakfast in King Ardit's dining room. I, for one, was looking forward to bathing tonight and cleaning the grime from my skin.

I glanced around our small campsite and noticed Foulke was with the horses. He was always the first to rise and the first to start prepping for the day. He was adjusting their saddles and readying them for another day of riding.

He was one of the most patient males I knew, but the last day of travel always saw him urging the others to hasten their pace. He was practically twitching with anxiety.

"The sooner we start, the sooner we arrive," was his motto.

We mounted our horses and started the slow descent from the plateau of the moor down toward the lower lands of the rocky Eurus coast. As we descended the hill, the prickly gorse gave way to yellow cow wheat and wild grasses. There were a few trees scattered across the plains that danced in the breeze but for the most part, the moor was barren.

We crested the last hill, and the ocean spread out in front of us. Ardit's castle was perched upon a peninsula off the west coast of the kingdom. I had always liked Ardit's castle as it reminded me of a larger version of my own home. Instead of sitting on a small island at the edge of a lake, his castle was perched atop a headland on the coast.

It was late afternoon by the time we finally arrived. The impressively large stables on the mainland came into view first. Beside the stables were the guard houses and beyond them was the stone gatehouse.

My eyes trailed along the bridge, from the gatehouse across to the island, where the great hall sat in the shadows of the castle towers. The various towers rose in height as they climbed the island's rocky terrain, making the castle appear far larger than it actually was.

Not that the castle was small by any means, but the illusion created by the shape of the island gave the castle an imposing presence.

We approached the gatehouse and dismounted our horses. The only way to reach the castle from the gatehouse was via a narrow bridge made of rope and wood. It was strong enough to hold a battalion of men, but no horse would attempt to cross it. Because of that reason, Ardit had stables built near the gatehouse on the mainland.

As we approached, a few stable hands came to take our mounts. Then we passed through the gatehouse and made our way toward the bridge.

"What about the law?" Faolan asked, his eyes glancing backward to the gatehouse.

"What law?" My head tilted as I looked at him. A slow smile crept on my lips as realization dawned on me. "You mean the law about guards not being allowed inside the gates of a castle without invitation? Do you know why that law exists?"

"Yes." A petulant frown appeared on his face. "Because one of the kingdoms—"

"Not 'one of the kingdoms,' Caecias. Your kingdom. One of your ancestors brought a large number of warriors with him to Leuconotos and claimed they were just guards for the journey. They ambushed the Leuconotan king from inside his own castle and after he defeated them, he called a Conclave of the Kings and put the law into effect." I took a deep breath, then let it out slowly, turning to look Faolan in the eyes. "Let me guess, you were never told which kingdom ambushed Leuconotos?"

Faolan's eyes were downcast as he replied, "I was told it was your kingdom."

"Of course you were," I huffed as I set out on the rickety rope and wood bridge.

As I crossed, I peered below at the waves crashing against the rocks. Ardit's castle was well-defended due to the craggy nature of the coastline. It was too treacherous to access the castle from the water, as proven by the remains of several boats that had crashed into the coast.

And there was no safe, passable beach to speak of. At high tide, the waves crashed directly against the cliffs, while at low tide the waves hit the small stretch of rocky beach that was directly below the sheer cliffs.

I glanced back at Faolan, who looked a bit unsteady as he attempted to cross the narrow bridge. The winds were always strong at this stretch of coastline and whipped against the bridge causing it to sway, often dangerously.

After a small stumble, Foulke laughed at Faolan, "You alright, little prince?"

I pressed my lips together and suppressed a laugh. I would never admit to him that the first time I crossed this bridge I had fallen on my ass.

As we stepped back on solid ground, we found King Ardit awaiting us from outside the great hall. He was tall and muscular, his golden-brown skin glistening in the late afternoon sun. He wore his black hair short and kept his beard and mustache neatly trimmed. He was dressed in his usual colors of brown and burgundy with accents of gold.

His simple gold circlet crown rested atop his head, marking him as the royal he was. He smiled that familiar, warm smile as he outstretched his arms in greeting.

"Melisende," he exclaimed as I walked into his embrace.

"Ardit, my friend, it has been entirely too long," I said as I hugged him.

Of all the kings in the Etesian Isles, Ardit was my favorite. Unlike the others, Ardit was empathic and optimistic, led progressively, and chose peace over war—and when war came to his gates, he chose defense over offense.

I pulled back to smile at him. Faolan stepped up behind me, and it was only then that Ardit realized that I was accompanied by someone other than my personal guards. Ardit's eyes flashed to Faolan, and a brief look of surprise crossed his face.

"And who is this?" Ardit looked over Faolan appraisingly, and I realized that they must have never met.

But why would they have met? Faolan wasn't even out of warrior training and according to customs wouldn't have been allowed on any missions outside of his own lands.

"Hello, Your Majesty, my name is Faolan," he said as he inclined his head and reached out an arm to Ardit, who shook his hand.

"He's Rian's youngest and the newest general of Caecias," I added.

Ardit's gaze darted to me, and curiosity and disbelief shone in his eyes, not surprising given that two enemies showed up at his door together.

"Well, welcome to my home anyway, Faolan." A little chuckle left his mouth.

"Hello, Your Majesty," Foulke said when he finally caught up with us.

"Foulke, my friend. Always good to have you," Ardit remarked as he threw an arm around Foulke's shoulders.

Foulke winced a bit. The wound from the Raider's arrow was bandaged but still needed to be tended to and redressed.

The king added, "I believe Sigeweard and the other guards are imbibing a new cider in the great hall if you would like to join them."

"Say no more," Foulke laughed. He looked at me, then nodded. "Faolan, you should join me." He grabbed Faolan by the shoulder and led him away.

Faolan glanced at me over his shoulder before letting Foulke lead him toward the great hall. Foulke knew that I wanted time to talk to Ardit alone, so I appreciated him pulling the prince away. The two of them walked to the great hall, and as Foulke opened the door, I heard the raucous sounds of the guards from inside.

They disappeared into the crowd, and I turned to smile at Ardit.

Ardit led us past the great hall and up a path that led to the walled gardens. The gardens were at the top of the peninsula near a small chapel and had breathtaking views of the north and south coasts of the peninsula.

As much as I loved my own kingdom, the wild, rocky coasts of Eurus always took my breath away. Ardit opened the door to the gardens and gestured for me to enter. The space was lush and filled with flowers; it was my favorite place to talk as it was beautiful, but it also provided privacy and was rarely visited by others.

"So, are you going to tell me why you are traveling with a Caecian prince?" Ardit asked as he joined my side.

He placed his hand on my elbow as we walked along the perimeter of the gardens until we reached a small bench surrounded by flowers at the far side.

"Rian appointed him as general after Cathal's death. And apparently his first duty as general is to form some kind of peaceful alliance between Caecias and Boreas." I looked at Ardit and took a seat on the bench, crossing my legs and brushing some of the dirt from my trousers.

Faolan may believe in the mission he was sent to my lands to accomplish, but I still doubted his father's intentions. As long as Rian was King of Caecias, there could be no peace between our kingdoms.

"Well, that's new." Ardit looked surprised. He remained standing and crossed his arms.

"Only if that is what you believe Rian *actually* sent him to Boreas for." I snorted and shook my head. "I'm assuming you've heard of the portals that have opened in the kingdoms of Argestes and Leuconotos?"

"Of course. Aleksander Winterbourne visited me a couple weeks back and told me of his father's suspicions. Do *you* really think someone is opening portals?"

His gaze searched mine. I could tell that he didn't necessarily believe what the Leuconotan prince had told him but that he would believe me. Ardit was one of the most intelligent males I had ever met. He was a fierce warrior, but also extremely smart and capable. He had a sharp mind and cunning wit, so he was unlikely to believe idle gossip.

"I didn't at first," I started. "You know as well as I that no one has been capable of the kind of magic required to open portals in over a thousand years."

"And you've since changed your mind?" He finally took a seat next to me on the bench.

"A portal opened in my lands." I shook my head and sighed. "There was an attack on one of my villages. It was razed to the ground. Few of the villagers survived and even less of their homes."

"I'm so sorry, Meli." He placed his hand on my knee in an attempt to comfort me.

"All but one building was lost and over half of the villagers were killed either from the fire or the attackers. Thankfully, Maelys was there and able to call for help." I paused and took a deep breath. The thought of how close I was to losing him racked my brain. I shook the thought from my mind. "He told me what he witnessed. He said that the attackers vanished into thin air. The way he described it, it sounded like a portal."

"Shit. So, there have been portals in Leuconotos and Argestes, and now in Boreas as well?" Ardit shook his head. "Where do you think they are coming from? Who do you think is powerful enough to conjure them?"

I shrugged. "That's the mystery. So far there have been portals opened in Argestes, Leuconotos, and Boreas. If we assume that all three of the royal families are innocent and didn't conjure the portals, that only leaves the royals of Caecias and Eurus."

Ardit's eyebrows drew together, giving him a sour expression, when I included his kingdom in that statement.

I reassured him, "Don't worry, Ardit, I don't believe for a second that you have anything to do with this." I offered a genuine smile.

"Then do you think Rian is behind it?" he asked incredulously.

My lips pursed tightly, and I rolled my eyes. "King Rian doesn't have the power. And he's scared of anyone that *does* have power. I can't imagine someone in his kingdom not only having that kind of magic but also being able to conceal it from him while launching these attacks." I stood up and started pacing along the stone path. "I think what is bothering me is that I can't figure out who has the motive *and* the ability."

"So what are you thinking, Melisende?" Ardit stood and took my hands in his to stop my pacing.

"Faolan and Foulke have both brought up the possibility that Leuconotos could be responsible, as their portal was the only one that didn't lead to an attack. That and the fact that Cyrus believes the attack on his lands was led by Leuconotos. But do you really think Lancaster would make up a portal just to throw suspicion off both himself and his kingdom?"

"He doesn't seem the type," Ardit replied after a moment of consideration.

"Exactly. Alcina had once mentioned that she knew of a fae in Leuconotos that has powers, but who knows how strong they are."

The king gave me a pointed look. "It seems unlikely that some unknown fae has been hiding powers strong enough to conjure portals."

Ardit turned and started walking down the stone path back toward the garden's entrance and rolled his head from side to side. I braced myself, as every time he did that, something absurd came out of his mouth.

He mused, "So portals are opening in the Isles, and you are traveling the length and breadth of Eastern Etesia with your enemy's son? What nonsense will be next?"

Ardit laughed, and I rolled my eyes, saying, "Whatever Faolan's original purpose of coming to my kingdom, he hasn't actually attempted to kill me, and he's even proven himself a bit helpful." Ardit feigned shock, and I glared at him. "But if you ever tell him I said so, I'll stick a knife in your throat."

He chuckled at that, "Just as peaceful as ever, Meli."

"Oh, Ardit, you have no idea."

***

The sun was just starting to set over the ocean as we returned to the castle. Ardit summoned one of his servants to show me to my room. The guest wing overlooked the north cliffs of the peninsula and as we entered the space, I could see the waves splashing against the cliffs from the window.

I watched the tumultuous ocean for a few minutes before pulling a book from the bookshelf in the corner of the room. I returned to the large picture window and sat on the bench below it, reading for about an hour before a knock on the door disrupted me.

I opened the door to find a servant standing on the other side with a note in hand. Unfolding it, I found it was a message from Ardit. He had invited me to join him and his advisor for a drink before dinner and wanted me to wear the dress he had set up for me in the bathing chamber.

I glanced up from the note and immediately made my way to the bathing chamber. When I entered, my eyes landed on a light silvery-grey gown hanging from a hook on the wall.

Normally I would balk if a male insisted on dressing me, but I knew instantly why Ardit had picked the gown. It had belonged to his late wife, and my best friend, and I had complimented her every time she wore it. I even remember joking with her stating, "Someday, I will steal this gown from you!"

Tears stung my eyes as I took in the dress. It was beautiful, just like Guenevere. The color was unusual for her, as she always wore warm earthy tones of brown and burgundy. I also admired the way the dress wrapped around her body as if a wind had carried the fabric and draped it to fit her every curve. I ran my fingers over the fabric; it was soft and supple under my touch.

Someone cleared their throat behind me, and I turned around. The servant who had showed me to my room earlier entered carrying a large jug of hot water. She brought it over to the washing basin and informed me that I could call for more if I wished to take a bath.

"A bath would be lovely, thank you," I replied, and she nodded then left.

After washing, I pulled the gown down from the wall and slipped it on. The soft fabric easily slid down my body, and I fastened the straps on the back of the gown. I smoothed the dress with my hands and turned to face the large mirror in the corner of the bathing room. It was bittersweet seeing my reflection in my late friend's gown.

I made my way downstairs from my room in the guest wing to the small sitting room that was next to the dining room. Ardit and his advisor, Erwan, were already waiting for me.

Erwan had the same warm brown skin and hair as Ardit, but his eyes almost glowed gold instead of brown. He had permanent wrinkles on his forehead from constantly furrowing his brows in concentration yet still had a lean warrior's frame. They stood at the far end of the room near a sideboard covered in bottles of wine, carafes of whiskey, and various other bottles of alcohol. And in the center of the room were burgundy-colored velvet couches surrounding a low table made from the trunk of a felled tree.

Ardit poured himself a glass of clear liquid before handing the bottle to Erwan. I entered the room and cleared my throat.

Both of the males glanced in my direction, Ardit's eyes suddenly shimmering with unshed tears. I smiled and mouthed the words, "Thank you," as I approached them.

The king embraced me in a warm hug and whispered in my ear, "She would have wanted you to have it."

Our moment was interrupted when Erwan exclaimed, "Melisende, it's been entirely too long!" He embraced me in a hug as well and continued, "It's good to see you."

I grinned back. "You too, Erwan."

"Kirsch?" Ardit asked as he raised his glass. I looked over to him and nodded.

He reached for another glass and poured a large portion of the clear liquid before offering it to me. I took a sip and let the luscious cherry flavor cover my tongue.

The three of us moved to the sumptuous velvet sofa surrounding the fireplace and sat down. I took another sip of my drink before placing it on the table to my right. "So, what has Ardit told you so far?" I asked, looking at Erwan.

He shrugged. "Not much. He told me that you came because a portal has opened in Boreas, but then we decided this conversation required having a drink," he laughed.

I looked over at Ardit and smirked. He always liked to have discussions over a glass of something. Usually it was wine, sometimes it was mead, but today it was kirsch.

"I never thought I'd live to see the day Boreas and Caecias cooperated," Erwan added with a raised brow.

At that, I made a face. "*Cooperated* is a strong word. Rian sent his youngest pup to my kingdom under the guise of forming an alliance between our kingdoms, but I don't trust their intentions. At least, not Rian's. The last son he sent to my castle attempted to murder me."

"Yet you're still alive," Ardit said with a warm laugh. He was always laughing, and I was in awe of his unwavering optimism and ability to see the humor in any situation.

"Faolan has, however, been helpful as an escort through his kingdom. We made it here with only one small incident," I said, reaching for the necklace covering my scar.

"Why do I get the feeling that the incident wasn't that small?" Ardit narrowed his eyes at me.

"We were found by some of the mortal Raiders that plague Caecias. Foulke took an arrow to the shoulder, but we were otherwise unharmed. And before you worry about him, I already told Foulke to see a healer while here."

"Hmmm…" Ardit didn't seem convinced, but he continued on anyway. "Despite Faolan's behavior so far, do you think it is still Rian's intention to conquer your kingdom?"

"When is it not, Ardit? I'm sure he sent Faolan to kill me, just the same as he sent Cathal before him." My voice was filled with a conviction I no longer had. I still believed that Rian wanted me dead, but I was starting to doubt that Faolan would actually follow through.

202

Ardit's gaze traveled away from me to a figure just on the other side of the door. "Faolan?"

All the blood left my face.

CHAPTER TWENTY-THREE
Faolan

Shit. Ardit saw me. I took a deep breath and stepped into the room as if I had just happened to be passing by and not been in fact listening to their conversation by the door.

I hadn't actually intended on eavesdropping; I was on my way to the dining room when I heard my name and couldn't help but listen. I straightened my shoulders and stood a bit taller. "Good evening," I said to Ardit, nodding in greeting. "I was just heading to dinner and heard voices, so I thought this might be the dining room."

"It's next door," Ardit informed me with a knowing look. "We were just enjoying an aperitif if you'd like to join us. Dinner should be served soon enough."

I entered the room and took a seat next to a male I assumed was Ardit's advisor. After hearing Melisende's confession from the hallway, I wanted to avoid her gaze at all costs. A servant rushed to my side. He set a goblet on the table in front of me and poured a clear liquid from the jug he held.

"It's kirsch," Ardit explained as he raised his own glass in toast.

"Thank you." I nodded at the servant before he retreated, taking a small sip of the liquid and being pleasantly surprised by the cherry flavor.

"This is Erwan, my advisor." Ardit waved a hand toward the male I was seated next to.

I turned to him and inclined my head in respect and acknowledgement.

"It's nice to meet you, Faolan." He extended his hand, and I shook it. "Have you been to Eurus before?"

I glanced at Ardit, who took a long swig from his glass. His eyes remained on mine, waiting for me to answer.

As a soldier, you generally weren't allowed to travel to other kingdoms until you had completed training, but as a member of the royal family I could have had opportunities to visit with the other royal families on diplomatic trips. My father, however, had never taken me on trips outside of Caecias, only my older brothers.

My gaze returned to Erwan. "I've only been to the borderlands during my training."

"That's right. I forget how young you are," Erwan replied, then looked toward Ardit.

"Were you even able to finish warrior training before becoming your father's general?" Ardit interrupted. "Do you not have to go through the aibithe before finishing training in Caecias?"

"Normally, yes, but my situation was outside of the normal." My thoughts drifted back to my brother Cathal returning to the kingdom under a black shroud after unsuccessfully attempting to assassinate Melisende. His death was the reason I was now the general of Caecias and was here alongside Melisende. I cleared my throat. "Technically, I haven't completed my training as I haven't reached the aibithe yet, but my father had me put through the completion trials anyway. Then he promoted me to general."

"Surely you have other older, more qualified brothers to take on the position of general?" Ardit said as his eyes narrowed slightly. His question irritated me, but only because I had often wondered the same.

If my father disapproved of me so much, why would he promote me? Especially if he had no faith that I could succeed. He expected me to fail, to die trying to slay the queen, yet he still promoted me to general first instead of Brenhin.

"I have learned to stop questioning why my father makes the decisions he does." I took a sip of my kirsch and looked toward Erwan, hoping that he would interject and save me from Ardit's line of questioning.

He just stared back as though he, too, was enjoying my discomfort. My gaze fell to my hands, and I twisted my turquoise ring around my finger.

"Following decisions blindly isn't the best way to lead as a general," Ardit continued, his voice growing more gruff with each sentence.

"Does it look like I am leading anything?" My voice came out louder than I had intended, and my face flushed, my grip on the glass tightening. "My father was devastated when Cathal died." *If only because Cathal was his perfect ruthless general.* "Brenhin was the obvious choice for general, but he chose me. And then these portals opened up and he needed to send one of us on this diplomatic mission.

"My brother Bradach was the obvious choice, but again he chose me. I don't know what future plans my father has for me, but for now he has sent me on a diplomatic mission to form an alliance between himself and Queen Melisende, as well as you, King Ardit."

He laughed, "Your father wants to form an alliance with me? This is the first I'm hearing of this."

"It was my intention to send a letter to inform you of my visit after I had formed an alliance with Melisende." I glanced toward Melisende and sighed. She was watching me with slightly narrowed eyes.

"And how is that going, Little Wolf?" she asked, and the right side of her mouth pulled up into that signature smirk that annoyed me but also caused a tightness low in my stomach.

"Do you think an alliance is necessary or even possible?" Ardit inquired.

I was growing increasingly uncomfortable with King Ardit's line of questioning. When we had first arrived at the castle, he was joking so easily with Melisende that I believed he would be welcoming, but the longer I was here the more I felt as though I was being interrogated.

I wondered if his attitude toward me was a result of my family's reputation or because he wanted to protect Melisende.

"Father." A head popped into the room, interrupting our conversation. I let out the breath I was holding and tried to relax my shoulders. "Dinner is ready."

The female had the same brown skin and eyes as Ardit. Her dark hair was braided, and she wore a burgundy gown.

"Thank you, Aurelia. We'll be in shortly." Ardit smiled warmly at his daughter.

She turned and walked away. At least dinner might stop this train of conversation.

We all moved to the dining hall, following Aurelia. Ardit took a seat at the head of the table and his daughter sat on his right.

Erwan took a seat at Ardit's left, and Melisende took a seat next to him.

I looked at the chair next to Ardit's daughter, which would have put me directly across the table from Melisende, but before I could even decide whether or not to sit there, another noble and his mate approached the table and took the chairs next to Aurelia. Resigned, I sat down next to Melisende.

Sigeweard, Ardit's personal guard, whom I was introduced to while drinking with Foulke and the guards when we arrived at the castle that afternoon, took up the seat across from Ardit at the opposite end of the table.

"Will Auryn be joining us tonight?" Melisende asked as she drained the last of her kirsch.

Ardit replied, "No, Auryn isn't at the castle right now. I sent him out on a reconnaissance mission to check the supplies in the villages on our northern border."

"Any further news on the betrothal?" Melisende probed as she set her empty goblet down.

"Nothing yet." Ardit took a breath before continuing, "It's not a love match, and King Cyrus pushed for the betrothal when Chiara was young, too young to know what was even happening. I wouldn't push my son into anything he doesn't want to do, but I fear Cyrus will force Chiara to marry him anyway."

"That's a shame." Melisende's eyes lowered to the table, and she let out a sigh. I didn't believe in the archaic mating traditions of the Etesian Isles, and it appeared neither did Ardit or Melisende. They had mostly died out, but occasionally you would hear of two nobles being betrothed by their families.

Once everyone was seated, the servants started bringing platters of food to the table. There was grouse and pork, apples, various breads, and vegetables so fresh they must have been picked from the castle's garden that very day. There was thick gravy, small plates with fresh butter, and little pots of spices adorning the table.

The scent of all the food wafted into my nose, and I could feel my stomach grumble.

Everyone at the table started plating their food while the servants started pouring wine into the goblets at each place setting. It was a rich red wine and smelled of cherries, which reminded me of the kirsch we'd enjoyed before dinner.

Melisende lifted her wine and took a sip. My gaze lingered on her mouth, and I watched as she swallowed, then licked her lips. "This is delicious, Ardit," she complimented as she placed the goblet back onto the table.

"Auryn brought it back after visiting one of our southern villages. They have vineyards full of the grapes that produce this excellent wine." Ardit took a long draw from his own glass.

I followed suit and took a sip. It really was delicious. I couldn't help but wonder if the warmer climate of the southern coasts added to the richness of it.

"It's almost as good as the wine we drank during your coronation, Ardit. Do you remember?" Melisende laughed.

The sound was so melodic and beautiful, and it caused my stomach to tighten and blood to rush to my cock. I took a deep breath, then stabbed a carrot with my fork, trying to distract myself from the feelings I didn't want to have.

"What are you insinuating, Melisende?" Ardit said with a wink.

"Oh gods!" Aurelia exclaimed, smacking her forehead with her hand. "Not again."

I glanced in the princess's direction. She was clearly embarrassed about the story that was about to unfold. My gaze turned to Ardit in anticipation.

"It all started at the celebration after my coronation. Lanston had a bit too much to drink…" Ardit started the story.

"Guenevere and I were late coming down to the celebration, as she had wanted to change into a more comfortable gown. Why did you make her wear that stuffy thing to your coronation, Ardit?" Melisende chimed in.

"I did no such thing!" Ardit shouted.

I listened, completely enraptured by Ardit's storytelling. He recounted the story of how his then personal guard, Lanston, had been drinking so much that he had admitted his feelings for Guenevere. How Lanston, realizing what he had done, then began to throw up on Guenevere's shoes.

Ardit continued, "He was so embarrassed he told me, 'Banish me from the kingdom…'"

"…and feed me to a dragon!" Melisende piped up and said in tandem with Ardit. The two of them laughed at the story that only they remembered.

I glanced at Aurelia, who was rolling her eyes. I couldn't imagine how many times she'd heard the story. I then turned my attention to Ardit, whose expression had gone a bit darker, recalling both his deceased wife and guard.

Finally, my gaze shifted to Melisende, who had the most beautiful smile on her face. One I had not seen since arriving in her kingdom a week ago.

It was the kind of smile that a male would sacrifice the world for.

If only she would smile like that at me.

CHAPTER TWENTY-FOUR
Melisende

After dinner, we retired to one of the drawing rooms in the southern tower. It was a lavish room covered with rich velvet fabrics. The large picture windows were swathed with sumptuous burgundy velvet curtains.

There were plenty of plush chairs and sofas scattered around the room, all facing the large ornate fireplace. Above the fireplace was a painting of Ardit and his late wife, Guenevere. There were finely woven rugs covering the hardwood floors and a long sideboard table lined with decanters of whiskey and spiced rum, as well as multiple glasses. I'd be lying if I said this wasn't my favorite room in the castle.

Ardit took a seat in one of the large armchairs, crossed his legs, and waved his hand toward the other seating, beckoning for Faolan and me to join him. He looked toward the two servants that were standing at attention by the sideboard.

"A whiskey for Queen Melisende and me," he ordered. I smiled at Ardit, and he returned the gesture before turning his attention to Faolan. "Faolan, what will you have?"

"I'll have a whiskey as well, thank you," Faolan replied.

He was much quieter now than before dinner. Ardit had been critical of Faolan earlier, but I was surprised when Faolan snapped during our pre-dinner drinks.

He didn't seem to want to be general, and it occurred to me that his father could have treated him as poorly as his cousin. I'd almost feel sorry for him, but I knew the Dulaines were great actors. Whether or not his outburst was a ploy was yet to be seen.

The king spoke, "I know I was giving you a bit of a hard time earlier, Faolan, but Meli here says that you have actually been of some help to her. Both in assisting the village that was attacked, but also in protecting her from some Raiders in your lands."

I shot Ardit a murderous glance. Gods, I was going to kill him. I was actually going to kill him in his sleep tonight. Slice his throat right open and shut him up for good.

Ardit just smirked at me. "Oh, come on now, Meli," he drawled.

I gritted my teeth. "Do you even remember what I told you in the gardens, Ardit? I'd sleep with one eye open tonight if I were you."

Ardit's boisterous laugh filled the room, and he turned toward Faolan. I took a long draw of whiskey and relished in the burning sensation down my throat, taking a deep breath.

"So, what do you make of all this portal business, Faolan?" Ardit took a long sip of his drink, peering at him over the rim.

The prince hesitated. "To be honest, I don't know what to make of them. I haven't seen a portal myself yet, but I saw the damage that ensued when warriors used one to attack the village of Morvern in Boreas."

He took a deep breath and looked at me, an expression of sorrow on his face. It mirrored the haunted look he had the morning after the attack.

Grimacing, Faolan turned his attention back to Ardit. "Prince Lancaster came to Caecias to share the news of the portals in the Western Isle. My father didn't believe him, but after seeing what I did in Morvern, not only do I believe him, but I also want to do everything I can to help."

"It's so strange, Ardit," I remarked, tapping my fingers on my goblet. "There doesn't seem to be any rhyme or reason to the attacks."

"Aleksander explained everything he knew while he was here, but I'm still a bit confused. So, Leuconotos was the first to have a portal, but they weren't attacked? They only had a mortal pass through?" Ardit asked, his brow creasing.

"A mortal?" I started. There was nothing about a mortal passing through the portal in Leuconotos in the letter I had received from King Lancaster.

"Prince Lancaster didn't say anything about a mortal," Faolan added, frowning in confusion, and I shook my head. At least he was as surprised as me.

I focused on what was important. "Regardless of whether a mortal did in fact pass through the portal in Leuconotos or not, the timeline remains the same." I slid my hands down the arms of my chair and uncrossed my legs. "Based on both the letter I received from King Lancaster and what Faolan has told me, the first portal was the one that opened in Leuconotos, but no warriors came through nor any attacks launched. Then a portal opened in Argestes, but they *were* attacked."

Ardit set his drink aside, steepling his fingers in thought as he processed this.

"Lancaster mentioned that he *believes* it was a portal in Argestes, however King Cyrus doesn't believe it was a portal; he believes it was an attack by Leuconotos," Faolan added. "We only have what the Winterbournes have told us to go on when it comes to the attacks and portals on Western Etesia."

"The next portal that we know of was the one that opened in my lands. It was a bigger attack than the one in the Argestes, but there were similarities," I continued.

"The masked warriors wearing black," Ardit suggested.

I nodded. "Yes. Maelys also told me that the masks were fashioned to look like some kind of bird. I don't know how relevant that information is, but it may be important."

Faolan paused, eyes darting between Ardit and me. "If someone created portals and sent warriors through to attack Argestes and Boreas, why would they open a portal in Leuconotos just to send a mortal through?"

"Do you think it was a test?" Ardit wondered. "Maybe whoever is creating the portals was testing their powers. It takes a lot to conjure a portal, let alone make it strong enough and large enough for someone to pass through. Maybe whoever is responsible for conjuring the portals chose a mortal to test them with rather than risking one of their own."

The prince pondered this. "That would also explain why it was seen in Leuconotos. Practice with a mortal on your own lands before attempting to send any of your warriors elsewhere," he provided.

I watched Ardit and Faolan as they continued talking and played absentmindedly with the stone on my necklace.

The portals were a threat to us all. If fae were regaining powers, especially ones as strong as the original god-born fae, we were likely to see another war on a massive scale. The last time any fae was known to have conjured a portal was a thousand years ago when the then King of Argestes launched a war with the Kingdom of Lacusia on the continent.

The king opened a portal so massive that he sent his entire army through. After years of fighting along the beaches and borders of the kingdom, he enlisted the other monarchs of the Isles and arrived at the capital to attack the Queen of the Rusalki fae, Nyneve. His attack resulted in him losing his head and the Gods deciding to remove the elemental magic from all fae. No one had been able to conjure a portal since.

"Either way, that doesn't get us any closer to figuring out where the portals are coming from and who is capable of conjuring them," Faolan said, interrupting my thoughts.

I sighed. "Nyneve is the only one I know of that was alive to see the last portal. By the time I was born, no fae retained enough of their magic to conjure one. No one should be *capable* of conjuring one."

"Have you written to Nyneve yet? She might be able to shed some light on the situation," Ardit mused. "Maybe she has heard whispers of fae regaining their powers?"

"Nyneve... I think I've heard of her. She's the Kingmaker, isn't she?" Faolan asked, and I glared at him. How could he not know about Nyneve? She was the longest ruling monarch of all the fae kingdoms.

"She is the Queen of the Rusalki fae in the Kingdom of Lacusia on the continent and one of the most powerful fae I know." I stared at Faolan, narrowing my eyes. "She helped my grandfather gain independence from Caecias, defeated the previous King of Argestes when he declared war against her kingdom, and she helped end the war between the Kingdom of Terraviridi on the continent and Eurus, resulting in Ardit being crowned. She doesn't make kings, she reveals them. If you ever find yourself on the opposite side of a war from Nyneve, you should think about if you are truly on the right side."

Faolan just looked at me, his jaw slack and his lips slightly parted. My attention remained on his lips, and I unknowingly licked mine. My eyes found his, and when they darkened, a shock ran through my body. I could feel my blood pumping through my veins, a flush of heat to my cheeks.

Stop it! my mind screamed. *He's the enemy!* But no matter how my mind argued, my body wasn't seeming to receive the message.

"Ah-hem," Ardit cleared his throat.

I turned slightly in my chair so that I was facing Ardit but lowered my eyes to the floor before me.

He continued, "We should definitely reach out to Nyneve to find out if word has made it to the continent about these portals. We should also take stock of any fae, royal or not, who still retain any powers no matter how minimal they are."

I shrugged. "As far as I know, Alcina and I are the only fae in Boreas that have any powers left."

Alcina lived in the far north of Boreas and was older than me. The children of Boreas called her 'the old crone,' but in actuality no one knew exactly how old she was.

I added, "And I haven't heard of anyone in Caecias with powers. Which isn't surprising given that King Rian would most likely have had them killed. What about Eurus, Ardit? Do you know of anyone besides yourself with powers?"

"What?" Faolan asked in surprise. "I didn't realize that you had any powers. My father told us that Melisende was the only ruler in the Isles left with magic."

"Meli can control the wind"—I scrunched my eyebrows in response to his exaggeration of my power, but Ardit just winked back at me, his lips curled in a cheeky smile—"whereas I can barely move the air."

Ardit lifted his hand, and I could see the concentration on his face. Soon I could hear the rustling of parchment as Ardit pushed the air over the table in front of us. A few pieces of parchment slid across the top of the table a few inches before Ardit lowered his hand again. He looked up at me, then at Faolan.

"My father was far stronger than me," he explained. "He could move carriages and knock down trees with his powers. Even my wife was stronger than me when she was alive, but it appears that neither of our children have inherited any magic."

"So, that's at least three fae in Eastern Etesia," Faolan remarked, counting on his fingers. "How many do you think there are in Western Etesia?"

"The Winterbournes have never spoken about having powers, but that doesn't mean they don't have them," Ardit stated, and while I didn't believe King Lancaster or his sons capable of that level of deception, Ardit had a point. We didn't know for sure.

"That's true, Ardit, but I did mention that one fae in Leuconotos with powers Alcina told me about. Although, the Winterbournes could have powers too. As Foulke and Faolan have said, they could have been behind the attacks, so keeping their powers hidden may have been by design," I added.

The conversation continued as we discussed who we thought was most likely behind the attacks and guessing at what their motives could possibly be. At one point, Faolan shifted in his chair, and his foot brushed up against mine. But just as quickly as it had come, it was gone again. I glanced at him, but his eyes were firmly on Ardit.

"Meli?" Ardit's voice interrupted my thoughts and brought me back to the present.

My cheeks flushed, and I straightened in my chair. "I'm sorry, my mind seems to have drifted away. What were you asking me about?"

"Nothing, I was just saying that I'm going to retire for the evening," Ardit replied.

"Oh, sorry. Goodnight, Ardit." I smiled. Ardit stood, then kissed me on the cheek before exiting the room.

And once again, Faolan and I were left alone.

CHAPTER TWENTY-FIVE
Faolan

"I didn't realize that you and Ardit were so close," I said, trying to keep my voice level.

The room had felt large when we first entered, but now it was as if the walls were closing in on me. The air felt as though it was being sucked out of the room.

It was only me and her. The entire universe shrunk down to this room, this moment, with her, alone.

Fuck.

"Was that a question?" Melisende asked as she picked up her glass of whiskey and took a long, slow draw of the caramel liquid, swallowed, then licked her lips.

Gods, I wanted to taste those lips. She was beautiful, yes, but I had come to learn that she was also strong and courageous, fair and reasonable, and above all kind and caring. I shoved those thoughts away and took a sobering breath.

"It's just… my father always made it sound as though you didn't have relationships, or at least *good* relationships, with any of the other kings in Etesia." I shifted slightly in my chair and turned to look at the painting of Ardit and his wife hanging on the wall. "But I've come to realize there is a lot my father didn't tell me, and a lot of what he did tell me isn't true, or is at the very least misleading."

Melisende laughed, and it was the most beautiful sound I had ever heard. She never laughed around me unless it was at my expense, and then it was a cold, bitter laugh. But then we arrived in Eurus, and I heard her genuine laugh for the first time.

That laugh was like a beautiful challenge, and from this moment until my last, I would do whatever it took to hear that sound again and again.

"Your father would think that." Another beautiful sound left her lips, and I subconsciously leaned closer to her. "I met Ardit during Eurus's war against Terraviridi. Eurus lost its previous king when they attacked Lacusia. They were without a king for over a century, and Terraviridi took advantage of the chaos.

"A few warriors from Eurus, including Ardit, stepped up and made claims for the throne, but with Nyneve's help, Ardit eventually won the war and claimed the crown.

"Ardit is high fae and has powers, but no royal blood, so he wasn't the other kings' first choice for the crown. And according to the other kings, I wasn't their first choice for Boreas either, so we had that in common. We were monarchs supported by our own citizens, but not the other kingdoms. I dare say we've been friends ever since." She shrugged.

I tried unsuccessfully to come up with something to say, but all I could do was stare at the exquisite female before me. We sat in silence, and she held eye contact for a moment.

A strand of hair slipped down and partially covered Melisende's right eye. My hand started to drift up slowly but stopped as she looked down at my hand. She leaned back in her chair, set her glass on the table, then brushed the hair behind her ear. I flexed my left hand and swallowed the lump in my throat.

"I plan on leaving for home early tomorrow morning, so you must excuse me as I head back to my room," Melisende said stiffly as she stood.

My eyes widened in surprise. "What do you mean *you're* leaving early? We've only just arrived. And do you really think I'd let you travel back through Caecias on your own?"

"Let me?" she snapped. *Sard*. I knew that was the wrong thing to say the second it left my mouth. I braced myself for her reaction. "Males don't *let* me do anything. I've lived over nine hundred years doing as I please and not giving a single fuck what males think. I don't need your permission, Little Wolf."

"Melisende…" I grabbed her by the wrist before she could turn and walk toward the door. "You can do as you please. If you want to leave, I won't stop you. But you can't control me either. If I want to protect you, I will."

"Protect me?" She laughed, but it was that harsh laugh again and hit me like a punch to the gut. "I don't need to be protected by you. I need to be protected from you! You think I don't know why your father truly sent you? And why you still haven't left my side even though I've told you to leave a hundred times? I didn't want you in Boreas and don't want you here, Faolan. I don't want…"

Her eyes went wide, and the silence that followed was deafening. With a start, she turned and hurried out of the room.

I took a breath and clenched my fists, steeling all of my resolve. I stood from where I was sitting and followed her, entering the hallway and looking both directions before spotting her at the far end, approaching the stairs that led to our rooms.

"I know you don't trust me," I shouted from behind her, and she immediately froze in place. I watched as her shoulders rose and fell as she took a deep breath.

She turned slowly and looked at me from the far end of the hallway. "Of course I don't trust you."

Our eyes were locked on one another, and neither of us moved.

After another tense moment, she lifted the hem of her dress and started up the long staircase, speaking over her shoulder, "And I know you overheard Ardit and me talking about your father. He has been vying for my kingdom for as long as he's been alive, your mother's father before him, and his father and grandfather before that. I wouldn't trust anyone from your family."

I quickly made my way down the hallway and followed her up the stairs. She reached the landing to the floor that housed our rooms and glanced back at me.

But just as quickly as she turned to look at me, she turned back toward the corridor and walked toward her room. I couldn't let her reach her room without finishing this conversation. I needed her to know that I'd changed. That I wasn't who she thought I was.

"I'm not my father, Melisende." The words came out like a plea.

She laughed loudly at me, another punch to my gut. "You Dulaines are all the same. You play the victims, meanwhile you are the ones that inflict the most damage." She stopped before she reached the door to her room and shifted to face me.

"Then tell me what damage I've inflicted since being in your kingdom, since being with you." I reached out and took her wrist once more.

Her eyes darted to where my hand gripped her, then slowly traveled up to my face. I knew I was playing with fire, but I didn't care. I would gladly burn if it meant I could remain in her presence longer.

I took a deep breath. "Regardless of why my father sent me, I'm here now. I'm with you."

"You're not *with* me. I barely tolerate your presence." She tried to pull her wrist loose from my grasp, but I refused to yield.

"I think you do more than barely tolerate my presence," I said as my thumb traced circles on the inside of her wrist. I heard a quick intake of breath.

My eyes traveled up her arm and met hers. It was the first time that I noticed the ring of grey that surrounded her hazel irises. They reminded me of silver moonlight bathing the landscape, swirls of golden brown, green, and grey.

"You're delusional." She narrowed her eyes at me, but I could feel her pulse quicken.

"Maybe I'm delusional, or maybe I have realized that I want more than what has been forced upon me. Maybe I want to forge my own path. Maybe I want you to finally trust me—"

"You want me to trust you?" she said incredulously, interrupting me. She pulled her arm free but remained where she stood.

"Yes," I promised. "How can I prove it to you?"

She stared at me for a moment before deciding, "Tell me why your father really sent you." She was seething, but I took a small step, closing some of the distance between us.

"You know why he sent me," I whispered as my eyes drifted down to her lips, then back up to her eyes.

She raised her chin in defiance. "I want to hear you say it."

I took a deep breath knowing that admitting the truth out loud would change everything between us. Any small amount of trust I may have garnered would evaporate.

And yet I would tell her, because I refused to keep this secret any longer.

"He sent me to kill you."

Before I could take another breath, Melisende launched forward, closing the distance between us and pushing me up against the wall just outside of her room. She braced me in place with her left forearm, resting it against my chest and shoulders. I could smell the sweet oranges and fragrant jasmine that had become unmistakably her.

I hadn't seen her grasp the small blade from a sheath concealed along her right thigh, but I felt it as she pressed it to the front of my throat.

CHAPTER TWENTY-SIX
Melisende

"*He sent me to kill you.*" His words echoed in my mind, my heart pounded like a war drum.

I couldn't move. My left forearm was frozen, pressed against Faolan's chest holding him in place firmly between the wall and my body.

I kept my grip on the dagger in my right hand. It was pressed right against his neck. It would only take the smallest movement for me to slit his throat, causing him to bleed out from his carotid artery. And I could do it, too; he wouldn't be the first male I had killed.

Being pressed against him, I could smell the subtle scent of lavender mixed with the bright citrus and sensuous leather he usually smelled of. I stared into his eyes just waiting for him to say something, say anything to give me reason to push the dagger in and slide it along his throat.

His eyes never left mine as he took a deep breath and slowly leaned forward, just an inch. That small distance was enough for the blade to slice into his skin. I could see a single drop of dark red blood form at the site and then slowly drip down his neck.

Before I could move or think, his lips captured mine, and time came to a stop. The kiss was electric, warming me from the inside out.

His lips moved like he was trying to convince me of his truth, and I almost believed them. And then his tongue pleaded for entrance, which I eagerly granted. Our tongues met in a battle for dominance.

There was a loud thud as the dagger in my hand clattered to the floor. Faolan's hands grabbed my hips, and he pulled me flush against his body. I inhaled quickly as I felt him stiffen against my hip.

The hand that had been bracing him against the wall now gripped the collar of his shirt. My right hand slid up his arm, along the back of his neck, and then my fingers tangled in his hair, pulling it tight and causing his head to angle back and expose his neck to me.

There was a small slice on his neck from where my dagger had nicked him. I could see the little drop of blood glistening down his neck and ending at his collarbone.

My tongue slowly licked up the trail of blood, reveling in the coppery tang on my tongue. When I finished, I licked my lips. His eyes darted to my mouth before he kissed me once more. I could taste his blood mixing with the taste of him. It was intoxicating, and I wanted more.

I leaned into Faolan's chest, but he grabbed me by the shoulders and pushed me across the narrow hallway and against the door to my room. Now I was the one trapped between the door and his body.

He kissed me again passionately. His hands moved from my shoulders to my breasts, and I wrapped my right leg around his hips, pulling his body closer to mine. I could feel his erection pressing up against me, and my entire body flushed with heat.

He moaned against my mouth. Suddenly all I could see, all I could feel, was him. But it wasn't enough.

My left hand dropped from his shoulder and landed on the door behind me. It moved around, searching for the handle. After a few seconds, I found the handle and turned it. The door opened and I stumbled back, dragging Faolan into my room with me. He stood just inside of the door, a starving man staring at the feast before him.

I took a few steps backwards and watched as Faolan pushed the door closed behind him, his eyes never leaving mine. Then I stood in the middle of the room, staring at the beautiful and dangerous male before me.

Faolan took a few steps forward and closed the distance between us.

I could feel his breath whisper across my skin as he leaned in further. He captured my lips with his again and started to reach for my clothes, but I pulled back and stopped his hands.

His lips parted, but he didn't say anything. I smiled, knowing that I had the upper hand. I took one slow step back, creating some space between us.

I slowly loosened the ties along the back of my dress, maintaining my gaze with Faolan the entire time. Once the last tie was loosened, I let the dress slip down my body, pooling on the floor.

Faolan's eyes darkened, and he attempted to take a step forward, but I stopped him with an upraised hand, shaking my head.

"Stay. Good pup." My hands came up to caress my breasts, then slowly traveled to my stomach, gently roaming over every curve. Just as my right hand started to make its descent lower and lower, Faolan attempted to touch his growing arousal. I shook my head again. "No touching."

The look of desperation on his face was delicious and told me everything I needed to know. I took a few steps back until my legs met the end of the bed. I sat on the very edge and started stroking my core. Faolan let out a low groan.

"Get down on your knees," I ordered. Without hesitation, Faolan kneeled. I loved an obedient pup. The right side of my lips curled up in a smirk. "Crawl to me."

My core pulsed at the sight of this gorgeous male crawling on the floor toward me. He stopped in front of me, his eyes locked on his prize. He licked his lips, and my stomach tightened.

I couldn't wait any longer. "You can touch me—"

"Fuck," the word left his mouth so quickly as he leaned forward. His hands raised toward my thighs, but I stopped him, grabbing both of his hands and interlocking my fingers with his.

"…But only with your tongue," I whispered.

Faolan's eyes flashed for a moment, arousal clear in his gaze, then he dipped his head between my thighs and licked up and down my core. My back arched, and I threw my head back in pleasure.

He reached the apex of my core and sucked on the little bundle of nerves.

"Gods!" I shouted as my grip on his hands tightened, my nails digging into the back of his hands.

Only when my breathing became more rapid did he thrust his tongue inside me. Stars shot across the back of my eyelids. I felt like I was floating in the ether, and Faolan was my only tether to this world.

He pulled his tongue out of me only to find that little bundle of nerves again and again.

Faolan stopped momentarily, leaning back far enough that I could see my juices dripping down his chin. He winked at me before returning his attention to his prize. He sucked on that little bundle again before biting it, then plunging his tongue inside me again.

"Fuck!" I no longer had control of my body. I could feel every fiber of my being vibrating with pleasure.

The walls of my core were spasming around Faolan's tongue as he continued to plunge it in and out of me in the most delicious rhythm. Only when the waves of pleasure from my orgasm stopped did I look down at him.

I dropped his hands and brushed my thumb across his chin, wiping away my juices. I sucked the sweet liquid from my thumb and looked down at Faolan.

"Very good, Little Wolf."

CHAPTER TWENTY-SEVEN
Faolan

One taste was all it took. I was addicted to her and would gladly spend the rest of my life on my knees worshipping her. She motioned for me to stand, and I complied, slowly rising from my position on the floor of her bedroom.

I stared down at her, desperate for another taste, for anything she would allow me to have.

She stood from her spot on the bed and approached me before her hands found the hem of my tunic. I took a deep breath as she slowly lifted my tunic up over my head and discarded it on the floor, her eyes never leaving mine.

A small shiver ran through my body as her hands returned to my stomach. They traced the lines of my abs before resting on my chest.

She lifted her eyes from my torso to my face. I licked my lips in anticipation.

The right side of her mouth lifted slightly in that signature smirk before she leaned in and kissed me. The kiss was gentle, yet pleading and passionate. I hoped it was a hint of what was to come.

Her kisses moved from my mouth to my jaw and then to my neck, and I let out a low groan. My right hand fisted in her hair and held her in place while my left hand drew lazy circles on the back of her shoulder.

Her hands traveled back down my stomach and stopped at the waistline of my trousers. I could feel as she slowly loosened the tie and pushed them down my hips. I took a small step back to remove my trousers, then looked back up at the resplendent female before me.

Melisende's eyes drifted down to my erection, her gaze full of lust. "What do you want to do to me, Little Wolf?" she crooned.

"Everything." I closed the distance between us and crashed my lips into hers.

I needed her more than I needed air to breathe. I needed her more than water or food. My entire existence depended on her.

My hands slipped down her back and to her thighs. I picked her up, then walked to the edge of the bed. I laid her down and she inched back until her entire body was splayed upon the mattress before me. Then I climbed on the bed and crawled over her, leaving a trail of licks, kisses, and bites along her skin.

When my face met hers, I leaned down and kissed her gently as I positioned myself at her entrance.

Melisende slowly lifted her pelvis to meet me, but I pulled back slightly and just winked at her. Two could play this game.

I captured her left nipple in my mouth and alternated between sucking and biting the little nub while sliding my cock along her entrance. She felt incredible, and I wanted so badly to thrust inside her warmth, but I also wanted to make this feeling last as long as possible.

I kissed a trail from her left nipple to the center of her chest, then licked the entire length of her sternum until I landed at the little dip between her collarbones. I placed a kiss there before lifting my head slightly.

I saw the small scar on the left of her sternum and placed a sweet kiss on top of it. "How——"

"No," she stopped my question before I could finish.

"Okay," I responded, filing that conversation in the back of my mind for later. I kissed the small scar one more time before moving across to her right nipple.

My hand slid along her waist and across her hip. My fingers replaced my cock and slid along her warm, wet core.

I sucked on her nipple as I plunged two fingers inside her.

She arched her back, closing her eyes, and a breathy sound escaped her lips. "Faolan."

Upon hearing my name, I nearly lost it. My cock twitched, and I needed to be inside her. I pulled my fingers from her and slid my cock along her entrance again. I captured her lips and continued rolling my hips, my cock sliding along her core, begging entrance.

I was about to thrust inside Melisende when she opened her eyes, placed her hands on my shoulders, and rolled me over so she was on top of me. I let out a breath as she grabbed my cock and lined up her entrance.

One quick downward motion and she was seated to the hilt.

"Gods!" I cried out, pleasure coursing through my body.

"You don't pray to the Gods in here, Little Wolf. I'm your goddess now." She locked eyes with me and started moving up and down, milking my cock. I reached for her arms and pulled them behind her back, restricting and guiding her movements.

I shifted my hips and thrusted, my cock burying further into her warmth.

"You're no goddess, but you might just be my salvation." I thrusted again, deeper this time, and the world fell away. In mere seconds, an orgasm ripped through my body, shredding through the very fiber of my being.

Moaning, I released her arms from my grip and her hands moved to cup my face. I closed the distance and kissed her once more like she was my only source of oxygen.

Because at this moment, she was.

CHAPTER TWENTY-EIGHT
Faolan

The sun streamed in from the window and landed on my face, waking me from the best sleep I'd had since leaving home. I slowly opened my eyes and caught the sight of Melisende asleep in bed next to me.

Sard, she's beautiful. Her scent of sweet oranges, jasmine, and fir filled my nose, so I took a deep breath and held it, hoping to imprint her scent in my memory. I closed my eyes and took another deep breath, inhaling her intoxicating scent once more, reveling in the serene look on her face, the soft curve of her lips.

Being with her was better than being with every other female combined, including Etaine. And unlike with Etaine, I wanted this moment to last forever. This wasn't some fleeting romp with someone who meant nothing to me. No, *this* meant everything.

Unfortunately, my peaceful moment was interrupted by a loud knock on the door.

Rousing from sleep, Melisende slipped out of the bed and walked across the room, rubbing her groggy eyes with a yawn. She was still naked and completely resplendent.

I had been with plenty of other females, but all paled in comparison to the queen before me. The early morning sunlight caressed her curves as she reached for a robe hanging on the wall. She slipped her arms through the sleeves and tied the straps around her waist.

I wanted to cross the room, strip her of the robe, and pull her back on the bed again. My thoughts were interrupted as the knock sounded again, and she sighed before turning and walking toward the door. She opened the door about a foot wide, and I could see Foulke on the other side. His gaze quickly shifted from Melisende to me, and I could have sworn a smirk appeared on his face before it vanished.

"Yes, Foulke?" I could hear the irritation in her voice. Was she embarrassed that he had seen me in her bed, or angry? I hoped neither.

Foulke turned his gaze back to Melisende, expression turning grave. "There's been another portal. Another attack." At his words, my heart dropped and the color drained from my face.

Melisende readjusted the straps on her robe and stepped just outside of the room, closing the door behind her. After everything that had passed between Melisende and me, I wasn't about to be excluded from this conversation. I slipped out of the bed, not bothering to look for my clothes, and walked quietly to the door. Then I leaned in and held my breath as I attempted to listen in on their conversation.

"What do you mean there was another attack? Where?" Melisende's voice managed to remain calm in the aftermath of the news, but I could sense tension in her tone.

"Ardit received word this morning that another portal opened in Leuconotos." He paused for a moment, then sighed. What wasn't he saying?

"Foulke?" Melisende pressed in a tone that was more a command than a question.

"A large contingency of warriors came through the portal, but this time they weren't hiding behind any masks. The attacks are coming from the Kingdom of Terraviridi on the continent."

Terraviridi. My brain started buzzing with a thousand new questions. I slowly moved away from the door and began collecting my clothes. I could still hear Melisende's voice as I pulled on my trousers.

"What? What possible motive could Terraviridi have to attack the Etesian Isles?" Melisende sputtered, her tone rising.

"Beyond revenge for the war they lost seven hundred years ago, I can't think of a single reason. But that was so long ago, not many are still alive who would remember those times," Foulke answered, voice severe.

"Okay. But why attack without the masks? Why reveal themselves now?"

"This attack was much larger than the previous ones. Ardit thinks it's possible they wore masks before because their king was still harnessing his portal abilities. He thinks they didn't want to reveal who they were until they were sure he could portal an entire army through."

I pulled my tunic over my head and snuck back over to the door.

Foulke continued, "This time they wanted us to know who was responsible..."

"Spit it out, Foulke. Responsible for what?" I could tell Melisende was getting impatient.

"Lancaster Winterbourne II, the King of Leuconotos, is dead."

Melisende gasped. I slowly stepped back and sat down on the bed. This threat just became a lot greater than any of us had anticipated. We had worried about the strength required for a portal to span the islands, not the Etesian Sea.

Jumbled thoughts swirled through my head. I stared at the door, not sure what to make of the news. The sound of Melisende dismissing Foulke pulled me out of the haze. I heard him retreat down the hallway before the door handle started to turn.

Melisende quietly opened the door and slipped inside. When she turned around, her eyes widened upon seeing me awake. "Faolan."

"Meli," I replied and an expression, surprise maybe, flashed across her face. It was the first time I had called her by her nickname.

"I'm assuming you heard?" she asked as she took a few steps closer to me.

"I heard Foulke say there was another attack," I admitted. Eavesdropping at doors was not something that I wanted to be known for, and this was already the second time I'd been caught doing it here in Eurus.

"I don't have all the details, but Ardit received word that there was a large-scale attack on Leuconotos and that the attack was led by Terraviridi. This was the first time the attackers weren't hiding behind masks." She paused and took a seat on the bed next to me. The robe slipped from her shoulder, and my eyes skimmed the naked skin along her collarbone. I swallowed before returning my gaze to her face as she continued, "King Lancaster is dead."

"Gods," I breathed. "So, does Ardit believe it has been Terraviridi behind all of the attacks?"

She shrugged. "It has to be. The idea that two fae can conjure portals…" she trailed off. I watched as she pulled the robe back up over her shoulder. "That's all I know. Ardit wants to meet with us this morning to discuss it further."

"I should go back to my room so you can get ready." I stood and walked over to the door.

This was not at all how I'd wanted this morning to play out, and I wasn't ready for my time in Eurus to be over. I wasn't ready for my time with Melisende to be over.

Before I reached for the door handle, I turned back to look at her. "I'll see you downstairs."

I exited Melisende's room and walked across the hall to my own. Upon entering, I leaned back and placed all my weight upon the door with a sigh.

Memories of the previous evening flashed in my mind. I took a long, slow breath and walked across the room. There was a water jug waiting by the washing basin, but when I dipped my finger inside, it was cool. That was probably better for me anyway. I poured the water into the basin then splashed a handful of it on my face.

After washing, I walked to the wardrobe and reached into my pack for a clean tunic. I quickly dressed, then glanced in the mirror and ran my fingers through my hair.

No matter what the future held, the last twelve hours had changed absolutely everything.

***

King Ardit was pacing the length of the dining room when I finally arrived. Melisende was already seated in one of the chairs, sipping from a glass of juice. I walked over and took a seat in the chair next to her. She didn't acknowledge me, her attention instead solely on Ardit.

"This is worse than we thought," Ardit grumbled as he stopped and turned toward us. "At first there was just a portal in Leuconotos. Then there was a small attack in Argestes. Then an entire village was destroyed in your kingdom, Meli. And now... now, King Lancaster is dead."

Melisende stood and walked over to Ardit, placing a hand on his shoulder. Ardit looked at her and tried to force a smile before he continued to pace the far side of the table.

"We'll figure this out, Ardit." Melisende offered a weak smile, and Ardit returned one equally as feeble. I hadn't experienced war the way these two had and couldn't imagine the horrors that were inevitably running through their minds.

Melisende returned and took her seat next to mine. The door at the far end of the room opened, and Foulke entered along with Sigeweard and Erwan. They sat across the table from us, and Ardit finally stopped pacing. He stood behind his chair at the head of the table and placed his hands on its back.

"We need to call a Conclave of the Kings," Ardit said as he finally took a seat.

Melisende grunted, saying "When are we going to change the sarding name of the Conclave? Conclave of the Monarchs works just as well."

"That's not the most pressing matter right now, Meli," Foulke said with a hint of a smile from his seat across from me. Melisende stared daggers at him, and I suppressed a laugh.

"Regardless of the name, we still need to call a Conclave," Ardit continued. He placed his elbows on the table and steepled his fingers.

"Agreed," Melisende replied. "Ardit, you more than any other monarch know the trouble Terraviridi can create for us. If they really mean to start another war with the Isles, we must be prepared."

"Are there any Terraviridian warriors left in Leuconotos? Did they take any hostages?" I asked, furrowing my brows.

"Leuconotos was able to execute most of them, but not before losing King Lancaster. They have kept a few hostages, and the fighting has stopped for now," remarked Erwan.

"It seems as though most of the hostages are low-level grunts. They haven't gotten any intel from them, but one…" Ardit paused. "One is the nephew of the king."

Shock rippled through my body. I didn't know much about the royal families on the continent, but capturing a royal as a hostage was serious. We finally knew who was behind the portals, but would we be able to learn why?

"The Winterbourne princes have kept him hostage in their castle. They are hoping that he is worth enough that they can draw out the Terraviridian king," Erwan added.

"I know they have been using portals to travel between the continent and the islands to launch their attacks so far, but has anyone checked to see if they have sent a fleet of ships? I wouldn't be surprised if they attempted a multi-pronged approach. Ships could be landing on our shores while we are distracted by the portals," Foulke said, and all eyes darted to him.

Gods, if they had sent ships too, they could divide our forces. There was no way, even if all the kingdoms in Etesia worked together, that we would be able to defend against attacks coming from the sea and portals spread across our lands.

"Foulke's right," I interjected, and his eyes darted to me. I could feel him assessing me. "The portals could be a distraction from a larger attack they are planning. It would be hard to defend against attacks on both fronts known and unknown."

"Shit," Ardit groaned, running a frustrated hand down his face.

The conversation continued for an hour. Foulke and Erwan offered their suggestions while Melisende and Ardit weighed everything carefully. Sigeweard talked about getting the numbers we could amass if all the kingdoms worked together. We discussed different approaches if the attacks were solely coming from portals as well as if the attacks were coming by sea too.

Occasionally I would offer my opinions and for the first time in my life, I was listened to. No one ignored or tried to silence me.

And here, in a foreign kingdom, sitting side by side with my kingdom's worst enemy, I finally felt respected and that I belonged at the table.

CHAPTER TWENTY-NINE

Melisende

During the discussion, it had become increasingly obvious that this latest attack had changed the threat from the chance of a random portal opening to the real possibility that war was looming before us. And not just a war amongst the kingdoms on the Etesian Isles, but with one of the largest and greatest kingdoms of the continent.

I knew I needed to inform Redwald and Maelys about what we had discovered, but when I thought about the extent of information I wanted to convey, the more I realized that I needed to send Foulke, not a raven. He wasn't going to be happy with me, but I couldn't send one of the guards; they weren't in the room when we had the discussion.

I would send him back to Boreas with two of the guards and remain in Eurus for another night with Faolan and Bevan before heading north tomorrow.

Everyone had left the meeting room except for Ardit, who was talking to one of his servants in the corner. I exited the dining room and returned to my quarters. There, I penned a message for Maelys about my intentions for Foulke and the guards upon their return. I pulled a wax block from the desk and retrieved my royal seal from my pack, sealing the parchment and leaving my room.

I walked the hallways looking for Foulke so I could inform him of my plans and give him the letter. I knew he would be staying in the same wing of the castle that Ardit's personal guards and advisors took up residence.

Crossing through the castle and making my way to the guards' wing, I saw him about to enter his room.

"Foulke," I called just before he turned the door handle.

He looked up and nodded at me. We walked the length of the hallway and stopped at the end beside the window overlooking the cliffs.

"Good, I need to talk to you," he said as he rolled his shoulders and straightened to his full height. "I was talking to Sigeweard and —"

"I need you to head back to Ardelve today."

"But…" he tried to interrupt me, but I put up a finger, halting him.

"You need to tell Redwald and the advisors what has happened in Leuconotos. Let them know that I will meet with them when I return," I instructed.

"You can put that in a note and send a raven, Meli," he argued, his tone taking on a sharp edge. I narrowed my eyes at him.

"I want *you* to go, Foulke."

"Send Bevan. He's fast on a horse. My place is at your side," he said, almost pleading. It was rare that I ever sent Foulke off on a mission, leaving me behind, but he fought me every single time.

He had never successfully been able to get me to change my mind, and I wasn't about to start changing it now.

"Bevan wasn't in the room when we were discussing what happened. I'm asking you to go, Foulke. No arguments. And I need you to give this to Maelys," I said, handing him the letter. "I will return with Faolan and Bevan when I am done with my business here."

His eyes turned cold, and his nostrils flared. "So, you sleep with the little prince once and now you trust him enough to lead you safely through his father's land? The father who wants you dead, I might add," he scolded.

I narrowed my eyes. "Careful, Foulke. I allow you to speak your mind, but remember you are speaking to your queen."

He sighed in resignation. I turned and walked back down the hallway, stopping outside Foulke's room.

I added, "Besides, I'm in no danger here in Eurus, and I can protect myself from the little Caecian prince." After last night, I knew Faolan wasn't a threat to me, even if his father still was.

At that, Foulke's expression changed from irritation to amusement, and he let out a low snort. "Oh, I'm sure you can," he said as he followed me down the hallway and stood by my side.

I glared at him, embarrassment bubbling up from my stomach. Foulke had seen his fair share of males in my bed, but none of them had ever made me embarrassed before. And I wasn't ready to explore why that was.

I elbowed Foulke in the stomach, and he grunted. "What was that for?" he exclaimed.

"You know what that was for. Keep your mouth shut and do as you're told."

He rolled his eyes, and I couldn't help but smile at him in return before he turned and entered his room.

I walked back down the length of the hallway and stopped in front of the large picture window once more, watching the waves crashing against the cliffs of the peninsula that the castle sat upon while pondering our next steps.

With such a blatant attack from one of the kingdoms of the continent, war was most certainly headed our way.

I wasn't sure how long I had been staring out of the window before I heard Ardit call out from behind me, "Meli?"

I turned and smiled at him. "Hello, Ardit."

"Is everything alright?" he asked as he placed a hand on my shoulder.

"I'm sending Foulke and two of my guards back to Boreas to inform my council of what we have discussed. I need Maelys and Redwald to handle the kingdom and deal with the council while Faolan and I meet with Rian."

"You're going to meet with King Rian? Do you think that is wise?" Ardit looked at me as though I had lost my mind. Perhaps I couldn't blame him.

I laughed at the thought and realized I must be going a little bit mad. "No. I don't think it is wise, but I think it is necessary."

"At least meet him in a neutral location, Meli. I fear for what will happen to you if you head directly into the den of wolves." His eyebrows knitted together, a look of concern in his eyes.

"I don't have the time to arrange a meeting in a neutral location." My lips tightened into a straight line before I continued, "Besides, I have to pass through Caecias to return home anyway."

Ardit's gaze shifted to the ground, and a long sigh left his mouth.

I shook my head and exhaled. "What is happening, Ardit? We haven't seen portals in over a thousand years and not only is someone conjuring them, but they are using them to launch attacks on the Isles."

Ardit placed his left hand on the window, his mating band still sitting on his third finger. "I had hoped that I was finished with war.

After losing Guenevere in a battle with Caecias, I hoped that my children and I could live peacefully. I've seen enough war for multiple lifetimes."

"Haven't we all, Ardit?" I said as I turned to face him fully. "While I know that peace between Caecias and Boreas is unlikely, I had hoped that I wouldn't have to see war on a large scale ever again."

Ardit's hand slipped from the window, and his usually cheerful face held a mournful expression. "As did I, Meli. As did I."

***

I sat at the small table in the corner of my room while two servants flitted around the room preparing my lunch. One of them was shifting plates of food from the small cart they had wheeled into my room to the table where I was seated while the other was pouring tea into the cup in front of me and asking if I would like some wine with lunch as well.

I liked wine as much as the next fae, but Ardit had wine with nearly every meal. I shook my head, and she bowed slightly before returning the bottle to the cart, leaving the pot of tea on the table for me. I reached for a slice of hard cheese and took a bite.

There was a knock on the door before it opened and Foulke entered my room. "Meli, we are packed and ready to leave," he informed me.

"Be quick but careful, Foulke," I said as I stood, reaching for his hands and holding them in mine.

"Are you sure it's necessary for me to ride out with the guards? I can just relay the information," he reminded me. I shouldn't have been surprised that Foulke was still attempting to change my mind, yet I shook my head.

"Yes, it is necessary, Foulke." I steeled myself for what I was going to tell him next; I knew he was not going to allow it, but as queen it was my decision and mine alone. "Besides, Faolan and I are going to meet with King Rian on our way back—"

He pulled his hands free from mine and took a step back, aghast.

"Meli!" It was rare that Foulke ever raised his voice to me, but I had expected this. "I will *not* allow you to go to Rian's castle alone and unguarded."

"Since when do you *allow* me to do anything? Besides, I'm not going alone or unguarded!" I protested.

"Faolan?" He snorted and shook his head. "You think you know him? You think you can trust him? You think he'll protect you? He's a Dulaine, Meli!"

I stiffened. I wasn't about to have this conversation with him.

"Don't you think I know that?" I said, raising my voice in return. "Do you really think so little of me that I would trust any of Rian's pups after one night?"

"No." He looked down at his feet, avoiding my gaze.

"Of course I don't trust him. But he did keep us alive on the way through Caecias once, and I believe he will do it again. He owes us that much."

"But I don't know if I trust him to keep you safe in Rian's home." He shook his head and sighed in frustration, running his hand over his face. "My father almost lost you to a Caecian once. I won't be the one to lose you to a Caecian for good."

"Foulke." I ran my hand from his shoulder down to his hand and held it. "I need to go to Caecias and see for myself how Rian reacts to the news. I need to know if he sees these attacks as a real threat. I need to know if he is going to continue to be a threat to Boreas while there is a war with Terraviridi."

I sat back down and motioned for him to take a seat as well. He shook his head and remained standing, expression stern.

I continued, "I need to go to Caecias, which means I need you to head back to Boreas. I trust you, Foulke. I need you to return as quickly as possible to warn Maelys, Redwald, and the advisors of what has happened. I need you to protect them from any new threats that might arise before I return."

He slowly nodded his head, the gravity of what I was asking of him finally setting in. "I understand," he said quietly.

"Good." I smiled at him, yet the prospect of war didn't ease my mood in the slightest.

"But that doesn't mean I like it," he added.

I laughed loudly, and he smirked at me. "I would expect nothing less."

Foulke placed his hand on my shoulder. "Be careful, Meli, you're playing with fire." Before I could respond, he turned and walked out of my room.

CHAPTER THIRTY
Faolan

"Faolan, join us. The generals are going to talk." Foulke leaned across the table after the meeting between Ardit and Meli had ended and invited me to join him and Sigeweard for a discussion.

I watched as this large man pushed back his chair and stood up, rolling his head and shoulders. It was the first time I looked at Foulke as a general, not just Melisende's personal guard. I followed him and Sigeweard out of the meeting room and to a room on the ground floor of the southern wing of the castle.

"We need to find out if Terraviridi has sent any ships across the sea. Until we know whether we are fighting on two fronts or one, it will be hard to make plans," Foulke explained as we took seats in the small, comfortable lounge.

"It's late in the season to sail, but I have two crews on standby. I can send one out to search the coast of Western Etesia, but it would probably be quicker to have either Leuconotos or Argestes send out scouts," Sigeweard added.

"Leuconotos has just lost their king and countless warriors. And we don't know where Argestes stands on this matter yet. According to the letter we received from King Lancaster, Argestes didn't believe in the portals to begin with, and I don't know if they do now. I fear we are on our own until the Conclave of the Kings," Foulke sighed and rubbed his beard. "How many fighters can you assemble in a month?"

"In a month? Probably fifteen, twenty thousand," Sigeweard replied.

Foulke turned to me then. "What about you, Faolan? How many fighters does Caecias have on reserve?"

Gods, did I even know? I had been general less than a month before being sent to Boreas and neither my father nor brothers were very willing to divulge intel. Based on my training, I knew our military had twenty-one divisions and that the largest held close to two thousand males.

"I don't know," I admitted, shaking my head. "My father hasn't exactly been forthcoming, but if I had to guess, around thirty-five thousand in total. Trying to convince him to call on all of them is going to be the challenge."

Foulke offered me a look that could have passed for sympathetic. "And Boreas has around ten thousand. That's at least sixty thousand fighters on East Etesia."

"Estimates said Terraviridi sent around ten thousand warriors to Leuconotos. And that was just a small army. I've heard they number over one hundred thousand," Sigeweard said.

"Shit!" Foulke exclaimed, mirroring my thoughts exactly. "We need to start talking to Leuconotos and Argestes to get numbers ahead of the Conclave. I need to speak with Melisende."

Foulke stood from his chair and pushed the sleeves up his arms. He nodded at Sigeweard and me briefly before turning and exiting the room. I ran my hands along the chair arms and took a deep breath. So much had happened in the last twenty-four hours, my head was spinning.

"If you'll excuse me, I have some matters to attend to," Sigeweard said as he stood. I watched as he left the room and took another long, deep breath.

I didn't know how long I had been sitting by myself before Ardit's voice drew my attention.

"Faolan!" He crossed the room and poured two glasses of wine, handing me one and sitting down across from me. It wasn't yet noon.

I took a sip of wine as Ardit cleared his throat and looked at me.

"I've known Queen Melisende for a long time; she doesn't trust anyone from Caecias. Your father has killed thousands of her citizens. Your grandfather before that and his father and grandfather before that. And with the looming threat of war, her top priority is going to be protecting her kingdom. There is no room for anything, or anyone, else."

"I…" I stuttered. I wasn't sure why he was telling me this. "I don't understand."

He frowned. "I've seen the way you look at her. Meli doesn't do relationships. You'd be better off returning home and forgetting about her."

He downed the remaining wine and set the empty glass on the table next to him, then stood and strode across the room. Before he reached the door, he turned back to me. "Just think about what I said." With that, he departed and left me alone with my thoughts.

That was… I don't know what that was, but I knew he was right.

Melisende and I didn't make any sense, but that didn't stop me from wanting her even more now that I'd had a taste. Being with her was like finally seeing a light in the endless darkness of my life.

I took a deep breath and set my glass down on the table. Why did everything have to be so godsdamn complicated?

***

It was early evening when the servants cleared the remains of my lunch as I stood by the window and watched the waves crash against the cliffs. I was feeling restless and needed to stretch my legs. The skies had grown dark and grey, but the rain was holding off, for now at least.

I left my room, exited the castle, and headed toward the gardens to walk off some of my unease. The gardens were at the highest point on the peninsula, and the views were stunning.

My mind drifted back to what Ardit had told me, *"Meli doesn't trust anyone from Caecias."*

I was not ignorant of all the atrocities my family had committed against her and her kingdom, but I wasn't my family. Was there anything I could do to earn her trust?

And even if I *did* earn it, what would that mean for us if she didn't do relationships?

Last night, she pulled me from the darkness I had been living in, and I wasn't ready to give that up. I wasn't ready to give *her* up. Nor the light she had brought to my life.

I only managed to enter and briefly walk the perimeter of the walled gardens before I felt the first drops of rain. I sighed and decided to turn back, closing the wooden door of the gardens behind me as I left. I walked back toward the main castle tower, but before I entered the building, I noticed a group of fae saddling horses on the mainland side of the bridge near the gatehouse.

I walked past the castle entrance to the edge of the footbridge and saw Foulke was amongst the group getting ready to ride out.

Shit. "Foulke!" I shouted, the waves drowning out my voice. He merely nodded at me and then turned his horse and followed the group of riders galloping away.

Shit. Shit. SHIT! I couldn't believe they had left without me. After everything we'd been through, after everything that had happened, I couldn't believe that Melisende would just leave without even saying goodbye.

I didn't want to believe Ardit when he told me she didn't do relationships and that I would be better off forgetting her, but I guess this was the proof.

The rain continued and soaked me to the core as I watched the riders retreat into the distance. Once they were nothing but specs on the horizon, I returned to the castle with a heavy heart.

Maybe last night didn't mean anything to Melisende, but I had to believe our relationship was more than that. More than just sex. I had helped when Morvern was attacked. I protected her and her guards from the Raiders while traveling through Caecias. I was the only ally from Caecias she would have in facing the threat of portals and war.

I climbed the stairs towards my room as questions swirled in my mind. What was I supposed to do now? Where should I go? Would Ardit even allow me to stay in his kingdom while I figured everything out?

I didn't have the answers to any of those questions, but one thing was clear: I couldn't go home. I had failed in the one thing my father had asked of me, and I didn't want to see how he would respond.

I crested the top of the stairs and headed down the long hallway to my room, stopping outside the door and punching the wall beside it. My knuckles stung, pain wracking through the bone, and I sucked in a breath.

Above all, I couldn't believe that Melisende had left without saying goodbye.

Just as I turned and faced her room, Melisende opened the door and stepped into the hallway. My heart stopped beating. She was still here!

Her hazel eyes met mine, and all the resentment I had been feeling melted away. She glanced down the hallway, looking for the source of the loud bang. I rubbed my stinging knuckles.

When her eyes returned to mine, I swallowed. "I just saw Foulke leaving."

"Yes," she said, and her eyes softened ever so slightly.

"I thought you were with them." My voice came out more desperate than I would have liked. I took a step closer to her and cleared my throat.

"No. I sent Foulke back to Boreas to inform Maelys and Redwald of what we have learned here." Her eyes darted to my lips quickly before returning to meet my gaze. "It is important that they hear the news as quickly as possible, and I didn't want them to wait until after you and I returned from Caecias. We need to discuss this new attack with your father."

It was as if she stabbed me in the gut. "Absolutely not! He will kill you, Meli," I urged as I closed the distance between us and placed both of my hands on her shoulders.

"Get your sarding hands off of me, Faolan." She narrowed her eyes, and I could see the anger bubbling under the surface.

"Your fury is going to be my undoing."

"Fury? You haven't seen fury yet." She tried unsuccessfully to step away from me. "War is coming, Faolan. We actually need an alliance between all the kingdoms of Etesia. You can wait for Ardit to call the Conclave and see how your father reacts at that meeting in a month's time, or we can go talk to him now."

"Wait for the Conclave! My father wants you dead, Meli. If we go to the castle, he will kill you!" I dropped my hands from her shoulders and reached for her wrist. I pulled her close, her body just a hair's breadth from mine. I could feel her breath against my neck and her intoxicating mix of orange and jasmine scents filled my nose yet again.

"If your father thinks he can kill me, he is mistaken. He underestimates me. He underestimates all females, and that will be his downfall." She pulled her wrist from my grip and pushed past me. I watched as she descended the stairs.

The sky was darkening as I returned to my room. I wasn't sure how I was going to convince her, but I knew we couldn't go to Cathair Mor; it was bad enough that we had to pass through Caecias once more on the way back to Boreas. And there was no talking to my father.

Not only would Melisende die, but I knew what fate awaited me if I returned home with Melisende in tow alive rather than dead.

**

Dinner was a much smaller affair tonight. Foulke had returned to Boreas, Sigeweard was absent, and Aurelia had decided to dine with a male who was courting her. It was only Ardit, Erwan, Melisende and me. Talk steered clear of the portals and war, but the tension was still thick enough to be cut with a knife.

After dinner, I followed Melisende down the hallway to our rooms. "What can I do to convince you not to visit my father?" I pleaded, making her pause.

"Nothing, we're going."

"No, we're not," I insisted.

She looked me in the eye. "Maybe you haven't learned this about me yet, Little Wolf, but I don't care what males think."

"You might not care what I think, but I'm telling you, my father will kill you if you step foot in his castle. We're not going." I reached out, pulling her closer to me. *Why is she being so stubborn about this?*

"Yes, we are. This isn't a discussion." She turned away from me, but my grip was unrelenting. I stepped forward and pushed all of my weight against her, trapping her between the wall and my body.

My chest pressed against her back, and I reached for her left wrist with my left hand. I pulled both of her arms above her head and pinned them against the wall. I leaned in even closer, my nose pressed against her neck. Her scent was like a drug I couldn't resist, and I inhaled greedily.

My cock throbbed as it pressed up against her backside. Her head turned to the side, and she tried to glare at me. That murderous look in her eyes just turned me on more.

"You're going to be the death of me," I whispered in her ear, then I moved ever so slightly, just enough for my erection to rub against her ass again. "You know, I could take you right here against this wall."

I adjusted my hold on her, grabbing both of her wrists with just my left hand. My right hand slowly moved down her body until I reached her waist.

"You could try," she said as she tried to wiggle free.

The only thing she succeeded in doing was rubbing her ass against my throbbing cock. I suppressed a groan.

I squeezed her waist with my hand, then turned her around to face me. Her back was pushed against the wall, and I slid one of my legs between hers; I could feel the warmth between her thighs beckoning me.

She let out a breath as her head fell back, and I leaned forward to lick along her collarbone. A small whimper left her lips, further enticing me. I moved my right hand from where it rested on her waist to the slit of her dress.

Slowly I slipped my fingers under the fabric of her dress along the skin of her thigh. Eventually, my fingers found their destination.

"Fuck, you're so wet for me," I moaned as I bit the delicate skin on her neck.

Just then, she slipped one of her hands free of my grip and pushed against my chest. I stumbled back a step. For a moment we just stared at each other from this short but impassable distance.

She turned down the hallway and started walking away.

Sard if that didn't make me want her more.

She turned her head to look back at me as she reached for the handle on the door to her room. "Are you coming, Little Wolf?"

CHAPTER THIRTY-ONE
Melisende

It was still dark when I woke up, and I stared at the ceiling as my mind raced. It was the second night in a row that I had slept through the entire night. That hadn't happened in over eight hundred years.

I turned my head slowly to the side, seeing Faolan was still asleep in the bed next to me. I took a deep breath, the smell of lavender and leather filling my nose. The scent had become so distinctly his, and it was delicious. *Gods, Meli, what are you doing?*

I knew I shouldn't have slept with Faolan, let alone twice, but I couldn't help it. It's not like I didn't occasionally enjoy the efforts of the males in Boreas, but none of them, *none of them*, compared to Faolan. What was it about this little prince that captivated me so?

I needed to remind myself that Faolan was a Dulaine. He was a Caecian. And I could never trust a Caecian, something I repeated to myself as I brushed the scar on my chest.

I took a deep breath and slipped out of the bed. The sheets rustled behind me as Faolan woke. I looked over my shoulder and offered a small smile before grabbing my robe and entering the bathing chamber. The servants hadn't brought hot water in yet this morning, so I poured the remaining water from yesterday's jug into the basin and splashed a little on my face. Water droplets ran down my face and neck as I looked up into the mirror.

Regret. The look on my face was the look of regret. I shouldn't have given into my lust. Maybe Faolan didn't want to kill me, but that didn't mean that I could trust him either. I needed to be stronger than my desires.

Reaching for the soap, I rubbed it between my hands before gently scrubbing my face. After I finished washing, I grabbed the towel hanging by the basin and wiped my face dry.

Upon returning to the room, I saw Faolan pulling up his trousers. The muscles in his back and arms shifted as he tugged them over his thighs and ass.

Swallowing, I told myself to enjoy the view because it was the last time I would see it. I had bedded the young prince twice, and now that I had, I would move on. We would meet with his father, then go our separate ways.

I walked to the wardrobe and pulled it open. Inside were a clean pair of trousers and the tunic that the servants had washed for me when we arrived in the kingdom a couple days ago. I pulled on my clothes and turned back toward Faolan.

"There is still time to change your mind," he said after pulling his tunic over his head. I didn't need to read his mind to know he was talking about going to meet with his father.

He sat on the bench at the foot of the bed and started lacing up his boots, his eyes flicking up to me expectantly.

"Faolan?" I said a bit hesitantly. He looked up at me, and my stomach flipped as his eyes met mine. "What happened here, what happened between us, it can't happen again."

"What?" He stood, and there was a brief surge of pain in my chest.

"This,"—I waved my hand between us—"can't happen again. I won't let it happen again."

"Why? Because of my father?" He took a step closer and held my stare. Because of his father, because he was Caecian, because he hadn't even reached aibithe yet?

All of the above, but mostly because I knew what would happen if I let him in. If I let down the walls I had built to protect myself. I barely knew him, but I already doubted I would survive the hurt and betrayal that would inevitably ensue. "If your father wanting me dead so he can claim my kingdom for his own isn't enough for you..." I trailed off, my voice thick.

"My *father* wants you dead. *I* don't. And this is exactly why I said we shouldn't go to Cathair Mor. But—"

"But nothing," I cut him off. "You're the Prince of Caecias, I'm the Queen of Boreas. We are enemies. There is no version of this story that doesn't end badly."

My stomach knotted as I turned toward the door, everything in me screaming to turn back, to go to him. I squeezed my eyes closed, trying desperately to clear the vision of Faolan's pained expression from my mind and attempting to take a steadying breath, but when I opened my eyes, instead of feeling resolve, I only felt remorse.

Unwilling to let Faolan see my resolve slipping, I walked out of the room and let the door swing shut behind me.

***

Later that morning after we had finished breakfast and packed our belongings, Faolan and I joined Bevan at the stables where he was readying our horses.

Ardit crossed the footbridge to join us and say farewell. My arms wrapped around him in a tight embrace as I reassured him that this war was not the end. That this too we would overcome. He squeezed my shoulders before kissing me briefly on the cheek. We bid our final farewells and mounted our horses before heading north and back into enemy lands.

Our first day passed with no problems. We neared the border and camped in a clearing on the moor. The following morning, we crossed into Caecias and continued our trek north toward Cathair Mor to meet with Rian.

We had been traveling for nearly two full days and Faolan had barely talked to me. At least Bevan managed to keep me entertained with stories of his youthful misdeeds.

That evening as we ate dinner around our small campfire, Bevan told us an embarrassing story from when he was only six years of age. He had been trying to catch a fish for his mother and when he leaned down to pick it up with his hands, it swam away and he lost his balance, falling face-first into the water.

I laughed so hard my cheeks hurt, and I noticed Faolan's gaze snap to me. His eyes locked on mine, and that familiar tug pulled low in my stomach. I swallowed, then forced my eyes back to Bevan.

The following morning, I arose just as the sun was starting to crest the hillside. Bad dreams had plagued my sleep as usual. I stretched from where I lay, then rolled over to see that Faolan's bedroll was empty and packed up. Bevan was still asleep on my other side but would most likely be waking soon.

I slipped out from under my blanket and stood, surveying the campsite, but Faolan was nowhere to be seen. Frowning, I reached for a cloak to help keep the morning chill off of me and headed in the direction of the creek.

Just before reaching the small creek, I saw the glint of something metallic. It looked like the sun reflecting off a sword, but I didn't hear the sounds of struggle.

I slid behind a large oak tree and peered in the direction of the glinting metal. What I saw caught me by surprise. Faolan was standing by the creek, shirtless, practicing with his sword. His form was impeccable and his motions breathtaking. I felt rooted to the ground but managed to lean away from the tree just enough to get a better view.

He raised the sword, and I watched as the different muscles in his arms and back engaged. His movements were slow and disciplined, his body powerful and strong. I was completely awestruck.

I watched how well he handled the blade with grace and precision and couldn't help but be reminded of how he handled my body with the same devotion. My body flushed with heat as I took a step away from the tree trying to compose myself.

"You're staring," Faolan said without so much as looking in my direction.

I balked at him, then steeled my expression. "Don't flatter yourself, Little Wolf. I was coming down to the creek to wash," I attempted to deflect.

"Whatever you need to tell yourself, Fury."

My eyebrows narrowed. "Fury?"

"It's only fair that you have a nickname as well," he said as he resumed his practice.

I walked down to the creek, hearing the sound of his sword cutting through the air behind me. I desperately wanted to do nothing more than continue to watch him, but I wasn't about to give him the satisfaction.

I set my cloak on a rock along the bank before slipping my trousers and tunic off. I folded them and set them on my cloak before removing my chemise as well. Then I stepped into the shallow creek and scooped up a handful of the cool, crisp water before splashing it on my face and letting the little water droplets run down my chest and arms.

I stepped further into the stream and listened as Faolan's steps and sword movements slowed to a stop. "Now who is staring?" I teased.

I continued to wash in the stream until I could no longer bear the cold of the water. Turning toward the bank, I noticed my clothes were no longer resting on the rock where I had left them. Instead, they were hanging from Faolan's grip.

He was standing at the edge of the creek, just waiting for me with a devilish smirk. My gaze slowly traveled from his lips to his eyes as I strode out of the water. Standing before him, I stretched my hand out to retrieve my clothes, but he just pulled his arm away. I glared at him before attempting to reach around him, but he took a couple of steps backwards.

"Faolan…" He stared at me. I reached out again, but just as before he took another couple of steps back. "Give me my gods-damned clothes," I snapped impatiently.

This time as I reached out, I could feel tingles erupt across my palm as a strong burst of wind came forth and caused Faolan to stumble backwards. There was a look of shock on his face.

But then his lips twisted into a smile. "Oh, Fury… now *that* is interesting."

***

The afternoon sun beat down on us as we continued our trek north. My horse let out a deep breath, and I patted his neck a few times. My mind had been racing since the incident at the stream with Faolan this morning.

I had only ever been able to summon a weak breeze or small whirlwind, but this morning my powers had actually caused Faolan to stumble backwards. I had only ever seen my father, Alcina, and Nyneve have that much control over their magic.

My stomach growled, and my mind shifted from my new, stronger powers to stopping for a small meal. Bevan located a clearing near some tall oak trees where we could feed and water the horses. I dismounted and handed my reins over to Bevan, who led both of our horses to a nearby pond.

Nuts, a bread roll, and some dried apricots were all I had left in my pack. Thank gods we would reach the castle before nightfall.

After our lunch break, we mounted up and continued on our way. Bevan took the lead and was currently whistling, while Faolan and I silently rode side by side behind him. I glanced over and noticed Faolan deep in thought.

"My father isn't a good male," Faolan finally announced, breaking the silence, and Bevan's whistling came to an abrupt stop.

"I'm sorry to tell you this, Little Wolf, but that's pretty much common knowledge throughout all of the kingdoms." My face softened, but I could feel the battle between empathy and validation playing out through my lopsided smile.

"I know why *you* don't like him, but…" he trailed off. I looked over at him again, and he adjusted slightly in his saddle.

His eyes had that same haunted look they did in the aftermath of the attack in Morvern. For the first time, I felt sorry for Faolan. Knowing the atrocities King Rian had committed against my kingdom, I could only imagine what he may have done to his own kingdom, or even family.

I rode in silence next to Faolan, hoping he would continue sharing his thoughts.

"You saw how my cousin lives," he said quietly. "My aunt is the daughter of the late king and grew up in the castle. And now… now, she lives with her daughter in a little, nondescript village on the outskirts of the kingdom. Why? Because my father wanted to assert his dominance the second he got the crown. He might as well have pissed all over the castle."

He shook his head and took a long, slow breath.

"He barely treats my mother any better, and she was born into the royal family. He wasn't. He married into it. And he dotes on my brothers but calls me a bastard. I guess… I guess time outside of Caecias has given me perspective and a chance to see him more clearly. To see how he treats the individuals who are closest to him. No wonder our citizens fear him."

"Faolan…" I couldn't find the words to comfort him. His father was the biggest asshole in all the kingdoms and not just in the Etesian Isles. To my surprise, Faolan halted his horse and faced me.

"And you, Meli. I see the way you treat those around you," he said reverently. "My father would never let his advisor or personal guard talk to him the way you allow Redwald and Foulke to talk to you. You took in Ethann when his family was killed, and he loves living at the castle with you. He *loves* it, Meli. Your citizens love you."

"I…" My eyes softened, and I started to reach out my hand before I thought better of it.

Faolan's expression hardened. "We are walking towards a death sentence. My father will try to kill you. I'm pretty sure he will try to kill me, as well."

I paused. "Faolan, your father is the worst male I've ever met, but I can't believe he would kill one of his own sons." My nose wrinkled; he couldn't be right.

"That's where you are wrong, Fury." He turned his horse back toward the trail and nudged him forward, leaving me sitting in place, staring at him.

I didn't know what to make of this male.

CHAPTER THIRTY-TWO
Faolan

The late afternoon sun was getting weaker as clouds started rolling in from the south-west. I looked up at the large oak trees that surrounded Cathair Mor. The last of their leaves were falling, smattering the forest trail with various shades of gold and auburn. We were less than an hour to the castle, and my stomach tied itself in knots.

Melisende thought she could just show up unannounced and demand to speak to my father. But I knew him better. I knew what awaited us.

"Meli, I'm asking you one last time to reconsider. It is not too late to turn around and continue north to Boreas," I pleaded, my heart sinking in my chest the closer we drew to my home.

She shook her head. "I didn't come this far just to turn around —"

"You think this will be easy? That you can just stroll into his castle? My father will kill you if you step foot inside the gates." I could feel my temperature rising with my ire, and my jaw clenched tightly.

"Grow up, Faolan! Nothing is easy, and there will always be someone trying to kill you." She raised her voice, and my eyes widened as I looked over at her.

"Yes, but that doesn't mean you need to ride straight to their door and present yourself on a silver platter!" I shouted back at her.

"Are you lovebirds alright back there?" Bevan asked from the lead.

"Shut up!" Melisende and I yelled in unison, and Bevan just laughed from up ahead of us.

"Do you want to spend a day on the rack when we get back to Boreas?" Melisende asked, and I watched as her chest rose and fell with each heated breath she took. Bevan just laughed harder. "Fine!" She threw her hands up. "We won't go to the castle, but I'm still meeting with your father."

And just like that, the glimmer of hope was snatched away from me. "What do you mean you still want to meet with my father?"

"Take me to the White Stag; I can meet your father there. You do have a White Stag, right?" she demanded, her tone turning condescending.

The White Stag was the other solution that came about from one of my ancestors ambushing the Leuconotan royals in their own castle; it was a public house built in each kingdom's capital city in order for both sides to meet on so-called neutral grounds.

Melisende nudged her horse forward until she caught up with Bevan. I could hear them talking amongst each other, but I couldn't make out what they were saying.

It wouldn't have mattered anyway. My brain was firmly locked on trying to come up with a way to appease my father. At least Melisende agreed not to go to the castle, but now I just had to find a way to get her—as well as Bevan and myself—out of Caecias after the meeting and back into Boreas. *Alive.*

I wasn't sure whether my father had heard about the latest attack in Leuconotos or if he even cared. My guess was that he still thought the portals were fake and that his biggest threat was from Melisende.

And that was precisely what worried me. Our best chance, our only chance, was to convince him of the threat posed by the portals. If he knew they were real, if he knew that Terraviridi was behind them, maybe, just maybe he would cease his attempts on Melisende for the time being.

My father wasn't alive during the war between Terraviridi and the Etesian Isles, but all Sylph children in Caecias learned about how King Ardit won the war and claimed the throne of Eurus.

Melisende slowed her horse and rejoined me as we made our descent into the valley where Cathair Mor lay. I looked over the place I used to consider home and realized I now felt like a stranger in my own lands.

"You should pull your hood back up." My tone was flat, and I adjusted in my saddle. "The villagers of Holbeach may not have recognized you, but in the capital everyone will."

Melisende obeyed, the shadows of her hood obscuring her face. She tightened her grip on the reins, her knuckles turning white. Was she nervous? She should be. Cathair Mor was a dangerous enough place for its citizens.

We finally arrived at the outer gates of the city, and I dismounted Dulachan, handing his reins to Bevan. There was a guard standing outside of the gatehouse, and I approached him. After exchanging a few words, the guard lifted the gate, I remounted my horse, and we entered the lower ring of the city.

Cathair Mor was a large walled city. The lower ring was filled with muddy dirt roads, shoddy wooden houses, and was home to the poorest of the capital's citizens.

I swallowed thickly as I led Melisende and Bevan past a family begging on the street, an injured male limping toward a healer's hut, and children running around barefoot in scraps of fabric. Eventually, the road brought us to the middle ring of the city where the majority of the citizens lived. We passed houses comprised of wood and stone, smiths, traders, and the market square.

As we turned a corner, the White Stag appeared. It was an unremarkable building but had a large sign hanging out front with the image of a white stag painted on it.

We dismounted our horses and tied them to the rail outside before entering the building. There was a bar and tables to the left and a crackling fire burning in the hearth to the right. The room smelled of freshly baked bread and stale mead.

I strode up to the bar and stood facing the male on the other side. "We need three rooms for the night," I informed him.

"Only 'ave two," he remarked, voice gruff, as he slammed two keys down on the bar.

"Two is fine," I replied, though that meant that two of us would be sharing a room. I knew who I preferred to stay with, but the queen had made her choice obvious before leaving Eurus.

I tossed some coins down and snatched the keys, turning toward the stairs.

The barkeep called out, "Oi, you look familiar. Do I know ya?"

My blood ran cold. I was so concerned about Melisende not being recognized that I hadn't worried about myself.

Clearing my throat, I said, "No, I just have one of those faces."

The male behind the bar just grunted as I started climbing the stairs, with Melisende and Bevan trailing close behind.

The large brass keys had numbers etched into them. Six and seven. As we reached the second floor, I handed one of the keys to Melisende. "Bevan and I will share a room for the night."

Melisende took the key, inclined her head, then walked to her room.

Once she was inside, I turned to Bevan. "I'm going to head to the castle to inform my father that the queen would like to meet tomorrow."

"Good luck," he said in a tone that indicated I would need it, but not necessarily that he cared if I succeeded. *That's fine.* His job was to protect Melisende; he didn't owe me any allegiance. He turned and opened the door to the room and entered.

Alone in the hallway, I pulled the hood of my cloak up and took a deep breath. How was I supposed to navigate this situation?

The White Stag was the safest place in Caecias for Melisende as it was built as a safe house for anyone visiting a foreign kingdom, but that still didn't mean much.

My father was determined to kill the queen, and while there was a chance he might respect the law and not harm her in the White Stag, nothing was preventing him from hurting her the moment she stepped outside. This was a horrible idea, and for the life of me I couldn't figure out why Melisende was being so stubborn about it.

I closed my eyes and took one final deep breath before descending the stairs and heading back out into the city.

***

The sky was turning darker as I made my way to the city's innermost gatehouse that protected the castle and its grounds. As I approached, a guard stepped out and pointed his halberd toward me. "Who approaches?" His voice boomed.

Lowering my hood, I turned my face toward the light from the torch hanging on the side of the gatehouse.

The guard's eyes widened as recognition dawned on him. "Your Highness." He straightened his halberd and bowed before returning to the guard room and raising the portcullis.

I passed through the gate and looked out over the large bailey that surrounded the hill where the main castle resided. It wouldn't be long before my father was informed of my arrival. I followed the path past the stables and guard houses until I reached the castle gatehouse at the base of the hill. The home that I grew up in stood tall before me, dominating over everything in Cathair Mor.

Again, a guard came out to meet me and once he realized who I was, raised the portcullis. Past the castle gate, the gardens sprawled out before me, and I glanced appreciatively at all the different kinds of roses. My mother loved to plant flowers and while the wild roses had mostly gone dormant by this time of year, the care she took in the garden kept these ones blooming almost year-round.

I passed the rose gardens and walked toward the castle. Any hope for a quiet arrival was dashed as I approached the long marble staircase that led to the entrance and saw my father storm out, rage painted over his features.

His black-brown hair shone in the last rays of sun, and his cape billowed behind him. His black tunic was tucked into his leather trousers, and his boots were shiny like they had never seen a speck of dust. His face soured when he saw me, and his right hand drifted closer to the sword strapped at his side.

"What is the meaning of this?" he demanded, nostrils flaring and a vein throbbing in his forehead. I winced.

Swallowing, I tried to calm my breathing. I wasn't the same naïve, young prince I was when I'd first left the castle. I looked my father straight in the eyes, willing my resolve to stand strong.

"There have been developments," I said carefully.

"Developments?" he bellowed as he took a menacing step closer. "What developments could warrant you abandoning your mission and turning up on my doorstep?"

"Faolan?" My mother's voice interrupted my father's tirade. My shoulders relaxed slightly at the sight of my mother appearing from the castle entry and standing next to my father. "It's cold, come inside."

My father grunted but followed my mother back into the castle. I stood, staring at the castle that used to be my home for a few more moments before eventually following behind them.

The scent of lavender filled my nose as I entered the foyer. It was my mother's favorite flower, and she always kept bouquets of lavender throughout the rooms of the castle. The entry hall was massive, with black marble floors and pillars reaching high to the vaulted ceilings. The walls were covered with rich velvet fabric which added to the opulence of the room.

"I'll have some food and drinks brought to the small dining room," my mother said, a smile gracing her lips. She touched my father on his forearm and nodded before leaving to fetch some servants.

"If you'll excuse me, I was finishing a meeting when I was informed of your arrival. Go to the dining room and wait for me there." My father didn't even look at me as he spoke, spinning on his heel and stomping out of the room.

I shouldn't be surprised by the icy reception; my father had never been a kind male, and I had failed at the one thing he'd sent me to accomplish.

A few servants passed me heading for the dining room, carrying trays of food and a large decanter of mead. I looked past the servants and to the large portrait hanging on the wall opposite. It was of my father, his disapproving scowl just as venomous in painted form as it was in real life.

I shook my head and reminded myself that my visit tonight was just to inform my father that the portals existed and that Melisende wanted to meet with him at the White Stag.

Following the servants, I entered the dining room and took a seat at the table. I reached for a bowl of nuts and snatched up a handful, eating them while one of the servants poured me a glass of mead. It wasn't more than five minutes later that I heard a commotion in the hallway outside.

"You have a lot of explaining to do, Faolan," my father barked as he pushed the double doors open and stormed into the small dining room. He stopped in front of the mead and poured himself a glass before approaching his seat at the head of the table. He didn't sit, rather he chose to remain standing, his towering form exerting dominance over the room. "I haven't received any news of the queen's death and yet—"

I hurried to speak for myself. "I—"

"Why is the witch queen still alive?" he cut me off as he slammed his drink on the table in front of him, his dark brown eyes locked on mine. "You've been with her for more than a week now; there should have been plenty of opportunities for you to kill her. What the sard have you been doing all this time if not what I asked of you?"

"There have been developments." I rolled my shoulders in an attempt to portray an air of confidence, false as it may be.

He scoffed. "Developments? I told you to kill her. What developments do you think warrant keeping her alive?" His eyebrows narrowed, and he leaned over his chair.

"There was a portal in her lands—"

"And?"

My jaw clenched, my lips thinning at his response. "There was an attack. I saw the destruction it caused. The queen wanted to meet with King Ardit, and I thought it prudent to gather all information about the portals before... slaying her."

"So why isn't she dead now?" He was clearly losing patience and interest in me and what I had to say, his expression twisted into a scowl I knew all too well.

"She wanted to meet with you to discuss the portals before the Conclave that will likely be called in a month." My eyes darted away quickly before returning to my father.

"You brought her to my *home*?" His voice was getting louder each time he spoke.

"She's at the White Stag."

"So, you follow her orders now?" It was then that his eyes darkened and he growled just inches from my face, "Are you fucking her?"

My blood ran cold, and I struggled to formulate a response. "I saw the aftermath of the portal that opened in Boreas firsthand. I saw the destruction that these portals are causing. They are a real and dangerous threat to Caecias."

I stood from my seat, my fists clenching tight.

"She is the threat! See? She's worked her dark magic on you!" His arms waved wildly. "She will die for all that she has done!" He stormed out of the dining room, and I stood frozen, watching as the doors slammed closed behind him.

***

The long corridor was empty and silent, save for the sound of my footsteps, as I made my way back toward the foyer. I wanted to get out of the castle and to the White Stag as quickly as I could.

When I entered the foyer, a familiar voice interrupted the tense silence. "Little brother."

I turned to see Brenhin leaning against one of the walls, under a large portrait of our grandfather. He was immaculately groomed and donned his ever-present smug expression.

His eyes left mine as they drifted to the cuffs of his tunic, which he slowly adjusted before placing his hands in his pockets. He pushed off the wall, and his gaze slowly traveled up my entire body.

I had seen this intimidation tactic before, and annoyance dripped from my tone as I icily replied, "Hello, Brenhin."

"I don't know if you are wise or stupid in bringing her here." He narrowed his eyes as if he was actually debating. After a moment, he continued, "Father is enraged that you not only haven't killed the queen, but that you've brought her here, to our kingdom. Of course, you know this already from his *warm* welcome."

He smirked. I could barely contain the urge to punch him in the face.

I took a deep breath, attempting to calm my racing heart. "What do you want, Brenhin?"

He took a couple steps toward me, cocking his head to the side. He reached for his dagger and slowly pulled it out of its sheath.

"It's not too late, you know," he crooned as he pointed the tip of the dagger at my chest. My gaze dropped down to the blade before returning to his face. I stared at him, waiting for him to continue. "Do what he asked of you."

I narrowed my eyes. "What?"

Brenhin started picking at his nails with the tip of his dagger, feigning disinterest. "You heard me, do what he asked of you. Kill her. Whether the portals are real or not—"

"They are," I interrupted.

Brenhin shot me a sharp look before returning to his nails. "Whether the portals are real or not, slaying Queen Melisende would benefit our kingdom greatly."

I couldn't help the scoff that burst from my lips. "How exactly would it benefit Caecias? By killing her we would ensure a war on two fronts," I reminded him.

He rolled his eyes. "Little brother, you think on such a small scale. War is already here, but with her dead we eliminate the threat from the north. With her out of the way, we give her citizens two choices: either they accept us and we take them back under Caecian rule, or we will kill them all. By ending her, you could help reunite the kingdom and make it stronger.

"And Father would not only accept you, but he would also praise your name. This is your destiny, Faolan." Brenhin cleaned his dagger against his trousers and sheathed it at his side before turning and retreating down the long hallway toward the dining room.

Destiny. I'd come to hate that word. Alone with my thoughts, I crossed the large foyer and exited the castle.

Ethann's words echoed in my mind again, *"Is it really your destiny? Or is it just something that you have been forced to believe? What is it that you really want?"* If you had asked me that question a month ago, I would have said that I wanted my father's respect. I wanted him to be proud of me. I wanted to have a place in my family.

But now… Now, I just wanted respect. I wanted to belong. And I wanted Melisende.

CHAPTER THIRTY-THREE

Faolan

It was dark and a light rain had started falling when I finally returned to the White Stag. The male that had been behind the bar when we arrived was now replaced by a female with red hair that I knew as one of the representatives from Argestes.

The White Stag was run by representatives from each of the kingdoms to help maintain peace, neutrality, and ensure the law was followed. I nodded my head in the female's direction, and she offered a small wave in return.

The stairs creaked as I made my way up to the second floor, a few oil lanterns illuminating the space. I stood outside of the room I would be sharing with Bevan and knocked.

Silence. I knocked again, louder. Still silence.

"Bevan," I said as I grasped the doorknob, my brow furrowing. The door opened without resistance, and I glanced around the room, finding it was empty.

I entered the space and closed the door behind me. My eyes fell on a piece of parchment sitting on a table in front of the fireplace. *Discussing plans with Melisende. -B*

Setting the paper back on the table, I looked around the room. There were two small beds, one on each side of the space, with a window that faced the alley behind the White Stag between the beds, and in front of the bed on the right, which held Bevan's discarded pack, was the fireplace.

Slowly, I made my way to the bed on the left and sat. I kicked off my boots and laid down on the mattress. My thoughts drifted to Melisende, and I wondered how I was going to get her out of here alive.

Could I somehow lie to my father about her departure? Would he even believe me? I could try to sneak her out a back door, but I assumed my father had stationed spies outside of the building as soon as I told him she was staying here. They would be watching all exits and even if they didn't recognize her, they would recognize me. No, I needed to be more clever than that.

My thoughts were interrupted by a knock on the door, startling me. Bevan wouldn't have knocked on the door, and I wondered who would be coming to my rooms at this time of night.

A spark of hope flashed through my chest. Was it Melisende? Had she changed her mind?

"Coming." I crossed the room in a few paces and opened the door with my right hand, bracing my left against the doorframe.

Etaine was on the other side. *Fuck. What is she doing here?*

She slipped inside, dipping under my arm, and I huffed out a loud breath through my nose before closing the door and turning to face her.

How did she even know I was back in Caecias? And how did she know where I was staying? Having her here with Melisende across the hall was making me feel twitchy, and I just wanted to get rid of her as quickly as possible and without too much commotion.

The last thing I needed was for the queen to catch me with another female in my room.

"You will be soon," Etaine said with a smirk as she pulled off her coat and tossed it onto the table in the corner.

I grimaced slightly as a bitter tang filled my mouth. She was only wearing a thin chemise, and she smiled at me as she slipped the straps off her shoulders, leaving her completely naked before me.

"How did you know where I was?" I demanded.

I had only been in the city for a couple of hours and somehow, she not only knew I was here, but that I was staying at the White Stag.

She shrugged, feigning nonchalance. "A friend of yours told me."

"Etaine—" I started, but she stalked toward me and put a finger to my lips to shut me up.

"Shhh. You've been gone for so long, and I've missed you. I'm going to have you on every surface of this room." Her hand slipped from my lips to my chest before she reached for the hem of my tunic.

I grabbed her by the wrist and stopped her. "Etaine."

Her eyes shot up to mine, wide with surprise.

I took a couple steps back and reached down for her discarded chemise on the floor. Before Melisende, I might have taken her up on her offer, but now… Now, I couldn't even think of touching her.

"No!" she shouted when she realized what I was doing.

I turned to face her, her chemise hanging from my hand. "No?"

"No. You don't get to turn me down. I let you come to my room whenever you wanted to fuck." She prowled toward me and put her hand on my chest again. "Now it's my turn." She stretched up on her toes and started kissing my jaw.

"Get dressed, Etaine." I recoiled, shoving the chemise towards her.

She snatched it out of my hand and looked at me, eyes narrowing. "What the sard is wrong with you, Faolan?" she snapped.

"There's nothing wrong with me. I just don't want to fuck you, Etaine," I snarled.

She stared daggers at me, then slipped the garment over her shoulders. She turned her back to me and grabbed her coat from where it was draping over the table. I watched as she pulled it over her shoulders and tied it at the waist.

She slowly turned to face me again and then shook her head. "You're going to regret this, Faolan."

"Doubtful."

Etaine took a couple steps forward and then slapped me across the face. Pain blossomed through my cheek as shock registered.

"Fuck you, Faolan!" She turned and walked over to the door, not looking back as she opened it and left. The door slammed closed behind her.

I crossed the room and sat on the edge of my bed, rubbing my cheek in disbelief that she'd had the gall to slap me. As a prince, I could have her thrown in the dungeon for such an improper act.

But I didn't have long to ponder the matter before another knock sounded on the door.

"Sard," I groaned as I stood up, ripping open the door and expecting to see Etaine again. "I told you—"

"You didn't like my gift?" Fionn interrupted as he grinned at me from the hallway.

I stared at him. "You sent Etaine? Why?" I opened the door a bit wider to let him in.

"Hello, by the way…" Fionn laughed as he entered my room. "You've been gone for a while, so I thought you might enjoy some… stress relief. I have to say, I'm quite surprised you turned her away."

"And why is that, Fionn?" I sighed, giving him a level look.

"The Faolan I know used to jump through hoops to get out of the castle and meet Etaine." His eyes suddenly narrowed as he fixed his gaze on me. "Unless…"

My gaze lowered as I rubbed the back of my neck. "I don't know what you're hinting at."

He scoffed, as if unable to believe what he was about to say. "Are you crazy, Faolan? You've fallen for the queen, *our enemy*. That's a death sentence for both of you!" he sputtered.

"That's ridiculous!" But my protest was weak, and Fionn saw right through it. "I'm not—"

He held up a hand to stop me. "Don't worry, I won't tell anyone, but you'd better pray to the gods that your father doesn't find out." Fionn pinched the bridge of his nose, and I knew he was reluctant to keep my secret. I bit the inside of my cheek and watched as he shook his head and sighed. "Look, you've had a long day, I'll let you get some sleep."

He turned around and exited my room, closing the door behind him. Leaving me alone with a reality I wasn't sure I could face.

***

The following morning, I awoke and rolled over to find Bevan asleep on the other bed across from me. He snored loudly, and I wondered how late he had been over in Melisende's room last night discussing *plans*, whatever those were.

I rolled my eyes and crawled out of bed, throwing on my tunic and trousers and reaching for my boots. The hallway was quiet as I tugged them on and laced them up, slipping out of the door. I glanced toward Melisende's room before heading down the stairs.

The redhead from last night was still behind the bar, and I smiled as I approached her and took a seat on one of the stools.

"Good morning, Your Highness." She nodded, then reached for something behind her. "This message was left for you." She handed me a piece of parchment before disappearing into the kitchen behind the bar.

I snapped the wax seal open and unfolded the parchment. According to the message, my father would be coming at noon to meet with the queen. Crumpling up the paper, I crossed the room to the fireplace and tossed it in the fire. The flames flashed a brighter yellow as they consumed the parchment before settling back down to their normal amber hue.

***

My father was seated at the head of the table when I entered the private meeting room in the White Stag. My brother, Brenhin, was seated on his right.

I approached the table slowly as I heard my father announce, "Ah, the disappointment finally arrives." His lips curled in disgust.

Fighting to keep my expression neutral, I lowered myself into a seat at the far end of the table. The silence was stifling as the three of us sat, glowering at each other.

Finally, the door opened and Melisende entered. She was wearing the same dark gown she wore at my cousin's house, the one that was practically backless, and it took all my strength to keep my focus on the meeting and not her soft, velvety skin.

"Melisende." My father's voice dripped with disdain.

"Rian." Melisende's tone was equally venomous.

"Nice of you to invite us for lunch, Your Majesty," Brenhin said snidely as he sipped from his glass of whiskey, eyes peering over the rim.

"I wasn't aware that I had," Melisende replied as she sat in the seat next to me and directly across the table from my father.

Brenhin opened his mouth but shut it again. My father adjusted in his seat and reached for the decanter on the table. He slowly topped off his whiskey then took a long draw of the caramel-colored liquid, as if readying himself for battle.

"So tell us, Melisende, what could you possibly have to tell us about these portals that warrants a visit here to our kingdom?" he drawled, voice thick with disdain.

"Actually," she started as she snatched the decanter and poured herself a glass, "I was visiting King Ardit in Eurus. I only stopped by Cathair Mor as a courtesy to you."

My father scoffed, and her eyes snapped to his. If looks could kill...

"I know you are aware of the portals that have opened on Western Etesia," she continued, shifting her attention from my father to Brenhin, then back again. "Since then, there has been an attack on my lands. My cousin witnessed the warriors escape through a portal, but not before they laid waste to his village."

"And why should we be concerned about some insignificant village in your kingdom?" The king waved his hand dismissively.

"I know you don't give a shit about the villages or citizens in my kingdom, but what you should be concerned about is the escalation of these portals. The first portal in Leuconotos didn't lead to any destruction. The second portal in Argestes led to the death of a few warriors. The third portal in my kingdom destroyed an entire village, but the latest portal—"

"The latest? We haven't heard about another," Brenhin interrupted.

Melisende shot him an icy glare. I knew her fury really would be the death of me, but I would gladly embrace death's bitter grasp if she was there beside me.

"It only happened a couple days ago. Another portal opened in Leuconotos. This time, a large contingency of warriors came through. King Lancaster was murdered."

The look of shock her words elicited on my father's face was oddly satisfying.

She continued, "It appears that the portals are coming from the continent."

"The continent? What makes you say that?" Brenhin asked, brows creasing.

Melisende tipped her glass towards him. "The attack on Leuconotos was made by Terraviridi."

Brenhin narrowed his eyes and leaned forward slightly. "And how do you know it was Terraviridi?" he challenged.

"Because this time the warriors weren't hiding behind black clothes and masks. From what I understand, the princes of Leuconotos were able to capture a few hostages from Terraviridi, one of whom is the king's nephew."

My father opened his mouth, then shut it again, at a loss for words. I still thought this was a horrible idea, even now, but I did enjoy watching the effect the queen had on him.

Melisende went on, "Ardit is calling for a Conclave of the Kings. He thinks it would be prudent for all the kingdoms of the Etesian Isles to work together against this threat. You wanted an alliance, well, here's your chance. Unless that's not the reason you sent the youngest of your brood into my kingdom." She cocked her head to the side and stared at my father.

This was it. This was why she fought so hard to meet my father. She didn't want to inform him of the portals and what had transpired on her lands; she wanted to confront him about my mission. She wanted to see his reaction when she accused him of sending me to assassinate her. She wanted to see his reaction when he realized that I had failed.

My father dared to look shocked and offended. "Of course it was! Why else would I send one of my ilk on such a dangerous journey?"

Melisende rolled her eyes, and Brenhin shifted his attention to me.

My father shook his head slowly, adding, "But I fear the time for alliances is over. If these portals are becoming more frequent and more dangerous as you say, it is each kingdom for themselves. King Ardit can call a Conclave of the Kings if he so desires, but I am not going to waste any of my men to protect your sham of a kingdom."

He stood and motioned for my brother to follow him out of the room. I shifted my attention to Melisende and noticed the way the right side of her mouth quirked up. I assumed she got the reaction from my father that she wanted.

But at what cost? My father wasn't going to allow her to leave the kingdom. He wasn't going to allow her to leave the White Stag. She was safe inside the confines of these walls but would be dead the moment she stepped outside.

Which meant I had to find a way to get her out.

"Father!" I yelled as I followed him out of the room. He motioned for Brenhin to continue and turned slowly to face me, a sneer curling his lips.

"Ah, the traitor." He looked as though he had little patience, so whatever I was going to do, I had to do it quickly. "Well?" he demanded.

"The queen didn't want to come here," I blurted out.

"What?" His eyes narrowed in confusion.

"The queen didn't want to come to Cathair Mor. She knows that you sent me to kill her. But I convinced her to come. I told her that she needed to inform you about the other portals, that if you knew the threat from the portals was real, you might be willing to put aside the war and form an alliance."

"Have you gone mad? Why would you believe that I would ever form an alliance with that witch?" He shifted his weight, the vein in his forehead pulsing with ire.

"I said what I had to say to convince her to come here." I took a deep breath and looked my father in the eyes. "I brought her here so we could hold her captive."

Father scoffed, "Why would I do that when I can just kill the evil wench?"

"If you kill her, you'll have twice as many threats to contend with at once. Her citizens won't just roll over and accept Caecian rule. But if you keep her alive, you can force her to sacrifice herself for her kingdom."

I was walking a fine line. To pull this off, I would have to deceive both Melisende and my father. I didn't want to lie to the queen, but if it meant that I could give her a chance to escape, I would, even if I would lose her in the process.

"And what makes you think she would do that?" he challenged.

"Because I've watched her this past week. I've seen how she acts when it comes to protecting her citizens. If the choice is 'defy us and we kill everyone in your kingdom' or 'surrender to us and we will spare them,' she will surrender. She will do whatever it takes to save the lives of everyone in her kingdom."

Father stared at me and for the first time ever, he didn't look at me with disgust. He didn't look at me with respect either, but at least his stare didn't leave me with a pit in my stomach. "What are you suggesting?" he said quietly.

"She will want to leave early tomorrow. Have someone keep watch at the front door of the White Stag and station some guards nearby. Have them arrive early in the morning, just before dawn. When she leaves, your watch can alert the guards, and they can apprehend her."

A smile crept upon my father's lips, and I suppressed a shudder. "This is your last chance, Faolan. If this doesn't work, you'll find yourself dead in place of her."

I offered him a solemn nod, then turned and retreated back down the hallway toward the private meeting room.

CHAPTER THIRTY-FOUR
Melisende

Muffled voices from the hallway reached the private meeting room, but I couldn't decipher what Faolan and his father were arguing about. The look on Rian's face as I accused him of sending Faolan to kill me was priceless, but my stomach curdled as Faolan followed his father into the hallway after our meeting. During our time in Eurus, I would have sworn that Faolan had renounced his father, but now I wasn't so sure.

Sighing, I reached for the decanter. After filling the glass for a third time since arriving at the meeting, I drained all the liquid, letting it burn my throat on the way down. I knew I shouldn't have come here, but part of me wanted to see how Rian treated Faolan. I needed to see it. Or maybe I was just a masochist and wanted to punish myself for desiring Faolan and giving into my lust.

The sound of the door opening captured my attention, and I turned to see Faolan returning to the room. His eyes were downcast, and he ran a hand through his hair.

A stray curl fell on his forehead, and I desperately wanted to brush it away from his face and kiss his jaw. But my thoughts screeched to a halt. What happened in Eurus could never happen again. I wouldn't let it. I'd been hurt enough before.

Faolan was still a Dulaine and therefore still my enemy.

Something I would be remiss to forget. My eyes followed him as he took a seat at the table, pausing before he spoke.

"My father wants you dead," he finally said, his gaze refusing to meet mine.

"And?" I pressed, leaning closer.

"He won't let you leave Caecias. He won't even let you leave Cathair Mor. He's planning on having guards kill you as soon as you leave the White Stag." Faolan was spinning the turquoise ring on his finger and avoiding looking at me. This wasn't some grand revelation, so what wasn't he telling me?

"Faolan?" My mouth went dry, and my voice was brittle.

"I convinced him not to kill you. That it would be beneficial to hold you captive instead. That if you were killed, Foulke, Redwald, and Maelys would start a full-scale war in retribution, but if you were captured and held captive…"

His voice trailed off. I leaned away from him, my heart racing in my chest as dread pooled in my gut. What did he do?

"If you were held captive," he continued, "we could give you an ultimatum: surrender your kingdom or, if you don't, we kill all of your citizens. My father expects you to depart the White Stag just before dawn. He will know the moment you attempt to leave."

No. I scrambled to my feet and reached for a knife, clutching it in my hand, my breathing becoming rapid and shallow.

How could I have let this happen again? How could I have trusted a Caecian, just to let them betray me? Because that is what he was attempting to do, right? Betray me?

He stood from his chair and took a step away from me, still not looking me in the eye. "I told him that is the reason I brought you here instead of killing you, so that he could take you as a captive." Slowly, his gaze lifted from his hands to my face. The moment his eyes met mine, it was like being struck by a thousand lightning bolts, fire and pain radiating throughout my entire body. I nearly crumpled to the ground. "Meli, you have to understand—"

I gripped the knife tighter in my hands, my knuckles turning white. "No!" I shouted and thrust the knife toward him. But I was too far away, and the blade was too dull to do any damage. Still, I threatened him just the same. "I knew I couldn't trust you!" I took a step closer to the door, my pulse a war drum in my veins.

"Meli—" Faolan's voice broke. What else could he possibly have to say to me? I wasn't about to stay to listen.

"Don't you fucking follow me!" I screamed as I bolted through the door and up the stairs to my room.

I needed to get out of this kingdom before it would be the end of me.

"Bevan!" I shouted when I reached the second floor. He threw open the door of his room and stormed into the hallway with his dagger drawn, bracing for an attack. "We need to leave!"

"What happened?" His eyes scanned me up and down, looking for injuries. When they didn't find any, his eyebrows furrowed in confusion. "I take it the meeting with Rian didn't go well?" he guessed.

"Faolan betrayed us. He betrayed me." I pushed the door to my room open and entered quickly. Bevan followed, and I shut the door behind him, locking it from the inside. I crossed the room and peered out the window, the hairs raising on the back of my neck. Did Rian have a spy waiting for me already?

"Meli, what is going on? I need you to calm down and tell me what happened," Bevan said as he took a seat on the edge of my bed and patted the space next to him.

I took a deep breath, then walked over and sat on the bed next to him. "The meeting with Rian went about as well as you would think," I started as I dragged my gaze from my hands in my lap to my guard's face. "Rian stormed out, then Faolan followed. I could hear them shouting in the hallway for a few minutes.

"When Faolan returned, he told me that he instructed his father to have a guard stand watch outside the White Stag, that I would be captured the moment I tried to leave."

"Captured? Not killed?" Bevan's eyebrows pulled together, and he rubbed his forehead.

"No, Faolan had the brilliant plan to have his father's guards capture me and force me to surrender Boreas or they would kill everyone. They want to make me choose between my crown or my citizens." I buried my head in my hands.

How could I let this happen? Foulke warned me not to come here and I ignored him. My pride had blinded me, and I couldn't see common sense. Now I was in the heart of enemy territory with only one guard to protect me.

"We need to leave now," Bevan said, standing and moving toward my pack. "Grab your things. I'm going to check the surroundings."

"They will be expecting us to try and leave now. It's too risky." I shook my head at his suggestion.

"You want to wait until tomorrow morning?" Bevan asked, his face scrunched in confusion.

"No," I replied. "Faolan told his father we would leave in the morning, so they should position the guards just before dawn."

He spun to face me. "Why would he tell you that?"

"What do you mean?" I stopped shoving a tunic in my pack and looked up at him.

"Why would he tell you his plans? If he's trying to capture you, the element of surprise would be better." Bevan rubbed his forehead again.

Why would he tell me? No, you can't fall for this again. I shook my head. "You're missing the point. They will be on high alert right now, expecting us to make a run for it while there is still daylight. If we don't leave now, they will expect us to leave in the morning and will be on high alert again just before dawn."

"So… what are you suggesting?" He raised a brow at me.

"I don't know exactly, just that I think the worst times for us to try and leave are right now or at dawn tomorrow." I exhaled loudly. We didn't have a plan, but we desperately needed one.

Bevan stared out of the window as I began pacing the room.

"There are three exits," Bevan announced, turning around and facing me. His gaze was alert and his voice was steady. "The front door, the back door, and the kitchen door. They will probably focus on the front and back doors but also keep an eye on the kitchen door. If we want to slip out of here unnoticed, then we need to leave another way. I think I have an idea."

Bevan crossed the room and reached for my pack, throwing it over his shoulder. He walked to the door, unlocked it, and passed into the hallway.

I inquired, "Are you going to share your plan? Or are you going to leave me here wondering what you are up to?"

"Follow me." His tone was determined as he walked down the hallway.

I followed Bevan into the room he had shared with Faolan the previous evening. He locked the door behind us and assured me that

Faolan would be a fool to try and come back here after his betrayal. He then told me his plan in full.

"They expect us to exit the building through a door, right?" Bevan asked as he began to shove his items into his pack.

My eyes narrowed. "Yes, and?"

"And we will exit through a window."

I scoffed, "Don't you think they will be watching my window as well? Faolan knows what room I am staying in."

"They'll be watching your window, yes." He set his pack on the floor then continued, "It faces the front of the building. This window faces the alley to the rear. We can exit through the window and climb to the roof."

"Are you serious?" I exclaimed.

"Yes, it is the only chance we have to get out of here unnoticed, and it isn't guaranteed."

"Fine," I relented. "When do you want to attempt to make our escape?"

"Sometime after midnight but before dawn, and hopefully just before a guard change when they might be more likely to miss us."

Now, we just had to wait for the opportune moment.

I sat on the bed that Faolan had slept in the previous evening, my pack laid across my lap as I picked at my nails. Bevan stayed low and peered out the window that faced the alley behind the White Stag.

After a couple hours of observation, he managed to identify the watchguard. It was a lanky male who leaned against the side of a shed behind the blacksmith two doors down on the left side of the alley. Five hours into the shift, a second male replaced the first. The new watchguard was much larger and paced the distance from the blacksmith to the White Stag and back again every hour.

"This guard is good," Bevan remarked, cursing under his breath. "Let's hope he is replaced with someone a bit less competent and vigilant."

Our assumption was that the guards were changing duty every five hours, a theory proven correct when the second guard was replaced right on time at ten o'clock. Luckily for us, the new guard started yawning within the first hour of his shift.

Three hours in, Bevan lowered himself from where he was crouched by the window and sat on the ground.

"He's looking more and more tired by the minute. I think the best time to head out will be within the next hour. Do you want me to go over the plan again?" he asked.

"No." I picked my pack up off my lap and tossed it over my shoulder, securing it tightly. I adjusted the jacket I was wearing and smoothed the leather of my trousers. "I'm ready. I just want to get out of here."

Bevan stood, crouched to avoid detection from the window, and walked over to the door. He knelt down on the floor and pulled his dagger from its sheath.

He slid the dagger under the door and tilted it. The shiny surface served as a mirror, and he was able to glance down the hallway outside our room. The White Stag had been silent for a few hours, and we were safe inside according to the law, but Bevan wasn't taking risks.

"Still empty," he said as he withdrew his dagger from under the door and straightened.

We left the single candle burning in the corner of the room as the two of us slowly approached the window. Bevan peeked through the edge of the window, finding the guard sitting on a barrel near the blacksmith's. He turned to me and nodded before quietly unlatching the window.

The window was a single pane of glass set into a wooden frame, attached to the wall by a set of large brass hinges at the top of the opening. It was designed to allow a small amount of fresh air in under the angled glass while still keeping the vast majority of the heat in the room.

Bevan watched the guard for movement before pushing the window out. He angled the window about fifteen degrees before stopping.

We sat in silence for minutes just watching and waiting to see if the guard, or anyone else for that matter, noticed that the window was now ajar. Satisfied that we were still unnoticed, Bevan pushed the window open further. He stopped when the window sat at a thirty-degree angle and he was met by some resistance.

If we were going to sneak out of this window, we would need to push past the point in which the window was built to be open.

After another ten minutes of silent watching and waiting, Bevan pushed the window to its limits. He stuck his head out and looked down the alley, checking to see if anyone else was outside this late at night.

Then he ducked back in and looked at me. "It's clear. Are you ready?"

I took a deep breath, letting it out slowly. "Yes."

"There is a cross beam to the left of the window. Use it to climb onto. You should easily be able to reach the roofline and pull yourself up." He placed his hands on my shoulders and looked in my eyes. "You can do this, Meli."

I poked my head out of the window and peered down the alley. The guard was still sitting on the barrel, keeping watch. I glanced down the other direction, and like Bevan had said, the alley was blissfully clear.

I leaned out of the window and reached my left arm out, grasping the cross beam. It was only sticking out the side of the wall by about six inches. I closed my eyes and took a fortifying breath.

Pushing myself further out of the window, I reached for the crossbeam with my right hand, then swung my right leg over the window frame. I was now straddling the window frame and unsure how to proceed. *You're a sarding idiot, Melisende. You've survived numerous assassination attempts, but you are about to die falling out of a window.*

Bevan must have sensed my uncertainty as I heard his voice sound from behind me. It was quiet, but sure. "You're going to have to hang from the crossbeam first."

I let the weight of my body slowly guide my hips and left leg out of the window, they slid down along the wall until I was hanging onto the crossbeam by my hands. Gathering all my strength, I pulled myself up and managed to get an elbow over the top of the beam. That one move gave me the leverage I needed to pull the rest of my body up until I managed to get a toe on the beam.

I pushed upward, clinging to the side of the building when my fingers finally found the roof. Thankfully, the roof wasn't that much higher than the window, and it was far easier for me to pull myself up onto the roof.

Once I was safely on the top of the White Stag, I sat and watched as Bevan joined me. He slid his legs out of the window first, then grabbed onto the crossbeam with only his left hand as he let his body fall. He reached for the crossbeam with his right hand and easily pulled himself on top of it, then stood and practically jumped onto the roof.

I let out a sharp burst of air, "Show off." He just laughed as he sat next to me.

We sat on the roof for quite a while, just watching the guard and ensuring we hadn't been noticed. It was nearly three in the morning and almost time for the guard to change again, and not wanting to risk having the current one replaced by another vigilant one, we decided to make our move.

Bevan rose and walked along the edge of the roof. I watched as his eyes made their calculations, then he motioned for me to join him. I walked over and stared at the building to the right of the White Stag.

"Are you sure it's safe?" I asked, furrowing my brow.

He shrugged, sighing, "Safe enough."

Bevan backed up a few paces, then ran and leaped off the edge of the White Stag. I watched as he sailed over the six-foot gap between the buildings with ease and landed on the roof of the adjacent building.

The thump from his landing echoed down the alley, and he immediately dropped flat on the roof. I followed his lead and when I turned my head, I noticed the guard was surveying the area as he walked in the direction of the White Stag.

Fortunately, his line of sight remained low along the street. He tugged on the back door of the White Stag and found it locked, then grunted and continued his search. He looked around for a few more minutes before returning to his post outside the blacksmith.

After the alley remained silent for a while, Bevan signaled for me to make my way over. I stood up and took a few steps back, giving myself enough room for a running start.

Bevan nodded at me, and I steeled myself for the jump. Sprinting as fast as I could, I leapt across the expanse and landed with a thud on the neighboring building, slamming my body flat against the roof as the guard once more surveilled the alley in suspicion.

Bevan and I lay on the roof, and I rolled onto my back to stare up at the sky. The moon was partially obscured by clouds, with only a few stars visible.

We stayed like that until we heard the guards changing their shifts. From this distance, it was hard to get a good look at the new guard. After ten minutes or so, the guard settled next to the blacksmith's shed.

"Let's go," Bevan whispered, urging me on.

We walked along the roof until we reached the far side. He scaled the side of the building first; it was only two stories which made the height more manageable than the White Stag.

I followed behind him and shortly found myself back on solid ground. From there, we kept to the shadows and dark corners as we slowly made our way to the stables to retrieve our horses.

"I saw an empty cart in here when I brought the horses." Bevan opened the door, and we slipped into the side of the stable.

Just as he remembered, there was an old cart abandoned in the back. He placed his pack in the back of the cart, then brought our horses out. I helped him attach the cart to the saddles and replaced the reins with the long driving lines.

It was nearly half past five in the morning as we finished readying the horses. Bevan stepped onto the cart and lifted the seat. He dropped my pack inside, then waved his hand toward the opening.

"Get in, Your Majesty," he instructed.

I narrowed my eyes at my guard, who seemed to be enjoying this a little bit too much. I climbed onto the cart, then stepped into the chest. As soon as I was situated in the small space, Bevan lowered the seat and sat down.

He slowly led the horses out of the stable and down the lane. It was still dark but the streets were now starting to fill with merchants getting ready for their day. I couldn't see anything from inside the storage chest under his seat, but I could hear the sounds of the city waking up.

No one stopped or questioned Bevan as we made our way through the city, until we reached the outer gate. "Where are you headed?" asked one of the guards.

"I'm headed to the hills to collect some wood," Bevan lied.

"Mind if we check your cart?" another guard asked, and my heart began to beat faster.

"It's empty. I haven't collected any wood yet, but you can check it if you like," Bevan replied.

I heard the two guards walk around to the back of the cart to inspect the empty bed. Satisfied, they waved him on, and we made our way out of Cathair Mor.

CHAPTER THIRTY-FIVE
Faolan

Birds started singing, waking me from a fitful sleep. I opened my eyes and blinked a few times, taking in my surroundings. The room was dark, as the sun hadn't yet risen, but I could still make out the shape of the wardrobe and the chair in the corner.

I was in my bedroom, the bedroom in the castle I had lived in my entire life, but strangely, it didn't feel like home. I didn't want to be here any longer. I wanted to be where Melisende was. She was my home. Melisende…

Melisende! Memories of the previous day flooded my mind.

I wasn't sure what fate had befallen her since yesterday, but I knew what fate would befall *me* if I stayed any longer. There was no place for me here as long as my father was the king, and while Melisende might not allow me to have a place with her, I still needed to ensure she was safe.

I quickly dressed and packed a few of my belongings in a small bag, shoving one dagger into the sheath on my thigh, another into the sheath along my calf. I also retrieved my sword, which leaned against the rack in the corner of the room with a few of my older blades and one with a large blue stone in the hilt that I recognized as Fionn's.

I hoped that Dulachan was still in the stables near the White Stag, and I walked as quickly as I could from the castle down to the middle ring of the town.

The stables were quiet when I arrived, but I did notice that Melisende's and Bevan's horses were gone, leaving my horse alone.

Thank the gods. Dulachan snorted as I led him out of his stall and put on his saddle and bridle. He clearly wasn't happy that I had woken him so early.

"Sorry, boy," I said, mounting him and heading toward the outer city wall.

A guard slowly exited the gatehouse as I approached. "You're up early this morning, Your Highness."

Nerves wracked my stomach. "I couldn't sleep. Figured I might as well start on patrol." I shrugged, trying to appear casual.

The guard just nodded and let me pass. His nonchalance led me to believe that he wasn't aware that the queen had made an escape. I wondered how she had succeeded but was glad that she had. For now, I just had to catch up with her and ensure her safety until she reached the border of Boreas.

About an hour's ride past the outer walls of Cathair Mor, I discovered an abandoned cart. Pulling Dulachan to a halt, I dismounted and started to examine it.

The tracks were fresh, and it appeared that the cart had been deserted recently. I searched for any clues but came up empty-handed. It was possible they had used the chest under the bench seat to hide the queen from view when leaving the capital.

I lifted the top, and the scent of jasmine filled my nose. It was them; they had made it past the city walls.

Dulachan and I followed the trail of hoof prints that led away from the abandoned cart, and I figured we would catch up with Melisende and Bevan within a few hours. By the time we were on the southern edge of the Coill Forest, however, the clouds were getting darker. Another storm was swiftly rolling in. I only hoped it would hold off long enough for me to catch up to the queen and make camp for the evening.

In the distance, I saw some movement in the bracken that prompted me to pull Dulachan to a halt. My eyes widened as a wolf jumped out from the bushes and onto a rock.

He was large and would have seemed more imposing had I not come face to face with the amarok as a child. His yellow eyes stared in my direction, and I held a breath. He slowly lowered his head, then turned and retreated into the forest.

I watched until he was gone from view before continuing my pursuit of the queen. This wasn't the first time this had happened, and I filed the thought away to revisit after I knew Melisende was safe.

Finally, in the early afternoon, I spotted Melisende and Bevan in a clearing sitting on a fallen tree, eating. I dismounted Dulachan and cautiously approached, but Bevan stood and unsheathed his sword. As soon as he realized it was me, he sheathed it again but kept his grasp firmly on the hilt.

"What are you doing here?" Melisende stood and stepped in front of Bevan, eyes narrowing on me.

"Look, Meli, you might not want me here, but I know my father and I know what he was planning—"

"Because it was *your* plan!" she shouted, her eyes full of hatred.

"I said what I did to try and keep you alive!" I fired back.

She scoffed. "Telling your father's guards to capture me the moment I left the White Stag is a funny way to do that."

"He wanted them to kill you the moment you left the White Stag! I convinced him to capture you instead."

I could see Melisende's shoulders rise and fall every time she took a breath, her rage barely contained. "Oh, so noble of you. Is that what you are here now to do? Capture me and bring me back to your father?" she challenged.

I raised my chin in defiance. "I'm here to protect you."

"Protect me, ha! And why should I believe you?"

"I don't think there is anything I can say or do to convince you." I looked down at my hands and spun the turquoise ring on my finger. "Just know this: my life was nothing before meeting you. My father and brothers have always treated me as if I am nothing, a bastard to be ignored and pushed aside.

"To be sacrificed in the never-ending war between our kingdoms…" I looked up at Melisende. "My family casts darkness over everything, but meeting you was like seeing the moon for the first time. I finally felt hope because I knew that there could be light even in the darkest of times."

Melisende's eyes softened, and my chest felt infinitesimally lighter. She turned to Bevan and inclined her head before retaking her seat. Bevan remained standing, dropping his hand from the hilt of his sword, but his eyes remained focused on me.

"Don't think this means that I trust you," she said as she crossed her legs. "How did you get out of Cathair Mor?"

"I lied—"

"Seems to be a pattern," she muttered under her breath.

I ignored her slight and continued, "When I was at the outer gates of Cathair Mor, I realized that no one seemed to suspect you were gone. But I'm sure my father has sent his guards in your pursuit by now. And one guard to protect you is not enough."

Melisende scowled. "I don't have the luxury of time to be able to send a raven to Foulke and wait for more guards to come."

"That's why we need to keep moving. Travel as far as we can before making camp for the night," I insisted.

"We?" She raised a disbelieving eyebrow at me.

"Yes, we. You may not want my protection, Fury, but you're still going to get it."

A dagger suddenly flew through the air, slicing into Bevan's chest and catching us both off guard. Horror twisted Melisende's features, and she gasped when his body slumped to the ground, the blade protruding from his heart as blood poured from the wound.

"Meli…" His voice was a quiet rasp as blood started dripping from his lips.

"Bevan!" Melisende screamed, falling to her knees next to his body as his final breath left him in a strangled gasp.

A single guard approached from beyond the tree line, and I positioned myself between him and Melisende, raising my blade.

"Hand the queen over. I don't want to have to kill you too, Prince," he commanded.

I glanced around the trees, not seeing anyone else, but I knew others wouldn't be far behind. Still, I narrowed my eyes, my grip on my blade tightening. "I'd like to see you try."

He jumped down from his horse and unsheathed his sword, taking a few steps forward. As he neared, I finally recognized him; he had been in the same division as me during training. He was strong and quick, but sloppy. He favored his right side and exposed his left quite often.

I glanced back at Melisende who was still on the ground, hovering over Bevan's body. She placed her hand on his face and slowly closed his eyes, then reached for the dagger that had pierced his heart.

"Don't get any ideas, Fury," I warned. "Stay the sard down and out of the way."

In a flash, the guard lunged forward and swung his sword in my direction. I deflected easily, then shifted my weight, adjusting the grip on my own blade. He swung again and again, but I dodged each of his blows. In truth, I was biding time. I knew eventually he would get sloppy and attempt to slash his sword back and forth quickly, leaving me the perfect opportunity to duck to his left and attack.

Out of the corner of my eye, I noticed Melisende shift her weight. Then the dagger she had been holding landed in the guard's left thigh. He cursed and swung high, aiming for my neck impatiently.

He slashed left and then quickly shifted his stance, cutting back to the right, avoiding weight on his injured leg. Just as I expected, his left side was unguarded, and I thrust my sword forward and into his chest.

A small, gurgled grunt left his mouth as I pulled my sword out, blood spewing over the grass at our feet. He collapsed, and I stabbed him again, this time directly in the heart.

"I told you to stay out of the way!" I spun to find Melisende standing behind me.

"You're welcome for giving you an opening." She gestured to the dagger she'd thrown. "Besides, I thought you said the guards didn't seem to know I was missing when you left. How was he so close behind you if you didn't lead him here?" she challenged.

"I didn't!" I shouted, wiping my blade on my trousers then sheathing it along my back. "He must have seen me leaving the outer gates and decided to follow me."

Melisende narrowed her eyes, untrusting of my words.

I huffed, "I swear I didn't lead him to you. But if he was able to catch up to us, others won't be far behind. We need to keep moving."

"How am I supposed to trust you, Faolan?" She stepped closer to me, her chest lifting with every manic breath.

"I just killed a guard from *my* kingdom to protect you!" I closed the remaining distance between us and stared deep into her eyes. "What else can I do?"

"Nothing! There is nothing you can do!" Her voice was filled with rage, but her eyes betrayed her as they quickly darted to my lips.

My voice quieted and became husky. "Do you want me to grovel on my knees? I will. My favorite place in the world is being on my knees in front of you."

***

We needed to take a path that the guards wouldn't expect us to. Rather than continue north towards Boreas, there was a small village due east that we could take cover near. It was far enough off our original path that I hoped we would lose the King's Guards.

We rode for hours, not even stopping to rest the horses, until night fell and bathed the forest in darkness and silence. Eventually, we reached the outskirts of the village I had in mind.

I pulled Dulachan to a halt amongst the trees behind an abandoned barn. "We'll stay here tonight."

Melisende hadn't said anything to me since the attack, so I wasn't surprised when she just took a deep breath, then dismounted her horse. I took the reins from her and loosely tied the horses to a tree, turning around to find Melisende sitting on a stump, staring at the forest floor.

I knew she was angry and mistrusting of me, but the look on her face was one of grief. I couldn't even begin to comprehend her feeling of loss over losing Bevan.

"Drink this," I said as I handed her my waterskin.

She took a long draw, and despite her sorrow, I couldn't help but watch as her lips wrapped around the opening. Her throat bobbed as she swallowed the water. She pulled the skin away from her mouth and licked her lips. My mouth suddenly went very dry.

"Thank you," she said as she returned the waterskin to me. Her eyes were haunted, and a sympathetic smile crossed my lips.

I prepared a meager dinner for us, then set up both of our tents and bedrolls. We ate in silence before turning in for the night. A small storm passed through, and I listened to the rain from inside my tent.

Normally, the sound of rain would lull me to sleep, but my brain raced knowing that the King's Guards were on the hunt for us. We needed to make it to Boreas before they could catch up. I tossed and turned for hours before my mind eventually relented and darkness took hold.

***

The following day was much the same. We rode in silence, taking forgotten trails and avoiding major roads. As the sun started to set, we found a small area to camp in the foothills near the border of Boreas.

"I think this is as far as we should go tonight," I said as I brought my horse to a stop in a clearing. "The foothills are just past the creek. The woods will provide ample cover, and there is plenty of gorse and hawthorn for the horses to eat. I'll do a quick patrol before we set up camp for the night."

I dismounted, then headed off into the surrounding woods to check for any dangers. Walking around the perimeter of the area we were going to camp in, I noticed the ground looked undisturbed, and the stream was free from animals. The rain from the previous evening had stopped, but the clouds remained dark, threatening another storm.

When I returned, I found Melisende sitting on a stump. "Everything clear?" she asked, her voice dull. I nodded at her.

I set up our camp while Melisende started pulling food from our packs. We had some dried meat, a few crusty bread rolls, a wedge of hard cheese, and some apples. She had also managed to keep a skin of wine, a gift from King Ardit.

After camp was prepared, I joined Melisende and reached for an apple. We ate in silence; I hated this new dynamic but understood that the queen was grieving. I also knew she didn't trust me since Cathair Mor, and that's why she kept me at a distance.

Once we'd finished eating, I untied our horses and led them down to the creek to drink as I filled our waterskins. While I was lowering one of the skins to the bubbling water, the forest rustled nearby, and I paused, looking toward the source of the sound and spotting a wolf. It had to have been the same one I had seen yesterday. Was it following us?

Just as before, it merely looked at me, then retreated into the distance. It started to feel like a harbinger of doom every time one appeared, so I kept my guard up, turning back to the horses and reaching for their reins.

Melisende was sipping from the wine skin as I tied the horses to a nearby tree. I walked back over to her, and she handed me the skin. But something caught the corner of my eye.

I didn't have time to react before an arrow lodged itself in the wine skin. Burgundy liquid started dripping from the leather, staining the ground. The black arrow had the same red feathers we had seen days before when we were attacked by a group of Raiders on our way south to Eurus.

Before we could move, a loud whinny sounded from behind us, and I turned to see an arrow protruding from Melisende's horse's neck, blood spurting from the wound.

"Faolan!" I whipped around toward where Melisende was pointing. I didn't say anything, just grabbed my sword and bolted in the direction of the Raider.

I raced through the gorse bushes, the sharp needles cutting through my trousers and stinging my skin, but I didn't care. Adrenaline coursed through my body; I just needed to find and kill the Raider.

I charged through the woods and unsheathed the dagger at my hip, the sword still gripped in my left hand. The Raider stepped out from behind a tree, and I launched my dagger. It found its mark as it sunk into the man's shoulder.

He stumbled a few steps, grunting in pain, and it gave me the opportunity to catch up with him, grab him by the arm, and turn him around.

"Who sent you?" I shouted, murder in my eyes.

"I sent myself. Do you know who you travel with? That's the Queen of Boreas!" he sputtered. I twisted the dagger in his shoulder, and he groaned before continuing. "The king made a proclamation that whoever brings in the queen, dead or alive, will receive their weight in gold."

My eyes widened as I yanked my dagger from his flesh. The Raider grunted again. "You've just made a huge mistake," I growled. "No one touches her."

At that, his eyes lit up in recognition of who I was. "Except for you, *princeling*?" he scoffed, and ripped his arm from my grasp.

Shit. I tightened my grip on my sword.

He sneered, "Maybe I should take a turn before I kill her. That pussy must be magical if you are willing to betray your family and kingdom for it."

My vision turned red. I didn't even think; I just raised my sword and cut his head from his body. It landed with a thud as his corpse crumpled to the ground, sputtering blood.

I took a deep breath and looked down at my sword, glistening crimson. More blood dripped down my face and neck from where it had sprayed as I dealt the killing blow. I peered down at the Raider one last time before turning around and walking back to the camp.

CHAPTER THIRTY-SIX

Melisende

Blood dripped from where the arrow pierced Philippe's neck, and I struggled to maintain pressure on the wound as the horse neighed in agony. Faolan had gone after the Raider who attacked us, but I was frozen, just watching as my horse slowly lowered his body to the ground. He was losing too much blood and must have been in immense pain.

I knelt on the ground next to him and cradled his head in my lap, his breathing growing more labored by the minute. "It'll be alright," I lied as I ran my fingers down the length of his nose. I knew what I had to do. "You're free now..." I whispered as I sliced my dagger across his throat, putting him out of his misery. A single tear ran down my cheek.

"I'm sorry," Faolan said as he reemerged from the trees.

I laid Philippe's head on the ground and slowly stood, rage coursing through my veins towards Rian's guards and his pathetic kingdom.

I spun toward Faolan, my eyes widening at his disheveled appearance. "You're covered in blood."

"It's not mine."

It was the Raider's then. *Good.* Based on the amount of blood covering Faolan, the bastard probably suffered a violent death.

A sigh escaped my lips, and I looked down at my hands and clothes, both stained red with death. I had been struggling after the death of Bevan, but now after losing Philippe as well... Loss was a familiar friend, but this was too much too soon. I couldn't process it.

I looked up again and scanned the clearing. We had camped on the Caecias side of the border, but I knew this area well. There was a small creek just north of us. Beyond the creek were the foothills and the border of Boreas.

My gaze slowly returned to Faolan. "Follow me."

Neither of us said a word as we walked down to the creek. I was tired. I was in pain. I wanted to feel something, anything other than the immense agony threatening to pull me under.

I stopped on the bank and stripped my clothes off. Faolan just stood and watched as I took a few tentative steps into the icy water. I turned and waited while he looked at me, his eyes scanning every curve of my body.

"Come." It didn't take any more encouragement than that before Faolan stripped out of his blood-soaked clothes and walked forward, into the creek.

I dipped my hands into the water and slowly started washing the blood from Faolan's chest and arms. He stood absolutely still and closed his eyes as my hands continued to wash his neck and face.

Then I ran my fingers through his curls, and he slowly opened his eyes, those dark umber irises pleading for a chance. "Meli..."

I had told myself over and over again that he was my enemy, that he would betray me. And he had. But he had also left his home to come and protect me, and it was the second day in a row that he had killed someone for threatening me.

My head told me to stay guarded, but my heart told me otherwise. I leaned in slightly and just before my lips met his, he reached for my waist, pulled me close, and kissed me.

***

The following morning, memories of the previous evening came flooding back in. I glanced in the direction of my horse, Philippe. His body still lay cold on the ground, a large pool of blood surrounding his neck. I swallowed past the lump in my throat.

There had been a storm two nights ago, but last night we had been lucky; the rain had yielded. I had a feeling we wouldn't be so lucky today.

I wanted to leave as early as possible to try to get ahead of the storm and further my distance from Rian's guards. I also wanted to get home to the safety of my castle. I sat up in my bedroll and looked over at where Faolan lay a few feet from me.

"You're staring again," he said, and I rolled my eyes before reaching for my boot. I chucked it at him, and it hit him square in the shoulder. He winced. "What was that for?"

"Get up. I want to get out of your godsforsaken kingdom and stay ahead of the rain," I said as I stood, brushing dirt off my clothes.

I pulled my tunic and trousers over my chemise, then added a second tunic for warmth. Finally, I pulled my cloak from my pack and fastened it over my shoulders. Faolan stood and stretched before getting dressed while I finished packing my supplies, food, and bedroll.

We only have one horse. Bitterly, I felt the loss of Philippe all over again, pain wracking through my chest. I sighed and looked down at all the supplies we had between us.

Dulachan was a strong, large horse, but he wouldn't be able to travel as quickly as I wanted if he carried both of us and our packs. As if reading my mind, Faolan walked up behind me and said, "I wish we had brought Bevan's horse with us."

We had been in such a rush to get as far away from King Rian's guards as possible that we left his horse and supplies behind. We hadn't even been able to properly bury Bevan.

Tears blurred my vision, threatening to fall, and I swallowed the lump in my throat. If it hadn't been for my stubbornness and had I listened to Foulke, Bevan wouldn't be dead. Philippe wouldn't be dead.

Faolan reached for my pack and secured it to one side of Dulachan's saddle before securing his own to the other side. "You ride Dulachan, and I'll walk," he suggested.

"Why?" My eyes narrowed at him.

"Why is it that you always think the worst of me when I'm simply trying to do something nice for you?" He held the reins in one hand and steadied the stirrup with the other.

I winced at my reaction; I had snapped at Faolan again. It had always been easier for me to dismiss his actions as having a sinister or ulterior motive. I offered a weak, "Thank you." My left foot slipped into the stirrup, and I swung my right leg over the saddle.

After a few hours, we stopped to eat and relieve ourselves. Faolan fed and watered Dulachan, then sighed as he sat down next to me. I felt a drop of rain hit my cheek and looked up at the sky. Shit, the storm was coming fast and unlike the other night, this one looked far worse. We were still a few hours' ride from the castle, but if Faolan continued walking, we wouldn't arrive before nightfall.

"Can Dulachan carry us both?" I asked. Faolan looked at me, his eyebrows scrunching. "It's just… the storm is coming, and if you continue on foot, it'll take us almost twice as long. We need to travel at a gallop."

"He can handle it," he said as he stood. He helped me back into the saddle, then mounted Dulachan and settled in behind me. Faolan's chest pressed against my back, and his arms wrapped around me as he took hold of the reins.

When we arrived at the valley just south of Loch Mor where the castle resided, we slowed down to give Dulachan a break.

The storm had arrived and was now a constant rain. Faolan pulled his cloak around both of us in attempts to keep us dry. I wriggled a little in the saddle to try and get more comfortable, as I was used to riding alone. Suddenly, Faolan inhaled sharply, and I felt him harden against me.

"Are you always sarding hard?" I bit out, unable to help myself.

"Only when I'm around you, Fury." He laughed.

I rolled my eyes and shook my head, but a small smile graced my lips.

The gatehouse at the banks of the lake soon appeared before us. We had finally arrived back at the castle and relief settled deep within my bones. We crossed the narrow stone bridge, and I spotted Foulke waiting outside of the castle.

I dismounted and left Faolan to take Dulachan to the stables. Foulke stormed over to me, the scar on his forehead deepening as he furrowed his brow.

"Where's Bevan? What happened?" he demanded, his voice gruff. I knew Foulke well enough to know that he wasn't going to let me out of his sight for the foreseeable future.

"We were attacked by a Caecian guard. A *single* Caecian guard."

"Meli, I told you this was dangerous!" He grabbed me by the shoulders, his eyes locking with mine, a mix of frustration and disappointment appearing.

"I know, Foulke, I've beaten myself up enough about Bevan's death. I don't need it from you too," I sighed.

"Bevan was a good guard, but that could have been you, Meli!"

"But it wasn't," I protested.

"But it could have been!" His harsh tone was gone, replaced by overwhelming concern.

I stepped around him and started walking toward the entrance to the castle. "I'm tired, Foulke. Leave me alone."

"Too bad." His tone shifted again, hardening, and my stomach soured. "The advisors are assembled in the banquet hall. They want to speak with you immediately."

I stopped. "I know this is urgent, but can't they wait for me to take a bath?"

"Sorry." He passed me and held open the castle door, waiting expectantly. Sighing, I walked inside and headed toward the grand banquet hall for the meeting.

All eyes turned to me when I entered the room full of advisors.

"Queen Melisende, finally," Malcolm greeted. He stood from where he had been sitting and inclined his head toward me.

This room was the largest of all the rooms in the castle. I never liked it and never used it outside of these kinds of meetings with the advisors. It was too large and stuffy, and the wooden table in the center of the room, which could easily seat twenty, was too formal and impersonal.

"Meli, it's good to have you home," Redwald said. He looked tired as though he hadn't slept much the past week, but his eyes sparkled with relief.

I embraced him, then walked to the head of the table. I looked around the room, seeing most of the advisors were here, but Maelys was absent.

"Redwald, did Maelys—" I started.

"Did Maelys what?" I heard a familiar voice enter the room. I turned and saw his trademark smirk that pulled up the left side of his mouth.

"Maelys!" I exclaimed as I rushed over and hugged him tightly. I whispered in his ear, "I'm happy you're here."

"Me too, cousin," Maelys said as he stepped back slightly. My hands slipped from his back, down his arms, and when they reached his hands, I gave them a little squeeze before dropping them.

"Are you staying for the winter solstice celebration?" I asked.

"Yes, but we can talk about that later. The advisors have been waiting for you for days. I'd hate to see what would happen if you made them wait any longer." Maelys sniffed the air, his nose scrunching in disgust. "Ugh, you smell."

"Thank you, Maelys." I narrowed my eyes and playfully smacked him upside the head.

I walked back to the large chair at the head of the table and finally took my seat. The rest of the advisors sat down as well. Maelys was on my right and Redwald on my left.

"We have much to discuss. There have been new developments while I've been traveling to and from Eurus," I said as I made eye contact with every single advisor sitting at the table. Malcolm and Ragnall were sitting in the seats nearest to Redwald, while Alethea and the other advisors sat next to Maelys.

"There have been developments here as well. We've received correspondence from Nyneve," Malcolm added, and my eyes darted in his direction.

Malcolm was the most stubborn of my advisors. He had more traditional views better suited for backwards kingdoms like Caecias, but his family has been in Boreas since its inception and been part of the advisory board for nearly as long.

"Nyneve? What does she have to say?" I asked.

I had wanted to send her a letter about the recent events on the Isles but was unsure how long it would take to get to her as the last ship to sail the Etesian Sea before winter had already left. She would have had to send her letter a couple weeks ago for us to receive it. Did she even know about the portals opening here?

Before the battle in Leuconotos, we had no idea where the portals had been coming from and assumed they were contained to the Isles. It was only after that battle we found out it was Terraviridi who had been responsible for them.

Malcolm lifted some pieces of parchment and shuffled through them, looking for the letter from Nyneve. "I have the letter here somewhere."

I rubbed my forehead. "I don't need to hear what she wrote word for word. You can just give me the general idea."

"She has heard about the attacks on our lands," said Redwald. "Well, she received a letter from King Lancaster after the first two portals opened. She sent her correspondence immediately after, before the seas became impassable."

"So, she doesn't yet know about the attack on my lands or the death of King Lancaster?" I looked at my advisor, worry etched on my brow.

"Ah, I have the letter here." Malcolm interjected, shaking the piece of parchment and pointing to the top of the page. "It is dated a fortnight ago. King Lancaster sent her a letter about the portal on his lands and the attack by portal in Argestes. He asked her about portals, as she is the only monarch alive who has seen them."

"Did she mention if any portals had opened on the continent?" I asked.

"No, none," Ragnall responded, and I turned my attention to him.

Of my advisors, he was the pensive one, always wanting to gather all information before acting. Malcolm was the opposite, as he liked to act first and think later.

Ragnall added, "She said she would send correspondence to the other kingdoms on the continent to inquire if they had heard about any portals being opened, but she feared she wouldn't be able to send a letter with her findings in time."

"So she didn't know that it is Terraviridi behind the attacks? I would send her a letter to warn her, but ships don't usually sail the sea this time of year." I frowned.

The seas were much too treacherous in the winter months which meant no ships ventured between the continent and the Etesian Isles.

"Unfortunately, Nyneve will be on her own until spring," Redwald said, and I shifted in my chair, my lips pursing in a tight line. I didn't like the idea of leaving my friend to battle Terraviridi on her own. He continued, "We will just have to hope that she can guard against her neighboring kingdom until then."

"Your Majesty, Foulke managed to fill us in on what you learned in Eurus, but we'd like to hear it from you, Melisende," Alethea said, and my attention shifted to my female advisor.

I smiled meekly, then recounted what I had heard from Ardit. "The morning after we arrived in Eurus, Ardit received a letter from Leuconotos. Another portal opened on their lands, but this time it was a large contingency of warriors. They were no longer dressed in black and wearing masks. They slaughtered hundreds of Leuconotans, including King Lancaster."

"So, it is true…" Malcolm said, thoughtfully stroking his beard with his fingers.

I nodded. "Yes. King Ardit plans on calling a Conclave within the next month, if not sooner. The kingdoms of the Isles must come together if we have any hope of defeating an army from Terraviridi, especially one that has the use of portal magic."

"I'll be on the lookout for his letter and make all the necessary arrangements," Redwald said.

"Now, what are your plans with the Caecian prince, Your Majesty?" Malcolm inquired after a brief pause.

"I don't understand," I replied, weighing my words carefully.

Malcolm splayed his hands. "Some of us are concerned about the idea of him returning to Ardelve and staying here in the castle. He is still our enemy, after all."

"The prince betrayed his father and killed a Caecian guard to help me return home. Those are not the actions of an enemy," I pointed out.

"So you trust him not to betray you?" Malcolm asked, and my jaw clenched. He gave a sidelong look to the other advisors. "We are just worried about history repeating itself."

I knew why my advisors didn't trust Faolan, why they didn't trust any Caecian. It was the same reason I didn't trust Caecians, but they weren't with me when Faolan helped in Morvern, saved us from the Raiders in Caecias, and saved my life—twice—on the ride back to Boreas. They didn't know him the way I knew him.

I stood abruptly. "This meeting is adjourned." With that, I stormed out the hall as their protests rang out behind me.

CHAPTER THIRTY-SEVEN
Faolan

Rain drenched my skin as I watched Foulke lead Melisende inside to meet with her advisors. But at least the air felt different after returning to the castle, less electrically charged, the threat of lightning disappearing.

I turned Dulachan toward the stables, noticing Ethann waiting for me. He reached for my reins as I dismounted and removed Melisende's and my packs. Together we took off Dulachan's tack, brushed him down, and fed and watered him.

After finishing in the stable, I returned to the castle, my mind swarming with thoughts of what was to come.

Would Melisende allow me to stay here in Boreas? Would my father send another son to the castle to try and assassinate the queen? When and where would the next portal appear? There were too many questions and I had answers to none of them.

The scent of limestone mixed with night-blooming jasmine and pine trees filled my nose as I ascended the stairs to the first floor of the castle. This late in the year, very little sunlight made it into the north tower, and I appreciated the extra torches lining the walls of the staircase and corridor.

Muffled voices made their way toward me, and I surmised that Melisende must have been meeting her advisors in the banquet hall. It was odd to me that the advisors would choose to meet in such a formal hall given Melisende's penchant for using the castle's smaller rooms and parlors.

My stomach suddenly growled, and I turned to enter the small dining room. The scent of food cooking made my mouth start to water.

"Hello, Balfour!" I greeted as I entered the kitchen and grabbed a wedge of cheese from a table next to his workstation. I tore off a chunk and popped it in my mouth.

"I have some roast chicken and vegetables if you would like a plate," Balfour said as he reached for a plate from the shelves behind him.

"That would be great, thank you." I nodded and returned to the dining room as I chewed on another piece of cheese. Just as I sat down at the table, Foulke entered.

"Faolan," he said with a slight incline of his head. There were dark circles around his eyes, accentuating his exhaustion, and somehow even the scar on his forehead seemed deeper.

"I'm surprised you're not in the meeting." I looked up at him as he approached the table and took a seat across from me.

"I'm not one of Meli's advisors." He reached for the wedge of cheese and a knife, cutting a slice and placing it in his mouth.

"That may be, but I know she values your opinion," I replied.

Balfour exited the kitchen with two plates in his hands. He set one in front of Foulke and the other in front of me, the delicious scent of food making my mouth water.

"She does," he sighed and sat back in his chair, running his fingers over his salt and pepper hair, and I wondered if I would get any grey hair before reaching the aibithe.

I continued to watch him as he looked out of the window, expression distant. I picked up my fork and knife and cut a slice of roast chicken, taking a bite. It was delicious, as expected, but after days of eating on the road, I'm sure anything would taste amazing.

After I finished chewing, I looked at Foulke again. "So why—"

"I'm her personal guard. Some of the advisors would take offense to my joining the meeting as I am not an advisor. And yes, Meli does listen to me, and I advise her in my own way, but the main reason I'm not in that room has less to do with the advisors or Meli. I don't *want* to be in that room." He leaned forward again and stabbed some vegetables with his fork before eyeing me intently. "Can I ask you something?"

"Of course," I answered, preparing myself to answer for Bevan's untimely death.

"Meli told me that you killed a Caecian guard on your way back to the kingdom." I opened my mouth to say something, but he held up a finger to silence me. "That's not what my question is about."

"Okay…" I looked at him a bit puzzled and shifted slightly in my seat, taking another bite of food.

"Meli also told me that you confessed that your father sent you to Boreas to try and kill her. I know… well, let's just say I saw the aftermath of that conversation."

Blood rushed to my cheeks at his implication. Did he really want to talk about Melisende and I having sex… now… at dinner? He looked directly in my eyes as he leaned forward. "What are your intentions with Meli?"

I balked at him. *My intentions?*

"I don't know what all she's told you, but whatever happened while we were in Eurus is over." I cleared my throat and shrugged. "So… nothing. I have no plans, no intentions when it comes to her."

Foulke's lips curled into a smirk. "Sometimes I forget how young you are."

I clenched my jaw, and the grip on my fork tightened.

He added, "And sometimes I forget that you don't know Meli like I do."

"What's that supposed to mean?" I snapped.

The smirk disappeared from his lips, and he sat back, placing both of his hands on the table. "I see how you look at her. I've seen a lot of males look at her the same way."

I rolled my eyes, grumbling, "Really, it's over, so you don't have to try and act like an overprotective father."

"I'm not trying to protect her. I'm trying to protect you," he clarified, voice sharp. "You might be from an enemy kingdom, but it's clear that you care about her."

"You're trying to protect me?" My eyebrows furrowed as I set my fork down.

"I've seen many males attempt to pursue Meli only to betray her. They want her crown, her kingdom, her power. So she's learned to put up walls. Walls so high, I fear no one will be able to scale them. She doesn't let anyone in." He shrugged.

"I…" I didn't know what to do with this information. I already knew that Melisende didn't trust me. I knew that she would never let me in. And I knew I would never be the one she wanted.

"She'll hurt you before you ever have the chance to hurt her," Foulke added.

I wasn't surprised by that statement, Melisende had already tried to push me away. But despite her efforts and despite knowing that we didn't make sense together, I couldn't help but hope. Hope that someday, I would be the one to break down her walls and earn her love.

But that's all it was... hope. My chest ached as I replied to Foulke, "Well, as I said before, she made it very clear that it was over."

"I'm going to tell you something that not many know." He adjusted his position at the table, a frown curling his lips. "Meli has survived a lot of loss. She lost her mother, her father, and her aunt and uncle. Thousands of Boreans have died over the years. Countless battles lost. And all of that loss was at the hands of Caecian kings."

That's not entirely true, I thought. Melisende's mother died shortly after childbirth, and she killed her own father. Caecias wasn't responsible for those deaths.

But I did know Caecias was responsible for the death of her aunt and uncle as well as more than our fair share of her citizens, a grim reality that was hard to swallow.

Foulke sighed. "It's not my story to tell, but Meli was betrayed by someone she believed cared for her. Someone she believed loved her. But it turned out that he was a Caecian spy sent to seduce her. Since then, she has put walls around her heart, and she doesn't let anyone in."

"I... I didn't know." I shook my head in disbelief.

"It was long before your time, long before your father's time even. Before the betrayal, Meli hoped they were anamchara; that's how deep the deception went."

A burning sensation filled me, and my stomach twisted. "I didn't think fated mates existed anymore," I mumbled.

There were old stories about two fae from rival kingdoms, Anam and Chara, who fell in love and despite their ill-fated romance, chose to be together. One day Chara went to meet Anam at their secret meeting place, but he never showed. When she went to look for him, she found his body on the battlefield, cold and covered in blood.

The gods watched as Chara screamed and cried over her lost love and decided that if these two enemies could overcome their kingdoms' rivalries and fall in love, they deserved another chance, so they brought Anam back to life. Thus came to be the idea of gods-blessed mates known as Anamchara.

"They do, they are just extremely rare," Foulke said, and I wondered what it was that made Melisende believe that male was fated to be her mate. "Just think about what I said." Foulke pushed his plate to the middle of the table and stood up. "Goodnight, Faolan," he said before departing the room.

I looked out the window, processing everything he had told me. I had hoped after Melisende and I kissed in the stream last night there might be another chance for us. But after her tears dampened my cheeks, I knew it wasn't the right time.

If there really was no chance for us, what did that mean for me? I couldn't return to Caecias. And if Melisende didn't want me here, then where did I belong?

I finished eating the chicken and vegetables before returning my plate to the kitchen, thanking Balfour for the food, and reaching for an apple as I exited the room. I took a bite as I passed through the dining room on my way across the corridor and up the stairs to my room.

I paused outside of my room and sighed, standing there for a moment before finally raising my hand to the handle and opening the door.

Upon entering the room, I crossed to the wardrobe on the far wall, removed my jacket, and hung it before discarding my dirty tunic and trousers as well. It had been a long few days, and I was physically and emotionally drained.

Sighing, I lay down on my bed and stared at the ceiling. My thoughts drifted from Melisende to the portals. I wondered if there were any fae that still possessed powers in Caecias, or if my father had actually killed them. My mind then wandered to how powerful Nyneve was, as she was the oldest of all the fae monarchs. If she wasn't strong enough to conjure a portal, who was?

I pulled myself out of my thoughts and stood up, crossing the room to the washing basin. The water was cold, but I didn't care. Wanting to feel something other than confusion and hopelessness, I splashed the cold water on my face.

Tiny droplets ran down my neck and chest. I reached for the small bar of soap on the side of the sink and lathered it up between my hands, washing the dirt and grime from the past few days off my body. If only it was as easy to get rid of the pit in the bottom of my stomach.

I splashed more water to wash away the soap and then finally reached for the cloth hanging near my sink, drying myself off and returning to the wardrobe.

I reached for a clean pair of trousers and started pulling them up when a loud knock on my bedroom door interrupted me.

CHAPTER THIRTY-EIGHT
Melisende

The sound of my footsteps echoed down the corridor as I stormed out of the banquet hall and toward the kitchen. It was one thing to remind me that Faolan was from our enemy kingdom; it was another entirely to assume I was not capable of deciding who I could and could not trust.

There were a few candles lit on the small dining room table and a plate of abandoned food that had hardly been touched. I walked around the table and pushed open the door to the kitchen.

"Good evening, Your Majesty," Balfour greeted when he saw me, stirring a pot on the stove.

I smiled back at him. "Good evening, Balfour."

"I'll make you a plate," he said as he scurried around the kitchen, filling my plate to the brim with food.

I suppressed a laugh. Balfour had a habit of trying to overfeed me after trips. I returned to the dining room and took a seat at the table. A minute or two later, Balfour emerged from the kitchen with a plate overflowing with roast chicken and vegetables and a large goblet of wine.

"Thank you." The smell of the food wafted up to my nose, and my stomach growled. I hadn't realized how hungry I was.

A few moments later, Redwald entered the dining room and took a seat across from me. He reached over and snatched a carrot from my plate and took a bite. I watched and waited while he chewed.

He finally sighed, "They just want to protect you."

"I'm not a child, Redwald," I snapped as my fists came down on the table.

He took a deep breath before continuing, "They just—"

"They just see me falling in love with another Caecian and think history will repeat itself." My eyes widened as I realized what I had said. *Love*. I wasn't in love with Faolan. I couldn't be. I had closed off that part of my heart a long time ago.

Redwald's expression softened, and he took my hands in his. "Melisende." My eyes traveled from our joined hands up to his face. "I trust you to know your heart and mind, and I know you will do what is best for the kingdom."

With that, he exited the dining room, leaving me alone with my thoughts.

I ate my dinner in solitude, my mind returning to my previous confession. It was impossible for me to be in love with Faolan; I hadn't even known him that long. Besides, he was from Caecias and was young.

But the more excuses I came up with, the more they sounded like just that... excuses. My head started throbbing, and I closed my eyes to stave off the pain.

After taking a final bite of chicken, I pushed my plate to the middle of the table, abandoning the remainder of my dinner. Standing, I straightened my tunic, then walked around the table and left the dining room. I started ascending the stairs as my mind returned to my feelings about Faolan once more. Acting on my desires felt like betraying my kingdom, but denying my feelings felt like a betrayal, too.

I soon reached the landing of the floor Faolan's room was on. I paused, not knowing what to do. Sard, I didn't know what I *wanted* to do.

I walked down the hallway until I was outside of his room. My heartbeat increased, and there was a tightness low in my stomach. Finally, I shook my head and turned back toward the staircase. My foot barely touched the first step before I paused and turned around again. I stopped outside of Faolan's room a second time and just stared at the door.

I took a deep breath and raised my hand up. Unsure of what I was going to do, I exhaled and knocked on the door.

After a few moments, it opened.

"Meli…" Faolan said, his eyes wide with surprise. It was then, in that moment, I knew what I wanted to do. This was my choice, and I was choosing him.

"May I come in?" I asked, and he stepped to the side, allowing me to enter.

My eyes traveled up and down his frame. His leather trousers were slung low on his hips, unfastened as if he was in the process of pulling them off when I knocked.

I swallowed over the lump in my throat. He wasn't wearing anything else, no tunic, no boots, just the trousers I was dying to rip off his beautiful body. My eyes traveled up to the defined muscles of his chest and stomach, which were highlighted by the candlelight dancing around the room.

"You're staring," he said, a smirk curling his lips.

"Shut up, Little Wolf." I walked over to the bed and sat down at the foot of it. He just stood where he was, looking at me. Assessing me.

"I won't say another thing," he replied with a laugh.

"I just finished the meeting with my advisors."

The smirk fell from his face at the change in topic. "And?"

"And they don't trust you," I said quietly.

"Do you?" His voice was soft and almost wistful, and I watched as his eyes darted down to my lips, his tongue gently licking his own with cautious hope.

He slowly took a step closer to me and my pulse started to race.

"Should I?" I looked up at him through my lashes.

He took another step forward until he was standing directly over me. My chest rose and fell as I took deep breaths, waiting. He leaned down and brushed the hair behind my shoulder before kissing the nape of my neck. My eyes closed, and my head fell back.

"Faolan…" His name was barely a whisper on my lips before he captured them with a kiss. I spread my knees and pulled him closer to me.

He started kissing me with more urgency, and when his tongue pleaded for entrance, I granted it eagerly. He kissed me until all I could taste was him, all I could feel was him, and all I could think of was him. He slowly reached for the hem of my tunic and pulled it up over my head. Then he pushed me down so that I was lying on the bed and trailed kisses back down my body from my chin to my neck, then to my chest.

"I'm yours," he murmured as he kissed my lips again before reaching for my trousers.

He stood up and slowly pulled them down the length of my legs, discarding them on the floor. I held my breath as he slowly lowered his trousers down and stepped out of them.

"You are so beautiful," he said as he stared at my body laid bare before him.

I moved further back on the bed and smiled at him, a silent invitation. Faolan climbed up on the mattress and crawled over me. I licked my lips in anticipation as his eyes locked with mine.

"I'm yours, if you'll have me," he promised.

He kissed me again as he slowly entered me. A soft moan escaped my lips as his hips started their delicious, tortuous rhythm, but it wasn't enough; I wanted more. I wrapped my legs around his waist and pulled him closer, tighter. My nails dug into his back, and he kissed me deeper, biting my lip until he drew blood.

He licked the corner of my mouth where a small pool of blood had gathered, then kissed me gently. It was sweet, but I didn't want sweet.

I pushed on his shoulders and rolled over until I was on top of him, repositioning his cock at my entrance and then slamming down with all my force. A groan escaped his lips before I captured them with another passionate kiss. I continued to ride him until my body started shaking with pleasure.

I was on a precipice; if I only let go, the orgasm would overtake my body. I quickened my pace, attempting to push my pleasure over the edge when Faolan suddenly rolled me back over. I let out a little whimper at the loss of connection.

I wanted to feel him inside me again.

No, I *needed* to feel him inside me again.

He looked down at me and said softly, "I'm yours completely. Tell me you want me, tell me I'm yours."

He thrust slowly back in, and every nerve in my body lit up with pleasure.

"You're mine," I gasped, arching my back.

"Look me in the eyes and say it again," he commanded as he pulled back out.

My eyes locked with his, the emotion there enough to make my heart skip a beat. "You're mine," I replied as he thrust back in one final time and the climax ripped through my body.

Thunder sounded loudly outside, echoing the intensity of our orgasms. It was like nothing I had ever felt before. Heat surged through my body from the orgasm but as Faolan's eyes traced my skin, it felt as though tiny snowflakes followed in their wake. I knew instantly what happened. What it meant.

Slowly, the shivers of pleasure faded, and I looked at Faolan as he slumped against me, his body a comfortable blanket covering mine. He peppered my jaw with kisses before he slid off me and laid down next to me.

"I know why you don't trust anyone from Caecias, and I know to you I am just another male, but to me…" He reached up and cupped my cheek with his hand. "…To me, you are everything. You are my entire reason for being."

I opened my mouth to reply, but he shook his head.

"And if another portal suddenly opened up and swallowed the entire world, I would fumble through the darkness just to seek your light again."

My lips pulled into a small smile before I placed a single kiss on his lips. "A long time ago, I trusted someone that I shouldn't have, and it went badly." I took a breath. "I had loved him. I had trusted him. And he had waited ten years to ensure both of those before attempting to kill me."

A single tear ran down my cheek, and I turned away from Faolan in shame. Sighing, my fingers absently made their way to the small scar on my chest, where the male had attempted to kill me.

I whispered, "It wasn't until after his death that Foulke's father learned my lover was actually one of Senach Neville's elite guards sent to kill me. As you can imagine, I haven't trusted anyone from Caecias since."

Faolan reached for my hand and took it in his, gazing in my eyes as he softly said, "Meli…" He lowered his head and reverently kissed the small scar over my heart. "My Fury."

He kissed the scar again, then kissed a path up my chest and past my collarbone to the crook of my neck. I could feel his soft breath on my skin, and a shiver ran down my spine. I arched my head back, exposing my neck to him.

"I wish I could take it all away," he said, kissing my jaw. "Your scar, your pain. If I could take it all away, I would." He kissed me on the corner of my lips.

I tangled my hand in his hair and pulled him closer. Our tongues tangled and danced around each other as he guided our bodies together once more.

CHAPTER THIRTY-NINE
Melisende

He's my anamchara. My gods-blessed, fated mate.

I hardly believed it, as anamchara were extremely rare. But Faolan was mine. I knew the second the orgasm ripped through my body. Those little icy kisses on my skin that followed in his eyes' wake.

I had heard about what it was supposed to feel like when the bond snapped in place, but I had never expected it to be so intense.

Lying in Faolan's bed, I stared up at the ceiling. He had fallen asleep after we made love for the second time. But my mind was a conflicted, jumbled mess. I had been fighting my feelings for Faolan. And just when I decided to give into my desires and choose him, I found out he was my anamchara.

I hadn't chosen Faolan after all; we were fated to be together. I didn't know how to feel about my choice having been torn away from me. And what did it mean to have a gods-blessed bond, to be fated?

I had lived most of my life on my own, not needing or wanting anyone else. Part of me wondered whether this was some kind of sick joke the gods were playing on me.

My family had fought for our independence for so long. My father had prepared me to be the first ruling queen in the Etesian Isles. And now fate decided to mate me with one of the sons of my enemy.

If Faolan knew, would he want to take my kingdom away from me? By tradition, if we officially mated through ceremony, he would be the rightful King of Boreas and I would be relegated to queen consort, without any power over the lands that were my birthright, my destiny the same as his mother's.

I rolled onto my side and stared at the window. Maybe tomorrow would bring me more clarity. I closed my eyes and took deep breaths, trying to quiet my mind. Eventually, darkness overcame me.

The following morning, I didn't wake up until the sun crested over the mountains. It had taken me a while to fall asleep, but the sleep I had was gloriously deep and free from my usual nightmares.

I rarely slept this well. The last time… the last time I slept through the entire night was in Eurus, when I had slept with Faolan. My stomach twisted at the thought it could have been a sign that we were anamchara.

Taking a deep breath, I tried to steady myself. There was no use in worrying about my thoughts while I was still in Faolan's bed.

I stretched my arms up over my head—my entire body felt like it was buzzing with energy—then I turned on my side. Faolan was still asleep next to me. I watched him breathing, his chest rising and falling with each breath.

"You're staring again," he said with a slight laugh, peeking an eye open with mirth.

"Shut up, Little Wolf." I rolled my eyes and sat up. I started to slip my legs over the side of the bed, but Faolan pulled me back down and against his body.

"Stay." His lips brushed against my neck, and he inhaled deeply. The tightness low in my stomach returned.

"Faolan…" I sighed.

"I love the sound of my name coming from your mouth," he whispered, then captured my lips with a kiss.

My hand drifted up to his cheek as his hands pulled my body flush against his. I could feel his erection pressing up against my stomach, and I smiled coyly against his lips.

Eventually, I was able to extricate myself from the bed and make my way to Faolan's bathing chamber across the hall. I poured water into the basin and washed myself before returning to the room in a robe. Faolan was now sitting at the edge of the bed, with only a thin slip of sheet covering him.

Sard. I wanted to be strong; I wanted to distance myself from him to allow myself time to think about the fated bond and what it meant to me, but every time I looked at him it felt as though the wind was being knocked out of me.

I walked across the room and picked up my clothes that had been discarded on the floor the night before. "I'm going to meet with Maelys this morning," I informed him. "We have to plan the winter solstice celebration. I want to try and keep a bit of normalcy for my citizens until the Conclave. There is no need to worry them before we have the meeting, know all the facts, and have a plan."

Faolan stood, and the sheet slipped away from his form. I forced myself to keep my eyes on his face as he walked up to me.

"Whatever happens next, whatever the fates have in store for us, I'm grateful for the time I've had with you." He placed a chaste kiss on my cheek, then turned and walked toward his wardrobe. I clutched my clothes tighter to my chest and left his room, heart pounding.

Thankfully, I didn't see anyone on my walk up the stairs and back to my own chambers. I quickly dressed and called for a servant to arrange breakfast for Maelys and me in the parlor. The winter solstice was fast approaching, and there was a lot of preparation that still needed to be done.

***

Maelys was already sitting in a large, comfortable chair near the fireplace when I entered the parlor. "Good morning," I said as I took a seat in the chair opposite his.

He reached for his cup of tea and smiled, the left side of his mouth pulling up in that recognizable smirk of his. Usually, I found it endearing, but this morning it hit differently. Rather than being cute, it annoyed me.

I nodded to the servant near the side table, and she brought over a large tray of food and set it between Maelys and me. Once she finished serving our food and tea, she left the room, leaving us alone to speak in private.

"Did you sleep well, cousin?" Maelys asked, and his lip pulled up further.

"Spit it out, Maelys," I snapped, reaching for my tea with a scowl.

"I went to your room last night, as I wanted to make sure you were alright after the meeting. You weren't there."

"And?" I exhaled.

Maelys was smart and extremely observant. I hated when he pretended like he didn't know something just to get me to confess. It was a clever tactic but also annoying when he turned it on me.

"*And* it was late, and you weren't in your room." He leaned forward, resting his elbow on the table and tapping his fingers on the wood.

"Clearly, I'm fine. Thanks for your concern, Baby Bird." I placed my tea back down on the table with a bit too much force, and a few drops splashed over the side of my cup.

He winced at my use of his childhood nickname. "Don't 'Baby Bird' me. Something is different." He stared at me, his brows furrowing thoughtfully.

I looked down at my hands and sighed. Something *was* different. My hands had been humming, like my powers were barely contained beneath my skin. I flexed my fingers. "You're right. I can't quite explain it, but I woke up this morning and it felt like my powers had woken up with me." I shrugged.

"What do you mean? Have you tested them?" he pressed.

"Are you kidding me?" I scoffed. "With all these portals opening and tension rising in the Etesian Isles, the last thing I need is for my powers to be acting up. Besides, my powers should be the least of our concerns right now." He raised an eyebrow, and I huffed. "Fine."

I lifted my right hand, flexed my fingers, then swiped my hand through the air. The book that had been sitting on the small table to Maelys's left flew and smacked him on the side of the head. My eyes widened.

"Sard, Meli!" He rubbed his head as blood rushed to the surface in a large splotch of red.

"I... I'm so sorry, Maelys!" I shot to my feet and rushed to his side, brushing his hair back from his forehead and examining the growing bruise along his temple. I pursed my lips as I held in a giggle. "You *did* ask me to test my powers."

"I didn't ask you to hit me in the sarding head." He scowled. "What do you think caused this?"

I didn't want to admit it, but I had a pretty good idea of what had caused it. I said quietly after a few moments of tense silence, "He's my anamchara."

"I'm sorry, what?" Maelys's eyes widened, and his hand lowered from his head.

"Faolan. He's my anamchara. I felt the bond last night when we —"

"Gross, don't finish that thought," he interrupted, and I laughed.

Maelys and I were close. He was my last living relative, and while we didn't live physically close to each other, we had a bond that made us more like siblings than cousins.

"So you're mates. What do you think that has to do with your powers?" he wondered.

"I don't know, it's just a feeling. Something changed. It's like he's... *unlocked* me."

"Does he know that you are mates?"

I bit my lip. "I haven't told him that I felt the bond, if that's what you mean."

I didn't even know how I felt about the bond. I needed time to think, but with the Conclave coming and the threat of war on our doorstep, time was something I didn't have.

"Are you going to tell him?" Maelys asked.

I shook my head. "I don't know. I know I should, but..." But I wasn't sure how I felt about it. I needed time to sit with this information. I needed to know what being his anamchara meant to me before I told him.

"Are you going to take him to the Conclave with you?"

"I don't know. Sard, Maelys, I just found out that Faolan, the son of my greatest enemy, is my fated mate." I exclaimed. Shaking my head, I continued, "I don't know how I feel about it, and I don't know how he would react. I need time."

Maelys placed his teacup on the table and reached for a chunk of bread. He took a large bite and chewed slowly before changing the subject. "The winter solstice is in a couple days. Are you still planning on having the celebration in the village?"

I exhaled the breath I was holding and relaxed my shoulders. "I think it's best if we go ahead as if the portals and attacks aren't happening. I want to keep things as normal as possible until the Conclave. Let's not worry our citizens until we have more information."

As we continued to eat our breakfast, we discussed our plans for the winter solstice celebration. It was the largest celebration in Boreas. Citizens would travel from all over the kingdom to attend. There would be food, dancing, and gifts.

Maelys had been hard at work preparing the gifts. We always gave out baskets full of food, blankets, clothes, and other supplies our citizens needed. "I have requisitioned the baskets, and most of them have been filled with non-food items," he said as he pulled out some pieces of paper covered in various scribbles. "We just need to add the food once Balfour agrees on what items to include this year."

"And the extras?" I asked. We always kept extra stock on essential items our citizens needed so we could help support the neediest in the kingdom.

"Yes. We have them in the storage barn with the baskets."

"Thank you, Maelys."

He shuffled his papers and continued, "I have also been working with Balfour on the dinner menu. We have three courses set and he is obtaining all of the ingredients he will need in order to feed everyone."

"Have you reached out to the village elders to arrange the table settings?" I inquired. Every year, the villagers would bring their dining tables and chairs into the street running through the center of the village, and we would have dinner together as a kingdom.

"Of course," he replied. "We've never come up short and I don't think we will this year either."

Not all citizens could make the trip to Ardelve for the solstice, but all were welcome. Some villages on the furthest edges of the kingdom would host their own winter solstice parties. I'd always liked to think that even apart, the kingdom celebrated together.

After dinner and after dispersing the gifts, the rest of the solstice evening was typically spent listening to music and dancing under the canopy of stars. Eventually, the aurorae would light up the skies, and the kingdom would fall into a peaceful silence. The festivities would continue until sunrise as the kingdom would spend the longest night of the year together looking forward to the sun, warmth, and longer days returning.

***

Rain pattered against the window, and fire crackled in the hearth as I read a book in the lounge later that afternoon. My reading was interrupted when Redwald entered the room. He was a bit flushed; whatever he had come to tell me was important.

I closed the book and set it in my lap, waiting for him to speak.

"We've just received a letter from King Ardit," he said as he handed me the letter in his hands.

"I'm assuming it's the invitation to the Conclave of the Kings. Has he picked a date?"

"Yes… but there is more," he said warily. I looked up at Redwald, seeing his grave expression, and felt the bottom drop out of my stomach. He took a seat on the edge of the chair opposite me, leaning forward.

"More?" I asked, setting my book on the table next to me and unfolding the letter.

Ardit had indeed set a date for the Conclave, and it was less than a week away. I would have to leave the day after the solstice to make it to the Middle Isle in time. But then I saw it, the *more* that Redwald had mentioned.

There had been another attack. This time in Ardit's own kingdom. Thankfully, there was minimal loss of life as Ardit had alerted his guards to the potential threat. They had been scouting the lands and were luckily present when the enemy appeared from thin air.

What worried me more than the fact a new portal had opened was the fact that there was less and less time between attacks. The Terraviridians were ramping up their efforts, but why? The longer I looked at the words on the page, the more convinced I was that another all-out war between the continent and the Isles was looming.

CHAPTER FORTY
Faolan

It was the day of the winter solstice. I had hardly seen Melisende since the morning after we returned from Caecias. She and Maelys had been busy with preparations for the celebrations, traveling between the castle and the village of Ardelve nearly every day.

The winter solstice wasn't celebrated in Caecias. We knew it was the shortest day of the year and marked the eventual return of spring, but beyond that it was just another normal day in the kingdom. But here in Boreas, it was the biggest celebration of the year. I didn't know what to expect, but I was looking forward to participating.

As the northernmost kingdom in the Etesian Isles, the winter was especially bleak and the days incredibly short here. It made sense to me that they would celebrate the eventual return of the sunlight and longer days to their lands.

Leaving the darkness behind to bask in the light was something that I had come to appreciate after having met the queen.

I had also heard that gifts were passed out to each family in attendance, that the kingdom ate together as one, and that the remainder of the evening was spent dancing under the stars and watching the aurorae.

I may not have been born a Borean, but the more time I spent in the kingdom and with Melisende, the more I realized that this was where I wanted to be. Not the destiny forced upon me by my father, but the life I chose for myself.

If only I could prove to Melisende that I had chosen her over my family and kingdom. That I would always choose her. That my life would be nothing without her in it. She had called me hers during the throes of passion, but did she mean it?

The sun started setting and the late afternoon light was shining on the floor as I returned to my room. I dressed in my best tunic and clean trousers. As usual, I was wearing head to toe black. I pulled my boots on and tried to tidy my hair.

When I was done getting ready, I exited my room and made my way down the stairs. As I approached the lower ground floor, I noticed Foulke and Redwald waiting near the guardroom at the exit of the castle.

Foulke was dressed in exceedingly nice clothes; I had never seen him dressed up before. He always seemed to prefer the rough attire of a warrior than those of a nobleman. But tonight he wore black trousers with a navy tunic that had silver stitching along the cuffs of the sleeves.

I smiled at him. "You clean up well, Foulke."

His laugh was loud and filled the small space. "Thank you, Faolan. As do you."

"Are you looking forward to the solstice?" Redwald asked. He was also adorned in elegant navy attire with silver embellishments. They were both wearing the royal colors of Boreas.

I nodded. "Yes, I am. We don't celebrate the solstice in Caecias."

Redwald smirked. "Not many outside of Boreas do, just as not many outside of Eurus celebrate the summer solstice."

Foulke's and Redwald's eyes shifted behind me. The hairs on the back of my neck stood on end as I turned around. Melisende was descending the stairs, wearing a shimmery skin-toned gown that was covered in tiny blue and silver gems. It was as if the stars had fallen from the sky, dripped down her skin, and wrapped her body in a cage of liquid starlight.

Every curve was accentuated by the fabric, and the slit in the front showcased her long legs. I swallowed and stood up straighter.

When her eyes met mine, the world faded away. She was my entire universe, and I would spend the rest of my life trying to prove my worth to her.

"Little Wolf," she said as she joined me at the bottom of the stairs.

I smiled and extended my arm. She glanced briefly at my arm before looping hers through mine. Foulke cleared his throat, and heat flushed my cheeks. I turned to look at him.

"Shall we?" he asked as he opened the door. I led Melisende out of the castle behind Foulke and Redwald.

There was a carriage sitting on the island near the stone bridge. We approached the carriage, and Redwald opened the door for us.

I placed one hand on the handle and helped Melisende in. She sat on the velvet bench seat and patted the space next to her with her hand. Once I climbed into the carriage and sat down at Melisende's side, Redwald closed the door and sent the carriage on its way.

"Redwald and Foulke aren't riding with us?" I asked as I shifted and looked from the empty seat across from us to Melisende.

"No, another carriage will come to take them. Besides, I wanted to talk to you before the evening runs away with me." She glanced down at her lap, then reached for her necklace and adjusted it over the small scar on her chest, a habit I had come to know well. What was making her anxious? She cleared her throat and continued, "Faolan…"

I put a finger up to her lips, silencing her. "Before you say anything, I just want to make something clear. I was nothing, *nothing* before meeting you, Meli. I understand why you can't trust me, but I'm not him. I'll never be him. You are the light of my life, the moon that shines on the darkest night. You are my entire universe, and I would sacrifice everything in this life just for a chance to prove that I am worthy of your love."

A single tear ran down her cheek. I wiped it away, then brushed her hair behind her shoulder and kissed her neck. Her hand moved to the back of my head, and her fingers tangled in my hair as my lips moved from her neck to pepper kisses along her jaw. Her grip tightened as she angled my mouth toward hers, and then our lips crashed together.

After a half hour drive, we arrived in Ardelve, the village in the mountains immediately north of the castle.

The carriage pulled to a stop near a small stable and Melisende attempted to smooth her hair down. My eyes glanced down at her lips, seeing they were swollen from kissing, and my heart leapt into my throat at the sight.

An attendant opened the door of the carriage, and I exited first before reaching out a hand to assist Melisende.

The storm that had followed us on our return to the castle a few days prior had finally cleared out, and the sky was full of stars which added to the magic of the evening.

We slowly walked into the center of the village. It was decorated with yew boughs and paper stars in varying sizes. In the middle of the street that ran down the center of the village were tables covered in food. It was a feast for everyone in attendance. In the market square, a band played music while the residents danced.

We approached a platform near the square where we found Maelys sitting in a large wooden chair that resembled a throne. There was a second chair next to him which sat empty. I wondered if Melisende would be required to spend most of the evening on her throne or if she walked, talked, and danced with her citizens throughout the night.

Maelys inclined his head in my direction as Melisende slipped her arm from mine. She kissed me on the cheek, then stepped up onto the platform and took her seat next to her cousin. I turned to walk along the main table when I noticed Redwald and Foulke approaching the village from the direction of the stables.

Redwald stopped at a side table and started to pour glasses of mead for the villagers. I joined them for a drink and listened as they talked about their favorite memories from winter solstices past.

I was in awe as I watched an entire kingdom come together to celebrate the solstice. There were villagers dancing in the market square while others were drinking and chatting with each other. Children were running around and playing swords with fallen tree branches. Everyone looked so happy.

While the villagers mingled, Melisende and Maelys started handing out the gift baskets. They consisted of small pouches of coins, a loaf of bread, and a bottle of mead that had been brewed in the east of the kingdom. Some of the baskets contained clothing and blankets, as well.

I watched as both Melisende and Maelys smiled and chatted with every single citizen that approached them to receive the baskets full of gifts. It was obvious that Melisende cared about every individual in her lands.

As the evening wore on, Melisende and Maelys invited the citizens to join them for dinner. Everyone found seats along the tables that ran for half a kilometer through the middle of town. Foulke sat with his guards, Redwald sat with the other advisors, and Melisende and Maelys sat at the head table.

I took a seat next to a family about halfway down the table from Melisende, then smiled as I watched her stand to make a toast.

"We have faced hard times with the countless attacks from our southern neighbors and we may face harder times still, but the solstice reminds us that even the darkest times will come to an end." She looked around at her citizens, before continuing, "Here's to making it through the darkness and finding the light."

Melisende returned to her seat and started serving food to the family next to her.

"She's beautiful, isn't she?" asked the female beside me.

"Beautiful doesn't begin to describe her," I sighed.

"Ah," the female replied with a knowing smile. I pulled my gaze away from Melisende and looked at her. "Is this your first winter solstice?"

"Yes. I'm… not from here." I replied, averting my gaze to my plate. I didn't want to admit I was from Caecias. Sard, I wanted to forget it myself.

After dinner, the villagers invited Melisende to dance with them. I watched as she spun and twirled on the dance floor. The smile on her face was resplendent, and I yearned to be the one to make her smile like that.

I continued to watch her from the side of the dance floor until a petite blonde female from the village approached me and asked me to dance. I glanced at Melisende, and when her eyes met mine, she nodded her head. I took the female's hand and led her out onto the dance floor. The musicians started a new song, and I danced with the blonde.

She was beautiful, laughing and smiling as I spun her around, but it was someone else I longed to have in my arms. As the song ended, I bowed toward my dance partner, then searched out Melisende.

I walked across the floor, zigzagging through the villagers until I spotted a tall, strong male extend his hand toward Melisende. She smiled as she placed her hand in his, and a pang of jealousy ran through my chest.

I watched as he pulled her close and the two of them moved in tandem. His hands trailed from her shoulders to her lower back. Seething, I couldn't watch anymore and walked to a fence at the edge of the village, trying to keep my jealousy in check.

I stared at the stars in the sky as I attempted to slow my breathing and remind myself that Melisende could dance with whomever she chose. *It was only a dance, right?* A few minutes later, I felt a hand on my shoulder. I turned, and Melisende's beautiful hazel eyes met mine. I was lost in the swirls of grey, green, and brown that danced in her irises.

"May I have this dance?" she asked, and I glanced back toward the dance floor. Her fingers brushed against my cheek as she pulled my gaze back to meet hers. "No, here."

We were at the edge of the village, with nothing but the stars as our witnesses. She stepped closer to me, and I took one of her hands in mine while the other slid along her waist to her back. This is where she belonged, in *my* arms.

As we started to dance, I pulled her closer so I could feel the entire length of her body against mine. I inhaled her scent of sweet oranges and jasmine as the blood rushed to my cock. I could never control myself around her, and honestly, I didn't want to.

My fingers brushed her hair behind her ear as I leaned in close. "I didn't like it when that other male was dancing with you," I dared to admit.

"Oh really?" she asked playfully.

"No. He was touching what is mine."

She pushed me back and her expression turned cold. "*Yours?* I may be your mate, but don't think for one second that I am your possession. I'm not some *thing* you can own."

Time stopped and the world turned blurry around me. *Mate?* My mind quickly replayed the words that she had said; clearly, I had misheard her, right? But no, she said mate. What did it mean? No ceremonies had taken place.

I blinked a few times, trying to refocus my gaze, then uttered, "I'm your mate?"

Her eyes widened as she realized what she had said. Then she sighed and looked down at her hands. "You're my anamchara, Faolan. The night we returned to the castle, I felt the bond snap in place."

Shock rippled through my body but was quickly replaced by a feeling of curiosity. That night hadn't felt any different to me than the others we had spent together.

"What do you mean you *felt* the bond? I didn't feel anything," I sputtered, trying to make sense of her confession.

"Bonds don't always happen at the same time for both mates. When the bond snaps in place for one of the anamchara, they feel a frisson, a shiver wherever their mate's eyes travel along their body. The other night, when we…" Melisende suddenly looked shy.

I had never seen her so vulnerable. I put a finger under her chin and lifted her face so her eyes returned to mine, willing her to keep talking.

She hesitantly continued, "When I called you mine, the orgasm ripped through my body but your gaze... your gaze cast icy kisses along every inch of my skin."

Suddenly, memories of the first time I saw Melisende swirled in my mind. She had been reading in the parlor, messy after having just returned from a ride, and she was the most beautiful female I had ever seen. And when she finally looked up at me... It had felt like tiny snowflakes were cascading down my entire body.

If only I had known then. Melisende, the Queen of Boreas, was my mate. My anamchara. My Fury.

I closed the distance between us, kissing her neck. My voice turned gravelly as I whispered, "Oh Fury, the things I would do to you if we were alone."

She leaned back slightly and looked me in the face. "What would you do to me, Little Wolf?"

"Don't play coy," I pressed my cock into her hip, and she bit her lip. The desire to have her overtook me; I needed to bury myself in her warmth.

My eyes scanned the area for somewhere private, and I noticed a large willow tree beyond a copse of fir trees. I took Melisende by the hand and led her to the tree, parting the curtain of willow branches before we ducked inside.

I pressed Melisende against the trunk of the tree and kissed her neck once before kneeling before her. My hands embraced her ankles before slowly sliding up her legs, pulling her dress up and out of the way as they went.

A smile graced my mouth when my hands finally reached her hips, and she was bare before me. I licked my lips before leaning in and trailing kisses from her hip down towards her entrance. My tongue slid along her core, and Melisende's hands gripped my hair, keeping me in place. I found her little bundle of nerves and sucked and licked while my fingers slid into her warmth.

Her moans spurred me on, and I continued to suck and bite and lick while my fingers pressed deeper and deeper.

Melisende's breathing soon became erratic, and I knew I had brought her to the edge. I withdrew and stood, a slight gasp leaving her lips. I slid my fingers into her mouth, wanting her to know how amazing she tasted as I loosened my trousers with my other hand.

As soon as my cock was free, Melisende reached out and took it in her hand and guided it to her entrance. In one swift move, I buried myself deep in her warmth.

"Fuck, Fury!" I cried, and she wrapped a leg around my hips, pulling me even closer. I slid in and out, in and out, lost in the rhythm of our bodies.

Melisende trailed her tongue up my neck, nibbling on my ear before returning her attention to my mouth. I welcomed her in and sunk my teeth into her bottom lip. My hips continued their relentless pace until we both teetered on the edge of oblivion.

"Let go," I whispered in her ear. I thrusted one last time, deep into the depths of her warmth, and stars exploded across my vision. The sky illuminated, and the sound of thunder crashed above us.

Melisende quickly cast her attention to the sky before slowly lowering herself off me. "There weren't supposed to be any storms tonight. I thought the sky was perfectly clear…"

I pulled my trousers back up and then straightened Melisende's dress. Her hair was mussed from the trunk of the tree, and I attempted to smooth it back down. "Yes, it was."

"Hmmm." She glanced through the willow branches again before running her fingers through her hair and checking her dress.

My lips met hers one final time before I took her by the hand, and we ducked under the canopy of the willow tree. As we headed back toward the village, my eyes scanned the sky, seeing nothing but stars.

Then it happened. Colors burst across the sky in waves. My jaw dropped slightly.

"The aurorae," Melisende said, her voice barely a whisper. "They are so beautiful."

But my eyes lowered and landed on the queen next to me. "Not as beautiful as you."

CHAPTER FORTY-ONE

Melisende

"Are you sure about this, Meli?" Foulke asked as he entered the small library near the armory on the ground floor of the castle.

I turned to face him. "Yes. We are traveling through our own kingdom. We don't need a large entourage. Besides, you know it is forbidden to bring weapons into the Meeting House, so there is no point in bringing multiple guards."

"Just because that is the rule doesn't mean that everyone will follow it," he insisted, and I could hear the irritation in his voice. "Besides, you know that isn't what I meant."

"I know what you meant." I reached for a book and pulled it off the shelf, pretending to scan the pages.

"What do you think Rian will do to you and Faolan when he sees the two of you together at the Meeting House? No, Meli, it is safer for both of you if he stays here."

"Foulke, there is something I need to tell you." I replaced the book but kept my eyes on the shelf, bracing myself for his reaction.

He balked at me. "Meli, please tell me you're not carrying—"

"Gods, Foulke, no!" My eyes shot over to him. I shook my head, attempting to clear the image from my head. "Faolan is my anamchara."

I had unintentionally told Faolan during the solstice last night that we were fated mates. I had wanted more time to think about what it meant to me, how fate had taken my choice away from me, but it didn't take me long to realize that I wanted Faolan in spite of fate, not because of it.

Foulke just stared at me. He didn't say anything for a long while, and I started to wonder if he heard me. Finally, his lips pulled up into a smile. "I'm not actually surprised."

"You lying asshole!" I shouted.

He shrugged. "There was just something about the first time you met."

"You weren't even in the room, Foulke!" I narrowed my eyes and threw my arms up in the air.

"I know, but you've never looked at anyone, and I mean *anyone*, the way you've always looked at him. Like you couldn't decide if you wanted to kill him or fu—"

"Ugh, that's enough, Foulke." I punched him in the arm, and he rubbed his muscles, feigning pain. I scoffed, "Oh stop, you big baby."

He schooled his features, turning serious once more. "But seriously, Meli, nothing good can come from Rian seeing you and Faolan together, anamchara or not."

"Thanks for your advice, Foulke, but my decision stands. Tomorrow morning, you, Faolan, and I leave for the Middle Isle."

***

The following day, I rose before the sun. I quickly washed and dressed, then packed for the trip. It would take Foulke, Faolan, and me an entire day of riding to reach the coast of Boreas. We would stay the night in an inn, which was in the coastal village of Ballantrae, where our boat to Middle Isle would depart.

It would take nearly four hours to sail to the Middle Isle where representatives would meet us and bring us to the Meeting House. We would then enjoy the evening in our private chambers before the Conclave the following day.

Years ago, when the five kings of the Etesian Isles called the first Conclave, they argued over where it should be held. They finally reached a truce and decided to hold all future meetings between the kings on the island situated between Western and Eastern Etesia. Two representatives from each kingdom were chosen to live on the island, build the Meeting House, and maintain its neutrality.

The Meeting House was made up of a central meeting room and five wings that extended out from the center. Each wing was reserved for a different kingdom and only the kings, their chosen escorts, and their representatives could access their specific wings.

I finished packing the last few items into my bag and sighed. The sun was just starting to peek over the mountains, its rays hitting my window and sending light into my room.

I picked up my pack, threw it over my shoulder, and slipped out into the hallway. Foulke and Faolan were waiting for me near the armory. Each of us took one sword and dagger for the trip to the island. All weapons would be stored in locked chests when we arrived on the docks of Middle Isle.

We exited the castle and made our way to the stables, where Redwald was already waiting. The young stable boy, Ethann, and the stable master had our horses saddled and ready.

I looked over at my mount, a young gelding named Arion. We hadn't had him for long, but the stable master assured me that he was fast, strong, and agile. If he was even half the horse Philippe had been, he would be a good successor.

"Thank the gods you haven't left yet!" I peered around Arion and saw Maelys jogging toward the stables, his voice calling out to me.

"Late as usual," I quipped with a grin.

"Not late," he laughed. "You haven't left yet." He threw his arms around me and squeezed tightly.

I leaned in and whispered in his ear, "I'm relying on you and Redwald to lead the kingdom in my absence."

Maelys leaned back, his eyebrows furrowing. He opened his mouth to speak but then closed it again. I placed a quick kiss on his cheek before leading Arion out of the stables.

Foulke, Faolan, and I mounted our horses as Redwald gave us a final rundown of the itinerary. "Luce will be waiting for your arrival in Ballantrae this evening. She has two rooms available in the inn. Her mate will take care of the horses while you're in the Middle Isle. Your boat will be ready to leave at ten tomorrow morning.

"I informed Luce that you would be at the Conclave for at least two days. She will hold two rooms for you for an entire week so that you'll have a place to stay when you return. There's no need to send her any notice of when you'll be back, as she'll be waiting for you. But please send a raven home when you return to Ballantrae."

"Of course, Redwald," I replied as I adjusted the reins in my hands.

"Farewell and travel safely," he said as he and Maelys waved us off.

The three of us crossed the stone bridge and exited through the gatehouse before following the road up into the hills above Loch Mor. Luckily, the sky was still clear, but the winds were cold and harsh. I pulled my cloak tighter around my body and hoped that the rain would hold off as long as possible.

***

The sun had set by the time we arrived in Ballantrae and just as Redwald had said, Luce was waiting outside of the small ivy-covered stone inn with her mate. She was a petite thing with curly brown hair and warm brown eyes while her mate, Bran, was as tall as Foulke but with short, light blond hair and sharp blue eyes. They were an unlikely looking pair, but deeply in love.

I brought my horse to a halt in front of the inn and dismounted. "Hello, Luce. Thanks for taking us in on such short notice," I greeted.

"It's no problem, Your Majesty." She smiled warmly, then turned and gestured toward her mate. "Bran will take your horses to the barn. Come quickly; let's get you out of this cold."

As we entered the inn, the warmth from the crackling hearth seeped into my skin, and the smell of cooking food filled my nose. If I had to guess, I would say it was pork, and suddenly I was ravenous enough to eat an entire pig myself.

Luce led us to a large sitting room with a grand fireplace and several animal hides hanging from the walls. I ran my fingers over an especially long-haired cowhide before moving closer to the flickering flames. When we finally took our seats, Luce and a servant brought us blankets and tea. I took a sip, finding it was rich and aromatic black tea with a tart and citrusy finish. My cup was nearly drained after my second sip.

"Dinner will be ready soon," Luce announced as she refilled my cup. "It's only pork stew and fresh bread, but it will warm you to the bones. Just what you need on a chilly night like this."

After we ate, Luce led us upstairs to a set of rooms at the end of the corridor. Faolan glanced at Foulke, then looked at me and said, "Foulke and I can share this room. Goodnight, Meli."

"Don't be ridiculous, Little Wolf." I grabbed Faolan's hand and pulled him into my room, winking at Foulke as I closed the door.

Foulke just smiled and shook his head in amusement. Faolan was my anamchara and now that Foulke knew, there was no reason to hide.

"What is the Conclave like?" Faolan asked as we lay in bed.

I pursed my lips in thought. "Honestly, it is a lot of screaming. Especially by your father and King Cyrus." I took a deep breath before continuing. "Imagine the five most stubborn fae—"

"I can see them very clearly," he said with a chuckle.

I narrowed my eyes at him. "Are you calling me stubborn?"

He smirked. "I think *you* called yourself stubborn."

My brain quickly replayed the conversation, and my eyebrows knitted together. "That's fair. Anyway, imagine the five most stubborn fae stuck in the same room, each wanting different things and unwilling to budge. But eventually, by some miracle, we manage to come up with a solution or reach a compromise.

"The Conclaves are held every five years, unless there is war. It has been almost five hundred years since the last war Conclave. Ardit and I are the only living monarchs who attended that one."

"Is it true that only the five kings... uh, monarchs are allowed in the room?"

"Not exactly." I shook my head. "Originally, that was the case. The only individuals permitted inside the meeting were the kings and their representatives, who would announce them or bring refreshments."

Faolan rolled over on his side, his eyes narrowing. "So, what changed?"

"War," I answered somberly. "It became clear that we needed the generals in the room with us. But while that was the case for war Conclaves, other meetings required a softer touch and an intelligent mind. Now, each monarch is allowed to bring one counselor into the room with them. Depending on the reason for the meeting, I will either bring Foulke, Redwald, or Maelys."

"That is why Foulke is here," Faolan mused.

I turned my face to the ceiling as a noncommittal "mm" left my mouth.

Faolan reached a hand over and cupped my cheek, turning my face back toward him. He kissed me gently before pulling me tight against his body. I breathed in his comforting scent and relaxed. It wasn't long after that I drifted off to a deep, dreamless sleep.

**

The following morning, we boarded our small boat and sailed it across the Middle Sea to the Middle Isle. The two Borean representatives met us at our designated dock when we landed. They greeted us, then locked our swords and daggers in a chest in the hut on the shore.

The representatives then led us up the hillside to the entrance of the Borean wing of the Meeting House.

My grandfather had the Borean wing built with only one bedroom, one washroom, and one kitchen. My father later expanded the wing, adding an additional bedroom, another washroom, and a sitting room. It was the smallest of the wings at the Meeting House, but it was comfortable.

The representatives brought our packs to our rooms while we sat by the fire in the sitting room. Foulke poured the three of us wine, which we drank, while also discussing plans for the Conclave. Soon after, the male representative called us into the kitchen to have dinner.

After eating, Foulke dismissed himself. "If you'll excuse me, I'd like to take a nice long bath and have an early evening."

He winked at us as he reached for an unopened bottle of wine before exiting the kitchen. I knew Foulke was still a little wary of Faolan, but he also trusted me to know that I wouldn't let history repeat itself.

"A warm bath does sound quite good," I remarked, turning toward Faolan. He stood slowly from his chair and reached out his hand.

I placed my hand in his and followed him to our bedroom and into the adjoining washroom. Steam billowed from the copper tub in the middle of the room, and the scent of jasmine flowers permeated the air.

Faolan slowly undressed me, and when I was naked before him, he sucked in a breath. "You are divine," he whispered, his words tinged with reverence.

I stepped forward and kissed him on the lips before undressing him. Once his trousers fell to the floor, he stepped out of them, and I admired the beautiful male in front of me. "Faolan—" Before I could tell him I loved him, his lips locked with mine in a searing kiss, one where we only stopped to breathe.

We made love in the bath and again after when we returned to our room. And for the first time in my life, I felt safe and cared for.

CHAPTER FORTY-TWO
Melisende

The sound of booming thunder woke me early. The morning of the meeting had arrived with dark skies and lingering dread.

I dragged myself out of bed and walked over to the window. Even in the darkness, I could see the crashing waves, their foam spraying the jagged rocks of the coastline. It was as if the weather was mirroring the tension building on the island.

Turning from the window, I walked over to the bookshelf and scanned the volumes. There was one in particular that caught my attention. It was covered in a thick layer of dust, and I knew it hadn't been read in quite some time.

Returning to the bed, I reached for a candle and lit it. Faolan shifted in bed but thankfully didn't wake. I flipped the pages of the book until I found the passage I wanted to read.

After about an hour of reading, daylight crested the horizon and Faolan finally stirred. I closed the book and placed it on the bedside table. Faolan called for breakfast while I bathed and when the food arrived, we ate in near silence, the impending meeting weighing heavy.

"When will the meeting start?" Faolan asked, breaking the quiet.

"As Ardit is the one who called the Conclave, he is responsible for arranging the date, inviting the other monarchs, and informing the representatives when he is ready to commence. The representatives will then instruct the remaining monarchs to proceed to the Meeting Room."

"So you don't know when it will happen?" he clarified.

"Not exactly, but knowing Ardit, it will be soon. He likes to start the meetings earlier rather than later." I took a final sip of tea and stood from the table. "I should get dressed."

Faolan nodded at me and headed into the washroom. After he disappeared behind the door, I approached the wardrobe, opening the doors and pulling out the navy dress I had worn the first night Faolan stayed in my kingdom. The neckline plunged all the way down to my stomach, and the diaphanous skirts parted at the slit that went nearly up to my hip.

After I dressed, I sat in front of the vanity and looked at my reflection in the mirror as I placed my crown on my head. Today was a day to project power.

The washroom door opened, and I looked in the mirror to see Faolan returning to the bedroom in his usual black garb. My eyes darted to a small package wrapped in dark blue velvet sitting on the vanity next to me, before I turned in my seat and smiled at him.

Faolan glanced at the package, then at me, and raised an eyebrow. "What are you up to, Fury?"

"Nothing," I drawled as I stood from my stool and approached him with the parcel. I kissed along his jaw and as I pulled away, I shoved the parcel into his hands. "Just a present for you."

Faolan's eyes darted down to the parcel, then back up to my face. A smirk graced his lips as he took a few steps over to the bed. He set the parcel down, then started to untie the strings that held the velvet wrapping in place. After undoing the string, he unfolded the fabric to reveal a navy tunic with silver embroidery. He held it up then looked at me.

I shrugged. "I thought it only appropriate that you have at least one item to wear in my colors."

"Your..." his words trailed off, thick with emotion.

"Faolan, you are my anamchara. If you wish it, Boreas can be your home."

He swallowed, his throat bobbing. "I would be proud to call you my queen, to call Boreas my home, and to wear its colors." His eyes shimmered, and he smiled at me. "*Your* colors."

I reached for the garment and took it from his grasp, setting it on the bed next to him. My hands reached for the hem of his black tunic, and I slowly pulled it up as Faolan raised his arms above his head. After tossing it to the floor, my hands skimmed along Faolan's chest. His eyes closed, and he let out a deep breath.

I licked my lips as my hands slid lower, but a loud knock on the door interrupted my movements, and I sighed.

"Meli, it's time," Foulke's voice sounded from the other side of the door. I sighed, then reached for the navy tunic and handed it to Faolan. He slipped it over his head, and I smiled at him before we exited our room to join Foulke in the hallway.

The three of us walked in silence toward the center of the Meeting House where the Conclave was held. Foulke stopped at the end of the hallway before we opened the door to the circular hall. Additional advisors and guards were allowed in the area that surrounded the Meeting Room but rarely ever waited in there, instead opting to stay in the comfort of their kingdom's wing. I nodded at him and then Faolan before entering.

The only other monarch I saw within the hall was the young king, Lancaster, standing next to his brother, Aleksander. The other kings were either already in the meeting room or running late. I looked at Lancaster and inclined my head to him. He returned the gesture, then faced his brother.

Aleksander whispered something to Lancaster before they entered the Meeting Room, leaving Foulke, Faolan and me alone.

I turned to Foulke and nodded. He inclined his head in return, then retreated back into the Borean wing.

I shifted to Faolan and took a deep breath. "Are you ready, Little Wolf?"

"Ready for what?" He furrowed his brows, puzzled.

I took a step closer to him and leaned in, my breath on his cheek. "For the Conclave of the Kings."

He was clearly taken aback by this. "But this is a war Conclave. Don't you want Foulke in there with you?

"As my anamchara, I want *you* in that room by my side. This meeting will determine the fate of all the Sylphs on the Etesian Isles."

"Are you sure?" His gaze searched mine. "But what about my father?"

"What about him?" I rolled my eyes. "Weapons aren't allowed in the Meeting House. He can't do anything here."

"But…" The protest died on his lips, but he still looked unsure.

"Faolan, forget about your father. The only thing that matters is that *I* want you in that room." I reached out and took his hand in mine, then kissed him on the cheek. "Whatever happens, whatever the future holds, I want to face it with you."

The corners of his lips turned up slightly, and he nodded at me. Under his breath, he said, "The strong may fall, but they never yield."

"What?" I asked, my eyebrows knitting together.

Faolan looked down at our joined hands. "It's something my mother used to say to me. We may stumble or fall, but we never give up and we *never* yield."

"Then let us not yield but instead face this together." Hand in hand, we walked up to the entrance to the Meeting Room. The Borean representative looked between Faolan and me, then down at our joined hands.

I mustered all the courage and strength I would need for the Conclave and announced, "We are ready."

Placing a hand on the door, the representative pushed it open to reveal the marble table in the middle of the circular room. I entered and stood behind my usual chair. Across the table, Ardit was talking with his advisor while Rian, who was seated to his right, argued with his representative. Lancaster sat in his late father's chair to my left, while King Cyrus of Argestes sat to my right.

The Borean representative had barely finished announcing Faolan's and my arrival when Rian exploded.

"What is this?" he growled as he slammed his fists on the table and stood, leering in my direction.

I looked around the room at the faces of the other three kings. Young Lancaster's brows furrowed in confusion as his gaze bounced between Rian and me, and Cyrus frowned at Faolan. Ardit's mouth shifted to a sly smile as he watched me take my seat at the marble table.

"What seems to be the problem, Rian?" I inquired, leaning back in my chair and crossing my legs. I shifted my attention to Faolan and tapped the armrest of my oversized velvet chair.

The other kings had designed their chairs like thrones, but I had opted for comfort instead. Faolan perched himself on the armrest as my gaze returned to Rian.

"This is unacceptable!" The vein in Rian's forehead pulsed as he leaned further over the table. "It is bad enough that we continue to allow you to rule, pretender queen, but now you sully the sanctity of the Conclave by inviting someone who isn't your general, advisor, or heir. And not just someone, but my son!"

Cyrus choked on his wine, spitting it onto the marble surface in front of him. His gazed shifted from Rian to Faolan as amusement curved the corners of his mouth. Ardit leaned forward, ready to defend me, but I beat him to the punch.

"*Allow* me to rule? I am the daughter of the former King of Boreas, Patrice. I took what was rightfully mine. You allow nothing!" I scoffed.

"Witch! You will not speak to me in this manner!" Rian's voice reached a fever pitch.

"Rian!" Ardit stood, attempting to diffuse the tension. "You will calm yourself."

My gaze traveled from Rian to Ardit. "Thank you, Ardit. We are here to discuss the portals, not my choice in advisor, are we not?"

I turned and motioned for my representative to bring a chair forward. As soon as the chair was placed next to mine, Faolan took his seat, and I returned my attention to Rian once more.

"Actually—"

"There is no actually," Rian interrupted. "You and my traitorous son should be ejected from the Meeting Room immediately and banished from the Isle for this insubordination!"

"Rian!" Ardit shouted again. "I called this meeting, and you will refrain!" Rian slumped into his chair and glowered at me, but Ardit just continued, "Melisende is correct. The purpose of this meeting is to discuss the threat from the portals that have now opened in four of our five kingdoms."

I glanced at Faolan whose face was rigid with shock. My hand reached for his, and his gaze slowly met mine. As I leaned closer to him, I whispered, "Breathe, Faolan. And remember, we do not yield."

CHAPTER FORTY-THREE
Faolan

A door flung open as Ardit returned to the Meeting Room. I watched as he walked to his chair and took a seat, surveying the remaining empty chairs.

The first hour of the Conclave consisted of each monarch recounting in detail the portal activities that had occurred in their respective kingdoms. Lancaster had started by discussing the original portals in both Leuconotos and Argestes. Cyrus interrupted him, adding new details about what had really occurred during the attack in his lands. Melisende then described the slaughter in Morvern as well as Maelys's description of the portal and the warriors. Ardit continued by sharing the particulars of the short battle in Eurus before asking Lancaster to finish by describing the fight that led to his father's death.

After hearing all of the new details that had come to light, everyone had a clearer idea of the magnitude of threat we were facing.

For the last half hour we had been on a recess. Ardit hadn't called it out of a necessity for a break or food, but because he wanted all the monarchs to digest the information they had just received before making decisions about the future of the Isles and the looming war.

Another door opened, and Lancaster and his brother, Aleksander, entered. They both approached the table, and Aleksander whispered something in his brother's ear. Lancaster inclined his head toward Melisende, then took his seat.

A loud crash sounded as yet another door swung open and slammed against the wall. My father entered the room by himself, a sour look on his face. He avoided looking in Melisende's and my direction, opting to stare at the door closest to the Argestan wing of the Meeting House. He slowly made his way to his seat and slumped against it.

Finally, Cyrus entered the room, followed by his advisor. The Argestan representative followed them in with a bottle of mead and placed it on the table as they took their seats.

Ardit cleared his throat, then sat back down in his chair, "Now that we have heard about the attacks and what Terraviridi is capable of, we need to discuss our plans going forward."

I sat back in my chair and settled in for the remainder of the meeting. Whatever was going to be decided here would have an impact on the future of all the Etesian kingdoms and potentially all of fae-kind.

Lancaster shifted in his seat, and Cyrus whispered in his advisor's ear. My father motioned to his representative, then said something before dismissing him. Ardit took a long draw from his wine, setting down the glass and reaching for some papers in front of him on the table.

"First of all, we know Terraviridi has the ability to travel to the Isles through portals, but I think we need to discover if they are planning a two-pronged approach. Melisende and I discussed the possibility of them also attacking by sea when she visited Eurus a couple weeks ago," Ardit started as he reached for a pair of glasses and shuffled his papers. "I think now is the time to discover how large-scale they intend on attacking. It is difficult to prepare for an attack by portals. It would be easier to prepare for and defend against an attack from the sea."

"They would be insane to attempt to travel the sea right now!" Cyrus interjected. His advisor pulled a piece of blank parchment out of a pile and started taking notes.

It would be incredibly dangerous for anyone to try to sail across the Etesian Sea this time of year; for two months, the seas became impassable, and storms capsized even the largest of ships, but then again, it didn't seem as though the Terraviridians were concerned with danger.

"Why would they send warriors by sea if they can travel by portal?" my father challenged.

His representative returned then with a glass and a bottle of whiskey. When he started pouring, my father snatched the bottle from his hands and poured the glass himself. He placed the bottle on the table in front of him, waved the representative off, then took a long sip.

"It might not be likely," Ardit said, "but think of the damage an entire fleet of ships could cause landing on undefended coasts while we are running around chasing portals."

"I see your point," my father replied, "but I still think any king would be ridiculous to send a single ship, let alone an entire fleet, out in this weather." He took another long swig of his drink before setting the glass down on the table.

"That's because they wouldn't be approaching your coast!" Cyrus shouted. "Ridiculous or not, if they are attempting to sail to the Etesian Isles, they would make land in *my* kingdom!"

"I have a ship ready to sail—" Ardit offered.

"No," Cyrus interrupted. "I will send a ship. My coasts are closest to Terraviridi."

"So your warriors can inform you of the threat, thus giving your kingdom the advantage and the time to protect your coasts while leaving the rest of us undefended? I don't think so!" my father shouted.

I rolled my eyes. Of course he didn't believe the Terraviridians would sail this time of year, but he still wanted the advantage of being protected from them if they did.

"You just said they would be ridiculous to sail this time of year!" Cyrus countered.

"I did." My father's voice increased in volume as he spoke. "But that doesn't mean my kingdom should be left unaware or undefended!"

"Order!" Ardit exclaimed, attempting to ebb the flow of shouting.

"I can send some warriors north to Argestes to sail alongside Cyrus's warriors," Lancaster offered. "I can send messenger hawks as well, to inform all kingdoms of our findings."

"I'm sending warriors as well," my father added. "If a ship is going out for reconnaissance, I want males I trust on board!"

"I know it is not your strong suit, but be reasonable, Rian," Melisende spoke up, and my father's head whipped in her direction. "We would be wasting precious time waiting for your warriors to travel to Argestes. The ship would sail much sooner with only Argestan and Leuconotan warriors aboard."

"I agree with Melisende," Ardit asserted, and my father rolled his eyes. "However, I do believe that all measures to secure the Isles on land should be conducted by members of all the kingdoms."

"And what exactly are these measures?" Cyrus questioned.

Ardit looked to his left. "That's what we are here to discuss. Have you been able to get anything out of the Terraviridian prince, Lancaster?"

"No, he remains tight-lipped," the young king answered with a frown.

"We are continuing to interrogate the other captives, but they don't seem to know anything of value. I have taken it upon myself to lead the prince's interrogations. As soon as I break him, you all will know," Aleksander added. He was the first advisor to speak, and all heads swiveled in his direction.

"Please keep us informed," Ardit responded. "It is crucial that we learn what Terraviridi is planning."

"Are all of your generals here?" Aleksander questioned, standing from his chair and peering around the room. "I have taken on the role of general in Leuconotos after my father's death, and I wish to speak to them. We will need to coordinate efforts and communication between all the kingdoms."

"Yes, my general is here," Cyrus answered.

"Seeing how my traitorous general is seated next to the Queen of Boreas," my father spouted, "I will need to arrange to have my son Brenhin travel here."

I winced at my father's slight, but I knew that it was my actions and decisions that left him without a general.

"We both know that you never really intended for Faolan to be your general," Melisende argued. "If you had really wanted Faolan to lead, you would have kept him in your kingdom and had him train with his warriors, not sent him to assassinate me!"

Gasps sounded throughout the room as my father sputtered, "Why... You... That..."

Melisende stood from her seat and leaned over the table. "What Rian? Are you saying that it is not true? Are you saying that your son lied to me?" My stomach curdled as I slouched back in my chair. My father's eyes darted between Melisende and me.

"That is *not* why I sent my son to your kingdom!" Father yelled as he shot up from his seat. His face was turning redder by the minute, and the vein in his forehead pulsed. "Faolan is young and must have misunderstood his task. He lacks the honor that comes with age."

"You want to speak of honor? Your son has more honor in a single finger than you have in your entire body!" Melisende slammed a fist down on the table.

"That's quite enough!" Ardit interjected, and both Melisende and my father looked in his direction before returning to their seats. "Melisende, is your general present on the island?"

"Yes."

"As is mine," Ardit continued. "Rian, send word to Brenhin and have him travel here immediately. After the Conclave is concluded, the generals will use the Meeting House to coordinate the efforts of our warriors."

"Fine," my father grunted. His voice had quieted but anger was still written on his face. He reached for a piece of parchment and scribbled a note before handing it off to his representative.

"I think we should reinstate the watchtowers," Melisende declared.

All the eyes in the room landed on her, and she sat up a bit straighter in her chair.

"What are the watchtowers?" Lancaster asked.

"When the Sylphs first fled the continent and made a home on the Etesian Isles, they built watchtowers on all of the highest peaks.

Guards would be stationed at each tower, and they could easily build fires or send colored smoke signals to indicate danger or threats," Melisende explained.

"Does anyone alive even know what the old codes they used are?" Cyrus asked. His advisor shuffled through his papers, and I could make out the words 'smoke signals' as he wrote them on a separate piece of parchment.

"Foulke does," Melisende shared, lips curling into a triumphant grin.

Father narrowed his eyes in suspicion as he watched the queen. I shifted my attention from my father to the female seated at my side. She placed her elbows on the table and laced her fingers together before continuing to speak.

"He can show the other generals how to create the signals and what each signal means. There are also some chemicals we will need to acquire, like iodine, that color the smoke. The sooner we can get guards stationed at the towers, the better."

"This is all well and good, but what am I supposed to do?" My father always found a way to make any conversation about himself. "Am I just supposed to wait for Melisende's smoke clouds or for Cyrus's ship to return while the Terraviridians continue to attack?"

A derisive snort left Ardit's mouth. "As I recall, your kingdom is the only one that hasn't been attacked yet."

Lancaster looked at his brother before shifting in his chair. "We have been reinforcing city walls and creating barricades around buildings we wish to protect. We have also started moving citizens from our most defenseless villages into larger cities. At least inside city walls they can be more easily defended." He may have been considered young by the other monarchs, but he was intelligent and seemed to be handling the transition from crown prince to king well.

"We should also start regular patrols in all kingdoms. Guards can be on the lookout for anything out of the ordinary," I added. It was the same suggestion I had made at the meeting between Lancaster and my father nearly a month ago. "The more eyes we have out there, the more likely we are to catch a portal early."

Lancaster and Aleksander nodded their heads, and Ardit looked at me with a satisfied smile.

"I agree with Faolan," Ardit announced. Pride swelled in my chest, and I sat up a bit straighter as he continued, "We need to be on constant watch for portals to appear. It is the only reason we were able to defend against the portal in Eurus so efficiently."

"I will visit Alcina," Melisende added. "She may know more about the portals. We need to know if there is any kind of counter-magic that can be used against them or if there is a way to track the origin of them. She might even know if there is a way to predict when and where a portal is going to be opened."

"Alright," Ardit declared as he stood and looked around the table. "Finally, we should make a plan to travel to Terraviridi in two months' time. We will take as many warriors as we can spare and bring the fight to their shores. They may have started this war, but we will end it."

"Agreed!" Cyrus's voice boomed as he slammed his glass down on the table.

Ardit continued, "So, to recap: the generals of all five kingdoms will meet to coordinate efforts as soon as Brenhin arrives. Foulke will instruct them on communication both by messenger hawks and watchtowers. Lancaster, you will send warriors to Argestes to sail out with Cyrus's warriors as soon as possible.

"Melisende will work with Alcina to research the portals and see if we can gain any insights that might be to our advantage. In the meantime, all kingdoms will reinforce city walls and barricades to protect their citizens as well as send out patrols to watch for new portals. And in two months we will set sail for Terraviridi. Are we all agreed?"

"Aye," Cyrus and Melisende said in unison.

Melisende looked at me and inclined her head.

"Aye," I added along with Lancaster and Aleksander.

"Fine, aye," my father begrudgingly mumbled. He rose from his seat and immediately turned to leave the Meeting Room.

I shifted my attention to Lancaster and his brother, offering a small smile. They returned the gesture before exiting the room as well. Ardit picked up his glass and took a sip of wine before Cyrus approached him, his advisor in tow.

As the three of them chatted, I turned my attention to Melisende. "That was..." I murmured, trailing off as I struggled to find the words.

"One of the more civil Conclaves I've been to." She turned and started walking to the door closest to the Borean wing. Just before she reached the door, she looked over her shoulder at me. "Are you coming?"

I smiled as I stood from my chair. Tonight, I would follow her to our room. Tomorrow, I would follow her back to our home in Boreas. And then... I would follow her to the ends of the world, until the end of my days.

***

"Well, how did it go?" Foulke asked when we returned to the sitting room in the Borean wing of the Meeting House.

He was sitting in a chair by the fireplace, reading from a book about the tactics of war, which was fitting given the present situation. He set the book down on the table next to him and looked at Melisende expectantly.

"Better than the last Conclave." She took the crown off her head and set it on the mantlepiece before slouching into the chair across from Foulke's. This meeting had started in disaster, but if it was better than the last, I dreaded to think what that one was like. "At least we came to some agreements."

I took a seat on the sofa situated between Foulke and Melisende as she waved over the representative that was sitting on a chair in the corner of the room. "Can you pour us some ratafia?"

The representative nodded at Melisende, then set down her knitting and headed toward the kitchen. Foulke uncrossed his legs and leaned forward, placing his forearms on his knees. "So, what was the conclusion? Where am I headed?"

"Nowhere," Melisende answered with a shrug.

"What do you mean, nowhere?" he blurted, sitting up straighter and looking between Melisende and me.

"Prince Aleksander wants to meet with the generals from all the kingdoms. Since four of the five of you are already here, you will convene when Brenhin arrives."

"Brenhin?" Foulke's brow furrowed, then he shot a glance in my direction before continuing, "Oh, of course."

I wasn't the General of Caecias anymore, not that I wanted to be in the first place. That wasn't my destiny. Ethann had been right; being general was something that my father had thrust upon me, but being with Melisende was what I wanted and was choosing for myself. At that moment, my chest felt lighter, and my shoulders straightened.

"You need to teach them the watchtower signals, as well," Melisende added.

The representative returned with three glasses of ratafia and handed them to us. She then sat in her chair in the corner and resumed her knitting.

"We're using the watchtowers?" Foulke asked as he relaxed back into his chair. "Smart play, Meli. That will be the quickest way to communicate between the kingdoms. And Rian agreed to this?"

"Begrudgingly, but yes." Melisende drained the rest of her drink, then set the glass down on a nearby table. "I'm heading to bed. Tomorrow, Faolan and I will return home to start preparing for the war."

CHAPTER FORTY-FOUR

Melisende

The patter of rain against the window and the distant rumble of thunder woke me from an otherwise restful sleep.

I rolled my head to the side to find Faolan still asleep next to me, his chest rising and falling with every breath. I pulled the blankets back and slid my legs off the side of the bed, pointing my toes, then flexing my feet before placing them on the cold tile floor.

As I stood, a flash of lightning sparked across the sky and momentarily lit up the room. I approached the window and stared at the storm raging outside. *Great.* Sailing home wouldn't be easy, but we couldn't afford to wait for the storm to subside.

CRACK. The subsequent thunder crashed, and Faolan stirred. He reached his arm across the bed, but when he felt empty blankets, he sat up looking for me.

His eyes met mine, and a slow smile graced his lips. "Come back to bed. It's still dark."

I glanced back at him. "Sorry, Little Wolf. I'm going to get dressed and pack. I want to set sail as soon as it's light out."

He grimaced. "I know you want to get home, but what's the hurry?" He rubbed the sleep from his eyes.

"The storm." I walked back over to him and took a seat on the edge of the bed. "In this weather, if we leave at sunrise, we won't make it back to Boreas until sundown."

I had sailed the Middle Sea many times and knew exactly how long the journey would be whether we were faced with calm waters or choppy waves, with heavy headwinds or a calm breeze.

Faolan frowned, then reluctantly sat up. The blankets pooled around his waist, showcasing his muscular chest and strong arms as he stretched. I licked my lips as my eyes scanned his body. "You're —"

"Shut up, Little Wolf." I smiled despite myself.

The sound of his laughter echoed in my head while warmth bloomed in my chest. I stood again and walked over to the drawers, pulling out a clean tunic and pair of trousers.

Faolan followed soon after and brushed my hair to the side, softly placing a kiss on my shoulder. I turned, clothes clutched tight against my chest, and kissed him on the lips before walking to the washroom to dress.

Once finished, I reached for my satchel and started packing my belongings while Faolan took my place in the washroom. Lightning flashed across the sky again, and I sighed while pulling my boots up over my leather trousers. We needed to beat this weather and fast.

The Borean wing of the Meeting House was still silent when I slipped out of the room. As I approached the kitchen, I found the female representative and asked her to have breakfast prepared for Faolan and me. She nodded and retreated back into the kitchen.

The rain started coming down harder, pounding against the roof like hundreds of hammers as I returned to the bedroom. Faolan was dressed and tightening the fastenings on his jacket.

"Breakfast will be ready soon, then we can head out," I informed him, wincing as thunder boomed through the house.

The smell of porridge filled my nose as we entered the kitchen and sat at the small table. The female representative set two bowls of porridge down in front of us. I took a large spoonful, the taste of honey sweet on my tongue, and the warmth heated me from within.

"This is delicious," Faolan said as he scooped some into his mouth.

"It's the honey," I said as I took another bite. "The bees make honey from the pollen of a local flower that only grows here on the island."

We ate in silence for a couple of minutes before the door opened and Foulke entered. He pulled out a chair across from us and slumped into it.

"So much for sleeping in," he grumbled, running a hand down his face in exasperation. "The rain is bad enough, but the thunder is excessive." He paused, glancing at us. "You're up and dressed early."

I dabbed my lips with a napkin. "Faolan and I are headed back to Boreas as soon as the sun comes up." I motioned for the female representative to bring Foulke some porridge.

"That's going to be a dangerous voyage, Meli. Do you really want to travel in this weather?" he asked as he took the food and nodded his appreciation.

"No, but I think we need to. I don't know how long the storm will last, and I don't want to delay." I could tell by the look on Foulke's face that he didn't agree with me sailing in the storm but wasn't going to argue either.

After we finished eating, Faolan and I returned to our room. I reached for my cloak and tossed it over my shoulders, securing it tightly in front of my chest and pulling the hood up over my head. Faolan picked up both of our packs, and after looking the room over one last time, we left.

Foulke joined us as we walked the hall to the external door of the Borean wing of the Meeting House and accompanied us down to the dock, where we waited for the representative to unlock the chest that held our weapons. After retrieving our things, we boarded the boat.

Foulke looked out at the water and asked, "Are you sure you want to sail in this?" He gestured to the choppy waves with his arms.

"I've sailed in worse with my father," I replied, turning to watch Faolan securing our packs and weapons under the small covering on the boat.

"But Faolan isn't your father," Foulke rebuked, his brows set with worry. "We don't know how experienced he is on the sea."

"We'll be alright, Foulke." I placed a hand on his shoulder and looked him in the eyes. "I promise."

A sigh escaped his lips, and I knew he would worry until he knew I was home safe in Ardelve.

"I'll send a raven when we return to the castle, but for now, focus on the meeting with the generals." I smiled softly, and my hand squeezed his shoulder before letting go.

"Right," he sighed.

"Goodbye, Foulke."

"Goodbye, Meli."

***

The waves had been choppy when we pushed off from the coast of the Middle Isle, but now, an hour later, they had turned into giant rolling swells. Faolan and I tried to squeeze under the covering near the mast. It wasn't a full cabin, but it did provide a small amount of protection from the deluge of rain.

"When did you learn to sail?" Faolan asked over the rumbling thunder as he adjusted his position and pulled his jacket tighter around his body.

"When I was young, my father would take me sailing every summer." I looked down at my hands and remembered the many times my father and I had gone out on the water, my chest tightening at the memory.

"My father never much liked the sea," Faolan remarked, spinning the turquoise ring around his finger with a shrug. "The only times I've been sailing was during my warrior training, and even then, it has been infrequent."

"I like the feeling of freedom you get on the sea—"

An impossibly large wave scooped up the boat and threatened to capsize us. As we leveled back out, I lunged toward the side of the vessel, clenched the railing, and emptied the contents of my stomach over the side.

I wiped my mouth with the back of my hand and returned to cover. Faolan pulled a waterskin out of his pack and handed it to me. I took a long pull of water, hoping to wash away the bitter taste of bile on my tongue.

A few hours later, I could see the coast of Boreas in the distance. *Thank the gods!* I stood and stumbled as I reached for the mainsail, making a few adjustments before calling out to Faolan, "We should reach land in just over two hours."

"Thank the gods. I was starting to wonder if we would ever make it back."

My eyebrows scrunched as I returned to my seat next to Faolan, "You have such little faith in my abilities?" I taunted.

"I have every faith in your abilities, but I also believe this storm wished us dead."

I couldn't help but scoff. "I've survived generations of your family trying to kill me. I'm not about to let a little storm succeed."

A brief smile flashed on Faolan's face before he let out a small chuckle.

The lightning had ceased, but the rain was still coming down in torrents when we finally landed on the shores of Boreas. Faolan assisted me in tying the boat's ropes to the small pier, where we unloaded our packs.

I heard a loud *gronk* and looked up to find two ravens sitting on some railing as if awaiting my arrival. I quickly scribbled a note to inform Redwald that we had returned home and would be arriving back at the castle the following day. One of the ravens lowered its head, and I placed the message in its open beak.

Once it had a firm grasp on the piece of parchment, I ran a finger down its back and whispered, "To the castle." It took off immediately, and the other raven followed soon after.

Faolan joined me by the now vacant railing, and the two of us walked into the village. Bran was outside of the inn, securing a window from the storm.

When he noticed us, he rushed to the door and called out to his mate, "Luce! Luce, the queen has returned."

Bran rushed us inside the inn while Luce tutted, "Oh, you poor dears! Please, sit by the fire. I will bring you some blankets."

"Can you show us to a room first, Luce? I'd like to change out of my wet clothes," I said as I unclasped my cloak and hung it on a hook, beads of water dripping to the ground.

"Of course, of course." She looked around for her keys, opening a drawer and pulling out a large ring with multiple keys hanging from it. She removed two keys, then continued, "Follow me."

Faolan and I trailed after Luce down a hall, up the stairs, and to a large room at the end of the corridor. She opened the door, then glanced between Faolan and me before handing me the key. "Your Majesty."

"The one room is fine, Luce," I stated as she looked between Faolan and me again.

"I will have blankets waiting for you by the fire downstairs, and I will heat some stew. Please let me know if you need anything else." Luce smiled awkwardly before leaving us to change into dry clothes.

I entered the room, set down my pack, and immediately stripped out of my soaked clothes. Faolan closed the door behind him, then just stared as I stood naked before him.

"Now who is staring?" I asked with a smirk as I strolled closer to him, placing a chaste kiss on his lips, and he groaned against my mouth.

There was a tightness low in my stomach as Faolan unfastened and removed his jacket, then pulled his tunic up over his head. I reached for his trousers and lowered them from his hips. When he was fully naked, he picked me up by the back of my thighs and walked me to the bed. We tumbled onto the bed together, and our lips met when the sound of the door opening stopped us in our tracks.

"I thought I would come and light... Oh my gods!" Luce dropped her candle to the floor and covered her eyes with a shriek. "I'm so sorry, Your Majesty!"

She knelt down on the floor, her hand fumbling for the candle she had dropped. Once she found it, she ran from the room, slamming the door shut behind her. Faolan and I erupted in laughter.

"We should get dressed and head downstairs," I said as I extricated myself from the bed. Faolan slowly followed my lead, and we both dressed in dry clothes.

When we arrived downstairs, there were two blankets folded on the couch nearest the fireplace and two bowls of steaming stew placed on the table nearby. I sat down and reached for a bowl, letting the heat seep into my hands. Faolan sat next to me, and we both giggled again.

The following morning arrived, and the storm had eased a little. Still, the idea of riding horseback for hours while being pelted with rain wasn't exactly appealing. But the sooner we left Ballantrae, the sooner we would arrive in Ardelve, and the sooner we could start enacting the plans that had been set forth in the Conclave.

Luce had some cooked meat, tomatoes, and cheese waiting for us in the dining room when we made our way downstairs. She greeted us but avoided looking either of us in the eyes. Faolan and I ate breakfast in silence, then returned to our room to pack our belongings once again.

There was a brief pause in the rain as Faolan and I mounted our horses. I reminded Bran that Foulke would be a few days behind us and that he would need to watch Foulke's horse for a little while longer. Luce and Bran both waved their goodbyes before retreating back into the inn.

"Ready, Little Wolf?" I asked as I turned my horse toward the road out of Ballantrae.

"With you by my side? Always."

CHAPTER FORTY-FIVE
Faolan

Home. We were heading home, and for the first time in my life I knew what that word meant. I had wasted so much of my life trying to fit in with my dysfunctional family and falsely believed that if I tried hard enough, I could. That trying to meet their expectations for me would somehow make me happy.

But then I met Melisende, and my entire world shifted.

I finally knew what it meant to be truly respected. What it meant to be accepted for who I was, not who I was supposed to be. And I hoped, what it meant to be loved.

As Melisende and I descended a hill along the River Ardelve, a calming sense of relief washed over me. Terraviridi and the portals were still very much a threat, but now we had a plan.

In two months' time we would bring the war to their doorstep, but until then we would send announcements to the citizens in smaller villages to seek shelter and protection in the larger cities. Leuconotos and Argestes would set sail and watch the coasts for any signs of Terraviridian ships. And all of the Etesian kingdoms would put guards in watchtowers and send patrols to reconnoiter their lands.

Aleksander would interrogate the Terraviridian prince for any knowledge of their plans, and Melisende would meet with Alcina to research portals. Terraviridi may have had the upper hand, but we weren't helpless.

By the time we reached the hills overlooking the village of Ardelve and Loch Mor, the rain had all but ceased. I peered up at the clouds which were still dark and grey but at least there were small patches of blue sky starting to appear in the cracks between them.

We had been riding for hours, and I was ready to stand on my own two feet. My ass needed a break, and I was looking forward to taking a long bath, not to mention eating a hot meal prepared by Balfour.

We rounded a bend on the trail and Melisende brought her horse to a halt. I pulled back on Dulachan's reins to stop him and watched the queen but her focus was on the woods before her.

"Something is wrong," she stated as she glanced around at the trees.

My gaze shifted to my right, then traveled back to my left. The woods looked exactly the same now as they had when we had ridden through them days before on our way out to the Conclave.

"What—?"

Melisende threw a hand out to stop me. "Shhhh!"

I watched as she scanned our surroundings before dismounting her horse. She handed the reins to me and slowly approached a nearby tree.

It was an old yew tree with a thick trunk and gnarled branches. She placed her left hand on the tree while her right hand moved to her thigh, unsheathing the dagger. Leaning to her left, she peered around the trunk and kept watch.

Dismounting my own horse, I pulled them off the path and between some bushes. I kept a firm grip on both sets of reins with my left hand keeping my right free should I need it.

A few bushes rustled as Melisende surveyed our surroundings, and I tried to see what she was seeing, to hear what she was hearing. After a tense couple of minutes, she re-sheathed her dagger, then crossed the path to join me.

"What is it, Meli?" I whispered, narrowing my eyes.

"I can't quite put my finger on it, but something just feels off," she answered, her eyes never settling on one spot.

"Do you want me to walk our perimeter?"

"No." She shook her head, her eyes finally meeting mine. "We are close to Ardelve, and there are always guards on patrol. I will send a raven to inform them we are descending the hill and to keep watch."

Melisende rummaged through her pack until she found a quill and some parchment. She scribbled a quick note and folded it twice before turning and scanning the trees for a raven. When she spotted one, she let out a sharp whistle, and it flew down to a low branch beside her.

The thing that amazed me about her ability to communicate with ravens was that she didn't need to train them the way messenger hawks needed to be trained. She didn't need to travel with a cage of ravens to be able to send correspondence back to a specified location, she could just call to a raven nearby and send it anywhere in her kingdom.

After she sent the raven off with our message, we remounted our horses and continued on our way down the hill.

My eyes kept scanning the forest; I was on constant vigilance. I may not have seen or felt what Melisende had, but I trusted her. These were her lands and her woods. If she said they felt off, then I believed her.

A half hour later, as we approached the final descent to the lake, I was the one to bring our horses to a halt. I grabbed Melisende's reins and pulled her horse close to Dulachan.

She glared at me. "What are you—"

A shadow shifted to our right, and both of us froze. We watched as the bracken swayed, parting for a large wolf. It jumped onto a boulder a short distance away and stared straight at us.

Melisende gasped, and I placed a calming hand on her thigh. "It's okay," I reassured her.

I inclined my head toward the wolf and watched as it slowly dipped its head, then jumped down from the boulder and continued on its path.

"You can communicate with wolves?" Melisende's voice was a mix of surprise and awe.

"Yes... No... I don't know." I shook my head. To be honest, I didn't know what this was. "When I was younger, I used to believe that I could talk to wolves. As a Dulaine, you have to spend a night in the amarok's cave as a rite of passage. It attacked me, but when it didn't kill me, I believed it was because I asked it not to.

"But recently, I've been seeing wolves shortly before terrible things have happened. It's almost like they are trying to warn me." I scoffed at the notion. "That's ridiculous, I know."

"No, it's not," Melisende said as she placed her hand on top of mine. "Long ago, when all fae had elemental powers, communicating with animals was more common. But sadly, with the loss of our powers came the loss of our connection to the creatures. Everyone assumes that I can communicate with ravens, and while technically true, it's one-sided. If wolves not only listen to you but are warning you of threats…" she trailed off.

I had tried to convince myself that the wolf sightings were just coincidences, but maybe she was right. The hairs on the back of my neck stood on end, and my heart started hammering against my chest. Maybe seeing the creatures was a harbinger of impending doom.

Swallowing past the lump in my throat, I nodded at Melisende. "Stay alert and follow me."

I pulled Dulachan forward and continued down the path. We didn't even make it five minutes before I saw a shape shift in the shadow of a tall oak tree.

I motioned for Melisende to slow down and stay behind me, but to my dismay, she pulled her horse next to mine.

Squinting, I watched as the shape slowly revealed itself to be a silhouette of a fae leaning against the trunk of the giant oak. Even obscured by shadows, I could tell it was a tall male with black hair and dark eyes.

Fuck.

A million thoughts started racing through my mind. Why was my brother here? Did our father send him? And when did he send him?

Our father had been in the Middle Isle for the past few days. For my brother to be here now, Father must have sent him before he left for the Conclave. And was he here for me, or for Melisende?

Panic gripped me as I watched my brother push off the trunk of the giant tree and take a few steps forward. He stopped in the middle of the path before us and his lips curved into a twisted smile.

"Hello, little brother."

***

"Bradach," I hissed as I watched my brother appear from out of the shadows.

Melisende tensed next to me, and I glanced sideways, scanning the trees. There were no guards standing with him, and I didn't see any hiding in the woods, but there was no way that he came here by himself.

A low rumble emanated from my throat before I continued, "What are you doing here?"

Bradach tilted his head and sighed loudly. "That's how you greet family?"

"That's how I greet someone who has just trespassed in these lands," I replied. I cast a sidelong glance at Melisende, my eyes begging her to stay put, before dismounting my horse. She took hold of Dulachan's reins as I stepped forward and placed myself between my brother and her.

Bradach's dark eyes had yet to seek her out. It seemed his attention was solely focused on me, but I wondered how long that would last.

"Oh, come on now..." Bradach drawled. "Is it trespassing if I have come to visit my brother?"

"Yes." I said, my voice loud and assertive. My right hand hovered an inch above the dagger sheathed at my thigh, and if I needed it, my sword was strapped to my back. I scanned the woods again but still I saw no additional guards.

"Fine. I'm trespassing," Bradach relented. "But only because I wanted to see what my little brother has been up to."

"Bullshit. You didn't come here to see me," I scoffed. I shifted my weight, my fingers twitching over the dagger. "What are you doing here?"

An exaggerated frown curved Bradach's lips, and he pouted, "You're no fun."

Melisende shifted in her saddle, preparing to dismount, but I threw my hand out to motion her not to come any closer. I could practically feel her rolling her eyes at me.

"I came to see if they were true," he said as he took a step forward, his eyes still trained on me. "The rumors."

I tensed but held my ground as my brother took another step forward, slowly closing the distance between us. Bradach's head tilted to the side as he stopped directly in front of me, then he straightened it again and his eyes shifted toward Melisende.

"But I see they *are* true; you have sided with our enemy."

"Your enemy, not mine." My hand finally patted the dagger, my fingers gripping the hilt. "I'm going to ask you one last time. What are you doing here, Bradach?"

Bradach's attention shifted to me as he took a step back and put his hands up innocently. "I'm just doing what I was told to do."

I spared a glance back at Melisende to find her pulling on the straps that attached the scabbard of her sword to her saddle.

"I wouldn't do that if I were you, witch."

Her eyes snapped up. "Or what, princeling?" she snarled.

Sard, we were going to have to have a talk about that fury of hers. I shifted and reached for my sword, and it sung as I unsheathed it. The air was thick with electricity as I raised it and pointed it at my brother. I didn't want to hurt him, but I would do anything to protect Melisende.

"Turn around, go home," I commanded. "You don't have to do this."

"Oh, but I do. You see, Father doesn't like failure. When he gives a command, he expects it to be executed. He gave Cathal a very important order but he failed. Then he gave you the very same order, and you failed him as well." Bradach paced back and forth across the dirt road like a predator stalking its prey. "Now, he has given me the same command, and I won't fail him."

Melisende dismounted, pulled out her sword, and came to stand by my side. Annoyed as I was that she was putting herself in danger, together we were two against one. Right now, we had the upper hand.

Suddenly, a low rumble sounded from the depths of the woods. I scanned the trees and in the distance, I could see bodies start to emerge.

Thank the gods, Melisende's guards have caught up with us.

But as I continued watching them, I noticed that they snuck out from under the brush, stepped out from behind trees, and jumped down from branches. They brandished their weapons and instead of wearing Borean blue, they were wearing the black and silver armor of Caecias.

Bradach's vile smirk returned to his face as the Caecian guards started forming a wall behind him.

I looked at Melisende, pleading, "Run, please."

"No." Those stubborn hazel eyes were locked on mine, a hurricane swirling in her irises. "We fight together."

"Meli—"

She lunged forward and kissed me. It was urgent and passionate and when she pulled away, she stated, "We do not yield."

Closing my eyes, I rested my forehead against hers and whispered, "We do not yield."

When I opened my eyes again, I nodded at Melisende, and she nodded back. We turned and faced my brother and the twenty or so guards lined up in an arc behind him. I watched as he raised his hand in the air and yelled, "Kill the queen!"

CHAPTER FORTY-SIX
Faolan

Everything moved in slow motion.

I breathed in…

Bradach's hand descended in a forward arc, eventually pointing forward and landing on Melisende.

The guards behind him pulled their weapons, some unsheathing swords and others gripping daggers. Their line broke as they started charging forward, boots stomping into the dirt.

I breathed out…

Bradach's smirk was frozen on his face as he watched his guards bolt past him, charging for the queen. His gaze shifted, and he winked at me before turning and retreating to a safe distance behind them.

I breathed in…

Melisende sent her dagger flying through the air. I didn't know if she had a target or just figured there were enough guards for it to strike someone. She raised her sword and braced herself for the onslaught.

I breathed out...

There were too many of them. There was no way out. We couldn't win. I closed my eyes and—

I breathed in...

The strong may fall, but they never yield.

I opened my eyes, and time sped up. The first guard to reach Melisende met my blade head on. The guard grunted and our swords continued to clash as another guard made his way around to Melisende. I could hear the squelch of blood as her sword plunged into his abdomen.

He toppled to his knees, and Melisende placed her boot on his shoulder as she extracted her sword from his body, blood spraying the dirt.

Two more guards ran forward, one attacking Melisende, the other heading for me. One guard on my right, the other on my left; I was constantly shifting my balance between the two, not allowing either of them to get the upper hand.

Eventually, I found my in, and I was able to thrust my dagger between the ribs of one of the guards, piercing his heart, while blocking a blow from the other with my sword.

Melisende and I fought side by side as we attempted to hold off the guards, but they kept coming. Deflect. Block. Evade. Thrust! As soon as one guard fell, another swiftly took his place.

I plunged my sword into the thigh of a guard and Melisende turned, her blade slicing through the air and decapitating him.

Gods, that was sexy. Disturbing, but sexy.

And then I heard it.

The sound of a blade piercing through skin followed by a soft grunt from Melisende's lips, "Uhngh."

She pulled a dagger from her shoulder. The wound wasn't too deep, but blood was still pouring from the gash.

Everything turned red. I flung my sword at the guard who had injured her. It struck him in the side and knocked him to the ground. I gripped my dagger in my hand as I ran to his fallen body, and I stabbed him in the chest repeatedly.

No one hurts my queen and lives.

Picking up my sword, I ran him through one more time, then blocked a blow from another guard who tried to sneak up behind me.

"Charge!" a voice yelled in the distance.

Behind the guards, Cyneweard led the assault with Maelys right beside him.

The Caecian guards' attention was pulled away from Melisende long enough for me to guide her away from the fighting.

We stopped under a tree just off the trail, and I looked her in the eyes. "Let me bandage your shoulder." She opened her mouth to protest, but I cut her off. "And don't try to tell me you are okay; there is blood running like a river down your arm."

She huffed, "Fine, but be quick about it." Even injured she was eager to return to the fight.

I ripped my jacket off and tossed it to the ground before pulling my tunic up over my head. Melisende looked at me, brows narrowing. I knew exactly what she was thinking. "I just told you I wanted to bandage your wound and *that* is where your mind goes?"

"You're the one stripping clothes off! The last time I wrapped an injury, I managed to keep all of mine on."

I ripped a large piece from the bottom of my tunic and Melisende looked down at my hands. I smirked as I replied, "The last time you wrapped an injury, I'm sure you had clean dressings."

She rolled her eyes. "Shut up, Little Wolf."

I couldn't help but laugh as I placed the fabric on her shoulder and started wrapping it under her arm. I circled her shoulder twice, then tied off the end to help staunch the flow of blood. Everything was dirty: her wound, her clothes, my tunic. She would need to have the gash cleaned out and stitched up, but she wouldn't die. At least not from this injury.

"How does it feel?" I asked as I picked up my tunic and jacket, putting them back on.

She waved her arm around, then rolled her shoulders a few times. "Good enough to slay a few more males."

As we returned to the fray, I noticed my brother in the distance. He was leaning against the same tree he had been when we first discovered him. My eyes locked on his, and I pointed at him with my sword. It was a warning and a promise: his fate was in my hands.

His eyes widened as I trudged forward. He pushed off the tree and reached for the sword at his back, holding it firmly in front of him.

To my left, Cyneweard was fighting two guards. They were both giant males, towering over him, but they were also slower. Cyneweard ducked under the blade of the first guard and managed to bring his sword to the back of the second's legs, slicing through the tendons at his ankles. The guard screamed out in pain as he slumped forward in the dirt.

Cyneweard turned and flipped his blade over, skewering the torso of the first guard. He thrust his sword upward before pulling it out. Blood and entrails poured from the gaping hole in the guard's abdomen as he toppled to the ground.

I stepped over the corpse of a Caecian guard that had been cut down by Maelys and from my periphery, watched as Melisende clashed swords with another male.

Even with blood running down her arm from the wound on her shoulder and gore from the slain staining her clothes, she was stunning. The guard kept lashing out, putting all his strength and hatred behind each blow. Melisende stayed nimble and deflected every blow, biding her time until the guard slowed, and when he did, she gutted him.

I shifted my focus back on my brother, who was holding his ground, sword firmly in his grasp, but his eyes… His eyes betrayed him. There was fear there.

I tightened my grip on the hilt of my sword as I called out to Bradach, "It doesn't have to be this way."

"Yes, it does," he replied, glancing at his dwindling number of guards. "Only one of us is making it out of this alive."

I sighed. "So be it." Lungeing forward, I lashed out with my sword.

Bradach blocked, a grimace on his face, and a grunt escaping his mouth. Had he not expected me to use my full force? I didn't want to kill my brother, let alone hurt him, but he was the one who declared it was him or me.

He parried and I deflected. I slashed out and he blocked. We had both been trained to wield a sword from an early age. It was an even fight, and I matched him blow for blow.

I heard a yelp and noticed one of Melisende's guards get cut down. But just as soon as the Caecian guard retracted his sword from the Borean's corpse, one of the queen's female guards struck. She came from behind and thrust her sword through the guard's torso, the blade slick and red with blood, protruding from his chest.

The loud clang of Bradach's sword meeting mine brought my attention back to the fight. He and I continued to parry, one attack after another until my muscles ached.

As my brother shifted his footing, he momentarily lost his balance, and I was able to land a blow. Red blossomed along his thigh as blood started pouring from the laceration. But my triumph was short lived. Bradach's sword swung out and sliced my left arm just above the elbow.

We were evenly matched in skill and strength, neither one of us being able to maintain the upper hand for long enough. Our swords clashed again, the force sending shockwaves down my arms.

Bradach took a step back and smirked at me. "I'm going to enjoy cutting that bitch down after I finish you."

At that moment, I looked at Bradach and I no longer saw my brother. I saw my enemy, someone who wanted to harm the one I loved. I lunged forward slashing left then right. I raised my sword above my head and swung it down in a chopping motion before I pulled it back and thrust it forward. The blade hit its mark.

Bradach's eyes widened, and a trickle of blood dripped from his lips. My eyes traveled from his face to his stomach, where my sword was currently embedded. I didn't look up as I withdrew the blade, crimson drops covering the ground with his essence.

There was a soft thud as his sword slipped from his grip and landed in the dirt. Bradach stumbled backwards and his hands covered the gouge in his abdomen. He looked down to find blood trickling past his fingers.

When his gaze returned to mine, I knew he knew. The wound was lethal, and he wouldn't survive it.

Bradach staggered back a few more steps before falling to the dirt. I stood over him, watching as the blood continued to pour from his stomach. My heart sank. "Why?"

He looked up at me and fixed a smug expression on his face. "Why what, little brother?" he sneered.

Why did every new Caecian king follow in the footsteps of their predecessor? Why could none of them break the pattern? Why did our father need to be the one to bring about the end of Boreas? Why couldn't we have found peace?

There were too many questions that bubbled up in my throat. All I could manage to say was, "It didn't have to be this way."

Bradach shook his head slowly before meeting my gaze again. "Yes, it did."

I leaned down, getting closer to my brother as he started gasping for air. My left hand joined his, and I put pressure on the wound knowing full well that it would do nothing to save him. He closed his eyes and leaned his head back as the gasps became more rapid.

The sounds of the battle behind me disappeared as I watched my brother fight for air. A few blood bubbles escaped his lips, and his hands went limp under mine.

His chest slowly rose, then sank for the last time.

He was gone.

Fuck!

I hated my father and brothers. I hated who they were and how they acted. I hated what they believed. But more than anything, I hated all the hate.

I might have just slain an enemy, but Bradach was still my brother. He didn't deserve to die because our ancestors couldn't find peace. He didn't deserve to die because of my father's jealousy and hatred. This was a petty war and needed to end. I closed my eyes and took a deep, slow breath.

As I stood, towering over the corpse of my brother, a million emotions clogged my throat. I wanted to scream, I wanted to cry, I wanted to...

Rage overtook me. When would this end? I raised my sword up over my head and in one swift motion, brought it back down to the earth. I thrust it into the ground, screaming, when lightning exploded from the hilt, illuminating the sky.

CHAPTER FORTY-SEVEN
Meli

I plunged my dagger into the neck of another Caecian, his blood splattering across my chest as I withdrew the blade. He placed his hands over the wound and stumbled backwards before falling to the ground, dead.

Over the sounds of the battle, I heard Faolan scream. My head whipped in his direction, and I found him standing over the corpse of his brother.

In anguish, he slammed his sword into the ground and lightning erupted from the hilt. The sound of thunder echoed through the trees, and Faolan slumped in the bloodstained dirt.

What in the gods...

Did he just...? I shook my head, filing the image away to dissect later, but for now there was still a battle to be won.

Cyneweard clashed swords with one guard, Maelys with another, while the rest of my guards started piling up the bodies of the defeated Caecians. I glanced around and noticed one male still writhing on the ground. I walked over to him and put him out of his misery by stabbing the end of my sword through his heart. We would leave no Caecians alive.

Maelys slayed the guard he had been locked in battle with, then dragged his corpse to the pile along with the others.

I watched as my guards checked pulses, ran daggers across still-breathing throats, and built a pyre at the base of the mountain of bodies. After generations of fighting, they were efficient at disposing of enemy remains.

Lailith, one of my guards, approached and placed a hand on my good shoulder. "Are you alright, Your Majesty?" Her eyes dropped to the bloody fabric wrapped around my arm, and she winced.

I smiled and reassured her, "Yes. Thank you, Lailith. A small scratch on my shoulder, but a healer should be able to stitch it up quite easily."

"I received your raven and informed Cyneweard straightaway." She looked down at her hands, her voice solemn as she continued, "I was worried we would be too late."

"You were just on time," I said, attempting to placate her. "What I really want to know is how they got past our defenses."

"Of course, Your Majesty."

"Meli, please, Lailith. You've been in my service for three hundred years, no need to be so formal."

Maelys wiped the blade of his sword on his trousers as he neared. He was soaked in crimson, but luckily it appeared none of the blood was his own. "That was too close, cousin," he chided as he shook his head.

"Agreed. I'm going to want a full report from Cyneweard as to how they got this far into the kingdom undetected." I rolled my shoulder, the pain finally radiating from the wound. I looked at my guard and commanded, "Lailith, ensure that all of the Caecian corpses are piled up and burnt. Leave nothing behind. And instruct Cyneweard to bring Bradach's body to the castle. We will need to shroud it and sent it to King Rian with a message."

"Yes, Your Majesty." She nodded, then turned and walked toward the other guards. I bristled slightly at her use of my formal title again.

Looking at my cousin, I noticed the left side of his mouth quirked up, that boyish smile gracing his lips. He leaned in and whispered, "A lightning wielder, huh?"

"You saw it too?" I questioned. "I thought maybe my eyes were playing tricks on me." In the heat of the moment, I couldn't have been sure if the lightning had struck Faolan's sword or exploded out from the hilt. He didn't have magic; no one in his family had possessed any elemental powers for generations.

How was it that this prince not only possessed magic, but one of the most powerful forms? No, it didn't make sense. It was far more likely that lightning had struck his sword.

Although the odds of that happening…

Maelys continued, "Maybe you weren't the only one to have their magic unlocked when you…" Maelys pretended to gag. "Ugh, you know, never mind."

I playfully smacked him on the arm, then looked toward Faolan who was slumped on the ground over his brother's form. He was staring at his bloody hands, deep in contemplation. Or grief. Or both.

"Go," Maelys urged.

The corners of my lips curved slightly upward, and I inclined my head before leaving him to join Faolan.

I walked across the dirt road and over to the tree underneath which Faolan had battled his brother to the death. He didn't seem to acknowledge my presence as I approached and knelt next to him.

His bloody hands were still outstretched before him, and his breathing was unsteady.

"Faolan," I said softly.

"Hmm…" His head lifted, and he briefly looked me in the eyes. The brown of his irises had lost their usual warmth, and his expression was mournful. He looked back down at his hands, seemingly lost to his grief.

I gently took his hands in mine, and his eyes snapped to mine once again. "He wanted to end you. He wanted to watch you die. If I didn't kill him…" he trailed off as a single tear ran down his cheek.

I wiped the tear away with the back of my finger before gripping his hands in mine once more. "I'm here, Faolan. I'm okay."

He gritted his teeth, his jaw feathering, and I could see the resolve return to his features. "It was him or you. I couldn't let him take you away from me. You are the single brightest thing in my life, and I wasn't about to let him extinguish you."

Faolan stood, and I followed suit, standing alongside him. His hands remained in mine, but his eyes returned to his brother's body.

Quietly, I informed him, "I instructed Cyneweard to have Bradach's body brought to the castle where we can shroud him before sending him back to Caecias tomorrow."

"Good," he replied, his voice taking on a darker quality I had never heard before. "There are a few things I would like to say to my father."

***

The following morning arrived with the sound of birdsong. The sun had yet to peek over the horizon, but the sky was becoming ever so slightly brighter, portending the dawn. I stretched and rolled over to find the bed empty and Faolan gone.

I sat upright and looked around the room. The faintest amount of light was streaming in from the south-facing windows, illuminating the foot of the bed and the wardrobe along the far wall. I glanced toward the bathing room, finding the door ajar.

I slipped my legs out from under the covers; they were covered in warm wool leggings that made me feel much more comfortable after weeks of travel and the bloodbath that ensued yesterday. Slipping my feet into a pair of slippers to protect them from the harsh cold of the winter floors, I crossed the room and pulled my robe down from the hook beside the washroom. Wrapping it tight around my body, I exited my bedchamber looking for Faolan.

He hadn't slept well during the night, waking from nightmares twice. I had brushed the hair, slick from sweat, away from his face and attempted to soothe him, but as soon as he had fallen back asleep, the nightmares resumed.

Reaching for a chamberstick from a recess in the stair walls, I took hold of it and let the flame from the candle light my way.

Eventually, I found Faolan in the parlor, asleep on the sofa with a book splayed open on his chest. I walked over to where he rested and gently picked up the book, placing it on the low table next to me. Walking over to the chair in the corner of the room, I grabbed the blanket and brought it back over to Faolan. He stirred slightly as I covered him with the warm fabric.

"Shhh…" I whispered as I sat on the edge of the sofa, my fingers drawing lazy circles on his chest. He closed his eyes and drifted back off to sleep.

Later that morning, after Faolan woke, we returned to my room to get cleaned up and dressed. Afterward, we had breakfast in the small dining room before I sent word to Cyneweard to meet us in the parlor. I wanted to discuss the attack, as well as our plans with Bradach and how we could start preparing for war.

Foulke would be returning to the castle within a couple of days, but I didn't want to wait that long to start moving our citizens to safer towns or stationing guards at the watchtowers.

Faolan and I entered the parlor to find Cyneweard sitting on the sofa, shuffling through some correspondence while waiting for us to arrive. He looked up and inclined his head, acknowledging us before waving a servant boy over and asking, "Can you bring us some teas? Thank you, Daniel."

I took a seat in a chair nearest the fireplace while Faolan sat in the chair to my left. Cyneweard set down the pieces of parchment he had been reading and looked at me, expression stoic.

"I've sent word to Foulke, informing him of what transpired here. The guards and I disposed of the bodies last night before I sent two patrols out to reconnoiter the surrounding hills. I will be visiting the border towns and villages after Foulke returns. I plan to interview them and see if anyone noticed anything out of the ordinary. I want to know how they made it almost all the way to the castle unnoticed on my watch."

"Thank you, Cyneweard. Now, about Bradach?" I asked, leaning forward in my chair, my fingers sliding along the leather of the armrests.

"Yes. We brought his body back and it is currently residing in the basement of the round tower."

"Good," I replied. I glanced at Faolan, seeing his eyes were fixed on the flames dancing in the hearth. He had barely spoken since last night. I reached out my left hand and placed it on top of his before continuing, "I need you to select four of your top guards to accompany the body back to Caecias. Shroud him in black—"

Cyneweard narrowed his brows in confusion, "Black? But black is for honorable—"

"He doesn't deserve it. Shroud him in any color but black," Faolan interrupted, shifting in his chair.

"Are you sure?" My eyes locked on his.

"Yes." Faolan asserted. "He wanted to kill you, Meli. He ceased being my brother in that moment. Shroud him in any fucking color, just not black."

He stood and strode over to the fireplace, leaning his arm against the mantle. I watched his back rise and fall with every breath he took. I looked at Cyneweard. "You heard him. Shroud Bradach in any color but black. We will have a message delivered to the round tower within the hour, then I want him gone."

"Yes, Your Majesty," Cyneweard acknowledged before standing to leave the room.

Just then, the door opened and Daniel returned holding a tray with three mugs of tea. He eyed the guard, who was standing, then looked at me.

Cyneweard approached the young servant. "I'll be taking my tea to go," he said as he reached for one of the mugs.

"Okay, very well, sir," Daniel replied.

After Cyneweard left the room, Daniel brought the remaining two mugs over and placed them down on the low table before me. I smiled at him, and he inclined his head, then turned and left the parlor as well.

Reaching forward, I picked up one of the mugs. The tea was fragrant and smelled of spiced oranges. I took a long, slow sip, then looked at Faolan. "Come back, sit down, and drink some tea."

He turned and his eyes met mine, that darkness still lurking under the rich mahogany. Slowly, he returned to his seat and picked up the other mug.

"We need to send a message with the body. I can write it unless…" I trailed off.

"No," Faolan insisted, clenching his jaw. "I will write it. I have a few choice words for my father. This feud ends now."

I took another sip from my tea before placing it on the table and crossing the room. I pulled a piece of parchment and a quill from the desk near my reading chair. Bringing them back to Faolan, I placed them on the table in front of him.

Faolan set his mug of tea back down on the table without even having taken a sip, then snatched the pen and started scribbling on the paper. It didn't take him long to finish, and I noticed he had only written two sentences. Two sentences was all he had to say to his father.

He stood up and handed me the piece of parchment. "Here, send this with the body." Not "Bradach's body". Not "my brother's body". Not even "his body". Faolan had said "the body".

I looked down at the piece of paper as Faolan exited the room.

If you ever come for Melisende again, I will gut you like the spineless dog you are. This war is over.

I exited the parlor and walked the long corridor that separated the two towers of the castle. When I arrived in the smaller tower, I found a servant and instructed him to take the note to the basement of the round tower.

Bradach would soon be returned to Caecias, and Rian would know that he had lost yet another son due to his lust for power and determination to have me killed. Perhaps now he would finally yield.

***

Later that evening, Faolan and I stood under the yew tree on the castle's island and watched the lake's waves lap up on the shore. The moon was a waxing crescent, and it poked out from behind the last remaining storm clouds.

I stared up at the moon and the few visible stars and sighed.

"Nothing will ever be the same," Faolan said, breaking the silence.

I gazed at him, watching as he skipped a stone along the surface of the lake. He bent down and retrieved another, examining it before discarding it for a smoother one.

"No, it won't," I replied. He stood and turned, looking at me. "But that doesn't mean it will be worse forever. I have lived for nearly one thousand years and I can tell you this, Little Wolf: Things will get bad. War will come at a cost. Thousands of Sylphs will starve and suffer. More beings you love will be hurt or killed.

"You will wish that you hadn't been around to see all the pain and distress. But life will go on. One day in the future, the fighting will end. And eventually we will find peace."

"How do you know?" Faolan dropped the smooth, round stone from his hand and came to stand beside me. "How can you be so sure peace will come?"

"If I could find you, my anamchara, after nine hundred years of betrayal and loss, I have to believe that anything is possible."

Faolan captured my lips with his, the kiss passionate and needy, and I melted into his touch. My back brushed against the trunk of the tree as Faolan pressed his weight onto me. My hands roamed his body while his caressed my face and tangled in my hair.

He held onto me like I was his only source of light in the darkness, and I drank him in like he was my only source of oxygen.

He pulled back slightly and searched my eyes before resting his forehead against mine. I inhaled his scent of leather and lavender and knew that no matter what lie ahead of us, we would face it together.

War could come to my doorstep, Rian could send a thousand assassins to try and kill me, but as long as I had Faolan by my side, I would not yield.

We would not yield.

ACKNOWLEDGEMENTS

To Ben:
You are my real-life anamchara, and I would have waited over nine hundred years for you.

To Tyler:
You will forever be my real-life Faolan. Thank you for the inspiration and being the book boyfriend the world may not have deserved, but desperately needed.

To Everyone Else:
I have a feeling the rest of the acknowledgements will read a bit like I've won a prestigious award and came ill-prepared with no acceptance speech. I'm sorry for the jumbled mess, but know you all mean so much to me.

To my parents: Thank you for always supporting my crazy dreams, whether it be starting a business, moving to a foreign country, or writing a book.

To my aunt Mary: I miss you every day. I know you would have loved following along with me on this adventure.

To the rest of my family: Thank you for supporting me. I love you.

To my editor, Ashley: You are a saint. You turned the flaming dumpster fire of a first draft into an actual freaking book! I couldn't have done it without you.

To my illustrator, Lia: Before you, this world only existed in my head. Thank you for the beautiful map, and thank you for sharing Faolan and Meli with the world.

To my cover designer, Jordan: You were such an amazing find! The cover is gorgeous and better than I could have dreamed of.

To my Beta readers, Verena, Anne, Amie, Sarah, Micaela, and Ashleigh: Thank you for not DNFing my horrendous first draft. Your encouragement kept me going.

To the Lost Court: We may have fallen, but we never yielded. Never stop dreaming and shooting for those stars.

To Canova Hall in Brixton: I miss the hours I spent there writing. I also miss your flat whites, po' boys, and gnocco fritto.

To Kettle on Grand in San Diego: Thank you for being my San Diego writing base. Writing at home is so boring.

To my London family, you all know who you are: I miss you all so much. Work hard, play hard, and be kind.

And to you, the readers: If you had told me five years ago that I would end up writing a book, I never would have believed you. The fact that people have actually read it blows my mind. Thank you for letting me take you on this adventure and I hope you enjoy the rest of the series.

Remember, the strong may fall, but they never yield.

ABOUT THE AUTHOR

K. J. Pearce has been a romantasy fan since she watched Disney's Beauty and the Beast as a child. One day, when she was much older, she decided to write her own book. Today, she is writing an "about the author" blurb for that book. She doesn't love talking about herself, but she does love talking about her fictional characters. She also loves traveling, Italian food, reading, and rainy days. She especially loves reading on rainy days. If she's not writing, you can usually find her adventuring in Southern California or London. She currently lives in Southern California with her partner and their two cats.

Join K. J. Pearce's little wolves pack on social media to stay up to date with her new releases.